MADDIE'S BABY

BY
MARION LENNOX

A SHEIKH TO
CAPTURE HER HEART

BY
MEREDITH WEBBER

MILLS
BOON

Wildfire Island Docs

Welcome to Paradise!

Meet the small but dedicated team of medics who service the remote Pacific Wildfire Island.

In this idyllic setting relationships are rekindled, passions are stirred, and bonds that will last a lifetime are forged in the tropical heat…

But there's also a darker side to paradise—secrets, lies and greed amidst the Lockhart family threaten the community, and the team find themselves fighting to save more than the lives of their patients. They must band together to fight for the future of the island they've all come to call home!

Read Caroline and Keanu's story in
The Man She Could Never Forget
by Meredith Webber

Read Anna and Luke's story in
The Nurse Who Stole His Heart
by Alison Roberts

Read Maddie and Josh's story in
Saving Maddie's Baby
by Marion Lennox

Read Sarah and Harry's story in
A Sheikh to Capture Her Heart
by Meredith Webber

All available now!

SAVING
MADDIE'S BABY

BY
MARION LENNOX

Published in Great Britain 2016
By Mills & Boon, an imprint of HarperCollins*Publishers*
1 London Bridge Street, London, SE1 9GF

© 2016 Marion Lennox

ISBN: 978-0-263-25435-8

Dear Reader,

Wildfire Island is my dream destination—a tropical paradise where all things are possible. Our island is breathtakingly beautiful, its weather wonderful one day, perfect the next. I close my eyes and imagine myself soaking up the sun as I float by the waterfall feeding the freshwater lagoon, preferably holding a drink with a wee umbrella.

Of course all tropical paradises have their bad days, and that's what happens in *Saving Maddie's Baby*. Maddie starts off with a *very* bad day. But this is Wildfire Island, where romance is always in the air—even if my hero, Josh, has to put himself in mortal danger to find it.

Saving Maddie's Baby is Book Three of the six-book Wildfire Island Docs series, written with my fabulous fellow authors Alison Roberts and Meredith Webber. We've had a lot of fun indulging ourselves in our Wildfire Island fantasy. I hope you have the same fun reading them.

Marion

To Meredith and Alison,
who make my writer's life fun.

Marion Lennox has written over a hundred romance novels and is published in over a hundred countries and thirty languages. Her international awards include the prestigious RITA® Award (twice) and the *RT Book Reviews* Career Achievement award for 'a body of work which makes us laugh and teaches us about love'. Marion adores her family, her kayak, her dog, and lying on the beach with a book someone else has written. Heaven.

Books by Marion Lennox

Mills & Boon Medical Romance

The Surgeon's Doorstep Baby
Miracle on Kaimotu Island
Gold Coast Angels: A Doctor's Redemption
Waves of Temptation
A Secret Shared...
Meant-to-Be Family
From Christmas to Forever?

Mills & Boon Cherish

A Bride for the Maverick Millionaire
Sparks Fly with the Billionaire
Christmas at the Castle
Nine Months to Change His Life
Christmas Where They Belong

Visit the Author Profile page
at millsandboon.co.uk for more titles.

PROLOGUE

HEROES AND HEROINES don't choose to be brave, Maddie decided. Mostly they have bravery thrust upon them. In her particular case, a heroine was created when vast chunks of rock trapped one doctor in an underground mine, a mine she should never have been near in the first place.

This heroine wasn't brave. This heroine was stupid.

Everyone knew the mine was dangerous. Ian Lockhart, the owner, had left Wildfire Island weeks ago, with salaries unpaid and debts outstanding. The mine had been closed for non-compliance with safety standards not long after Ian's disappearance.

So whose bright idea had it been to see if they could tap one of the seams close to the surface?

There were reasons this seam hadn't been tapped before. The rock was brittle. Without salaries, though, and desperate for income, the islanders had cut through the fence and quietly burrowed. No one was supposed to know.

But now... The call had come through an hour ago. A splintered piece of shoring timber and a minor rockfall had left one of the islanders with a fractured leg.

If it hadn't been badly fractured they might have

brought Kalifa down to the hospital, keeping their mining secret. Instead, his mates had had the sense to ring
Maddie, asking her to come across the mountains to
the overgrown mine site.

Maddie—Madeline Haddon—was heavily pregnant
but she was the only doctor available. The miners had
told her there were shards of bone puncturing Kalifa's
skin, so transporting him by road before assessment
meant the risk of cutting off the blood supply.

She'd had to go.

Once at the mine site, it had taken work to stabilise
him. Kalifa needed specialist surgery if he wasn't to be
left with a permanent limp, and she was worried about
the strain on his heart. She'd just rung Keanu, the other
island doctor, who was currently on his way back from
a clinic on an outer island. She'd been asking him to
organise Kalifa's evacuation to Cairns when there was
an ominous rumble from underground.

The mouth of the mine had belched a vast cloud of
dirt and dust.

She'd thought Kalifa and the two friends who'd
called her had been working alone. She'd never imagined there were men still in there. Surely not? But out
they came, staggering, blinded by dust.

She'd been helping lift Kalifa into the back of the
jeep—her jeep was set up as a no-frills ambulance, used
in emergencies for patient transport. She'd turned and
gazed in horror as the miners stumbled out.

'How many of you are down there?' The guy out first
had a jagged gash on his arm. She grabbed a dressing
and applied pressure.

'Tw-twelve,' the guy told her.

'Are you all out now?' When they'd rung about Kalifa she'd assumed… Why hadn't she asked?

'Three still to come.'

'Why? Where are they?'

'Malu's smashed his leg,' the guy told her. 'He's bleeding like a stuck pig.'

'Is he stuck? Has the shaft caved right in?'

'Just…just a bit of a rockfall where Kalifa fell against the shoring timber. Malu got unlucky—we were trying to shore it up again and he was right underneath where it fell. Macca and Reuben are helping him out but they had to stop to tighten the tourniquet. But the shaft's clear enough in front of the fall. They'll be out soon.' His voice faltered. 'As long as they can stop the bleeding.'

She stared at the mine mouth in dismay.

The dust was settling. It was looking almost normal.

Bleeding out…

Oh, help.

She'd done a swift, sweeping assessment of those around her. No one seemed in immediate distress. Men were already helping each other. The nurse who'd accompanied her, Caroline Lockhart, was taking care of a miner who looked like he'd fractured his arm. He was still standing, not in obvious danger. A couple of the men were crouched on the ground, coughing. They should be checked.

Triage.

One broken arm. Bruises, lacerations, nothing else obvious. Kalifa was waiting to be transferred to hospital.

Bleeding out…

Triage told her exactly where she was needed.

But she was pregnant. Pregnant! Instinctively her hand went to her belly, cringing at what she was contemplating.

What was the risk?

This had been a minor rockfall, she'd told herself. The shaft was still clear.

Along that shaft, Malu was bleeding to death. She had no choice.

'Help me,' she snapped at an uninjured miner. She grabbed his hand, pressing it onto the pad she'd made on his mate's bleeding arm. 'Push hard and keep up the pressure until Caroline has time to help you. The bleeding's already easing but don't let go. Caroline, can you radio Keanu?'

'He's on his way in from Atangi.'

'Tell him to land the boat on this side of the island and get here as fast as he can. Meanwhile, don't move Kalifa. He needs a doctor with him during transfer. The blood supply to the leg's stable, as long as he doesn't shift. But he has enough pain relief on board to keep him comfortable. Meanwhile, give me your torch,' she snapped at another miner. 'And your hard hat.'

'Y-you can't go in there,' the miner stammered. 'Doc, you're pregnant. It's dangerous.'

'Of course it's dangerous. You've been working in a mine that's supposed to be closed, you morons. But what choice do I have? Malu's got two children and his wife's my friend. Caro, you're in charge.'

And she picked up her bag, shoved on a hard hat and headed into the shaft.

'Doc, wait, I'll come with you,' one of the miners yelled after her.

'Don't even think about it. You have children, too,' she snapped back. 'We now have four idiots in the mine. Don't anyone dare make it five.'

CHAPTER ONE

DR JOSHUA CAMPBELL was so bored with solitaire he'd resorted to cheating to finish each game faster. It defeated the purpose, but he'd read every journal he could get his hands on. He'd checked and rechecked equipment. He'd paced. He was driving the rest of the staff at Cairns Air Sea Rescue Service nuts. He was going out of his mind.

No one in Northern Queensland seemed to have done so much as stand on a spider for the whole week. He'd been rostered for patient transfers, and every one of them had been routine. Patients had either been heading home, or were being flown from the city hospital to the country hospitals where they could continue recuperation among friends. There'd not been a single emergency amongst them.

'If this keeps up I'm joining the army,' Josh grumbled to Beth, his paramedic colleague. 'Maybe there's a place for me in the bomb squad. Do you suppose there's any call for bomb disposal any place around here?'

'You could try cleaning our kitchen as practice,' Beth said morosely. 'School holidays and three teenage boys? I'd defy a hand grenade to make more mess. You need to try a touch of domesticity if you want explosions. Consider marriage.'

'Been there, got the T-shirt,' he muttered.

'That's right, with Maddie, but that's ancient history.' Beth and Josh had joined the service at the same time, and after years of working together there was little they didn't know about each other. 'You hardly stuck around long enough to feel the full force of domestic bliss.' And then her smile faded. 'Whoops, sorry, Josh, I know you lost the baby, but still… It was so long ago. You and Karen, you think you might…?'

'No!' He said it with more vehemence than he'd meant to use. In fact, he startled himself. They were in the staff office, in the corner of the great hangar that held the service planes. The door was open and Josh's vehemence echoed out into the vaulted hangar. 'No,' he repeated, more mildly. 'Domesticity doesn't interest either of us.'

'And you're seeing less of each other,' Beth said thoughtfully. 'Moving on? Seeing we're quiet, you want to check some dating sites? We might just find *the one*.'

'Beth…'

'You're thirty-six years old, Josh. Okay, you still have the looks. Indeed you do. It drives me nuts, seeing the way old ladies melt when you smile. But your looks'll fade, my lad. You'll be on your walker before you know it, gumming your crusts, bewailing not having a grandchild to dandle…'

'I'm definitely applying for the bomb squad,' he retorted, and tossed a sheaf of paper at her. 'Just to get away from you. Sort these for a change. They're already sorted but so what? Give me some peace so I can download a bomb squad application.'

And then the radio buzzed into life. They both made a grab, but Beth got there first. She listened to the curt instructions on the other end and her face set.

The tossed papers lay ignored on the floor. Josh was already reaching for his jacket. He knew that look. 'What?' he demanded as she finished.

'Trouble,' Beth said, snagging her jacket, as well. 'Mine collapse on Wildfire Island. One smashed leg, needs evac to the orthopods in Cairns. Plane's leaving in ten.'

'Mine collapse?' He was snapping queries as he got organised. 'Just the one injury?'

'He was injured at the start of it. One of the supports collapsed. Fell on this guy's leg but the rest of the idiots didn't see it as a sign they should evacuate. But now...' She took a deep breath. 'The collapse looks serious. We're working on early information but one of the local doctors is trapped, as well.'

One of the local doctors.

Wildfire.

And something inside seemed to freeze.

Beth stopped, too. 'Josh? What is it?'

'You said Wildfire. Part of the M'Langi group?'

'Yeah.'

'That's where Maddie's working.'

'Maddie?' Her eyes widened as she understood. 'Your Maddie?'

'We're not married.' It was a dumb thing to say but it was all he could think of.

'I know that. You haven't been married for years. So how do you know she's there?'

'I sort of...keep tabs. She's working fly in, fly out,

two weeks there, one week on the mainland. Her mum's still in a nursing home in Cairns.'

'Right.' Beth started gathering gear again and he moved into automatic mode and did the same. There was a moment's loaded silence, and then…

'You mean you stalk her?' she demanded, but he knew it was Beth's way of making things light. Making a joke…

'I do not stalk!'

'But you keep tabs.' There was little to add to their bags, only the drugs they kept locked away or refrigerated. 'It sounds creepy.'

'We keep in touch. Sort of. Christmas and birthdays. And I take note of where she's registered to work. In case…' He hesitated. 'Hell, I don't know. In case of nothing.'

Beth's face softened. She clipped her bag closed, then touched his shoulder as she straightened. 'I know,' she said. 'I've been married twice, remember. Once your ex, always your ex. Unless it's nasty there's always a little bit of them under your skin. But, hey, there's a sizeable med centre on Wildfire. The trapped doctor doesn't have to be Maddie.'

'Right.' But suddenly he was staring into middle distance. He knew… Somehow he knew.

'Earth to Josh,' Beth said, not so gently now. 'The plane's waiting. Let's go.'

The crash had come from nowhere. One minute Maddie was working efficiently in the dim light, worried but not terrified.

Now she was terrified.

She needed to block out the dust and dark and fear.

Where was her patient?

She'd lost her torch. She'd fallen, stumbling in ter-ror as the rock wall had crashed around her. She was okay, she decided, pushing her way cautiously to her knees. There was still breathable air if she covered her mouth and breathed through a slit in her fingers. But she couldn't see.

Somewhere in here was a guy with a life-threatening bleed.

Where was the torch?

Phone app. She practically sobbed with relief as she remembered an afternoon a few weeks ago, sitting on the hospital terrace with Wildfire's charge nurse, Het-tie, while Caroline had shown them apps they could put on their cell phones.

Most she had no use for, but the torch app had looked useful for things such as checking it was a gecko on her nose and not a spider in the middle of the night. The disadvantages of living in the tropics. But now… Yes! Her phone was in her jacket pocket. She grabbed it and flicked it on.

One push and a surprising amount of light fought through the dust.

She could now see the big torch, lying at her feet. She grabbed it. The switch had flicked off when it had fallen. Not broken. She had light.

Next…

The guy she'd come in for.

She'd met them halfway in. Blood had been stream-ing from Malu's thigh and he'd been barely conscious.

The miners with him had tied a tourniquet but it wasn't enough.

'He needs more pressure,' she'd snapped. 'Put him down.'

And then she'd felt the rumbles. She'd felt the earth tremble.

'Run!' she'd screamed at the two guys who'd been carrying him, and she still seemed to hear the echoes of that yell.

They'd run.

She hoped they'd made it. Fallen rock was blocking the way she'd come. Please, let them have made it to the other side.

It was no use hoping. First things first. She was raking the rubble-strewn floor with her torch beam, searching for Malu. The combined beam of torch and phone only reached about three feet before the dust killed it.

He must have pulled himself back.

'Malu?'

'H-here.'

A pile of stone lay between them. She was over it in seconds. It hurt, she thought vaguely. She was eight months pregnant. Climbing over loose rock, knocking rock in the process, was maybe not the wisest…

She didn't have time for wise.

He was right by the pile. He was very lucky the rocks hadn't fallen on him.

Define luck, she thought grimly, but at least he was still alive. And still conscious.

Dust and blood. A lot of it.

He had a deep gash on his thigh where his pants were

ripped away. The guys had tried to tie a tourniquet but it had slipped. Blood was oozing…

But not pumping, she thought with relief. If it'd been pumping he'd be dead by now.

She was wearing a light jacket. She hauled it off, bundled it into a tight pad, placed it against the wound and pushed.

Malu screamed.

'I'm so, so sorry,' she told him, but there was no time to do anything about the pain. She had to keep pushing. 'Malu, I have drugs but I need to stop the bleeding before I do anything else. I need to press hard.'

'S-sorry. Just the shock…'

'I should have warned you.'

Go back to basics, she reminded herself, desperately fighting the need to cough, and the need to breathe through the grit. Desperately trying to sound in control. Don't start a procedure before explaining it to the patient, she reminded herself, even if she was trapped in a place that scared her witless.

Malu had relapsed into silence. She knew Malu. He was a large, tough islander from the outermost island of the M'Langi group.

He had a wife and two small children.

She pushed harder.

She had morphine in her bag. If she had another pair of hands…

She didn't.

His pants were ripped. Yes! Still pressing with one hand, she used the other and tugged the jagged cloth. The cloth ripped almost to the ankle.

Now she was fumbling one-handed in her bag for scissors. Thank heaven she was neat. There was so much dust… Despite the torchlight she could hardly see, but the scissors were right where she always stored them.

One snip and she had the tough fabric cut at the cuff, and that gave her a length of fabric to wind. The miners had tried to use a belt as their tourniquet but it was too stiff. The torn trouser leg was a thousand times better.

She twisted and wound, tying the pad—her exjacket—into place. She twisted and twisted until Malu cried out again.

'Malu, the worst's over,' she told him as she somehow managed to knot it. 'The bleeding's stopped and my hands are now free. I'll make us masks to make breathing easier. Then I'll organise something to dull the pain.'

And get some fluids into you, she added to herself, saying silent prayers of thanks that she had her bag with her, that she'd had it beside her when the collapse had happened, that she'd picked it up almost automatically and that she hadn't dropped it. She had saline. She could set up a drip. But in this dust, to try and keep things sterile…

Concentrate on keeping Malu alive first, she told herself. After so much blood loss she had to replace fluids. She'd worry about bugs later.

Malu was barely responding. His pulse… *His pulse…*

Get the fluids in. Move!

Five minutes later Malu had morphine on board and she had a makeshift drip feeding fluids into his arm. She'd ripped her shirt and created makeshift masks to keep the worst of the dust from their lungs. She sat back and held the saline bag up, and for the first time she thought she might have time to breathe herself.

She still felt like she was choking. Her eyes were filled with grit.

They were both alive.

'Doc?' Malu's voice was a whisper but she was onto it.

'Mmm?'

'Macca and Reuben… They were carrying me.'

'I know.'

'Reuben's my uncle. You reckon they've made it?'

'I don't know.' There was no point lying; Malu would know the risks better than she did. She grasped his hand and held. There was nothing else she could do or say.

The thought of trying to find them, trying to struggle out through the mass of rubble… Even if she could leave Malu, the thing was impossible. The rubble around them was unyielding.

Malu's hand gripped hers, hard. 'Don't even think about trying to dig out,' he muttered, and she thought that even though his words were meant as protection to her, there was more than a hint of fear for himself. To be left alone in the dark… 'It's up to them outside to do the rescuing now. Meanwhile, turn off the lights.'

'Sorry?'

'The lights. We don't need 'em. Conserve…'

'Good thinking,' she said warmly, and flicked off her torch. Then she flicked off the torch app on her phone. But as the beam died, a message appeared on the screen. When had that come in?

She wouldn't have heard.

The message was simple.

Maddie? Tell me you're not down the mine. On way with Cairns Air Sea Rescue. Josh.

Josh.

Josh was coming.

Her phone was working. Help was on its way.

It was amazing that the signal had reached down here, but this was a shallow tunnel, with ventilation shafts rising at regular intervals. The simple knowledge that she had phone reception made her feel better. And Josh was coming… All of a sudden she felt a thousand per cent lighter. She told Malu and felt the faint relaxation of the grip on her hand. Cairns Air Sea Rescue would be the forerunners, she knew. The cavalry was heading this way.

She gripped her phone hard, as if it alone was a link to the outside world. Help. Heavy machinery. Skill, technology, care. All the things needed to get them out of here.

Josh was coming.

It shouldn't make one scrap of difference that Josh would be one of the rescue crew. Their marriage had been over for years. They talked occasionally as casual acquaintances. Friends? Probably not even that.

But still… *Josh was coming.*

'So you still got reception?' Malu whispered, sounding incredulous, and she looked at the one bar out of five signalling a really weak link to the outside world.

'Just.'

'Tell 'em to hurry,' Malu muttered. 'And tell them if there's one single camera at the mine mouth then I need a new pair of trousers before they bring me out.'

She even managed a chuckle. He was so brave.

His pulse was so weak…

'I'll tell them,' she said and ventured a text back.

Yeah, we're underground. There's a bit of rock between us and the entrance. We're not very respectable. If you're coming in we'd appreciate a change of clothes. There's a distinct lack of laundry facilities down here.

She read it to Malu and he managed a chuckle. She should say more, she thought. She should give a complete medical update but for now it was enough that she was breathing and Malu was breathing.

She just had to keep it that way until Josh...

Until the cavalry arrived.

The plane was taxiing out onto the runway. 'Phones off now,' the pilot snapped, and Josh went to flick off his phone—and then paused as a message appeared.

If you're coming in we'd appreciate a change of clothes. There's a distinct lack of laundry facilities down here.

He swore. Then he swore again.

'Josh?' Beth was watching, all concern.

'She's down there,' he said grimly. 'Maddie's trapped.'

'Then all the more reason to turn your phone off so we can take off.' But she took the phone from his hands and stared at the screen, and her face tightened. This team were used to horror, but when it affected one of their own...

'Wait thirty seconds,' she told the pilot, and she started texting.

'What?' He tried to grab his phone back, but she turned her back on him and kept typing. Then the text sent, and she handed it back.

He looked down at what she'd written.

We're on our way. With Josh in the lead. He'll be in there with you, even if he has to dig in with his bare hands.

'Beth...' He could hardly speak.

'Truth?' she queried, and he tried to swallow panic. And failed.

'Truth,' he muttered, and he flicked his phone off and they were on their way.

CHAPTER TWO

WHAT BLESSED FAIRY had made her run into the mine with a fully loaded medical bag?

What bad goblin had made her run in at all?

In the hours that followed, Maddie tried to get a grip on what had happened.

There should have been systems in place to stop her, she decided as the darkness seemed to grow blacker around her. There should also have been barriers to stop the mine's ex-employees gaining access in the first place.

But who was in control? Where was Ian Lockhart? He owned this mine, or at least his brother did. So much on this island was running down. Lockhart money had dried up. There'd even been mutterings that the medical service would have to close.

At least the service had still been operating this morning, she thought, grasping at any ray of light she could find in this nightmare. The good news was that she'd been here. Yes, she'd been dumb enough to run into the mine, but she'd carried three units of saline and she'd only used two on Malu. The bleeding had slowed to nothing and his blood pressure was rising and…

And she was still trapped underground. A long way underground.

Her telephone beeped into life again. Ringing. Not a message.

A real person! But first she frantically sought settings to turn the volume down. The dust was still settling around them, and it seemed to her that any little sound might cause more rock to fall.

Malu was no longer aware. She'd given him more morphine and he'd fallen into an uneasy slumber. The ringtone hadn't woken him.

'H-hi.' It felt eerie to be calmly answering the phone in such conditions. She had to stop and cough. 'H-hold on.'

Let it be Josh.

Why did she think that? Josh was coming from Cairns. He couldn't be here yet. The coughing eased and she managed to focus again.

'Maddie?' The voice at the end of the phone was growing frantic. Not Josh.

She recognised the voice—Keanu, one of the other two island doctors. Sam, the island's chief permanent doctor, had decided to take leave before she had her baby, which meant she and Keanu were currently the only doctors on the island.

'What's happening?' he demanded. 'Are you okay?'

'We seem to be trapped but we're okay.' She glanced down again at Malu. 'You and me both, aren't we, Malu?'

Malu didn't respond but she didn't expect him to. The wound on his thigh was ugly. Without morphine he'd be writhing. She released the pressure from his makeshift mask a little, trying to get a balance between stopping the grit and making it harder for him to breathe.

Oxygen would be good. Why hadn't she lugged in an oxygen cylinder, as well?

She should have brought a wheelbarrow.

'Maddie?'

She jerked herself back to focussing on the call. 'Keanu? Malu has an impact injury, thigh.' She suspected broken ribs, possible internal injuries as well, but it was no use saying that in Malu's hearing. 'I suspect he'll need surgery when we get out of here, evac to Cairns, but I've stopped the bleeding and he's stable. Two litres of saline, five milligrams of intravenous morph…'

'You had that stuff down there?' He sounded incredulous.

'I was a girl scout,' she said dryly. 'I'm prepared.'

There was a moment's silence. Then…

'Are Macca and Reuben with you?'

'They ran when the second collapse came. They're not with us now.'

He must have her on speaker phone. She could hear sobbing in the background. He'd be in the operations room of the mine, she thought. The sobbing would be Macca's and Reuben's families.

Malu's family would be there, too.

No one belonging to her.

But then… Josh was coming. He'd said he would.

Josh wasn't her family, she reminded herself. In truth, he never had been.

'That last rockfall…' She was almost afraid to ask, but she had to. 'Was anyone else hurt?'

'Everyone's clear but you four.'

'Kalifa?

'Maddie, worry about yourself.'

'Should I worry?'

There was a moment's silence.

'It might take a while to reach you,' Keanu said at last. 'How's the air down there?'

'Dusty.'

'But?'

'But otherwise okay.' She sniffed. 'I can feel a bit of a draught. Do you reckon there might be some sort of escape hatch?'

'It's probably from a ventilation shaft. Thank God that's still working.' He hesitated. 'Maddie, we need to bring experts and machinery from the mainland.'

'The mainland... Cairns.'

'Yep.'

'Is that coming on the mercy flight?'

'How do you know about the mercy flight?'

'Josh told me.'

There was another silence. 'Your Josh,' he said at last.

'He's not my Josh.' And then... 'How do you know he's *my* Josh?'

'Hettie told me. She relayed the message from Cairns Air Sea Rescue. But... You've been talking to him yourself?'

'Yes.'

'Maddie?'

'Mmm?'

'You need to conserve your phone. It's probably not the time for chats with your ex.'

'He texted. I also have three battery backups in my bag. That's enough for two days.'

'That might not be enough.'

'You have to be kidding.'

'I hope I am,' he said. 'But for now…two days or not, conserve your phone.'

Two days or not, conserve your phone.

Maddie sat back on her heels and tried—really hard—not to panic.

Two days?

There'd been an incident, not so long ago, where miners had been trapped…where? Tasmania? The miners had been successfully brought to the surface after how many days? Fourteen? She couldn't remember the details but she remembered watching the rescue unfold on television. She'd been mesmerised by the tragedy of the mine collapse but even more mesmerised by the courage shown by the miners trying to keep their sanity as the appalling endurance test had stretched on.

Neither of them had been badly injured.

Malu was suffering from shock and a deep laceration, she thought, but what else? She wanted X-rays. She wanted him in hospital. She wanted a sterile environment and the necessary surgery for his leg.

She couldn't even see him.

Two days…

The darkness was absolute.

Her fingers were on Malu's wrist. His pulse was settling. There was no need to turn on the torch.

She flicked the torch on anyway, just for a moment. Just to see.

Their chamber was about eight feet in diameter. The roof was still up there, and there were shoring timbers above them. Where their tiny enclosure ended, the shoring timbers had splintered like kindling.

The floor was rock-strewn. She needed to clear it a bit to get Malu more comfortable.

She could do it without the torch. She had to do it without the torch. She flicked it off again and the total darkness was like a physical slap.

Her phone gave a tiny ping and the screen lit momentarily. She took three deep breaths—because she had been close to panic—and she let herself look.

Landed. You nice and safe down there? Got a couple of good rocks you can use for pillows or are you thinking you might like to come on up? Josh.

She could have kissed him. Except she didn't kiss Josh. Not any more. He'd always been uncomfortable with overt displays of affection. Even when they'd been married... Affection had been an effort, she thought, seizing on the excuse to get her mind off the dust. She'd never been in any doubt that he'd wanted her, but affection had been for behind closed doors. It was almost as if he'd been ashamed to admit he'd needed her.

He didn't need her. He'd figured that five years ago when he'd walked away from their marriage. But right now she needed him. She texted him.

I'm not going anywhere. Just trying to decide which rock pillow to use. It seems I have a choice. Have given Malu morphine. He's suffered major blood loss. Have given two litres of saline. I only have one more and want to hold it in reserve.

For drinking? She didn't say it. She couldn't.

Heart rate a hundred and twenty. Only just conscious. Worrying.

Damn Keanu and his ban on using her phone, she decided, as she hit Send. Okay, her battery life was precious, but Josh was a trauma specialist, a good one, and she needed advice. If she was going to be stuck down here with Malu, then the least she could do was keep him alive.

Which meant texting Josh. Didn't it?

She didn't get the little whoosh as her message sent. She stared at the single flickering bar of reception on her screen and willed it to send. Send. *Send.*

The screen went blank again and she was left with darkness.

Whoosh.

Sent. Delivered. At least she hoped it had been delivered. Josh would be on his way from Wildfire's tiny airstrip, and he had to cross the mountains to get to the mine. There were places up there where there was no phone reception at all.

How long before he saw it?

Did it matter? She was pretty sure there was nothing more she could do medically for Malu, except make him comfortable.

Comfortable? Rock pillows. Ha!

Josh will text when he can, she told herself, and the thought was comforting.

Why? Why Josh rather than anyone else?

She had lots of friends on Wildfire Island. She'd been working as a fly in, fly out doctor here for five years now, spending two weeks here, one week in Cairns. She was doing okay. She'd put her marriage behind her. This next stage of her life… Well, it was a gamble but it was something—someone—she desperately wanted.

Unconsciously her hand went to her belly. She'd been hit as the rocks had flown, but surely she'd protected her baby enough?

Why on earth had she risked her baby? It had been a split-second decision but now…it seemed almost criminally stupid.

'I'm sorry. I'm so sorry,' she whispered to the little one in her belly, and she felt like weeping.

She had to talk to someone.

Maybe she could text Hettie. Hettie, Wildfire's charge nurse administrator, was a real friend, whereas Josh was now merely a contact, someone she'd put to the back of her mind like she'd put old school photos to the back of her wardrobe. One day she'd throw them out.

But not yet, she decided as she told herself she couldn't phone anyone and started groping her way around the floor. She was shoving loose rocks to the side, clearing space so she could make Malu as comfortable as possible.

Photos. The thought was suddenly weirdly front and centre. Pictures of her mother before the stroke. Photographs of her wedding day.

They were all history, she told herself. She should get rid of them all. She touched her belly again, lightly, a touch that, all at once, seemed to be almost a prayer.

'I don't need any of it,' she said out loud, even though speaking was impossibly hard through the dust. 'The past is just that. I have a future now.'

But still…

Text soon, she pleaded silently to her phone. Please, Josh?

And she went on clearing rocks.

A truck met them at the airstrip. A chopper would have been more sensible, Josh thought grimly as they transferred gear from the plane to the truck, but the instructions had been explicit. 'We used to keep a solid clearing around the minehead but there's been cost-cutting,' Hettie had told them. The charge nurse at the hospital had put herself in charge of communication. 'The jungle's come back and even the parking lot got so rutted in the last rain it'd take hours to clear a landing site. We'll get you from the airstrip to the mine by truck.'

If they couldn't land the choppers, the injured would have to be trucked back to the airstrip for evacuation.

The injured…

Maddie?

The thought of where she was made Josh feel sick. He couldn't think of her. He had to concentrate on the job at hand—but it was taking too long to reach her.

To reach it. To reach the mine.

Maddie.

With the gear loaded he jumped into the front passenger seat of the lorry. Another jeep took Beth. They turned off the coast road, skirting the plateau to the other side of the island.

He checked his phone.

Nothing.

'There's no reception, mate,' the lorry driver told him. 'Not with the plateau between us and transmission.'

'Do you know anything more?'

'Not more'n you, probably.' The guy's knuckles were white on the steering wheel, but it wasn't because of hard driving. His face was grim as death. 'We haven't heard from Macca and Reuben. They're mates. We know Malu and Doc Haddon are alive but they're trapped.' The man's knuckles gripped even tighter. 'Bloody Lockhart. Rips all the money from the mine and what does he do with it? He's been told those shoring timbers needed replacing or the mine sealed. And where is he? Not here facing what he's done, that's for sure. It won't be him crawling down the mine trying to get them out.'

'That'll be Max Lockhart?' Josh ventured, trying not to think of anyone crawling down the mine to get… Maddie out. He was dredging up stuff he'd seen in the press about this island group. 'Isn't Max Lockhart the owner of Wildfire?'

'Yeah.' The guy spat out the window of the moving truck. 'But we've hardly seen hide nor hair of Max for years. Ian's his brother. He took over day-to-day running of the mine a few years back. He's supposed to be running the island for his brother, but as far as we can see he's just out for what he can get. He's somewhere overseas now. The mine got dangerous, the money stopped and he left. And now this mess… How the hell are we going to get 'em out?' There was a moment's silence and then he swore with an intensity Josh had never heard before and never wanted to hear again.

'And… Doc Haddon?' Josh ventured, not because he wanted to but because he was almost forced to say it.

The knuckles kept their death grip but the lines on the man's face softened. 'She's a great kid. Well, maybe she's not a kid any more but I'm sixty, mate, so she's a kid to me. She's been on the island for five years now. The wife got shingles last year. Doc saw her in the market, saw the bumps. We'd thought they were just bites but before we knew it Doc had her at the clinic. She gave her this fancy medicine right on the spot. The shingles was bad enough but Ally—that's our daughter—she looked it up on the internet and said if Mum hadn't taken the stuff it could have been ten times worse. And every day Doc found an excuse to pop in. When she was off island she got Caroline or Ana to come instead. You know that nerve pain they get? Real bad, it was, but Doc Maddie was right onto it. She cares for everyone like that.'

And then his face hardened again. 'They say she just ran in. Everyone else was running out and someone shouted that Malu was bleeding so hard the guys carrying him had to stop. She grabbed her bag and ran. She's a hero.'

And his voice cracked with emotion as he swiped his arm across his face and sniffed.

Josh's phone pinged. He glanced down, trying not to hope, but the word on his screen read *Maddie*.

He couldn't read the message. For some dumb reason his eyes were blurry, too. He had to do a matching swipe before he could make it out.

I'm not going anywhere. Just trying to decide which rock pillow to use. It seems I have a choice. Have given Malu morphine. He's suffered major blood loss. Have given two litres of saline. I only have one more and want to hold it in reserve. Heart rate a hundred and twenty. Only just conscious. Worrying.

How long since that'd been sent? While he was in the air? He swiped his face again and turned into doctor. Texted back, hoping whatever sliver of reception he had would last.

You're doing great. Heart rate will be high considering shock. Do what you can to keep him warm, cuddle him if you need to. If it's his thigh, see if you can get him sloped so his legs are higher than his heart. But you know this, Maddie. Trust your instincts. Love you.

And then he paused.

How many times in the past had he texted his wife and finished with the words *Love you*?

'You've never really loved me.' He remembered Maddie saying it to him in those last dreadful days when he'd known their marriage was over. 'Love shares, Josh. Love gives and takes and you don't know how.'

Love you?

She was right, of course. He hadn't loved her. Or not enough.

He stared at the screen for a moment and then he deleted some characters. Then hit Send. Without the love.

'I can't imagine what the wives are going through,' the truck driver said, almost to himself. 'And Pearl... Malu's wife... She's another who thinks the sun rises and sets with Maddie. Y'know, our local mums are supposed to go to Cairns six weeks before bubs are born but the docs can't make 'em so Pearl didn't. Maddie had to be choppered out to Atangi in the middle of the night. Breech it was, and Doc Maddie did an emergency Caesarean, right there in Pearl's kitchen. Pearl won't go to any other doctor since. And now Doc's trapped with Malu. Doesn't bear thinking of.'

Josh tried to think of something to say—and couldn't. He didn't trust his own voice.

'Married yourself, are you?' the guy asked at last. They were heading downhill now, through dense tropical rainforest, presumably towards the coast. Josh was trying to consider the terrain, thinking of what he already knew: that the rainforest had reclaimed most of the cleared land round the minehead, and how hard it was going to be to get machinery in.

He wanted to worry about machinery. About technicalities. He wanted to worry about anything but Maddie.

Married yourself? The guy's question still hung.

'No,' he said at last. 'Not now.'

He didn't deserve to be married. He hadn't protected…

He'd failed.

Born to useless, drug-addicted parents, Josh had been the protector since he could first remember. The strong one.

He remembered a social worker, one of the early ones, walking into their house to find Holly curled on the bed and whimpering. There hadn't been food in the house for days.

He'd been eight and Holly five. Josh had been big for his age, confused, helpless, as hungry as his little sister, but he hadn't been whimpering. He'd learned early not to cry.

And the woman had turned on him, shocked into an automatic attack. 'Why didn't you come for help?' she'd demanded. 'You're big enough now to protect your sister. Why didn't you at least tell a neighbour?'

He'd never made that mistake again. He'd protected and protected and protected—but it hadn't worked. He remembered the helplessness of being torn apart from Holly, placed in separate foster homes. The nightmares.

He'd learned to disguise even those. His job was to protect, not to share his pain. Not to add to that hurt.

And now? Once again Maddie was hurting and he was stuck on the far side of a mountain.

'Partner?' Maybe the guy was trying to distract himself. Surely he was. They were his friends underground.

And that was what Maddie was, he told himself. His friend. Nothing more.

'I guess… A girlfriend,' he told the guy and tried to think of Karen. They'd only been dating for three months but that was practically long-term for Josh. Karen was fun and flirty and out for a good time. She didn't mind that his job took him away so much. She used him as he used her—as an appendage for weddings and the like, and someone to have fun with when it suited them both.

Maybe she wasn't even a girlfriend, Josh thought. But that didn't matter.

Whereas Maddie…

'Here we are,' the truck driver said, turning off the main road—if you could call it a main road—into a fenced-off area. The main gates were wide open. The sign on the fence said Mining Area—Keep Out, but there was no trace of security.

There were a few dilapidated buildings nestled among the trees. Only the cluster of parked vehicles, an ancient fire truck, a police motorbike and a jeep with the Wildfire Medical insignia, told him that anything was wrong.

'Best place for the chopper's round the back,' the truck driver told him. 'The guys were starting to clear it when we left.' He pulled to a halt outside the first of the buildings and turned and clamped a hand on Josh's shoulder. 'Good luck, mate,' he told him. 'Thanks for coming. We sure need you.'

Josh climbed out of the truck and as he did his phone pinged. Maddie again.

We're warm enough. Could use a bit of air-conditioning. Do you think you could arrange it? Also a couple of fluffy pillows, two mattresses and Malu reckons he could handle a beer. I could handle a gin and tonic, though I suppose I'm stuck with a lemonade. Actually lemonade sounds brilliant. I'm happy to make do. That's my 'needs' list, Dr Campbell. Could you get onto it, stat?

A pillow would be nice. A pillow would be magnificent. Instead, Maddie lay on her back, with her hands behind her head, trying not to think how hard the rock was. And how much of a dead weight Malu's legs were.

See if you can get him sloped so his legs are higher than his heart.

That was easier said than done. She could have put rocks under his thighs—yeah, that'd be comfy. Instead, she'd emptied her soft leather medical bag and given that to him as a pillow. She'd given him a couple of sips of the water—not as much as he wanted but she was starting to figure that if Keanu said two days then she might need to ration. Then, out of options, she'd lain down and lifted his legs onto hers.

It helped. She had her hand on his wrist and she could feel the difference.

He'd objected but not very much. In truth, he was drifting in and out of consciousness. He could hardly assess what she was doing.

She wouldn't mind a bit of unconsciousness herself. She ached where she'd been hit by flying debris. She had a scratch on her head. Blood had trickled down and it was sticky. And grimy.

She'd kill for a wash.

Her back hurt.

Cramps?

That was her imagination, she told herself fiercely. It had to be.

Lie still and think of England.

Think of Josh? He's out there.

Josh. Her husband.

He was no such thing, she told herself, but for now, in the dust and grit, she allowed herself to think it. She'd married him. She'd made vows and she'd meant them.

When she'd signed the divorce papers it'd broken her heart.

'Josh…' She couldn't help herself. She said his name aloud, like it was some sort of talisman. She didn't need him, or at least she hadn't needed him until now. Josh hated to be needed.

But that wasn't true, she conceded. He loved to be physically needed, like he was needed now, flying off to the world's emergencies, doctor in crisis, doing what he could to help in the worst possible situations. But when she'd needed to share emotional pain?

That's when he'd been…divorced.

'Who's Josh?'

Malu asked his question sleepily. He stirred, winced, swore then settled again. His legs were so heavy. She couldn't do this for much longer, she decided, but she'd cope as long as she could.

'Josh is my ex-husband,' she said, more to distract herself than anything else. Doctors didn't reveal their personal lives to their patients, yet down here the lines between professional and personal were blurred. Two days? Please not.

'He's a trauma specialist with Cairns Air Sea Rescue,' she said, and the words seemed a comfort all by themselves. 'He's texted. He's on his way.

'Because of you?' Malu's words were slurred, but strong enough to reassure her.

'It's his job.'

'So not because of you.'

'We've been divorced for five years.'

'Yeah?' Malu must be using this as a means to distract himself from the pain, from the fear, from the difficulty breathing, she decided. It was so hard to talk through the dust.

She couldn't tell him to hush and conserve his energy. Maybe she needed distraction, too.

'So he's not the dad?' Malu asked.

'No.' She wasn't going there and it seemed Malu sensed it.

'I can't imagine being divorced from my Pearl,' Malu managed, moving on. 'So...five years ago? What happened? Wrong guy in the first place? He play fast and loose?'

'I guess...first option. He was always the wrong guy.' She thought about it for a bit and then suddenly she found herself talking. Talking about Josh. Talking, as she'd never spoken of it to anyone.

'Josh had it tough,' she said, softly into the dark. 'He had a younger sister, Holly. His parents were worse than useless and that the two of them survived at all was a miracle. They were abandoned as kids and went from foster home to foster home. Sometimes they were separated but Josh fought battle after battle to keep them together. To keep his sister safe. Their only constant was each other.'

'B-bummer…'

'Yeah,' she said softly. 'It was a bummer. But Josh was tough. He got a scholarship and made it into medicine, then worked his way through university, supporting Holly while he did it.'

'Where'd you meet him?'

'Just after I finished university. I was a first-year intern. We became friends and…well, one thing led to another.'

'To marriage.'

'That's right,' she whispered, thinking back to the precious months before that nightmare time. Lying in the dark, holding Josh. Feeling him hold her. Feeling his love unfold, feeling that they might have a chance.

'B-but?' He coughed and coughed again and then moaned, and she did a recalculation of morphine dosages and figured she could give him more in half an hour. She daren't give it sooner. She couldn't drug him too deeply, not with this amount of dust in the air.

So distract him. Tell him…the truth?

'I'm still not sure the reasons for marriage were solid,' she told him. 'My mum…well, maybe you already know? I told Pearl about her when she asked why I don't stay on Wildfire all the time. My dad took off when I was six. I'm an only child. We were incredibly close—and then she had a stroke. Major. She's unable to do anything for herself. She's permanently damaged. Anyway, as I said, Josh was my colleague and my friend, and when the stroke happened he was amazing. He cared for me when I was gutted. He cared for Mum—in fact, I think sometimes he still visits her. He did…everything right. And I thought…well, I fell so deeply in love I found myself pregnant.'

'Hey, that happens,' Malu whispered. 'Like me 'n Pearl. Never a better thing, though. So, your Josh. He was happy about it?'

'I'm not sure,' she whispered. 'He told me he was. But there's one thing Josh is good at, and that's hiding his emotions. All I knew was that he seemed happy about the baby, and he said he loved me. So we married. He still felt a bit…distant but I thought…maybe…'

'So what happened to the baby? What broke you up?'

'Knowledge,' she said bleakly. 'Learning Josh knows how to care, but not to share. Do you really want to listen to this?'

'Pearl says I'm a gossip,' Malu whispered, and grabbed her hand and held on. A link in the darkness. 'Tell me.' And then, as she hesitated, his grip tightened. 'I know it's not my business, but honest, Maddie, I'm scared. You could tell me it's all going to be fine but we both know that's not true. Distract me. Anything that's said in the mine stays in the mine.'

She almost smiled. 'That seems a really good arm twist to give you more gossip.'

She sensed a half smile in return. She was friends with his wife, but she barely knew Malu. Though maybe that was no longer true, she decided. There was nothing like hurling you down a mine and locking you in, with the threat of rockfalls real and constant, to make you know someone really fast.

And what harm to talk about Josh now? she asked herself. Somewhere he was out there, worrying. Caring. Caring was what he was good at, she thought.

Caring wasn't enough.

Tell Malu? She might as well. He needed distraction and she…well, so did she.

'They say troubles come in threes,' she said finally into the dark. 'So did ours. Mum had her stroke. We got married, which was the good bit, but there were two more tragedies waiting in the wings. We lost the baby—Mikey was born prematurely—and then Josh's little sister died.'

'Oh, Maddie.' What sort of doctor–patient relationship was this? she asked herself. It was Malu doing the comforting.

As Josh had comforted.

'You know, if it had been my sister and only my baby, like it was my mum, I'm guessing Josh would have coped brilliantly,' she said, and now she was almost speaking to herself. Sorting it out in her mind. 'But it was Josh's pain and he didn't know how to cope with it. It left him gutted and his reaction was to stonewall himself. He just emotionally disappeared.'

'How can you do that?'

'Normal people can't,' Maddie said slowly. 'But Josh had one hell of a childhood. He never talks about it but when I met him his sister was doing brilliantly, at uni herself, happy and bubbly. She told me how bad it had been but Josh never did. He used to have nightmares

but when I woke him he'd never tell me what they were
about. Sometimes I'd wake and hear him pacing in the
night and I knew there were demons. And then came
baby Mikey, too small to live. And Holly. One drunk
driver, a car mounting the footpath. So after all that,
Josh's care came to nothing and he went so far into himself I couldn't reach him. He finally explained to me,
quite calmly, that he couldn't handle himself. He didn't
know how to be a husband to me any more. He had to
leave.'

She shook her head, trying to shake off the memory of the night Josh had finally declared their marriage was over.

There was a long silence, for which she was grateful. And then she thought…

These *are* cramps. Stomach cramps.

Back cramps?

And that thought brought a stab of fear so deep it
terrified her.

She was lying on a rock floor, supporting Malu's
legs. Of course she had cramps.

Of course?

Please…

'I can top up the morphine now if you like,' she
managed at last, and at least this was an excuse to turn
on the torch. She needed the phone app torch, too, to
clean the dust away and inject the morphine. She held
the phone for a bit too long after.

The light was a comfort.

The phone would be better.

No word. No texting.

Cramps.

Josh…

Malu's grip on her hand gradually lessened. She thought he was drifting into sleep, but maybe the rocks were too hard. The morphine didn't cut it.

'So your Josh abandoned you and joined Cairns Air Sea Rescue?' he whispered at last.

Oh, her back hurt. She wouldn't mind some of that morphine herself...

Talk, she told herself. Don't think of anything but distracting Malu.

'I think that other people's trauma, other people's pain, are things he can deal with,' she managed, struggling to find the right words. Struggling to find the right answer. 'But losing our baby... It hurt him to look at me hurting, and when Holly died, he didn't know where to put himself. He couldn't comfort me and he thought showing me his pain would make mine worse. He couldn't help me, so he left.'

'Oh, girl...'

'I'm fine,' she whispered, and Malu coughed again and then gripped tighter.

'I dunno much,' he wheezed. 'But I do know I'm very sure you're not.'

'Not what?'

'Fine. You're hurting and it's not just the memory of some low-life husband walking out on you.'

'I'm okay.'

'I can tell pain when I hear it.'

'I got hit by a few rocks. We both have bruises all over.'

'There's room on my pillow to share.'

'It's not exactly professional—to share my patient's bed.'

'I'm just sharing the pillow,' Malu told her with an

attempt at laughter. 'You have to provide your own rock base.'

She tried to smile. Her phone pinged and she'd never read a text message faster.

Hey, you. Quick update? Tell us you're okay. Josh.

'Is that telling us the bulldozers are coming?' Malu demanded, and the threadiness of his voice had her switching on the torch again. 'Hey, it's okay,' he managed. 'You tell them…tell them to tell Pearl I'm okay. But I wouldn't mind a bulldozer.'

'I wouldn't mind a piece of foam,' she told him, and tried to think of what to say to Josh. Apart from the fact that she was scared. No, make that terrified. She hated the dark and she was starting to panic and the dust in her lungs made it hard to breathe and the cramps…

Get a grip. Hysterics were no use to anyone.

She shouldn't have come in in the first place, she told herself.

Yeah, and then Malu would be dead.

Josh wanted facts. He couldn't cope with emotion.

Yeah, Josh, we're fine.

CHAPTER THREE

JOSH WASN'T ON Wildfire to dig into a mine and pull people out. Not even Maddie. Josh was there to assess medical need, perform triage, arrange evacuation where possible and then get his hands dirty dealing with injuries needing on-the-ground treatment.

And there was a need. The locals were doing all they could, but the medical team here consisted of one doctor and two nurses. It had apparently taken the doctor—an islander called Keanu—time to get there, and the guy who had been injured first was taking up his attention. A fractured leg followed by a cardiac arrest left room for little else.

But there was more medical need. Apparently, before Keanu had arrived, the miners had fought their way back into mine, frantically trying to reach their injured mates. It hadn't worked. There'd been a further cave-in. Further casualties. Keanu barely had time to acknowledge Josh and Beth's arrival.

There was still a sense of chaos. Keanu had ordered everyone back from the mine mouth but no one seemed to be in charge of rescue efforts.

'Where's the mine manager?' Josh snapped as he surveyed the scene before him. A group of filthy miners were huddled at the mouth of the mine, with pretty much matching expressions of shock and loss. Keanu had organised the casualties a little way away, under the shade of palm trees. He and the nurses were working frantically over the guy with the injured leg, but he shook his head as Josh approached.

'We have everything we need here. It's touch and go for this guy and there's others needing help. The guy with the arm first.' He motioned across to where a miner was on the ground, his mate beside him.

'No breathing problems?'

'They've all had a lungful of rock—we could use a tank of oxygen—but…'

'I'll get Beth to do a respiratory assessment. Beth?'

'Onto it.' She was already heading for the truck, for oxygen canisters. 'Okay, guys,' she called. 'Anyone want a face wipe and a whiff of something that'll do you good? Line up here.'

'What's happening down the mine?' Josh asked.

'Hettie's called the mining authorities in Cairns. We need expertise. They're sending engineers and equipment now.'

From Cairns. It'd take hours.

Maddie was down there.

Keanu was adjusting a drip, watching the guy's breathing like an eagle watched a mouse. A tiny thing, the rise and fall of a chest, but so important. 'So you're the ex-husband,' he managed.

'Yeah.'

'Yeah, well, we all love Maddie, but she's in there now and it's up to the experts to get her out. Meanwhile, sorry, mate, but there's more work here than we can handle. We're still trying to stabilise. We have a suspected ruptured spleen, a guy with an arm so crushed he might lose it, a fractured leg with shock and breathing problems and more. Could you look at the spleen for me?'

And somehow Josh had to stop thinking of Maddie underground, Maddie trapped, Maddie deep in a mine where there'd already been two major rockfalls. He needed to focus on the here and now.

Triage…

He headed across to the guy with the suspected ruptured spleen. As long as he wasn't going into shock—which he could be if the rupture was significant—then the arm was the first priority. If he could save it.

Four underground. Including Maddie.

'Who's the mine manager?' he snapped, asking it not of Keanu, who was committed to the patient under his hands, but of the miners in general.

'Ian Lockhart,' one of the men ventured. 'At least, he's supposed to be in charge but he lit out when the debt collectors started sniffing around.'

'Was he in charge of day-to-day running of the mine?'

'That used to be Pete Blake. Max Lockhart owns the island but he's never here. He put Pete in charge but Ian reckoned he knew it all. He sacked Pete last year and took over the day-to-day stuff himself. Reuben Alaki's acting supervisor now but…' He hesitated and his voice cracked. 'Reuben's one of the guys stuck down there.'

'Is Pete still on the island?'

'He'll probably be out fishing.'

'Get him,' Josh snapped. 'Use one of the island choppers to bring him here—do an air drop.'

'What, pluck him off his boat and drop him here?'

'Exactly,' Josh snapped. 'We need expertise now.' He bent over the guy with the fractured arm. Compound. Messy. 'Okay, mate, let's get you assessed and see if we can do something for the pain. Meanwhile let's get things moving to get your mates out from underground.'

And then a nose wedged its way under his arm and he almost froze with shock. It was a great, bounding golden retriever.

Bugsy.

It was so long since he'd seen the dog it was all he could do not to shed a few tears into his shaggy coat. The big dog recognised him. That was amazing all by itself.

He'd given Bugsy to Maddie after their honeymoon, just before he'd gone back to work. His job was search and rescue. He spent days at a time in remote places, coping with emergencies like this one.

He'd been aware just how alone Maddie had been—that was one of the reasons he'd married her. Puppy Bugsy had been a great idea. He'd been their one constant when things had fallen apart, but when things had really fallen apart it had been logical that Maddie take him.

That he was here… On the island…

He couldn't focus on the dog, though. The fracture was severe. On first assessment he thought enough blood was getting through to keep the hand viable, but suddenly…it wasn't.

And behind him Keanu had the CPR unit set up on the guy with the fractured leg.

'Go find Maddie,' he said to Bugsy, pushing the great head away with a wrench that almost physically hurt. 'I can't go to her but maybe… Go fetch Maddie. Go!'

* * *

The cramping was hurting. Really hurting.

It's only my back, she told herself. It has to be only my back. I must have wrenched it when I fell.

The cramps were fifteen minutes apart…

Or more like ten.

Uh-oh.

'Josh, I need you here.'

Keanu wouldn't be calling if the need wasn't beyond urgent. He elevated the arm he'd been treating and called for Beth to hold it steady, as straight as possible. Please, let enough blood get through to keep it viable until he got back. The man needed two of him.

At least it stopped him thinking about Maddie.

'So tell me how you met Pearl?'

Malu might be her patient, Maddie thought, but the distinction between doctor and patient was getting blurred. The blackness was closing in, and her only link to reality seemed to be Malu's hand. But it was she who was doing the comforting, she told herself. Of course it was.

She'd asked the question to distract him from pain and fear. And she needed him to answer, because she needed to be distracted from pain and fear right back.

So she listened as, in a faltering voice that sometimes paused for long enough to make her worry, Malu told of growing up on the island, of diving, of fishing, of learning to show off to the girls.

Of being in sixth grade and kicking a ball between the desks with his mates. Of being punished by being made to sit next to a girl.

Of watching Pearl write a story about watching the boys dive, then listening to the teacher praise it and saying, 'You boys might dive any time you can, but by writing it down, Pearl keeps it forever.'

Of deciding right there and then that she was his woman.

Of it taking ten years before she finally agreed.

Then babies. Domestic drama. Love…

Maddie was blinking as Malu's voice finally trailed off and she realised he'd drifted into sleep.

Love, she thought. You didn't realise how rare it was until you lost it.

She'd lost her baby. Born so prematurely… Mikey. He'd lived for two hours.

And she'd lost Josh.

Actually, she hadn't lost him, she told herself harshly. She'd never had him. And now she had a baby to love on her own.

She'd brought her baby into a collapsed mine. How could she have done something so stupid? Even to save Malu… To risk her baby…

Josh was out there, she told herself, and, as if on cue, her phone rang.

It rang, didn't ping for an incoming message, and when she answered, miraculously it was Josh!

'Hi!'

Do not cry, she told herself. *You will not.*

'Maddie?'

She took a couple of deep breaths—or as deep as she could manage—and tried to talk.

'J-Josh.'

'Hey…'

'No. Sorry. I'm scaring you.' She was fighting to

get a grip, immensely grateful that Malu was sleeping. 'There's nothing to scare you for. Malu's settling. His blood pressure's rising. I think we can manage without the third bag of saline.' No need to mention why she wanted to hold it in reserve. 'Raising his legs seems to have helped. I've given him an additional five milligrams of morphine. He's... We're as good as we can be.' And then she cracked, just a little. 'Any idea when we might expect help?'

'We're working on it. Pete Blake's just been choppered in. He was out on the reef, fishing. He knows the old seams backwards.'

'P-Pete's good.' He was, too. She—and the rest of the islanders—had been appalled when he'd been sacked. 'But...'

'But he can't get you out on his own,' Josh told her. 'There needs to be careful appraisal before we do anything. I think you need to face staying where you are overnight.'

Overnight. Right. At least that was better than Keanu's two days.

'How will we know it's bedtime?' she managed, striving for lightness.

'The time will be on your phone, Maddie, but I'll ring you and tell you anyway. If you like, I'll even sing you a lullaby.'

'You!'

'My voice is improving with age,' he said, sounding wounded. 'You want to hear?'

'No!'

'No taste,' he said mournfully. 'I don't know why I married you.'

'I don't know, either,' she said, and suddenly it was

serious again. The past was flooding back—but also the present. 'Josh?'

'Mmm?'

'What's happening out there?'

'We've just saved a hand.'

She drew in her breath. 'Whose?'

'Max Stubbs.'

'Oh!' She thought back, remembering the stream of miners emerging from the mine mouth. Max had been there, staggering but on his feet. 'His blood supply was compromised? I missed it.'

'You're going to blame yourself?'

'If I'd stayed on top…'

'You made a call. Malu's need was greater.'

'I didn't even assess…'

'It wasn't compromised when you saw it. It was an unstable fracture and it moved. It's okay. We got it in time.'

She hesitated but she really wanted to know. 'What else did I miss?'

'Nothing.'

'Then why the sag in your voice? What aren't you telling me?' She knew this guy. He hid his emotions, but not well enough. Maybe that was why he'd had to walk away from her; because somehow she'd seen behind the wall.

'Maddie…'

'If you don't tell me I'll assume there's some sort of gas leak and it's on its way in here now, creeping in, inch by inch, ready to swallow—'

'Maddie!'

'So tell me!'

He hesitated again, but finally conceded. 'We lost a patient. The first guy out.'

'Kalifa?' She was incredulous. 'He had a broken leg.'

'Cardiac arrest. Sixty-seven years old. Overweight. He should never have been down the mine in the first place.'

'None of them should,' she said bitterly. 'But Kalifa... His heart... Oh, no. I should have—'

'Cut yourself some slack,' he said curtly. 'You were one doctor in the middle of a disaster. You did what you could. There were a couple more injuries from guys trying to be heroes after you disappeared but we're thinking they'll be fine. How's the battery on the phone?'

Her battery was okay. It had to be. This link to Josh seemed the only thing keeping her same. 'I have backup but I'll be careful. Josh?'

'Mmm?'

'You need to go back to work.'

'I do. We're stabilising, then we'll get everyone we can to the hospital here or out to Cairns. But I'll be staying at the mine mouth.'

Why did that make her feel a thousand times better? Why did his voice make something inside her settle, something that had been unsettled for years?

'Bugsy's been here,' he said tangentially. 'I saw him when I first got here. How come you get to keep him on the island when you're fly in, fly out?'

'He's become our hospital dog. Everyone loves him, but officially Hettie looks after him when I'm in Cairns. Hettie's our nurse administrator. She's tough on the outside, marshmallow on the inside.'

'Like me,' Josh said, and she heard his smile and why it made her want to weep again she didn't know.

Still that strange feeling. But she was over Josh, she told herself. She had to be.

'You're okay?' he demanded, and she struggled to make herself sound okay. The cramps... The pain in her back... But what was the point of worrying him? It wasn't like he could wave a magic wand and get her out of here.

'I'm fine.'

'You don't sound fine.'

'Okay, I'm sure my lipstick's smudged but I can't find a mirror.'

She heard him chuckle, but she knew the chuckle was forced. 'I'll ring you again in an hour, if Keanu's not watching,' he promised, and she managed to smile, and managed to tell herself the cramps weren't bad and she wasn't going to cry and she didn't need Josh here, now, holding her.

'And if he is?' she managed.

'I'll ring you anyway. I promise.'

She was trying not to think of Josh. She was also trying not to think of contra—of cramps. If she lay very still the cramps weren't so bad.

If only they weren't so regular.

They were every ten minutes or so, sweeping through her entire body. She had to fight not to gasp. Not to cry out.

If I lie very still...

She lay very still.

She lay in the dark and stared at nothing and her hands cradled the swell of her belly.

'I'm so sorry,' she whispered. 'I should have thought of you first.'

'Maddie…'

'Mmm?' Malu was stirring.

'Time for another of those wee jabs?'

'Pain scale, one to ten?' she asked, and he thought about it.

'Eight,' he said at last. 'And you?'

'I'm not—'

'Lying? I'm damned sure you are. You want to take your legs out from under mine?'

'No, I—'

'Or I'll shift 'em myself.'

'Malu…'

'There's two of us in this mess,' he said morosely. 'We keep things fair.' And then he hesitated. 'Though that's not true, is it? There's three.'

'Don't…'

'You are hurting. I can hear it in your breathing.'

'I told you, I got bumped.'

'How many weeks are you?'

'I… Thirty-four.' She was lying. Stupid, stupid, stupid. She'd gambled and she'd lost, big time.

Not catastrophically, though, she pleaded. Please…

'Maddie!'

'It's okay,' she managed. 'We just need to be patient. You want another sip of water?'

'Yeah.' But there was a world of meaning in that word. A sip… What they both wanted was a river. Or six.

'Pearl says you don't know who the daddy is.'

'Leave it, Malu.'

'You don't want to talk about it?'

'I don't want to think about it.' She'd just got through another cramp and her fear was building by the minute. 'I don't want to think about it at all.'

* * *

'No one's going near the mine until the engineers arrive from Cairns.' Pete, the sacked mine manager, had been lowered by chopper. He was still in his fishing gear and smelled of bait, but he was competent and authoritative. He was also adamant. 'The seam they're in...well, suicidal's not the word for it. Even Lockhart... He was greedy for every ounce of gold the mine'd give him. He knew it was a rich seam but the ground's unstable granite. Burrowing into it's like burrowing into rocky sand. It's a miracle the shoring timbers have stayed up as long as they have.'

'But we have two alive and two don't-knows in there,' Josh said bleakly. 'How—?'

'We worry about getting them out when the engineers arrive.' Pete was standing in front of the mine entrance and his body language said that anyone who wanted to go in there had to go through him. Which would maybe take a bulldozer. 'But initially we can check the ventilation shafts. There's a possibility we might be able to get lines through, enough to check air supply and to get them water.'

While they waited for rescue that might never happen? That might be too dangerous to even consider? The words were left unsaid but they didn't have to be said. They were so loud in Josh's head that everything else seemed muted.

The initial rush of trauma-related work had abated. The guys with the fractured arm and the suspected ruptured spleen were on their way to the airstrip, and then to Cairns. A doctor who'd been conducting research out on Atangi had been on the fishing boat with Pete. He'd agreed to fly back to Cairns as acting medical officer.

That was Josh's job, but Josh wasn't moving. Instead, he was pacing, like a trapped, caged animal with nowhere to go.

There was nothing to do.

Engineers were due to arrive at any minute. They had another couple of hours of daylight.

How much air was down the mine? How to get fluids down?

And then there was a shout.

'Hey, someone's down there. Someone's coming up.'

There was a surge towards the mine entrance but Pete was still in blocking mode. He spread his arms so no one could get past him—and then Pete saw who it was and forgot about security, making a surge himself.

And two minutes later he was helping Macca support Reuben for the last few yards. As the dust cleared, and the surge of miners parted, Josh got a clear view. Two miners, both islanders. An older man, in his fifties, staggering, dragging a leg behind him. A younger guy, tall, filthy, supporting his mate.

The younger guy's hand holding... Bugsy. Maddie's dog. Though it was kind of hard to tell—the usually gold of the retriever's coat was now matted black.

The big dog was wagging his tail, but even as Josh watched him he tugged sideways, looking back at the mine entrance.

'Hold, Bugsy,' he snapped. He was fifty yards away and he could see exactly what the dog intended to do.

And Pete was quick. He snagged the dog's collar and handed him over to the nearest miner before helping lower the injured guy to the ground. 'Doc...'

All Josh wanted to do was go to Bugsy, figure out how he'd done what he'd done and, more importantly, figure out if he could do more, but his attention had to be on the men.

Caroline, one of the island nurses, was with him, and judging by the fleeting embrace he'd witnessed between them, she was involved with Keanu. She had scissors out already, even as Pete was lowering Reuben to the ground.

Please, let him not need me.

It was silent prayer as he started work. Another compromised blood supply or similar would take all his attention.

But this leg was good. This leg was great.

Or…actually not. It'd hurt like the devil for a week or more but it wasn't broken. It needed careful cleaning, debridement, but it wasn't urgent.

The urgent stuff had been dealt with. And Keanu was here.

'You'll be okay,' he told Rueben. He glanced at Caroline, then at Bugsy, then back to Reuben again. 'We'll give you something for the pain and get you to the hospital but this looks like bruising and lacerations, not a break.'

And then he looked at Bugsy again.

'Do you think Bugsy could find Maddie?' Caroline whispered. He and Caroline were still kneeling over Reuben, but Caroline was following his gaze. 'He's Maddie's dog…'

He wasn't the only one thinking it, then. He glanced at Caroline and saw her fear.

'You're her friend?'

'Yes, not only am I her friend but I'm a Lockhart. My uncle was supposed to be taking care of this mine and these workers. He clearly failed at that. He's gone and now Maddie's in danger. This is partly my fault. I ordered the closure of the mine but I should have seen that the workers would be in desperate need. I just can't believe that Maddie went in there...'

She looked sick. This was bad for the outside rescue workers, he thought. How much worse would it be for those who'd lived and worked every day with those trapped underground?

And as if on cue, Caroline's phone rang. She flicked it open.

'Maddie. Oh, my God, Maddie, are you okay?' She cast Josh an uncertain look and then flipped the switch to speaker so he could hear. But all he heard was silence.

'Maddie, you've rung the duty phone,' Caroline said urgently into the silence. 'This is Caro.'

'I wanted...' Maddie's voice faltered. 'Caro, I wanted Hettie. I forgot you'd have the phone. Can I...? I need...' Her voice broke on a gasp.

It was too much for Josh. He took the phone from Caroline's hand and spoke.

'Maddie, what's wrong? We can get Hettie to ring you but it might take a few minutes. You sound distressed. Can you tell us what's happening?'

There was another gasp from the end of the line. Pain. Maddie was hurting, he thought. Worse. Maddie was terrified.

'Maddie...'

'I need Hettie,' she whispered. 'I need...'

'Hettie's doing the communication for transport. She's based at the hospital. We'll have her ring you as soon as we can, but you need to tell us why you're hurting.'

Silence seemed to stretch forever, or maybe it was

the fact that Josh wasn't breathing. The whole world seemed to be still. And finally Maddie answered.

'Hettie's the island midwife,' she whispered. 'I need… I need someone to talk me through this. My baby's coming. I think I'm in established labour.'

There were noises around them. Keanu was giving orders in the background. A truck was backing up, ready to transport patients. Beth was talking to someone on the phone.

All Josh could hear was white noise.

Established labour.

There was more silence. He could hear Maddie gasping through the phone. Breathing through a contraction? He knew she couldn't talk.

'How pregnant?' he demanded of Caroline, and it physically hurt to say the words. It physically hurt to wait for the answer.

'She says thirty-four weeks,' Caroline whispered, sounding terrified herself. 'But I suspect… She needs the money to support her mother in that gorgeous nursing home. I know she wants to work for as long as possible. She's due to finish here at the end of this week but I looked at her yesterday and thought the baby's dropped. There's a chance she's a couple of weeks further on.'

Thirty-four weeks. Maybe thirty-six.

Who's the father? But he didn't say it. He hardly even thought it.

Maddie. Underground. In labour.

Thirty-four weeks. A premature baby?

'Maddie,' he said, more urgently, but there was still no answer.

He thought suddenly, searingly, of Maddie five years

ago. Maddie lying in the labour ward, holding her tiny son. Mikey had been born impossibly early, never viable from the moment they'd recognised placental insufficiency. But the grief…

Maddie had held their son—*their son.*

He'd walked away. He'd been unable to share his grief and he hadn't been able to help her.

'Maddie?' And this time she answered.

'Y-yes?'

'How far apart are the contractions?' Somehow he kept his voice calm. He was desperately trying to sound like a doctor, when all he wanted to do was to drop the phone and start heaving rocks from the collapsed shaft.

'T-ten minutes. Maybe a bit less.'

'Thirty-four or thirty-six weeks, Maddie? Honest.'

'Thirty-six.'

He breathed out a little at that. It made a difference. For a prem baby, underground, with no medical technology at all, two weeks could make all the difference in the world.

'Malu,' he managed. 'The guy down there with you. Is he your partner?'

There was an audible gasp, and then, unbelievably, he heard the trace of a smile in her voice. 'No. Malu's married to my friend. He has two kids.'

'Can he help you?'

'No.' The sliver of humour disappeared as fast as it had come. 'I need… I need to talk to Hettie. She'll talk me through—'

'I'll put you back to Caroline,' he said in a voice he knew sounded strangled. 'She'll try and organise a line to Hettie. Hold on, love, and—'

'I'm not your love.' It was said with asperity.

'No.' He took a deep breath and somehow steadied himself. Asperity was good, he thought. Asperity meant she still had spirit, strength, the grit he knew and loved. 'The important thing is not to panic,' he told her, but he was all for panicking himself. There wasn't a shred of him that wasn't panicking. 'Hold on, Maddie. We need to do some fast organising.'

He handed the phone back to Caroline.

'Keanu,' he managed in a voice he hardly recognised as his own.

'Yeah?' Keanu was with him in an instant, thinking from Josh's voice it was something urgent, something medical.

It was.

'I want refills of morphine, saline, electrolytes,' he snapped, grabbing his bag then reaching for Keanu's and helping himself. There was a coil of thin rope lying nearby. He slung it over his shoulder. How much stuff could you cart down a collapsing mine? Not enough, but maybe enough to make a difference. 'Can you take over here?'

'What the—?'

'I'm heading down,' he snapped.

'You're going nowhere.' Keanu's hand landed on his shoulder. 'No one goes down that mine.'

'Bugsy's been down and come back again,' Josh snapped, reaching for one of the massive torches one of the miners had set aside. 'If he can, so can I.'

'Bugsy's a dog.'

'Yeah, he's a dog. He has no dependants and he's expendable if necessary. Mate, that's what I am. No one's waiting for me at home and I might make a difference. We have a pregnant woman in labour, an injured miner and the possibility that I might be able to reach them. I'm not trying to dig like the other idiots did. I'm following the path Bugsy's already found. I'm fit and I'm used to tight places. I'm asking no one to come in and rescue me—the responsibility's mine.'

'There's no way.' Keanu growled. 'I can't allow it.'

'You don't have a choice. As I don't. This is my wife.' And suddenly that's exactly what it felt like. He'd walked away from their marriage vows five years ago but she still felt...

Like part of him.

He wasn't married, he thought grimly as he sealed his bag. He didn't do marriage. He hadn't been able to help Maddie in her grief when he'd been unable to handle his own, and it'd almost killed him.

'Pete says the mining engineers are due here in the next half-hour,' Keanu said, urgently. 'They'll assess the risk.'

And he knew exactly what they'd say. They'd seal it. They'd work in inch by painstaking inch. They'd take days to reach her.

Reach *them*.

They'd have the manpower and the authority to stop him. Keanu did, too, if he gave him time to call Pete, to block the mouth by force, to muster all the sensible reasons why he shouldn't try.

'Sorry, mate.' He grabbed a discarded hard hat with attached head lamp and shoved it on his head. 'But this is my wife, my call. Clean things up here. Reuben, I'm leaving you in the best of hands. Oh, and if my boss calls, tell him I'm on family leave. Starting now.'

And then, before Keanu could respond, before another argument could be mounted, he grabbed Bugsy's collar from the miner who was holding him.

'Come on, Bugsy,' he told him, looping the collar hard under his hand. Bugsy had obviously figured the direction to go. He'd gone straight to the injured miners, and then, reluctantly, it seemed, accompanied them to safety.

'Come on, Bugsy,' he told the dog again, and he was at the mine mouth, heading in before anyone could move fast enough to stop him.

CHAPTER FOUR

'MADDIE?'

She'd had to disconnect from Caroline to try and reach Hettie but it hadn't worked. Hettie was manning the phone at the hospital and the line was continuously engaged. She grabbed the phone now, hoping it was Hettie, or, weirdly, hoping even more it was Josh.

That's crazy, she told herself. Just be grateful that you get reception down here, that you have any connection at all.

It wasn't Josh.

'Keanu?'

'Caroline's trying to get a message to Hettie to clear the line so you can talk to her,' he told her. 'Meanwhile, progress?'

'Things are stable. Nothing's changed.' She'd kill for a drink. The contractions were still steady at ten minutes. She ached. Malu was drifting in and out of his drug-induced sleep.

Yes, things were stable.

'Blood pressure?'

'Mine or Malu's?' It was an attempt at humour but it didn't work.

'Both,' he snapped, and listened as she told him.

'That's sounding okay.' But there was serious tension in Keanu's voice—deep tension—tension that told her something else was going on.

'You're about to tell me the sky's going to fall on our heads? If so, it already has.' She caught herself then and directed her beam upwards. 'Actually, no. No, it hasn't. Bad idea.'

'Can you see any light at all?'

'Um…no.'

'We were hoping you'd be near a ventilation shaft.'

'In which case we'd see light.'

'Not if it's blocked. No.'

'So…' There was still something he wasn't telling her. 'Anything else I can help you with?' She tried to make her voice chirpy, sales assistant like.

'You said you were feeling air.'

Another contraction. She gasped and forgot the sales assistant act. Keanu just had to wait.

'There is the faint whiff of air,' she admitted as she surfaced again.

'It's blowing hard out here, straight into the mouth of the cave. You have the torch? Can you shine it at the rocks, look for gaps?'

She shone. The torch beam simply disappeared into the dust and blackness.

'I can't see anything. Even if there was a way out, I could hardly wiggle. And not with Malu…'

'So if we got someone in to you…'

'No one's to come in.' She must have sounded shrill because Keanu didn't answer for a moment and when he did he sounded deeply concerned.

'Maddie?'

'It's just there's still stuff...settling,' she told him. 'Can't you dig us out from the top?'

'We're working on it. Maddie, you sound like you're in pain.'

'I'm not. I'm worrying. Keanu, no one else is to risk...' And then she stopped. She knew Keanu well. 'Someone's already trying, aren't they? Of all the... There's no room in here. Drill a hole down. Get us out from the top. We can't drag Malu out. There's no room for a stretcher and there are rocks still falling. Burrowing's impossibly perilous. I was an idiot to come in, but I've managed to keep Malu alive. There's no point in me doing that if someone else dies.'

Silence.

'What?' she said, feeling the weight of the silence. 'What aren't you telling me?'

'It's Josh,' he said heavily. 'And Bugsy.'

'What the...?'

'Bugsy went haring into the mine. He found the first two miners, the guys who were helping Malu when you went in. They came out, with him leading. It was almost as if Bugsy knew what he had to do. He got them to the surface but he was heading in again.

'And Josh?' She could scarcely breathe.

'Josh has gone with him. We couldn't stop him. The guy's either a hero or an idiot and I can't decide which.'

'Idiot,' she said, but only half of her meant it.

The other half of her unashamedly wanted Josh.

Torches were almost useless in the dust. The cabled lighting that usually lit the shafts had obviously been knocked out by the fall. The floor was covered with rock litter. Josh wasn't too sure where the roof was, and his torch beam seemed to disappear.

He kept his hand on Bugsy's collar. Bugsy was whining a little, but heading inward and down. He seemed to know exactly where he was going.

If Josh hadn't been holding him he'd have surged ahead. To Maddie?

Who knew? But the fact that he'd found the two miners was an excellent sign. The mine branched out in half a dozen different directions a little way in from the mouth. The miners had been in the tunnel Maddie was in, so he had to assume that was where Bugsy was heading.

To Maddie.

He stumbled on a loose rock and dropped to his knees. Bugsy whined and turned and licked his face, then tugged again.

'You need to go at my pace,' he told the dog. 'Four legs and half my height would be good.'

He tugged. Okay, there was no use sitting around waiting to shrink or grow new legs.

His phone went.

What was it with communications in this place? All the way across the mountains there'd been no signal, yet here…

Maddie. The name popped up on his screen as soon as his fumbling hand hauled his phone from his pocket. He almost dropped it in his haste to answer.

'Hey.' He tried to make his voice normal but the dust was too heavy. He ended up coughing instead.

'You're down the shaft.' Her voice was dull, dread-filled.

'Only a little way down,' he told her. 'Me and Bugsy.'

'Well, turn yourselves around and go back up again.'

'Bugsy won't and I don't know the way without Bugsy.'

'Bugsy took the miners out. They knew enough to say "jeep" and she obeyed. The whole island knows "jeep" to Bugsy means head back to the jeep and stay there. You can't have a dog trailing after you on every island emergency without a few ground rules.'

'So if I say j—' He stopped. 'If I say the name of your car...'

'Say it, Josh.'

'We're coming to find you. Me and Bugsy.'

'You'll kill yourselves and where will that leave us? The engineers will drill in from the top. It's not so deep. They'll find us.'

'It'll take days. Maddie, I'm disconnecting now. Bugsy's eager to keep going.'

'Josh, I don't want this. I didn't expect... You can't risk...'

'You know I always risk. It's what I do.'

'You're trained to swing from helicopters and abseil down cliffs. You're trained in emergency rescue. But for every single scenario you trained and trained. I'm betting not once have you ever trained to dig into a collapsing gold mine when even the experts are saying it's crazy.'

'I'm training now,' he said briefly. 'I'm coming, sweetheart.'

'I don't want you to die!' And it was a wail. She couldn't help herself. Her beautiful Josh...

She loved him. She always had and she always would. He wasn't marriage material. He'd never been her husband, not properly, and years ago she'd stopped hoping for that, and yet she still loved him. The thought of him being down in this appalling place was unbearable.

And then another pain hit. She whimpered before she could stop herself. She bit it off fast, but he'd heard.

'What the…?'

'I just moved on the floor. Sharp rock,' she lied, and heard silence on the end of the line. 'Josh, go home.'

'Conserve your phone batteries, love,' he told her. 'Any minute now you'll get to talk to me in person.'

'I'm not your love,' she repeated.

'Go tell that to someone who cares. I'm coming in anyway.'

He was coming.

She should be appalled. She was appalled.

But…he was coming.

'Help's on its way,' she whispered to Malu, but he was sleeping too deeply to hear.

He needed more fluids. Would Josh be carrying fluids?

'He won't get here.' She said it out loud, trying to suppress the flare of hope, of belief, of trust. 'Okay, Bugsy made it to where the last rockfall took place but there *was* a rockfall.

'It can't be too thick.' She was talking out loud to herself. 'Those guys were with us when it started falling and they ended up safe on the other side.'

She crawled across her little cavern to where the mound of fresh-fallen rock blocked the exit. At least, she thought this was the mound in the direction of the exit. It could be the one behind her.

She was pretty disorientated.

She was in pain.

Forget the pain, she told herself, fiercely now. Concentrate on ways out of here.

Ways Josh could get in.

The rocks were big. The fall wasn't packed with loose gravel, but rather a mound of large boulders.

Dear God, they'd been lucky.

Define luck.

'We have been lucky,' she said out loud. 'If any of these mothers had hit us we'd have been squashed flatter than sardines.'

They could still fall. Above her head was a mass of loose rock, and the shoring timber was cracking.

Don't go there.

Was there a way through the rocks? Was she even looking in the right direction? She played her torch over the mass. There were gaps in the boulders—of course there were—but there were more boulders behind. To try and crawl through…

'He's an idiot to try,' she said out loud. 'Ring him again.'

She knew it'd make no difference.

And for the first time a wash of fear swept over her so strongly, so fiercely that she felt as if she'd be physically ill.

Josh was out there.

There was nothing she could do. She crawled back to Malu and put her head next to his on his makeshift pillow. She pressed her body hard against his. She'd done this before when he'd needed comfort.

She was doing it again now but it was she who needed comfort. It was she who needed to escape fear.

'He's coming,' she whispered, and she linked her hands under her belly and held. Her belly was tight, hard.

Her baby...

'He'll come,' she said, and this time she was talking to her baby, talking to someone she'd barely been brave enough to acknowledge as a separate being until now. Was this why she'd been dumb enough to rush into the mine? Because she'd hardly had the courage to acknowledge that this baby could be real?

She'd lost one baby. Mikey's death had left a huge, gaping hole in her life, and it had been a vast act of faith, a momentous decision, to try again. Once the decision had been made, she'd gone through the process of finding a sperm donor, the months of hope, the confirmation of pregnancy...

But once that confirmation had come, joy hadn't followed. Terror had followed, that once again she could lose the baby.

She'd coped by blocking it out. She'd not bought any baby clothes. She'd hardly let herself think about it. It was as if by acknowledging she really did have a baby in there she'd jinx it. She couldn't let herself believe that she could hold a little one who might live.

But, belief or not, this baby had rights, too, and one of those rights was not being buried in a collapsing mine before he/she/it was even born.

'I'm sorry,' she whispered as another contraction started to build. 'I'm so sorry I got you into this mess. And I'm even more sorry we're depending on Josh to get us out.'

She was in labour.

The thought was unbelievable. The knowledge was doing his head in.

Somehow he had to put it aside, focussing only on

keeping his grip on Bugsy. He was inching ahead, making the big dog slow. Staying safe. He'd be no use to anyone dead. He was taking no unnecessary risks.

In labour.

Who?

Of all the stupid questions? Did he need to know who the father was?

They'd kept in touch. Theirs had been a civilised divorce, born out of grief. Maddie had understood why he couldn't stay married.

She'd said she felt sorry for him.

Why did that slam back now? That last appalling conversation as he'd tossed random stuff into his kit bag, ostensibly heading for a flood in Indonesia. The Australian government had offered help and Cairns Air Sea Rescue had asked for volunteers.

Maybe a month, they'd said.

They'd both known it would be longer. The pain of loss was so great Josh had curled inward inside. He couldn't bear seeing his loss reflected on Maddie's face. He couldn't help her. He couldn't help himself.

'You'll never heal by running away,' Maddie had said sadly, and even then he hadn't been truthful.

'I'm helping others heal. That's why I'm going.'

'You're hiding from the pain the only way you know how,' she'd said. 'But I can't help you, Josh, so maybe it's better this way...'

And then she'd walked out because she couldn't bear to watch him pack, and he was gone before she'd returned.

The end.

Who was the father of her baby? Why hadn't she told him?

This was important.

They got in touch on Christmas and birthdays. Formal stuff.

Babies weren't formal?

New partners weren't important?

He swore.

And then he reached the rock face. The tunnel ended with a mass of fallen boulders and loose gravel.

He raked the floor and saw evidence of the miners who'd been flung apart from Maddie and Malu. A tin canteen. He snagged it and opened it—sandwiches! Worth holding on to? If he could.

If there was anyone to eat them.

He stared at the massive rock pile. It was such a jumble—how could he ever get through?

But Bugsy was nosing forward, whining, clambering up and over the first couple of rocks. He'd let him go—now he made a lunge and grabbed him before he got down the hole he was intent on investigating.

Hole.

Bugsy.

Maddie would never forgive him if he risked her dog.

But contractions... What choice did he have?

He knelt and hugged the big dog close, and he knew what the choice had to be. If this was possible...

Please.

He hauled his coiled rope from his shoulder and tied an end to Bugsy's collar. Then he carefully unrolled the rope so Bugsy felt no pull. It was a light line. It shouldn't cause much friction.

But the chance of a collapse...

Don't think it, he told himself. He couldn't.

He hugged Bugsy one more time, thinking of him

all those years ago, thinking of Maddie's joy when he'd put a warm, wriggling bundle of puppy into her arms.

'I'll love him forever,' Maddie had said.

Dared he risk…?

How could he not?

'We're both risking,' he told Bugsy, and he sat back and let the dog go. 'For Maddie.'

And one minute later Bugsy had crawled his way across the first pile of rocks, pushed his nose into a crevice—and then his whole body.

He was gone.

Maddie lay in the dark and worried. A lot.

He could be anyone and I'd be terrified, she told herself. If he was some unknown rescuer putting his life on the line to save her, she'd be appalled.

But, then, no one else would have done it, and she knew it. To head into a mine shaft where the shoring timbers were collapsing, where the shaft was known to be unsafe, where a mass of rock was already blocking the way, was just plain lunacy.

'Idiot hero.' She said it out loud and Malu stirred beside her and she bit her lip.

But still… 'Idiot hero,' she said again under her breath.

But he'd be in his element. She knew that. Josh would do anything for anyone. He was brave, clever, fearless, giving…

But not taking.

If it was Josh stuck in the mine he'd be pulling down more rocks so no one could save him, she told herself, speaking under her breath. Josh being saved? Ha. No one saved Josh.

That was the trouble. When they'd lost Mikey, the

giving had been all one way. She'd sobbed and he'd held her but he hadn't wept, as well. He'd held himself close.

And then, when Holly had died, he hadn't even let her hug him. She knew how much he'd loved his little sister, but he'd held himself rigid within his grief and despair, with no way of letting it out.

I don't need help. That was Josh's mantra. How could he live like that?

He did live like that, which was why she couldn't live with him.

I don't need help?

Yeah, if that was the case for her then she should be over at the rock face, reinforcing the rubble so no one could get through. She should be telling Josh that the moment he emerged into her cavern she'd toss rocks at him.

As if.

I don't need help?

She was stuck in a collapsing mine shaft with a guy who was perilously ill. She was in labour. Caroline hadn't been able to put her through to Hettie.

Slowly but surely the contractions were building.

I don't need help?

Some things weren't even worth aiming for.

It was a good thing that Bugsy wasn't a fox terrier. Josh was very, very pleased that the dog was large.

Josh's current plan, albeit a weak one, was to let Bugsy see if he could find a way through the rocks. Bugsy wasn't much smaller than he was across the shoulders. If Bugsy could find a way, then he might be able to follow.

There were, however, a whole lot of unknowns in that equation. And risks.

The best-case scenario was that Bugsy would find a safe passage through, tugging the cord behind him. He'd find Maddie. There'd be a happy reunion. Josh could then follow the rope and get through himself.

The more likely scenario would be that the whole thing was completely blocked and Bugsy would have to back out.

A possible scenario was that Bugsy would become impossibly tangled and stuck.

Or there'd be a further collapse.

Both the final scenarios were unthinkable but beyond the mass of rock was Maddie, and Bugsy seemed as desperate as he was to get through. So there was nothing he could do now but sit and wait and watch the rope feeding out.

There was an initial rush of feed as Bugsy nosed his way past the first few boulders. Then the feed slowed.

And stopped.

Josh's heart almost did the same.

'Bugsy?' he called, but there was no response. And the line started feeding out again.

Was he going straight through? Dear God, had he turned? Could he trap himself?

He could cut the line at this end, as long as the dog didn't get impossibly tangled first.

Whose crazy idea had this been?

The line fed out a little further. And further.

Please…

He'd never pleaded so desperately in his life.

She could hear scrabbling.

It was almost like there were mice in the cave with her, but…scrabbling?

She moved away from Malu's side, almost afraid to

breathe in case she was wrong. Then she flicked the torch and searched the rock pile.

She could definitely hear scrabbling and it was getting louder.

It was high up where the rocks almost merged with the ceiling. Or what was left of the ceiling.

If it fell…

She couldn't breathe. She had no room for anything but fear.

Where…where…?

And then there it was, slithering down the face of the cave-in, a great, grey ball of canine dust, a wriggly, ecstatic ball of filthy golden retriever.

And Maddie had the presence of mind—just—to put the torch down before she had an armful of delirious dog, and she was hugging and hugging and pressing her face into Bugsy's filthy coat and bursting into tears.

He was going crazy. Or maybe he already was crazy. There'd been one last, long feed of line, like Bugsy had made a dash—and then nothing. Nothing!

According to the line, the dog didn't appear to be moving.

If he'd killed Bugsy…

Of all the stupid, risky, senseless plans. He'd worked for search and rescue for years. There was no way a plan like this could even be considered.

He knew the rules. You played it by the book. You got in the experts, you did careful risk assessment, you weighed up your options. You never, ever put people's lives on the line.

Or dogs'.

MARION LENNOX   81

Maybe his bosses would okay dogs, he thought bleakly, but surely not Bugsy.

What was happening? Dear God, what was happening?

And then his phone rang.

'Josh.'

She was crying. He could hear her tears. His heart seemed to simply stop.

'Maddie.'

'I have a dog,' she managed. 'I have a whole armload of dog. He's here. Bugsy's here.'

His heart gave a great lurch and seemed to restart. 'Does he still have a cord attached?'

'I…' There was a moment's pause. 'I'll see. It is dark in here.' She said it almost indignantly and he found himself grinning. His lovely, brave Maddie, who always rebounded. 'Yes. Yes, he does. But Josh, what the—'

'I'm coming through, then,' he said. 'Are you hugging Bugsy?'

'Yes, but—'

'Sandwich hug,' he promised. 'Stat.'

'Josh, don't you dare.' He heard her fear surge. 'We have a line through now. Wait for the experts.'

'How far apart are the contractions?'

'I don't… Josh, no!'

'How far, Maddie?'

'I'm not saying.'

'Then you don't need to say. I'm coming in.'

CHAPTER FIVE

JOSH WASN'T A DOG. Dogs were smaller than Josh and they bent more. He was carrying a backpack, necessary if he was to be useful in there, but it made things harder. After a while he tugged it off his back, looped the straps round his ankles and towed it. It was better but still hard.

The fallen rocks were large and angular. Where were smooth river rocks when you needed them? These seemed to have broken with almost slate-like edges, flat and sharp, fine if you walked over a nicely laid path of them but murder to crawl up and around.

But Bugsy had made it through and he would, too. He just had to be careful. Ultra careful. He was following Bugsy's cord, using the head lamp to see, but he was feeling his way, as well. He was testing every rock before he touched it, feeling the rocks above him, trying to take the fewest risks possible. Hauling his pack behind him with his feet. Halting whenever it snagged.

It was so dark. And sharp. And hard.

It was also really, really claustrophobic. He didn't get claustrophobia, he told himself, but another part of him was saying that in this situation claustrophobia was just plain sensible.

At the other end of the cord lay Maddie. Maddie, who was in labour.

He had to be so careful not to pull on the cord so it didn't become dislodged. He was feeding out another line behind him with the idea of ultimate rescue. These cords were lifelines. Meanwhile he was keeping his hard hat on, getting his body through the next crevice, figuring how Bugsy could possibly have got through. Every fibre of his body was tuned to survival.

Bugsy had done it in fifteen minutes. After half an hour Josh was still struggling...

How long could she bear it?

She wanted to ring him but how could she? How could Josh do what he was doing and calmly take time out to answer the phone? He couldn't. She wanted every ounce of his concentration focussed on keeping him safe.

She wanted him out of there.

And she could hear him. That was the worst part. For the last twenty minutes she'd been hearing him hauling his way through the rock. She could hear the occasional shift of earth, the silence as he waited for things to settle. Once she heard the echo of a muffled oath.

She sat and hugged Bugsy. Bugsy whined a little, tugging forward as if he'd go to him—after five years did Bugsy still feel loyalty?—but Maddie was holding tight.

Josh was trying—against all odds—against all sense—to haul himself through impossibly tight, impossibly dangerous conditions. Bugsy had been truly heroic but the last thing Josh needed now was a golden retriever in there with him, licking his face, blocking his way.

She was saying silent prayers, over and over. *Please, let him be safe. Please...*

She'd be saying them for anyone, but for Josh...

She couldn't even begin to understand what she was feeling.

He was her husband.

He wasn't her husband. He was...an old friend?

Liar.

She was no longer curled up by Malu. There was no way she could disguise the contractions now; they were so strong if she lay beside him he'd feel them.

Some doctor she was!

Malu was restless and she knew the pain would break through again soon, leaving him wide awake.

How could she ask a man with such injuries to help deliver a baby?

How could she deliver herself? To put her baby at such risk? This little one who she'd longed for with all her heart and yet hadn't had the courage to acknowledge might be real. This baby who had every right to live.

Could she depend on Josh manoeuvring through these last few yards? Could she dare hope?

Another contraction gripped and she stopped asking stupid questions. Only the one word remained.

Please...

This...had been...a really, really, really...dumb idea. He'd be trapped in here forever, a skeleton, hanging by his fingernails to a stupid rock that, if he could only find purchase, he could use to drag himself up and over.

Bugsy had done it but Bugsy had more toenails than

he did. Bugsy's back half wasn't nearly as heavy. She hadn't been hauling a backpack. This thing was imp—

No. He had it. He hauled and felt himself lift.

The cord now seemed like it was running downwards.

Please... It was a silent prayer said over and over. Let this be the last part. Let it open up.

Let me see Maddie.

He gave one last heave, up and over—and suddenly he was slithering, head first, downwards. He hadn't realised it was so steep. He almost fell, sliding fast on loose shale, the backpack slithering after him.

And then suddenly his head and then his torso were free from the tunnel. He saw light that didn't come from his head lamp.

Torchlight swung towards him, almost blinding him. 'J-Josh?'

And suddenly he was clear. He was on the floor of a cramped cavern that was still a tunnel but after what he'd been in seemed as wide as a house.

But he wasn't noticing. Nothing mattered except that he'd made it and he was holding Maddie in his arms. Holding and holding and holding.

Maddie. His woman.

She'd always felt like that. She'd always been that, from the moment they'd first met, but how much more so in this moment?

He could feel her heart beating against his. She was breathing almost as heavily as he was. He was hugging her and she was hugging right back, maybe even crying.

He wasn't crying. Crying wasn't his style, but holding was.

Why had he let this woman go?

It didn't matter now. Nothing mattered except that she was in his arms, she was safe and they were together.

'Maddie…'

He would have tilted her face. He would have kissed her.

But then there was the slight hiccup of the dog.

Bugsy wasn't letting interpersonal relations get in the way of his needs. He'd orchestrated this rescue and being left out now wasn't going to happen. The dog was wedging his way firmly in between both of them, turning a hug into a sandwich squeeze.

And then, from behind them, a voice.

'Have we got company? I wouldn't mind a hug myself.'

Malu. He put Maddie away from him, just a little, still holding her but loosely so he could see the man lying on the floor.

'Hey, how's the patient?'

'So who's the patient?' Malu managed. 'My Pearl's had two babies, with me beside her every step of the way, so I pretty much know my current treating doctor is well into labour. And her newly arrived backup seems to be one filthy doctor who looks—to my untrained eye, I'll admit—to be bleeding. You'd best fix him up, Maddie,' he told her. 'And then he can fix both of us up next.'

Malu was right. The first priority was actually him. The rocks had been hard and sharp. He'd sliced his arm on that last uncontrolled descent. It wasn't serious but it was bleeding hard and the last thing any of them needed was to lose fluids.

So he tolerated—barely—sitting back while Maddie put pressure on it until the bleeding subsided. She cleaned the cut, pulled it together with Steri-Strips and slapped on a dressing. He made a fast call to Keanu while she did it.

'I'm in.'

Keanu wasted no words. 'Is there a safe way to get them out?'

'No.' He thought about the way he'd had to clamber though. There was a good chance he couldn't get out himself.

If Maddie hadn't been here, maybe he wouldn't have made it. That tunnel was practically suicidal.

But he was here, with Maddie, who was calmly dressing his arm. Between contractions.

'We'll depend on the engineering boys to get us out,' he told Keanu. 'Short of another collapse, we're safe enough for now. But, sorry, mate, I have work to do. I'll ring as soon as I have things under control.'

Under control? That was a joke.

'It's not my neatest work,' Maddie said, a bit breathlessly, as she finished. 'But you'll do.'

She was breathless and her breathlessness didn't come purely from the dust. 'When was your last contraction?'

'Over ten minutes ago. I'm slowing down. Stress, do you think?'

'So you really are in labour?' Malu's speech was easier now, his body language showing how much it meant to him that someone had been able to get through. 'You didn't admit—'

'There wasn't a lot to admit,' Maddie said with as-

perity. 'You're not moving and there's no way we can
boil water and switch on humidicribs.'

'So you're thirty-six weeks?' They were sitting on
the ground. Josh had his arm cradled in front of him.
The more he rested it now the less likely it would be to
bleed again if...*when* he got busy. 'Tell me why you're
still on Wildfire?'

'I'm due to leave on Friday.'

'You know the rules for fly in, fly outs. Thirty-four
weeks and then only under strict conditions.'

'I wanted every day of my family leave to be spent
with my baby. Leaving six weeks before was a waste
of time.'

'Says the woman stuck underground in labour.'

'I didn't intend to get stuck underground,' Maddie
said—and sniffed.

The sniff echoed.

'You make our Maddie cry, injured or not, I'll get up
and shove you back in that tunnel,' Malu warned. 'And
I'll shove a rock back in after you.' He hesitated and his
voice faltered a little. 'I don't suppose... Maddie, you
can't get out that tunnel hero-boy just came in through.'

'No.' Josh and Maddie spoke together. Maddie, because the thought of crawling through rocks with the
massive bulge she had underneath her was unthinkable.
Josh...well, pretty much the same for Josh. He'd been
incredibly lucky to get here, he conceded. He could
well have got himself stuck at any number of places
on the way.

'They'll dig down from the top,' he said with more
confidence than he felt. He crawled across and lifted
Malu's wrist. 'Pain... Scale of one to ten.'

'I'm okay.'

'Answer the question.'

'Seven,' Malu said, reluctantly. 'But I can cope.'

'Forget coping. I have drugs.'

'Maddie has drugs.'

'I have more drugs. Nice drugs.'

'I'd give more for a mouthful of water.'

'I can do that, too. I have a backpack, fully loaded.' He helped the man drink, holding him up a little and then easing him back on his makeshift pillow. Noting the fierce effort it took him not to cry out.

He was in pain, Josh thought, but not from his leg. Ribs?

His breathing was a bit scratchy.

Fractured ribs? Pierced lung?

There weren't a lot of X-ray facilities down there.

'How long since you gave the last morphine?' he asked Maddie.

'I… Half an hour ago. Five milligrams.'

He cast a quick look back at her. She sounded strained.

She was strained. She was leaning against the rock wall, her arms were holding her belly, she was arched back and she was trying not to scream.

He flicked the torch away from her fast, so Malu couldn't see.

Triage. He'd like to do a very fast pelvic examination but Malu was breathing too fast. The pain would be making his breathing rapid and his heart rate rise.

The priority was Malu, but Malu got the world's fastest injection. He set up another bag of saline. Then he hesitated.

'Go to her,' Malu whispered. 'I'm imagining a nice

cubicle partition in my mind. I'll close my eyes. Those drugs you gave me...they'll make me sleep, right?'

'They will, but not for ten or fifteen minutes.'

'Tell you what,' Malu said. 'Those empty saline bags... Prop 'em up against the side of my face. Then tell Doc she has all the privacy she could ever want to get that baby out.'

'She's not... It can't be soon.'

'You're the doc and I'm the miner,' Malu whispered. 'But, hell, Doc, I'd go take a look if I were you.'

'I can't have my baby down here.'

That was pretty much what Josh was thinking. He had nothing. Nothing!

Well, that wasn't exactly true. He had basic sterile equipment.

Forceps, not so much. Equipment for an emergency Caesar? Not in his wildest dreams.

'Sweetheart—'

'I'm not your sweetheart.'

'Sorry,' he said, chastened. 'Maddie, I need to examine you.'

'I know you need to examine,' she moaned. 'And I heard what Malu said. Malu, thank you for the privacy but if a vacuum cleaner salesman could stop this pain right now I'd say go ahead, look all you like.'

Malu gave a dozy chuckle.

'Lie back,' Josh told her.

She lay back. He desperately wanted a decent bed. He was asking her to lie on rocks.

He could tug off his shirt to use as a pillow but he was already thinking ahead. If...*when* this baby came he needed something to wrap it in, and things to wrap it in were few and far between.

'So where's your layette?' he demanded, striving for lightness.

'Layette?'

'One of the mums we brought down from Weipa to Cairns last month had a suitcase with her she explained had a full layette. Her mum had knitted it for her. All white. Matinee jackets, bootees, christening robe, tiny wool dresses with pink roses embroidered on them. She went on to have a boy but at least she was prepared.'

'To live in Weipa?' She was gasping, trying to breathe as she obviously knew how to breathe when things got hard. 'With the red dust up there, everything will be pink at first wash.'

'So you don't have a layette.'

'Not here.'

'In Cairns?'

'Not…not even in Cairns,' she admitted. 'I have four weeks to shop.'

He'd helped her tug off her pants, laying them under her hips. That give her a tiny amount of protection from the rocks but not much. Her bra gave her a modicum of privacy, but there wasn't enough of that, either.

Four weeks…

'You're six centimetres dilated,' he told her. 'How many weeks does that give you in the layette-buying plan?'

'I can't…'

'Okay, don't think about it now. Keep doing the breathing. You know how. And stop fighting.'

'Josh, I can't.'

'You and Malu thought you were going to keep this

neat little cave a secret, didn't you?' He shifted so he was against the wall as well, then tugged her across him. She protested, but not too much—she was pretty much past protesting. She leaned back against him instead of the wall. He was holding her and that seemed sort of right. His arm was hurting, but in the scheme of things it was nothing. 'And then along comes Bugsy,' he continued, as if this was a completely normal conversation in a completely normal setting. 'And then Josh arrives—and now it seems someone else is coming, too.'

'Josh, you can't. Your arm. You can't hold me. Oh, my...' Her next words were lost in a silent scream. He felt that scream. He felt the contraction take hold of her. He felt her whole body spasm and he held her because it was the only thing he could do.

The contraction eased. She fell back against him with a gasp and his arms tightened.

'You're doing brilliantly. Has anyone told you lately that you're awesome, Dr Haddon?'

'I have.' It was a slurred interjection from Malu in the shadows, and he felt Maddie smile.

'And Bugsy tells me all the time,' Maddie managed.

And then another contraction hit and he thought, How did that happened? Didn't the texts say the rate increased gradually? That had been all of thirty seconds.

'I'm not pushing yet,' she said through gritted teeth as the contraction passed.

'Good for you. You show 'em. This baby comes on your terms or not at all.'

She even managed a wry chuckle.

'Maddie?'

'Mmm...?'

'Is there a dad out there who'll be frantic?'

There was silence at that. He wasn't sure if the silence meant she didn't want to answer, or she couldn't.

The next contraction rolled by without a word, just more of the silent screaming. This woman had courage. There was no way she'd scream.

Come to think of it, this really was a situation where she might literally scream the roof down. The vibrations of a woman in full labour might even be enough to…

Um…don't go there. Not.

Bugsy was whining a little, obviously sensing Maddie's distress. He was nestled as close to them as he could get. Josh had set one of the torches up, just one, aiming it off centre so it wasn't shining directly at them. They were in shadow.

He was still holding her. This was the strangest feeling…

To hold Maddie.

He'd loved holding Maddie. Holding her had been the only time in his life when he'd felt totally at peace.

But… He'd held her the night their baby had died. Or he'd tried to. He remembered the fierce struggle not to sob himself. Something had clenched inside, some hard knot of despair that he still didn't dare unravel, and the same knot had formed when Holly had died.

He hated it. They were two leaden weights he'd carry forever.

But what was he doing, thinking of the start of his marriage, a marriage that had never worked? Focus on now, he told himself. He had no choice. Maddie needed him.

'Just keep the breathing going,' he told her. 'Deep and even. You know the drill.'

'The drill's different when it's me,' she gasped.

'Breathe, sweetheart.'

'Don't call me sweetheart! Just get me out of here.'

He almost smiled. He'd heard that line before, from so many women in labour. *Take me home.*

Where was home?

He and Maddie used to have…

Don't go there, either.

'There's no father,' she muttered through clenched teeth. 'Or at least no one to slug right now. If it was you I'd be knocking your teeth out the back of your head.'

'Hey, it's not the guy's fault.'

'Who else's fault is it? I want someone I can sue.' She was beyond reason now, he thought, caught in pain and trying to find any way through it. 'Hold me tighter,' she demanded. 'Ohhh…'

He held her tighter. Her fingers clenched on his forearms. It was just as well it was his upper arm he'd injured. He'd have marks from her fingernails, he thought. Maybe she'd even draw blood.

But donating his arms seemed the least he could do. He so wanted to be needed.

If you don't need me then I don't need you. She'd thrown that at him that last appalling week. *You give and give and give, and you never take, not one inch. And what you give…it's all surface stuff, Josh. You hold yourself so tight, like you're in armour, and I can't get in. I don't want to be the taker forever. I can't be. You need to go.*

And he had. He'd walked away because he'd known she was right.

He couldn't let her in. He couldn't let anyone near the pain he was feeling.

'It was a test tube,' she muttered now. Her whole body

was straining, and the fingers were digging even tighter. 'A vial. Tall, black hair like yours, athletic build, smart, a university student doing his good deed for humanity— for me—by donating semen… What was he thinking? Oooh…'

And she tucked her chin down into her throat and pushed.

'Hey.'

He wanted nothing so much as to stay where he was, holding her. Someone had to hold her, but it could no longer be him.

He was needed at the other end. Someone had to catch.

He needed lights.

He had two torches, one head lamp and Maddie's phone app. He set them all up but still there wasn't enough.

It'd have to do.

He wanted towels. He wanted clean.

He ripped his shirt off but laid it aside. It was thick, serviceable cotton. It was filthy but it was the best he could do. But for a newborn baby with a freshly cut umbilical cord to be wrapped in such a thing…

'I used…I used my shirt for Malu…' Maddie gasped, and he gripped her hand and held.

'That's why I came. To bring you mine.'

'You always did…like an excuse to show your six pack…'

'There are a lot of people to admire it down here,' he told her, and then she moaned and pushed again and he had to deal with what he had: a woman lying in dirt he couldn't protect her from.

The head was crowning. A tiny dark head had

emerged at the last push, then gone back as the contraction had eased.

He'd grabbed lubricant from his bag, and gloves. And checked.

The cord… The cord!

'Maddie, I need you to back off.' He tried to make his voice normal, matter-of-fact. 'If you push any harder you'll tear.'

'I need… I need…'

'You don't need to push. Breathe through it, Maddie, and don't push. Don't!'

And she got it. She was a doctor. She knew.

'The cord…'

'It's fine. I just need a little space down here to get things organised. You have to breathe. Hold it, Maddie. Hold.'

And once again that little word was front and centre. Please…

The next contraction hit and he could feel the massive effort it took for Maddie to hold back. To somehow control her body.

The courage of this woman… He had to match it.

One dead baby… There would not be another, he swore. Please.

He had to wait until the contraction eased and it almost killed him.

'H-hurry,' Maddie muttered, and then she swore. 'Hurry, damn you.'

'Do you mind?' he said. 'There are patients present.'

'I'll swear, too, if it helps,' Malu muttered from the shadows, and Josh knew the big miner was feeling as helpless as he was.

Please.

The head had retreated. He had so little time. Where…?

There. He had it. Careful, careful, there was no way he was ripping it…

Hold that contraction.

Now! And somehow it came, slipping seamlessly up and over. The cord was clear and he felt like shouting.

Somehow he made his voice muted but the triumph was there. 'Houston, we have lift-off,' he said in a voice he couldn't possibly hold steady. 'Maddie, the cord's free. Next contraction, go for it.'

And she did. The contraction hit and, risk or not, fear of vibrations or not, there was no way Maddie could keep it in. She hugged her knees and she screamed, a long, primeval scream that echoed and echoed and echoed.

And ten seconds later a tiny, perfect little girl slipped out into that strange new world.

'You have a daughter,' Josh managed, and he couldn't stop himself. He was staring down at the slip of a baby in his hands and tears were streaming unchecked down his face.

'Let me…let me…'

What was he thinking? Every textbook in the land said bring the baby straight up to the mother, place the baby on the mother's breast while you cope with the umbilical cord, even let the mother discover the baby's sex for herself.

He slid the tiny scrap of newborn humanity up to her mother. Maddie's arms enfolded her.

Josh laid his shirt over the top of both of them—he wanted no dust or scraps of rock falling on this little one. He'd cope with the umbilical cord soon. It was good to leave it for a minute or two to stop pulsing, he told himself. And besides…

Besides, there was no way he was cutting anything through tears.

'A daughter.' It was Malu, whispering again from the shadows. 'Hey, a little girl. Congratulations to you both.'

And that was what it felt like, Josh thought. *Both.*

This little girl was nothing to do with him. She was the daughter of his ex-wife and an unknown donor. She had no biological connection to him at all.

But he glanced down at the woman cradling her new-born in her arms, at the look of unimaginable awe on Maddie's face, and he knew…

Biological connection or not, he'd defend this little family to the death.

There were so many emotions coursing through Maddie's mind that she had no hope of sorting them.

She was beyond trying. Josh had laid her tiny daughter on her breast. She was lying on her mother's naked skin, a tiny scrap of humanity.

Her daughter.

Josh had settled his shirt over the pair of them, but under the shirt she was cradling her daughter. Her hands enfolded her, feeling the warmth, the wetness, the miracle.

The tiny girl hadn't cried but she was making tiny, waffling grunts, as if she wasn't the least bit scared but rather she was awed at the amazing world she'd emerged into.

Her daughter.

She'd had the cord around her neck...

The tiny part of Maddie that was still a doctor let that thought drift.

If Josh hadn't been here...

He was. Her Josh, riding to the rescue.

It was what he was good at. It was what she most loved—and hated—about him.

But for now she was no longer capable of processing the whys and the wherefores. Too much emotion, too much pain, and now...too much wonder?

'She's snuffling,' Josh said, and she could hear him smiling. 'I can guess what she's looking for.'

'My bra... It unclips at the front...'

'Great forethought,' he said, but he had to use the torch again to help her unclip it, and he smiled and smiled as her baby girl figured exactly what was going on. He stroked the tiny face, she turned in the direction of his stroking finger, found what he was directing her to...and made her connection.

Maddie gasped and gasped again. How could this be happening? Something so wonderful?

She had a daughter.

A memory flashed back, or maybe not a memory. It was the bone-deep truth that she'd held Mikey like this. That she'd loved her son.

She glanced up and she saw in Josh's face that he knew it, too. It was a bittersweet moment, but strangely it didn't hurt.

And it was good that Josh was here to share it with her, she thought. Josh had never admitted how much Mikey's loss had hurt him, but she knew it had, and somehow, right now, it was important that he was here. Whether he'd admit it or not, this was a joy to be shared, but it was also the remembrance of sorrow. Somehow, Mikey was with them. Somehow, right now, she felt… married?

'Th-thank you for being here,' she whispered to Josh. 'Oh, Josh.'

'Hey,' he said softly into the shadows, and he touched her cheek, a feather touch, a caress, a gesture of love and admiration and…awe?

And then, because he couldn't help himself, or maybe it was her doing, maybe she'd turned her face to him, maybe because it seemed right, inevitable, an extension of this whole amazing moment… For whatever reason, he bent and placed his lips on hers. He kissed her.

'Josh?'

The phone was ringing. Maybe it'd been ringing for a while. No one had noticed and he didn't want to notice now.

The kiss was magic. The kiss was like putting back a part of his body he hadn't known had been removed. The kiss was…right.

But Maddie was stiffening a little and she'd managed to get his name out. She was right. The kiss had to end.

Obstetrician kissing mother?

He hadn't felt the least bit like an obstetrician. There were no foundations for how he'd felt, but still… For a few amazing moments he'd felt like a man in love with his wife. Remembering his son. Welcoming his daughter.

But that wasn't reality. Reality was that the kiss was over. Reality was that he was stuck underground in a mine. He was officially part of the rescue team and making contact had to be the first priority.

He was here to work.

Still, he'd missed the call and Keanu had to ring again, and by the time he answered, Keanu's first word was a shout.

'Josh!'

'I'm here, mate. There's no need to burst my eardrum.'

'What the hell's going on? We heard a scream. Hell, Josh.'

It had been quite a scream. It must have echoed up and out through the shafts.

If he'd been out there he'd have been going out of his mind.

He wasn't. He was in here.

All was quiet in the confines of the tiny cavern. He had a sudden, almost unbearable urge to cut the connection and keep the world at bay.

There was a dumb thought.

'What's happened?' Keanu was demanding. 'Another cave-in? Why haven't you been answering?'

Had the phone been ringing for a while, then? 'We've been busy.'

'The tunnel. Is it safe for me to come in?'

'No.' He knew that absolutely. He'd had amazing luck to get through himself.

'Hell, Josh. We're going out of our minds out here. Why didn't you answer?'

'Triage. We had a bit of a medical emergency but it's okay.'

'Medical emergency?' Keanu's voice was sharp with worry. 'It was a woman's scream. Was it Maddie? Is she hurt? What's going on?'

'Women's business,' he said, and he allowed himself a smile. 'We're on the other side of it now.'

'Women's business…'

'Yeah, and, Keanu…you know you were thinking there'd be three people and a dog to dig out?'

'Yeah?' Keanu sounded dazed.

'Make it four. We have a new arrival. Mother and daughter are doing fine. Malu and I could use cigars but if cigars aren't forthcoming a ruddy great bulldozer with a bit of finesse will do fine.'

CHAPTER SIX

A RUDDY GREAT bulldozer took time to organise. The experts had now arrived from the mainland. There'd be no more heroics. Things were being done by the book.

But because of Josh's forethought there was a further link to aboveground.

Josh had attached a cord to Bugsy when he'd sent the dog to find his mistress. When he'd come in himself, he'd hauled in another behind him. That meant they had two cords running through the caved-in rocks, cords that could be linked, like a raft fording a river. One cord got pulled in, with something attached. The attached thing was removed, the other cord was used to pull it back out. Back and forth. Josh had used the system in tight spots before, though never for himself.

Their team had bags designed for the purpose, tough and slippery. While the team from Cairns started their work aboveground the bags started their cautious way back and forth.

The first bag they tried contained tougher cable. The important thing was not to break the link. Then, with both cords set up as slippery cable rather than nylon, Keanu started sending in supplies.

First came fluids—not much on the first pull, as they

didn't want to risk anything getting stuck. But Keanu also risked sending in wipes and a blanket in which to wrap the baby.

Also a diaper.

There was also a card, very makeshift, written on the back of a mine safety notice.

A big welcome to Baby Haddon, the card said. *From all of us on the surface. But isn't the stork supposed to go down chimneys, not mine shafts?*

He read it to Maddie and it made her smile. Or smile more.

'That'll be Hettie,' she said, sounding a bit choked up. 'She's such a friend. I have so many good friends here.'

She had a whole life he knew nothing about, Josh realised as he retied the empty bag to the cord and sent a text for the guys out there to pull.

Then they went back to the waiting game while Keanu organised more stuff to come in.

Malu had finally let the effects of the painkillers take hold and was deeply asleep. Bugsy was also dozing, pressed close to his mistress. The baby had taken her first tentative suckle and drifted to sleep, as well.

Josh flicked the torch off and moved again to sit behind Maddie. She tried to object. 'I don't mind hard...' but he was having none of it. He was her pillow and they were alone in their cocoon of darkness.

It felt right. He was meant to hold her, he thought. His body thought so.

Danger or not, cradling this woman felt wonderful.

'So when did you decide to have a baby?' he asked into the silence, though he had no right to ask such a question and she had every right to refuse to answer.

Silence.

'Sleep if you want,' he murmured, letting her off the hook, but he felt rather than saw her shake her head.

'I don't feel like sleep yet. I know this is an appalling situation but all I can feel is happy. If you knew how much I wanted this...'

'I guess... I did know.'

'But you didn't want it.'

And there was a game-changer. The peace dissipated from the darkness and he let her accusation drift. Had he wanted this? A wife? A baby?

Not enough to take risks. Not enough to risk the pain he'd felt last time.

'I'm sorry,' she whispered. 'That was uncalled for. It's okay, Josh, I'm not about to dredge up the past. The truth is that I reached thirty-four last birthday and I thought if I don't do something soon I'll end up without a family. I know that sounds selfish but there it is. I wanted it so much.'

'Not enough to remarry?' He tried to say it lightly— and failed.

'I hardly have time for marriage.' She was trying for lightness, too, he thought. 'I work here fourteen days straight and then I have a week back in Cairns. I spend most of that time with Mum.'

'Wouldn't it have been better to get a job in Cairns?'

'Maybe.' This was none of his business and he could almost hear her thinking it, but she didn't say it.

'You know, it's really hard to say goodbye,' she said at last, hesitatingly, almost as if she was thinking it through as she spoke. 'The stroke damaged Mum mentally, but she still knows me and she still loves me visiting. But if I only have an hour, she clings and sobs when I leave. If I use a whole day, though... I take her out for walks, I give her meals and I read to her. Finally she goes to sleep happy. The nurses say the next day, when I'm not there, she's peaceful, not distressed. So if I worked in Cairns, I couldn't just pop in and out. It'd be too upsetting for all of us. But this way there are hardly any goodbyes. It's a private nursing home. It costs a bomb but fly in, fly out doctors get paid a bomb. This is the only way I can keep her there, and it works.'

'I told you I'd help!' It was an exclamation of anger, reverberating round the tunnel, and he felt rather than saw her wince.

'I told you, Josh. I'm done needing you.'

'You needed me today.'

'I did,' she said, and shifted a little and cradled her daughter just a wee bit tighter. 'And I'm so grateful.'

'So why won't you let me do more?'

'We've had this out,' she said, wearily now, and he flinched. The last thing he wanted was to make her tired.

'I'm sorry. We can talk about this later.'

'No, we can't. I shouldn't have kissed you.'

'You still...love me.' Why had he said it? But it wasn't a question. It was a statement of fact, and he waited for her to refute it.

She didn't. She was his woman, and he was cradling her with every ounce of love and protection he was capable of.

'Yes, Josh, I still love you,' she said at last, even more wearily. 'And I'm guessing... You're thinking you still love me.'

'I always have.'

'Within limits.'

'Maddie…'

'But loving's not for limits,' she whispered into the darkness, as if she was suddenly sure she was right. 'Look at my beautiful Lea.'

'Lea?'

'After a friend, here on the islands. And Lea Grace for my mum. I can't wait to show her to Mum. I know Mum's damaged but you know what? She'll think the sun rises and sets from her granddaughter. Unconditional love. That's what I'll give my Lea, from now until eternity.'

'I would have loved you…'

'If I let you. You said that. But your love had conditions.'

'It didn't.'

'It did,' she said, steadily and surely. 'As long as love is one-directional it's fine by you. You're allowed to love me all you want. But me…'

'Maddie…'

'No, let me say it,' she whispered. It was weird, sitting in this appalling place, locked in by total blackness. By rights they should still be terrified, but Lea's birth had changed things. This seemed a place of peace. Even Malu's breathing had settled, reassuring them all.

'Josh, when Mikey died it broke your heart.' She said it steadily into the stillness. 'I know it did, but you couldn't show it. You couldn't take comfort.'

'I didn't need to.'

'Yes, you did,' she said, still surely. 'But you were afraid if you showed it you'd break. You comforted me but when I cried you couldn't cry with me. You were my rock but I didn't need a rock. Mikey had two parents. Only one was allowed to grieve.'

'Maddie…'

'And then when Holly died it was worse,' she whispered. 'Because you were the one who was grief-stricken, but how could you let it out? How could you share? I could see the war you were waging but there wasn't a thing I could do to help. You have this armour, and it's so strong there's no way I can get through. And I can't live with armour, Josh. Just…loving…isn't enough.'

He didn't answer. Guilty as charged, he thought, but what could he do about it?

'It's okay,' she said, steadily now, and he wondered how she could sound so strong after what she'd been through. But she was strong, his Maddie.

His Maddie?

She wasn't his Maddie. They'd decided to end their marriage for the most logical of reasons and those reasons still stood.

His arms were around her. She was cradling her tiny new daughter and he knew if anything happened to either of them his heart would break.

But he couldn't share. That way… To open himself to such pain, to let the world see him exposed.

Maddie called it armour and maybe it was.

And, yes, he still needed it.

Out there be dragons.

She was right. He did have armour, and without it he had no weapon fierce enough to face them.

His phone rang. Thank you, he said silently as he answered. Thinking was doing his head in. Thinking while holding Maddie was doing his head in.

Keanu.

'Another bag coming in,' Keanu told him. 'This

one has air mattresses and a pump. It's safer if we pull in tandem.'

Which meant moving away from Maddie. She'd heard what Keanu had said and was already shifting slightly so he could move.

He hated leaving her.

But air mattresses... To lie on air rather than solid rock... It was imperative for both Malu and for Maddie.

'I'll miss my Josh cushion,' Maddie said, and he knew she'd said it lightly. But to Josh, right then, it didn't sound light at all.

Air mattresses. Dust masks. Food packs and drinks.

All the essentials to let them live.

And then Malu decided he might not.

He'd seemed okay. Josh had even let him use the phone to talk to Pearl. Pearl's terror had resounded through the shaft—there was no room for privacy here—but after a couple of moments the calm, gruff voice of her miner husband seemed to have settled the worst of her fears.

'We're looking after him,' Josh had told Pearl before they'd disconnected. 'He has two doctors dancing attendance every moment. He wouldn't get that sort of attention in the best city hospital.'

'Oh, but you have a baby.' Pearl was so weepy.

He had a baby? Not so much.

'Maddie has a daughter, yes,' he told her, and he couldn't help himself, he had to flick on his torch and let light fall on the woman holding her tiny bundle. No woman could look more contented.

You have a baby? No. This was Maddie's baby. They were separate.

Because he was afraid?

This was hardly the time to think about that. 'Are you telling me Dr Maddie can't cope with a newborn and any medical emergency that could possibly arise?' he demanded of Pearl. 'She's a superwoman, your Doc Maddie.'

And there it was again. *Your Doc Maddie.*

Not his.

'I...I know she is.' Pearl faltered.

'But we don't need her,' Josh said firmly. 'Malu's recovering. He'll emerge battered and bruised—we all will. But for now we have air beds, we have plenty of supplies, we have a new baby to admire and we seem safe. Pearl, we're okay.'

Except they weren't.

How late was it—or how early—when Malu's breathing changed?

Josh must have dozed but Maddie touched him and he was wide awake in an instant.

'What do you need?'

'Listen to Malu.'

She would never have woken him if there wasn't a worry. Maddie was a seriously good doctor. He flicked on the torch and was at Malu's side in an instant.

And he heard what Maddie was hearing.

He'd checked Malu before he'd allowed himself to sleep and Malu had been breathing deeply and evenly. The morphine was effective. He had an air mattress and pillow, and a light mask to keep the dust at bay.

Josh had checked him thoroughly, knowing the bruises and pain from his chest signified probable fractured ribs. There had, however, been no sign of internal problems.

There were problems now. Malu's breathing was fast and shallow. He was staring up at the roof, his eyes wide and fearful. As Josh's torch flicked on, he turned and gazed at Josh in terror.

'I can't… I can't…'

Pneumothorax? Haemothorax? The words crashed into Josh's mind with a sickening jolt.

His mind was racing through causes. Probable broken ribs… The ribs had caused no problems until now, but maybe in his relaxed state, with the morphine taking hold and giving Malu's body a false sense of security, the big man had shifted in his sleep.

And a fractured rib had shifted. If indeed the lung was punctured, every time Malu breathed, a little air would escape into the chest wall. And then a little more, and a little more…

There was no open wound. The air couldn't escape. The pressure would finally collapse first one lung and then the other.

Was he right? Almost before he'd thought it, he had Maddie's stethoscope in his ears, listening at the midaxillary line. Normally he'd listen at the back as well, but there was no way he was shifting Malu and risking more damage with those ribs.

Unequal bilateral breath sounds. Diminished on the right.

Very diminished.

If Malu had presented in an emergency room with suspected fractured ribs, he would have been X-rayed straight away, but up until now his breathing had been fine. That was all Josh had had to go on.

'What…what's happening?' Malu gasped, and Josh

took a moment to regroup. He needed to move fast, but panicking Malu would speed his breathing even more.

'I reckon you've somehow scraped your lung and made a small tear,' he told him. 'It's not too big or it would have caused problems before this, but if we're to get you breathing comfortably again we need to do something about it.'

'What...?'

Behind him Josh sensed Maddie reaching for the phone. They had two doctors, he thought, and the knowledge was reassuring, even if one was only hours post-baby.

'Keanu? We have a slight problem.' Maddie's voice was calmly efficient, as if a tension pneumothorax was something she saw twice a day before breakfast. 'We need a bag in here, with equipment...'

She knew that they didn't have the right equipment with them. She'd hauled her bag in when she'd run in. He'd brought in a bit more but now they needed specialist gear.

Part of his job was road trauma—actually, any kind of trauma. He had what he needed at ground level, in his emergency bag, the gear he'd packed so carefully back in Cairns.

'Let me speak to Keanu,' he told Maddie, and then he summoned a grin for Malu. 'Maddie's better at the bedside manner than I am. Is Lea asleep? Praise be. Our Maddie's just had the world's fastest maternity leave, and she's ready to move on.' And he held his hand out for the phone.

And Maddie had it figured, exactly what was needed of her right now. She edged forward—gingerly—who wouldn't edge gingerly so few hours after birth? Josh dragged his air bed to Malu's side so she had something soft to settle on.

'Let me tell you what I think's happening inside you,' Maddie said to Malu. 'It's really interesting. But, hey, I want you to even out your breaths while I talk. Nice and slow, nice and slow. I know it feels like you're a fish out of water, but we have time not to panic. Do you know what a pneumothorax is?' And she kept on talking, calm and steady, and Josh thought if he didn't know better he might even feel calm and steady, as well.

She was some doctor.

She was some woman.

But there wasn't time for focussing on Maddie. Keanu was on the end of the line, waiting with almost rigidly imposed patience. Maddie had said there was a problem. He'd know better than to demand details until they were ready to give them.

'Malu's developed a tension pneumothorax or hae-mothorax,' he said curtly, while Maddie's reassuring tones made a divide between Josh and his patient.

'Tension… Hell, Josh, are you sure?'

'Sure. A slight shift must have caused a leak. Un-equal bilateral breathing. Subcutaneous emphysema and tenderness, shortness of breath and chest pain. I'm thinking fractured rib is the only answer. Mate, I need gear in here fast. We need oxygen, plus local anaesthetic and equipment to get it into the intercostal space. I need a chest tube for drainage.'

'Mate—'

'Yeah,' Josh said, cutting him off. He knew exactly what Keanu wanted to say—that operating in conditions like this was unthinkable. How to keep a wound clean, a tube clear? 'But there's no choice. Send down a flutter valve but I'm thinking this place is too messy to rely on that alone. We'll use an underwater seal drain. I haven't used one for years but you'll find a three-chamber unit at the bottom of my kit. Also more saline. A lot more saline. Start getting it in now, drugs first. We have gloves and basic equipment here to keep things almost sterile.'

'Do you have enough light?' Keanu still sounded incredulous.

'Our Maddie will hold the torch while I operate. She's a hero, our Maddie. The lady with the lamp. Florence Nightingale has nothing on our Maddie.'

And Maddie heard. She turned a little and gave him a lopsided grin.

'Did you hear that?' she asked Malu. 'Josh reckons I'm great. Well, I reckon he's great so that's settled. We have two great doctors and one patient with a teeny, tiny tear in his middle. Nothing to this, then. Piece of cake.'

'What else do you need?' Keanu snapped, and Josh could hear the tension in the island doctor's voice. It was all very well playing the hero in the middle of hands-on action, he thought, but standing helplessly at the minehead, knowing there was nothing you could do to help, would be a thousand times harder.

But he needed to concentrate on practicalities. Thinking of others' distress only muddied the waters.

Focus.

'I need a fourteen-gauge angiocath and at least a four-centimetre needle,' he told Keanu, hauling himself back from the brink as he always did in a crisis. If there was urgent need, he had to block everything else out. 'We need anaesthetic, tubing, more antiseptic, more gloves. I need a good clean sheet—when this is done I want Manu and his drainage tube protected from grit. If you can get it in fast, we're good to go.'

'That's all?'

'Plus anything else you can think of,' Josh replied. He wouldn't mind a clearer head to think things through. His arm was throbbing. His own breathing was a bit compromised—the grit was working through the mask and there was still that piercing knowledge of the danger they were in. That Maddie and her baby were in…

Do not go there.

'Actually, a ruddy big hole for lifting everyone out would be great,' he added dryly, and was dumb enough to feel proud he'd kept the emotion from his voice.

'We're working on it,' Keanu told him. 'Is Maddie okay?'

'I'm a whizz,' Maddie said, hearing Keanu's sharp query and taking the phone. She even managed to grin happily down at Malu, as if popping down mine shafts and doing emergency surgery right after childbirth was part of her normal working life. 'I'm practically boring Malu to sleep now, but we might need to up the anaesthetic a bit. Keanu, just tie everything up with pink ribbons as my baby shower and send it right down.'

'What are their chances?'

In the clearing at the mine mouth the men and women were looking grim.

Caroline had been efficiency plus since she'd arrived at the site, but she'd suddenly broken down. Beth was crouched beside her, hugging her.

In the background things were happening. There could be no bulldozers here. One hint of heavy machinery and the entire shaft could crumble.

The odds were being spelled out to all. Caroline had been washing out grit from a miner's eyes. She'd finished what she'd been doing, calmly reassured the guy she'd worked on—and then walked to the edge of the clearing and sobbed.

Beth had been watching her. Helpless R Us, Beth thought. Usually in a disaster such as this there were things she could do. Work was the best medicine, the best distraction from fear.

Here, though, the work for the medical team had dried up. Keanu was acting as communicator, organising the bags that were being carefully manoeuvred underground.

Caroline and Beth were left with nothing to do.

Except fear.

'We have the best team possible,' Beth told Caroline now. 'The best engineers... We've been on to Max Lockhart—apparently he owns this mine. He, like all of us, assumed it was closed, and he's appalled.'

'He would be,' Caroline whispered. 'He's...he's my father.'

'Your father?'

'He lives in Sydney. My uncle Ian's been in charge here. Dad...Dad has problems.'

'No matter,' Beth said soundly. 'Whatever he is, he's moving heaven and earth to get resources here. There's a massive mining operation just north of Cairns. He's been on to them. See those guys over there? That's where they come from and this is what they do, deal with mine collapses. They're saying they'll drill side on to the collapsed shaft where the rock's more solid. Then they'll pick their way across to our guys.'

'But it'll take so long… And Maddie…' Once the tears had come, Caroline was no longer able to stop them.

'We have time.' This was what Beth was good at—that and shimmying down rope ladders and hauling people out of overturned cars, but, hey, she had a few skills, and reassurance was in her bundle. 'The bag pulley system seems to be working well.'

'But how can they stay there? Keanu says the blocked area is no longer than ten feet long. A woman who's just given birth…'

'They have food, water, air and light,' Beth said solidly, maybe more solidly than she was feeling. 'We even have little bathroom bags, like they have in spaceships. We pull 'em out every time the pulley comes this way. We can even send in deodorant if it's needed. Not that your Maddie would smell, but Josh and Malu in a tight spot… All that male testosterone… Come to think of it, I will send in some deodorant. Maddie must be just about ready to pass out.'

And Caroline chuckled. It was a watery chuckle but it was a chuckle all the same.

'But this operation…' she whispered. 'With the rock so unstable… You really think they can be okay?'

'We have two skilled doctors underground and the best mine experts on top of the ground,' Beth told her. 'Of course they'll be okay. You'd better believe it.'

And then Keanu came over to talk to them, to hug Caroline, to add his reassurances.

Of course they'll be okay.

You'd better believe it?

'Please, let me believe it, too,' Beth muttered to herself as she moved away. 'Please.'

CHAPTER SEVEN

THEY HAD ALL the gear. Malu was as settled as they could make him. The pneumothorax had to be fixed now.

There was one slight problem.

Josh's right hand shook.

Maddie had cleaned the gash on his arm and pulled it together with Steri-Strips, but it ran almost from his elbow to his shoulder.

He hadn't lost sensation. There was no reason why his hand should shake.

It shook.

Maddie had prepped and draped Malu's underarm. She'd used ketamine as an adjunct to the morphine, making Malu dozy but not soundly asleep.

What was needed now was local anaesthetic. It was a procedure that needed care, knowledge and a steady hand. The anaesthetic needed to be infiltrated through the layers of the chest wall, onto the rib below the intercostal space. The needle then had to be angled above the rib and advanced slowly until air was aspirated. The last five mils of the anaesthetic needed to be injected into the pleural space.

Josh knew exactly what to do. He'd done it before. He'd do it again—this was his job, trauma medicine.

His hand shook.

'Josh?' Maddie's voice was a soft whisper. She was holding the torch.

She'd have seen the tremor.

'I can do this,' he muttered under his breath, and he closed his eyes and counted to ten, trying desperately to steady himself.

He opened his eyes and his hand still shook.

I can't. But he didn't say it. Malu was still sleepily conscious. The last thing Malu needed was to sense indecision in his surgical team. Instead, he glanced up at Maddie, their eyes locked and held…

I can't.

'Slight change of roles,' Maddie said, without so much as a break in her voice. It was like this was totally normal, first cut one toenail, then cut another. 'Malu, Josh is looking at your ribs and thinking you don't need his great masculine forefinger to be making a ruddy big hole. Not when we have my dainty digits at the ready. So we're swapping. Hold on a second, Dr Campbell, while I scrub and glove. It now seems I get to play doctor while Josh plays the lady with the lamp.'

And Malu even smiled.

She was amazing, Josh thought as he took the torch from her. She'd made what was happening sound almost normal. She was stunning.

She was hours after giving birth. How could she?

'Maddie, can you?'

'Steady as a rock,' she said, smiling at him with all the assurance in the world, and she held up her hands to show there wasn't the hint of a tremor. There should have been. After what she'd gone through. 'Though we're hoping Malu's not rocklike. Malu, if you've been working out I might need to get a drill rather than a teeny, tiny needle. Why you guys think you need muscles is beyond me. Give me a guy with a one pack rather than a six pack any day.'

She was still distracting Malu. He was holding the torch—he could hardly help her on with her gloves but she used the backup method—using one sterile glove to tug on another. It wasted gloves but this wasn't the time to be arguing. Instead…he could do a bit of distracting, too.

'So you'd have loved me better if I'd had a bit of flab?' he demanded.

'The odd sign of humanity never hurt anyone,' she said, turning back to the instruments they'd laid out ready. Dust was still settling. Contaminants were everywhere. There were real risks here, but the alternative was unthinkable. 'I never did have much use for Spider-Man.'

'I guess that's what ended our marriage,' Josh said, managing a grin for Malu. 'Though I would have described myself more as Batman. He was so smooth in his other life.'

'Yeah, six pack in one, smarmy in the other. You ready, Malu? It's going to sting.'

'If he's Batman, I can do the hero bit, too,' Malu managed. 'Do your worst, Doc. Just get this breathing under control.'

He'd thought it would be the hardest thing in the world, to be aboveground, not knowing what was going on.

He was wrong. The hardest thing was doing what he was doing now, which was exactly nothing.

Except holding the torch. If Maddie wasn't totally reliant on the light he was holding maybe he could move behind her, support her a little. What he was demanding of her seemed impossible.

How dared his arm shake?

To have to ask for help... To be dependent on Maddie...

It wasn't him who was dependent on Maddie, he reminded himself. It was Malu. He was under no illusions, Malu's life was under her hands.

But they were steady hands, and there was no doubting their skill. He watched, every nerve attuned to what she was doing, as she carefully, carefully manoeuvred the anaesthetic to where it was needed.

Malu hardly responded as the needle went in. The morphine and ketamine were doing their job—but also, Malu was growing weaker. How much lung capacity did he have left?

To do so much and have him die now...

Stop thinking forward, he told himself. That was the problem with doing nothing—he had time to think.

Josh's work was his lifeline. When things hurt, when emotion threatened to overwhelm him, work was what he did. It stopped the hurt, or at least it pushed it so far onto the back burner that he didn't have to confront it.

They were waiting for the anaesthetic to take hold. Maddie was staring down at the sterile cloth holding her instruments. There was a risk dust would settle on the cleaned tools but there was little they could do about it. Josh was holding the torch with his steady hand. He couldn't do much assisting with the other.

She was practising what she needed to do in her head.

How many times had he watched her skill in a medical setting?

They'd met—how many years ago? He'd been a registrar at Sydney Central's emergency unit. Maddie had been a first-year intern, trying emergency medicine out for size.

She'd been one of the best interns he'd ever met. She'd been calm in a crisis, warm, reassuring and clever.

He'd tried to persuade her to stay, to train in the specialty he loved.

'Emergency medicine's great,' he remembered telling her. 'You live on adrenaline. You save lives. Every time you turn around there's a new challenge.'

'But you never get to know your patients,' she'd said, and she'd said it over and over as his professional persuasion had turned a lot more personal. Soon it hadn't been Dr Campbell trying to persuade Dr Haddon to change career direction, but it had been Josh persuading Maddie to marry him.

'Ready,' she said now, and he shoved the memories away and focussed. Even if his role was minor, the light was still crucial. Her fingers could never be allowed to shadow what she was doing.

But it nearly killed him to watch. What she was doing was so important. He was trained for this. This was his job, whereas Maddie...

This was still part of her job and, unpractised or not, she seemed to know exactly what she was doing. Her fingers were rock steady as she made the incision along the border of the intercostal space. She made it deep and long enough to accommodate her finger.

She glanced up at Josh then, a fast glance that said she wasn't as sure as her actions made out, but then she was focussed again.

'You're doing great,' he told her, but she wasn't listening.

She needed a nurse with swabs. Maybe he could swab, but if the light wobbled…

'In,' she said, and as the tissue was pushed aside by the insertion of her finger he heard the tiny rush of outcoming air.

She had the curved clamp now, using blunt dissection only, using the clamp to spread and split the muscle tissue.

She was in the pleural cavity. She'd be exploring, looking for adhesions. Making lightning-fast assessments.

He wanted to talk her through what was happening, but her face said it all. She was using all her concentration and then some.

'Going great,' he repeated, and then, as Malu flinched, not with pain, he thought, but maybe with tension because breathing was so darned hard, he took the miner's hand with his shaky one and gripped.

They both watched Maddie.

And watching Maddie…

He'd forgotten how much he missed her. He remembered that first time he'd seen her as a newly fledged intern. She'd been comforting a frightened child.

He'd been called to help but he'd paused in the doorway, caught by the sight of her. Something had changed, right at that moment.

Something he'd been denying ever since? That he needed her?

She was putting the chest tube in now, mounting it on the curved clamp and passing it along the pleural cavity. He heard Malu's breath rasp in and rasp in again, like a man who'd been drowning but had just reached the surface. Finally, blessedly, he saw the almost imperceptible shift at Malu's throat. It was imperceptible unless you were looking for it. It was imperceptible unless you knew that the lungs were re-inflating, that what was in the chest cavity was realigning to where it should be.

'Done,' Maddie murmured, and he did hear shakiness now, but it was in her voice, not in her hands. She was still working, but on the exterior, suturing the tube into place. She'd taken a moment to tug off her gloves and put on new ones before she worked on the exterior of the wound. She shouldn't have needed to. If she'd had an assistant...

She didn't. She was working alone.

He could have told her how to operate the underwater seal but he didn't need to. She knew how.

He could have helped her dress the incision area but he didn't need to do that, either.

She was a doctor operating at her best.

She didn't need him.

The words hung. A shadow...

Had he been too afraid to admit he needed her?

The tube was now firmly connected to the underwater seal. He could see the bubbles as air escaped the pleural cavity. The loss of this tiny amount of air wasn't enough to cause Malu major problems. Building up in the pleural cavity, it was lethal. Calmly bubbling out into water, it was harmless.

Job done. The dressing was in place. Maddie sat back on her heels—and he saw the energy drain out of her.

She swayed.

And finally, finally there was something he could do. She did need him. He moved before he even knew he intended moving. He took her into his arms and she let herself sag. She crumpled against him, let his strength enfold her, and let him hold her as if her life force was spent.

It wasn't spent, though. This woman had the life force of a small army. She let herself be held for all of two minutes and then he felt her gather herself, stiffen, tug away.

And it nearly broke him. For those two minutes he'd felt her heart beating with his. He'd felt himself melt into her.

He'd realised what he'd lost.

'Thanks, Josh.' Her voice was still shaky but she was back to being professional—almost. 'That's what you don't see in most theatres—doctors cuddling doctors. But I was a bit woozy.'

'You didn't seem woozy when you were operating,' Malu managed, and Maddie smiled and touched her patient's cheek. It was a gesture Josh knew—one of the things he'd noticed first about her. She was tactile, touching, warm.

He'd tried it out himself. It reassured patients. He'd learned from her.

Touching worked.

He wanted…

'I can pull myself together when I need to,' Maddie told Malu, and Josh knew her attention was back to where it ought to be—to her patient, to the situation— to her baby, lying peacefully on the air bed behind her. 'But now, if you don't mind, I'll let Dr Campbell take over my duty roster. Breathing easier?'

'You better believe it.'

'Excellent. That tube stays in place until we get an

X-ray upstairs, but there's no blood coming out. That's a great sign. It means you have a slight tear in your lung but nothing major. As long as you stay fairly still—no need to make a martyr of yourself but let's not roll over without giving me or Josh forewarning—you should have no problems.'

'I'll need an operation when we get out of here?'

When? There was no if. Even though the walls around them were made of crumbling rock, Malu seemed to have forgotten.

That was down to Maddie, too, Josh decided. She was showing not one scrap of fear. If she'd been a doctor at the end of a long shift in an emergency ward of a large city hospital she couldn't be more composed. She was weary and she was signing off, but she was calmly reassuring her patient before she went.

I'll need an operation...

'You possibly will,' she told Malu. 'One of those ribs must have broken with a pointy bit. Josh and I don't like pointy bits, do we, Josh?'

'No, we don't,' Josh agreed gravely. 'But after what you've been through, an operation to stick two bits of rib together will be a piece of cake. You reckon you might go to sleep now?' With the amount of drugs on board it must be only the adrenaline of what had been happening—plus the terror of breathing difficulties— that had been keeping him awake.

'Going to sleep now,' Malu whispered, his speech already slurred.

'And you,' he told Maddie. He wanted to hug her again but she'd already turned and gathered her baby into her arms, transforming again into a mother. With baby. A brand-new family—of which he was no part.

He tugged an air bed to the far side of the shaft. 'Here,' he said, roughly because emotion was threatening to do his head in. 'Keanu's sent down sheets. Settle. I'll cover you all. You and Malu and Lea. And then you sleep.'

'Yes, sir,' Maddie said, still wobbly, and it was too much for Josh. He did gather her into his arms, but not to hold her as he wanted to hold her. Yes, his arm was weak. No, he shouldn't be doing any such thing, but he lifted her anyway, carrying her bodily across to the air bed, setting her down, making sure she and her baby were safe.

He covered them both with the sheet.

'I need to turn the torch off now,' he told her. Keanu had sent down more batteries but they were both aware that the line into their cavern was fragile and the time until rescue was unknown. They had to conserve everything. 'I'll lie beside Malu so I can feel if anything changes.'

'You're a wonderful doctor, Dr Campbell,' she whispered. 'Thank you.'

Him? A wonderful doctor... He stared down at her, speechless. But she closed her eyes and slept and he was left saying nothing at all.

CHAPTER EIGHT

THE NIGHT CREPT ON, inch by pitch-black inch. It was a relief that Malu needed checking. Every few minutes Josh flicked on the torch and checked the underwater seal, checked Malu's vital signs, checked there was nothing wrong with his patient—and then he checked Maddie.

He never shone the light directly at her. There was no way he was risking waking her. She slept the sleep of the truly exhausted.

Her baby lay in the crook of her arm as she slept. He'd suggested they use his air bed, setting tiny Lea up in a separate space, but the look she'd cast him had been one of disbelief.

'When the roof of the cave could come down any minute? She stays right by me.'

The baby care 'experts' would have a field day, he thought. Mothers in the same bed as their newborn? He'd heard a lecture once by a dragon of a professor...

How easy would it be for mother to roll onto her child?

It wouldn't happen. Every ounce of Maddie's being was in protective mode.

She was instinctively caring.

She was holding her daughter.

And all at once he was hit by a wave of longing so great it threatened to overwhelm him. Family...

He couldn't do family. Families hurt.

He flicked the torch off and settled back on his air bed. Not to sleep, though. Malu's obs were vital.

But things were okay. They were as safe as he could get them. He'd done what he could.

But suddenly things weren't okay. Things were very much not okay.

He was shaking—not just his arm this time, but his whole body.

Why? He was fighting to suppress what was going on, fighting to make sense of it.

He was exhausted—he knew he was. He'd been working on adrenaline for almost twenty-four hours. He was injured. His arm throbbed.

He'd helped his ex-wife deliver her baby. It made sense that it'd affect him. If he could put it into logic, then he could control it.

He'd had to stand back and watch while Maddie had operated. He'd been helpless. He'd lost control.

Think it through logically, he told himself. Keep it analytical. Stop the shaking...

He couldn't.

There was no sound, no movement, and yet he felt like the walls were caving in. His head felt like it was exploding. Sensation after sensation was coursing through him. Black fear... Maddie with rocks raining down around her. Lea with the cord round her neck. Malu gasping for breath...

And more. The past. A dying baby. Maddie lying in hospital, sobbing her eyes out. Looking down at the tiny scrap who could have been his son. A child who *was* his son.

And Holly, his little sister, lying still and cold in the mortuary. A little sister he'd protected and protected and protected.

Until he'd failed.

He couldn't breathe. He couldn't think.

This is a panic attack, he told himself, fiercely, but he couldn't listen. The doctor part of him, the part that had been his all for so long, the Josh who was a crucial member of Cairns Air Sea Rescue was no longer here.

He was a kid lying in the dark, alone and terrified, during the time he and Holly had been separated in two different foster homes. Where was she? What was happening to her? How could he keep her safe when they were apart?

And then…he was a guy bereft, looking down at the body of his tiny son. Seeing Maddie's anguish. Trying to figure how to hide his own anguish so he could help her.

And then Holly's death. Maddie trying to hold him. The cold, hard knowledge that he'd failed. He'd failed everyone.

He must have made some sound. Surely he hadn't cried out, but he couldn't stop shaking. He couldn't…

And suddenly Maddie was there, kneeling on his air bed. Tugging his rigid body close so his head was on her breast. Holding him, despite the rigid shaking, despite the fact that he didn't know why, he didn't know what…

'Josh…Josh, love, it's okay. Josh, we're safe.'

Her words made no sense. The sensation of losing control was terrifying.

Her words faded but her arms tightened.

She held, and there was nothing he could do but be held, to take strength from her.

For the first time ever?

It couldn't matter. He was so far out of control that to pull back was unthinkable. There was no strength left in him.

And gradually the tremors eased. She was kneeling on the air bed, holding him against her, running her fingers through his hair and crooning a little. And as the tremors eased, the crooning turned into words.

'Sweetheart, it's okay. We're safe. The nice men with the digging machines will get us out. This might not be the Ritz but we have comfy beds and Keanu's saying the pulley system's even good enough for hot coffee in the morning. Maybe that's what this is, love, lack of caffeine. You always were hopeless without coffee. But it's okay, Josh. We're all safe. Thanks to you, love, we're fine and we'll stay fine.'

And then she added a tiny rider, a whisper so soft he could hardly hear it.

'I love you.'

And the world settled on its axis, just like that. The tremors stopped. He was a man again. He was Dr Josh Campbell, being held by…his wife.

Needing comfort?

He didn't…need. How could he?

How could he not? It was like he was being torn in two.

He broke away, tugging back, just a little but enough to break the contact. She turned and flicked on the torch, not shining it directly at him but giving enough light to turn blackness into shadows.

She touched his face—and he felt himself flinch.

He raked his hair and then thought he shouldn't have done that. The feel of her fingers in his hair was still with him. He wanted it forever.

He couldn't have it.

To lose control… To stand at the edge of the precipice and feel himself falling…

'Maddie, I'm sorry. I'm…'

'What is it, love?'

Don't call me love. Somehow he stayed silent but he wanted to shout it. Why?

Because he wanted those barriers up. He was in control. He had to be. He knew no other way.

'Maddie, I don't know what happened.' He did, but there was no way he could open the floodgates, explain terror he hardly understood himself.

'This is scary.' She said it prosaically, stating the obvious for the idiot who didn't get it. 'You've spent the day being a warrior, but armour can only hold you up for so long.'

'Yeah.' Like that made sense.

What was he doing, being this feeble? Shame swept over him, a shame so deep it threatened to overwhelm him.

'Sorry.' He spoke more harshly than he intended and he forced his voice to moderate. 'Nightmare or something—who knows? I'm over it. I don't need—'

'Me?'

Yes, he wanted to say. It would be so easy to sink against her again, to take comfort. But beyond that… How could he survive if he needed her?

He couldn't.

'I guess I needed a hug,' he admitted.

'Of course you needed a hug. You're human, Josh. Giving works both ways.'

'But I don't need anything more.'

It was the wrong thing to say. He saw her flinch. 'Of course you don't.' She was watching him, with the expression of a woman who knew everything she needed to know about her man, and it made her sad.

'That's why we could never make it,' she whispered. 'You've never let me share your nightmares. You've never let me close.'

'I can't.'

'I know you can't,' she whispered with desperate sadness, and then Lea stirred and whimpered behind her and she turned away.

'Try and sleep,' she told Josh as she lifted her baby to her breast. 'We'll leave the torch on. I need it to feed and you need it to keep the nightmares at bay.'

'I don't need—'

'And maybe you never will and that's a tragedy,' she snapped. 'Think about it.'

Lea settled. Maddie gently rocked and crooned and loved.

And he lay there in the dark and he felt more lonely than he'd ever felt in his life.

He'd loved loving Maddie. He'd loved holding her, making her laugh, helping her, comforting her.

Wasn't it enough?

But as he watched Maddie's face, as he saw the peace settle over her as her tiny baby settled, he felt like a prism had opened into a world he hardly knew.

Cradling her baby helped. Cradling Lea brought Maddie peace.

She'd wanted to comfort him. The night Holly had

died… He remembered coming out of the mortuary and Maddie had been there, white and shocked. She'd walked straight at him, gathered him into her arms and held.

And he'd pulled away. 'Go home, Maddie. There's no use for us both to suffer.'

To do anything else… To have let Maddie comfort him as she'd tried then…

It was still a precipice, and all he knew was to back away.

CHAPTER NINE

THE EXPERTS CHANGED their minds again. They didn't bore down from the top or the side; rather they cautiously picked their way through the existing shaft, inch by cautious inch, shoring as they came.

For those trapped, the wait seemed interminable, but they had what they most needed. Malu had stabilised and even improved. He slept.

Bugsy seemed resigned. He pinched half of Josh's air mattress. Josh used him as a pillow and he didn't mind. There was something comforting about using a golden retriever as a pillow. Josh slept fitfully while they waited, never for more than an hour at a time, keeping watch, but there seemed no drama. Maddie slept, too, waking only to feed and get to know her new daughter. If there wasn't the risk, Josh could almost imagine she was where she wanted to be. He watched the expression on her face as Lea's tiny mouth found the breast and suckled. He watched as Maddie's arms curved around her with love—and he was almost jealous.

Almost. He had himself back under control.

In the time he wasn't dozing, or attending to his little hospital's needs, he worked, and that was a relief. They now had netting above them, a sort of tent. He'd assembled it with care from materials sent in via the bags, small piece by small piece. It was made of wire mesh, and was supported by a series of triangular, snap-together poles. In the event of a full-scale collapse it'd be useless, but smaller loose stones were now less of a threat.

And the rescuers were on their way. Finally they could hear the miners through the rock.

'We reckon we're within six feet,' Keanu told him on one of their brief calls. Their supply of phone batteries was bearing up. The bag system could pull in more but the slightest rock slip could end their supply. Apart from that first indulgent baby parcel, only the barest essentials were coming in.

Malu was still drowsy but as the miners got closer Maddie stayed awake. Even Bugsy seemed restless. They all knew the last few feet were the most dangerous.

The more Josh thought about how he'd managed to get in here, the more he knew he'd been incredibly lucky—and maybe also incredibly stupid.

If Maddie hadn't been here...

Or not. Beth often told him he was crazy, that he had no fear, and maybe he didn't.

If there was an overturned car at the bottom of a cliff it'd be Josh who abseiled down to attend to an injured driver. He'd swung in a harness over a churning sea. He'd taken risks more times than he could remember.

Why not? It didn't matter if anything happened to him.

But now it mattered. He thought of the people dependent on Maddie and Malu. There were people outside who loved them.

'Do you have anyone back in Cairns you can hug when this is over?' Maddie asked into the silence, and he wondered if she'd been mind-reading.

'I… No.'

'No girlfriend?'

He thought about it before answering. He and Karen dated when it suited them. She was an adrenaline junkie, just like him, and for her birthday last month he'd taken her skydiving.

He remembered their dinner afterwards. She'd spent the night messaging about her awesome adventure to her mates.

No, he thought. She wasn't even his girlfriend.

'Earth to Josh…'

'Bachelorhood suits me.'

'That's fear talking.'

'Since when did you do psychology?'

'I had years to analyse you.'

'So why haven't you remarried?' he growled, and she snuggled down a little farther in her makeshift bed. Despite the earplugs they used during the worst of the drilling, the constant chipping of tools on rock was challenging.

Bugsy had abandoned Josh's air bed and was pressed hard against one side of Maddie, maybe sensing the increasing tension as the sounds of rescue grew closer. Lea was cradled in her arms. It was like she had a small posse of protection and he was on the outside.

'I tried marriage once.' She was speaking lightly, trying for humour, he thought. 'I don't have the courage to try it again.'

'So you'll raise your daughter on your own?'

'No.'

It was said sharply, and her words hung. For a moment he thought she wouldn't continue, but when she finally spoke her voice was reflective again.

'That's why I finally figured I could try again to have a baby,' she told him. 'When I realised I wasn't on my own. I guess…when I started working on Wildfire I was pretty much at rock bottom. I needed a job. The Australian government helps fund the medical services by supplying FIFOs. The pay's excellent and I was determined to keep Mum where she is. And, no, Josh, there was no way I was accepting help from you. But I hadn't been here for six months before I realised what a special place Wildfire is. The people are amazing, and the staff who are attracted to work here seem just as good. I guess all of us outsiders are running away from stuff, saving money, hiding, changing tracks… But the islanders welcome us all. Saying this place is like family sounds a cliché, but it's not.'

'That's why you ran into a collapsing mine?'

'Malu's wife is my friend. So, yes, in a way…'

'They're not your family.' He spoke more harshly than he'd intended. 'You're their doctor and colleague. They need you.'

'It works both ways. I need them.'

'How can you need them?'

'They accept me for what I am,' she said simply. 'When I ache, they ache. Last year Mum had another stroke. I went back to Cairns and had to stay for a month. When I came back, my tiny villa was a sea of flowers. Kalifa met me off the plane. Kalifa was one of the tribal elders, and he and his wife have practically been grandparents to me.'

She paused then and he knew she was thinking of

the eldery man, of a needless death, and of who knew what else waited for them on the surface.

That's what happened when you got attached, he thought. It was like slicing a part of you out.

He didn't have that many parts left.

'I think Kalifa organised it,' she said softly. 'Or maybe it was his wife, Nani, or Pearl, Malu's wife, or Hettie or any one of so many… Anyway, all along the path to my villa were hibiscus, and I think I was hugged by every single Wildfire resident that night. And you know what? That was the night I made the decision to have a baby. Because I'm part of a family. I'm loved and I can love back.'

The last few words were said almost defiantly. As if she expected him to reject them.

And then there was a sound of rubble, falling stones that made them both hold their breath. There was an oath from the far side of the rock and then the steady chipping restarted.

'I can't cope…with them putting their lives on the line for me,' Josh muttered.

'They're putting their lives on the line for all of us,' Maddie said, gentleness fading to asperity. 'You don't have a monopoly on heroism, Josh.'

'I don't—'

'No, that was mean.' She took a deep breath and winced again and he thought she was hurting. She'd given birth not twenty-four hours before. She'd already been bruised in the rockfall. Of course she was hurting. But she took a deep breath and kept on going. 'You know what I've figured?' she said, evenly again. 'I've figured that it's a whole lot easier to be the hero than the one dangling by her fingertips from the cliff.'

'What does that mean?'

'Why are you a doctor, Josh?' she asked, gently again. 'No, don't answer, because I know. It's because in medicine you can help. Add to that your search and rescue job and you can be the hero in every single situation. But when it comes to being rescued yourself, you can't handle it. That's what killed our marriage and it's killing you now.'

Silence. He watched her close her eyes and then saw her wince and put a hand to her neck.

Maybe there was something he could do.

'What's wrong?' he asked.

'Hero again?' she asked wryly, and she even managed a smile.

'Maddie, what is it?'

'I must have ricked my neck in the rockfall,' she confessed. 'I haven't had time to think about it.'

'Would a massage help?'

She thought about it. She looked at him for a long time in the shadowy light and then slowly she nodded.

'It might,' she said at last. 'But that'd mean accepting—again—that I need help.'

'You do need help. Maddie, being a single mother... You know it'll be hard. You still have your mother. You'll be doing a full-time job and trying to care for a baby, as well.' And then, because the sounds of rescue were growing closer and maybe there wouldn't be time to say it again, he said what he most wanted to say.

'Maddie, our marriage was good. The chemistry's still there. Maybe we can make it work again. Maybe we should try.'

'You'd be a father to Lea?'

'She needs a dad.'

'Need's no basis for a marriage. You must be the first one to tell me that.'

'But you need—'

'Josh, I don't need—at least, not from you. I have the community. I have my colleagues and my friends. Believe it or not, I even have my mum. She still loves me, even though she's so badly damaged, and her love supports me. I have everything I need. Marriage is something else. Marriage is for loving, not for dependency. It's for sharing and I don't think you ever will. I'm sorry, Josh, but I can't let you hurt me again.'

'I never would.'

'You don't understand how not to.' Then she smiled again, trying desperately for lightness, trying desperately to put things back on a footing to go forward. 'But in terms of need... Okay, Josh, more than anything else, I would love a head and shoulders massage. You do the best and I've missed them. That's what I need from you, Josh Campbell, and nothing more.'

Why couldn't she give in to him?

She was giving in to him, she decided as his fingers started their magic. If this was the last massage he ever gave her, she'd enjoy every second.

She'd pretend he was hers?

The first time he'd done this to her had been just after she'd started work. He'd been waiting for her at the nurses' station. She'd been supposedly watching an operation but the surgeon had thought hands-on training was best. The surgeon had stood and watched every step of the way at what should have been a routine appendectomy.

Except it hadn't been routine. The patient had been

a young mum with no history of medical problems, nothing to suggest the sudden, catastrophic heart failure that had killed her.

They'd had a cardiac team there in seconds, they'd fought with everything they'd had, but there'd been no happy ending. Maddie had walked blindly out of Theatre and Josh had been there. He'd gathered her into his arms and held.

He was good at caring was Josh. He was amazing.

They'd been supposed to be going out with friends. Instead, Maddie had found herself on a picnic rug on the beach, eating fish and chips, surprising herself by eating while Josh had let her be, just watched. And waited.

And then he'd moved behind her and started his massage.

It had started as gentleness itself, a bare touching, hands placed softly on her shoulders, resting, as if seeking permission to continue.

She hadn't moved then. She didn't move now.

Permission granted.

And now his fingers started their magic.

First they stroked over the entire area he wanted to massage, her head, her shoulders, her back, her arms and her hands. She was resting against him but as his fingers moved she slumped forward a little, so he could touch her back.

Skin against skin.

How could he do this with an injured arm?

She couldn't ask. Maybe she couldn't even care?

Then his fingers deepened the pressure and she forgot what the question was.

He was kneading the tight muscles on either side of her neck, kneading upward, firm now, pressing into

what seemed knots of tension. He worked methodi-
cally, focussing first one side then the other. His fingers kneaded, never so hard it hurt, never so hard she
felt out of control, but firm enough to make the tension
ooze upward and outward and away.

And then to her scalp. Her hair must be full of grit
and sweat, a tangled mess, but right now she didn't care.
Josh was stroking his thumbs upward, as if releasing
the tension that had been sent up there by his wonder
fingers. He was teasing her hair, tugging lightly, running his fingers through and through…

She was floating. She was higher than any drug
could have made her. Lea was nestled beside her, Bugsy
was at her other side, and Josh was turning her cavern
of hell into one of bliss.

She heard herself moan with pleasure. She was melting into him, disappearing into a puddle of sensual ec-
stasy… His fingers… His hands…

Josh.

She drifted and he massaged and she floated, every
single threat, every single worry placed at bay.

She loved… She loved…

And yet, as his fingers left her scalp and drifted
down, beginning their delicious movements at her
shoulder blades, an argument drifted back with them.

A long-ago conversation. After that night. They'd
ended up in bed—of course. She'd slept through the
night, enfolded by Josh's strong arms, and in the morning she'd woken to her beautiful man bringing her tea
and toast.

'Where did you learn…?'

'One of my foster-mothers,' he told her. 'She used to
have me do it for her after work.'

'Have you ever had anyone do it to you?'

'No,' he'd said shortly, and she'd set down her tea, looped her arms around his neck and drawn him to her.

'Well, I'm going to learn,' she'd declared. 'We'll massage each other every time we're stressed. Or even when we're not stressed. In fact, with massages like that, we need never be stressed again.'

He'd smiled and kissed her but then he'd drawn away. 'There's no need. I don't need a massage. Any time you want one, though...'

'So if I learn you won't let me practise?'

'As I said, sweetheart, there's no need.'

And there was that word again. It was like a brick wall, a solid divider that kept Josh on one side and the world on another. If he admitted need, then what? He'd fall apart?

She thought he'd crack. She thought if she loved him enough...

She was wrong.

He was stroking down her head now, across both her shoulders. There was grit on her shoulders and the remains of sweat and grime, but it made little difference. The finest oils couldn't have made her feel any more at peace than she was right now.

He was applying gentle pressure, running his fingers down her arms, using both hands, from shoulders to the tips of her fingers. She was totally subsumed by the sensation. If he wanted to make love with her right then...

Right... Less than two days after birth, in a collapsed gold mine, with her daughter, with an injured miner, with a dog...

The whole thing was fantasy. Her head was filled with a desire that could never be fulfilled.

His hands were stroking down her neck and shoulders, down her arms, breaking contact at her fingertips, over and over, but each stroke slower, slower, until finally his fingers trailed away from hers and held still.

Then a feather-light touch on her shoulders, a signal that it was finished.

Silence.

The end.

She wanted to cry.

She wanted to turn and hold him. She wanted to take him into her arms. She wanted him to be her…family?

She did none of those things. You couldn't hug a man with armour, she thought, no matter how much you might want to.

'Thank you,' she whispered into the shadows. 'Thank you, Josh, for everything.' And she gathered Lea back into her arms and held, not because Lea needed her— the baby was deeply asleep—but because she needed Lea.

'You need to sleep,' Josh said, and he held her shoulders while he moved sideways, so he wasn't right behind her, so she was free to settle back onto the air bed with her baby.

'Yes,' she whispered.

'Is there anything you need?'

'Nothing.'

Liar.

But it couldn't be a lie, she thought. She'd made her decision.

Or he'd made his decision years ago and nothing had changed.

And then a puff of dust surged out from the rocks above them and the dust had come from the gap Josh had used to get in, that they'd been using to haul bags back and forth.

'Anyone home?' There'd been scraping at the rocks that had grown so constant they'd hardly been listening— or maybe it was that they'd been just a bit distracted?

'Hey!' Josh called back, and his voice still sounded distracted. Maybe he was just as discombobulated as she was, Maddie thought, and was uncharitable enough to think, *Good!*

'I can see chinks of your light,' the voice called. 'You're eight feet away, no more. We've reinforced up to here. Another hour should do it. You guys almost ready to emerge?'

'You'd better believe it,' Josh said, but once again Maddie heard that trace of uncertainty.

It was as if they'd both be grateful to be aboveground, but neither of them was quite sure what they'd be leaving behind.

CHAPTER TEN

IT WAS MORE like three hours before the final break-through came, because no one was taking chances. By that time, however, there was a solid channel, a shored-up shaft that was deemed safe enough to risk moving them out.

They wasted no time. Safe was relative and any moment the ground could move again, so the move happened with speed. There was the moment's relief when a blackened face appeared, grinning and taking a second to give them a thumbs-up. Then there was skilled shoring work to make the entrance secure before a grimy rescuer was in the shaft with them and Maddie was being told she was to be strapped to a cradle stretcher, whether she willed it or not.

She didn't will it. 'Take Malu first.' She spoke it as an order, in her most imperious tone—a doctor directing traffic in the worst emergency couldn't have sounded more authoritative—and she couldn't believe it when she was overruled.

'Sorry, ma'am, orders are you're first,' the man said, and Josh touched her face, a light reassurance, but his touch was an order, too.

'They get two for the price of one with you,' he told

her. 'You and your Lea. Lea's a priority, even if you're not. Off you go, the two of you.'

And then, because he couldn't help himself, he kissed her, hard and fast, and it was an acknowledgment that being hauled out through the fast-made tunnel had major risks.

As if to emphasise it, another cloud of dust spat down on them.

'On the stretcher,' the man ordered, and Maddie had the sense to submit and then to stay passive, holding tight to Lea as what looked like a cradle was erected over her—the same shape as an MRI machine and just as claustrophobic. Once she was enclosed, the head of the stretcher was hauled up to the guy waiting, and she was lifted and pulled into the mouth of the shaft.

And then along. She didn't know how they did it. These guys were experts but she knew from their silence that they were working far closer to the limits of safety that they'd done before. And all she could do was lie still and hold Lea—and think of Josh left behind...

Josh, who didn't need anyone. Who'd be caring for Malu. Caring and never letting anyone care for him.

And then, amazingly, she was out of the darkness. The light was almost blinding and Lea was being lifted from her. She was being gathered into Hettie's arms and hugged and held, and Caroline was holding Lea and sobbing, and Keanu was there, giving her one fast hug, and she even saw tears in his eyes before he returned to his role as doctor.

They'd rigged up some sort of makeshift hospital tent. 'Let's get you inside,' he said roughly, trying to hide emotion. 'We need to assess—'

'I'm staying out here until the others are out,' she told him, and this time she managed to make them agree.

So Hettie organised washbasins and someone rigged up a sheet for a little privacy, and Hettie and Caroline did their midwife thing, as well as a preliminary assessment of scrapes and bruises, yet she could still see the mouth of the mine.

'She's perfect,' Caroline breathed, as she carefully washed Lea in one of the washbasins and inspected every part of her before wrapping her and handing her back to her mother. 'She's adorable, Maddie. Oh, well done, you.'

Surely Maddie should have beamed with maternal pride—and she sort of did but it was a pretty wobbly beam. She hugged her precious baby back to her, but still she looked at the mine entrance.

Malu's stretcher emerged next.

Keanu was ready to receive him, as was Beth. Hettie moved back to Keanu's side as well, so there was a receiving posse of medics moving straight into ER mode.

And, of course, Pearl was there. Pearl had greeted Maddie as she'd emerged, but even as she'd been hugging her, like Maddie, her eyes hadn't left the mouth of the mine.

As soon as the miners set Malu's stretcher down, Pearl was on the grass beside him, not saying a word, just touching his face, seemingly fearful of the drips, the oxygen mask, the medical paraphernalia Maddie and Josh had organised, but still…just touching.

And it was up to Malu to speak.

'Hey, girl,' he said, holding his wife any way he could. He spoke softly yet every person in the clearing could hear him. 'God help me, girl, I've needed you so much…' His voice broke on a sob and then, tubes or not, mask or not, everything was irrelevant, he was gathering Pearl into his arms and holding.

And Maddie couldn't help herself. Tears were coursing down her face. Happiness tears? There were matching tears on the faces of almost everyone around her, tears of relief, tears of joy, but mixed with that?

What sort of tears?

Jealous tears? To be loved like Pearl was. To be needed.

And then Josh was out, with Bugsy bursting out behind him. Josh had obviously refused the stretcher. He was bruised and battered. His arm needed urgent attention. She knew he'd lost strength so there was a chance of nerve damage, but he wasn't thinking of himself now. When was he ever? He stood blinking in the sunlight, gathering himself, and even as he did so Maddie saw him regroup, turn back into the professional, the doctor he'd become so he could help.

So he could hide?

But only she could see that. He saw her, half-hidden by sheets, lying in the shade, holding her baby. Their eyes locked for one long moment, a moment of recognition of all that was between them—and a moment of farewell?

And then he turned to Keanu.

'I'm fine,' he said roughly. 'We've got them out, now what else needs doing? Beth, what's the priority? What's the need?'

For once, however, Dr Joshua Campbell did not get things his own way.

Beth turned bossy. On his own turf he could have

overruled her, but backed up by the island medical team of Keanu, Caroline and Hettie he'd met his match.

'No one needs you, Dr Campbell. In fact, for the duration you don't even consider yourself a doctor.' Hettie, the island's nurse administrator, was doing the organising. She looked to be in her late thirties and was obviously a woman to be reckoned with. Keanu was testing his arm, making him flex, testing each of his fingers. Together they gave him no choice.

They propelled him into the temporary hospital tent, whether he willed it or not. Malu was on the next stretcher.

Maddie was still outside.

Another of the nurses was at the door of the tent—Caroline Lockhart. She stood, looking a little unsure.

'Caroline?' Keanu said.

'The plane's due to land in twenty minutes,' Caroline told him. 'I've been talking to Beth. There's another doctor coming from Cairns to fly back with the patients. Beth says there'll be room for her and for two patients, but Pearl's desperate to go with Malu. She has a sister in Cairns she can stay with, and another sister here, who'll look after the kids. But a tropical storm's closing in over Cairns and they say this could be the last trip for a few days. If we need to send Josh then Pearl can't go.'

'I'm fine,' Josh growled. What were they doing, sending another doctor? Tending to patients during transport was what he did. 'You don't need another doctor from Cairns. I can care for Malu.'

'The doctor's already on his way,' Caroline said, ignoring his protest, talking to Keanu, not to him. 'And

our little hospital's packed. Which leaves these two…
these three, if you count Maddie's baby…'

'I'm fine,' Josh growled again, but no one was listening.

'Maddie wants to stay here,' Hettie said, still excluding him. 'She's looking good—there's no medical reason to evacuate her.'

'I'd like them both in hospital,' Keanu growled. 'All
of them. Maddie and baby and Josh. Twenty-four hours'
observation. The conditions underground weren't exactly clean and this is the tropics. Josh, this cut's deep
and needs stitching. You get it infected, you risk long-
term damage. The rest of your scratches need care and
you need rest. So care it is. No one's growing infec-
tions on my watch.'

'Use the homestead,' Caroline said. 'You know we
have six bedrooms. I'll send a message to our housekeeper to make up beds. Keanu, you can do Maddie's
obstetric checks there. Once you've done Josh's stitching and you're happy with them they should be fine. I
can do obs.'

And Keanu stood back and looked at Josh—assessing.
Seeing him not as a colleague but as a patient. Someone
who needed help?

It was all Josh could do not to get up and walk out.
To lie on the examination table and be assessed like this
was almost killing him.

'I want gentle, gradual exercise,' Keanu said at last,
still talking to Caroline. 'Slowly, no sudden movements.
They've been cramped too long with injuries. So gentle movement with support, then food and bed. I'll give
Maddie a thorough check first but if she's okay… I'll
want them watched but the house should work. If we

clear you from hospital shifts, you can look after them, and I can organise one of the night shift to take over while you sleep.'

'And act as chaperone, too.' That was Beth, standing at the entrance to the tent. She had her cheek back. When Josh had emerged from the mine she'd looked whey-faced but now she was practically bouncing. 'These two have been married,' she told the tent in general. 'Josh and your Maddie. Once there were sparks, so separate bedrooms at separate ends of the house.'

'I don't think we need to worry about these two and red-hot sex,' Keanu said dryly, and managed a grin. 'When two sets of bruises unite—ouch—and there's nothing like a one-day-old baby to dampen passion. However, they're consenting adults. Whatever they choose to do or not to do is up to them.' And then his smile widened, and Josh thought for the first time in two days the stress had come off.

'No, actually, that's not true,' Keanu added, still grinning. 'For now Maddie has no obstetrician so I'm it. So, Dr Campbell, no matter what your intentions may be regarding your ex-wife, could you please take sex off the agenda?'

'I have no intention...' He paused, practically speechless. Of all the...

'She's a lovely lady, our Maddie,' Keanu said. 'If I wasn't otherwise engaged I'd be attracted to her myself.'

'Hey!' Caroline said, and everyone laughed, and the tension lessened still further.

Except Josh's tension didn't ease. He was stuck on this island. He was about to spend the night in some sort of private house, even if it was a big one.

If he was at one end of the house and Maddie was at the other—she'd still be there.

No sex… There was no chance of that, but a part of him was suddenly remembering sex from a long time ago, how it had felt lying in Maddie's arms—how it had felt to be needed by Maddie.

That was the only time when his world had seemed right.

His world was right now, he told himself savagely. His world was exactly as he wanted it. All he needed was to get away from this island and get home.

Home? To his base in Cairns? An austere apartment he spent as little time in as possible?

He glanced around the tent at this tight-knit medical community, and then out through the tent flap to where a huddle of women crouched around Maddie. They were readying her for transport to the Lockhart house but this wasn't medical personnel doing their bit. These were friends, and even from here he could tell how much she was loved.

But not by him. He could never admit how much he needed her.

Not even to himself?

But this was exhaustion talking, he thought. This was nonsense.

'You'll be fine.' It was Hettie, washing his already cleaned face again, as if she knew that the grit felt so ingrained it'd take months to feel as if he was rid of it. 'We'll take care of you.'

'I don't need—'

'Need or not,' she said cheerfully, 'you're trapped until the storm front passes over Cairns, so you might as well get used to it.'

* * *

The bedroom was amazing. Luscious. Or maybe luscious was too small a word to describe it. 'It was my parents' bedroom,' Caroline had told her last night. 'Best room in the house.'

'Caro, I can't.'

'Of course you can.' Caroline had helped her shower and tucked her into bed, brooking no argument, and Maddie had been too overwhelmed to argue.

And now it was morning. She lay in a massive bed with down pillows and a crisp white coverlet, surrounded by delicate white lace that served as a mosquito net but looked more like a bridal canopy.

The bed was an island of luxury in a room that screamed of age and history and wealth. Old timber gleamed with generations of layers of wax and elbow grease. Vast French windows opened to the wide veranda beyond. White lace curtains fluttered in the warm sea breeze, and beyond the lagoon and then the sea.

Even her bruises thought they were in heaven.

She did ache a little, she conceded, but this was a bed, a room, a house to cure the worst bruises she could imagine.

And Caroline was standing in the doorway, holding her daughter.

'Sleepyhead.' Caroline chuckled as she set Lea into her mother's arms. At some time in the small hours she'd come in and helped Maddie feed—surely Maddie remembered that?—but the rest... How deeply had she slept? 'Your daughter's been fussing so I took her for a little stroll and introduced her to her world,' Caroline told her. 'She seems to approve. At least she seemed to approve until five minutes ago, when...'

As if on cue, Lea opened her mouth and wailed.

And Maddie felt her face split into a grin. There was nothing she could do about it—she couldn't stop grinning.

And Caroline smiled, too, as she helped Maddie show Lea to her breast—not that Lea needed much direction.

'Hmm,' Caroline said, standing back as Lea started the important business of feeding. 'I don't think you two will need breastfeeding advice.'

'I had a booklet I intended reading before she arrived,' Maddie told her, smiling and smiling down at her tiny daughter. 'Stupidly I left it behind when I went in, but Lea and I figured it out all by ourselves.'

'You left a lot else behind when you ran in,' Caroline retorted. 'Including all our hearts. Maddie, how could you?'

'How's Malu?' Maddie asked, answering Caroline's question with those two words.

'He's okay,' Caro conceded. 'Keanu had a call from Cairns a couple of hours ago. He's settled and stable and sitting up, having breakfast. Thanks to you and your Josh.'

'He's not *my* Josh.' She said it automatically. She was touching her tiny daughter's cheek as she suckled, and she was trying to think about Lea. Just Lea.

Only Josh was in her thoughts, too.

'He seems very concerned, for someone who's not *your Josh.*'

'Josh always cares,' she said carefully. 'It's what he's good at.'

'He wants to see you.'

'I'm sleepy.'

'You mean you don't want to see him?'

She thought about that for a moment. Of course she wanted to see him. She had to see him. After all, without Josh Lea would be dead. The thought made her feel…frozen.

If only he wasn't… Josh.

'How about breakfast first, a shower, maybe even a hair wash and then think about audiences,' Caroline suggested, with a sideways glance letting on that maybe she saw more than her words suggested. 'If I can tell him that, I may be able to bully him back to bed. He has a nasty haematoma on his thigh and Kiera wants him to stay in bed for the day.'

'A haematoma…'

'Cork thigh for the uninitiated,' Caroline said, and grinned. 'Honestly, don't you doctors know anything? He has a ripped and stitched arm, he's bruised all over and we know he hurts. So can I tell him if he's a good boy and stays in bed you'll see him before lunch? A ten-minute visit before you both go back to sleep?'

'Caro…'

'Mmm?'

There was silence while she thought of what to say. It lasted a while.

'He's stuck on the island?' she asked at last, and Caroline nodded.

'We all are. FIFOs are cancelled. Cyclone Hilda's hovering just above Cairns and the weather gurus don't know which direction she'll swing.'

'It's okay here.' There was safety in weather, she thought. It was the only discussion to be had when there was an elephant in the room so big it was threatening to overwhelm her. An elephant by the name of Josh. She made herself look out the windows to where the glassy calm of the lagoon and distant sea gave the lie to any hint of a cyclone. Still, it was the cyclone season…

'You're not really thinking of the weather, are you?' Caroline asked, and Maddie sighed.

'No.'

'So Josh is your ex-husband—only he's not acting like an ex-husband. Do you know how many orders he's throwing around about your care? If he could, he'd swim back to Cairns and swim back, dragging an obstetrician behind him.'

Maddie smiled at that, but absently. That'd be Josh. Caring above and beyond the call of duty. 'I'll see him before lunch,' she managed.

'Can I do your hair?'

'I don't need to be made pretty.'

'It never hurts.'

You have no idea, Maddie said, but she said it to herself, inwardly.

It never hurts?

It still did hurt—so much—after all these years.

She glanced down at her tiny daughter and she knew she needed all her strength and more if it wasn't going to keep hurting forever.

'Ten minutes and not a moment more,' Caroline told Josh as she escorted him along the vast, portrait-lined hallway to Maddie's room. 'Lea's just fed and Maddie is tired. When I trained, it was the baby's dad and the baby's grandparents—immediate family only—in the first twenty-four hours, and that's not you.'

It was said as a warning.

He stopped, which was a mistake. He'd been walking quite well until then. Caroline had wanted him to use a wheelchair. The idea was ridiculous but in truth his leg was weak and when he stopped he wobbled.

Caroline held out a hand to support him but he pulled back. What was happening here? Down the mine he'd coped well, apart from the brief and overwhelming panic attack, but on the surface he was suddenly as weak as Maddie's baby. He was wearing boxers and a T-shirt borrowed from Keanu. His own clothes were ruined, ripped and bloodied. He wanted jeans and a shirt that fitted, but Keanu had had the nerve to grin and tell him clothes would be forthcoming when he, Keanu, deemed Josh fit to leave this makeshift hospital and not before.

For once in his life Josh Campbell was out of control and he didn't like it. Not one bit. He didn't like it that his legs had the shakes—and now this woman was warning him about visiting Maddie.

Only family—and that's not you.

'I may not be family,' he said through gritted teeth 'but apart from a bedridden and confused mother, I'm all she's got.'

'You think so?' Caro said, quite lightly. 'Let me tell you, Dr Campbell, that if you step one inch out of line, if you upset Maddie enough to even make her blink, you'll find out this island is what she's got. The entire island and beyond. The whole M'Langi group. She's loved by us all. Family comes in so many forms.'

'That's not love,' he snapped. 'She's your local doctor. You people need her. She needs someone—'

'To protect her? That's what I'm saying, Dr Campbell. That's what she has. She ran into the mine to protect Malu but if you hadn't gone in after her I can think of over a dozen islanders who would have, including me.

So let's not get carried away with heroics. Our Maddie might have needed saving in the mine, but she doesn't need saving from anything else.'

'Caro?' It was Maddie's voice floating down the hallway. 'What are you telling him?'

'Just normal midwifery stuff,' Caroline called out cheerfully. 'About not outstaying his welcome and new mothers need rest and not to cough anywhere near the baby. Oh, and there's antiseptic handwash on the bench…'

'He *is* a doctor,' Maddie called, and she was laughing.

'He might be a doctor where he comes from,' Caroline retorted, 'but from where I'm standing he's a patient wearing Keanu's boxers and learning to play by our rules.'

He was wearing boxers and a T-shirt. His dark hair was rumpled, tousled by sleep.

He had an ugly bruise on his thigh and his arm was wrapped in a stark white dressing.

He looked young, she thought, and absurdly vulnerable. She had a sudden urge to throw back the bedcovers and hug him.

He wouldn't let her. She knew it. Letting people close when he was vulnerable was not what Josh did.

She'd just finished feeding Lea. She cradled her close, almost as a shield.

'Hey,' he said, and she managed a smile.

'Have you remembered your antiseptic hand wash?'

He grinned back at her and held up his hands. 'Yes, ma'am. Do you think I dare disobey Commander Caroline? I stand before you, not a bug in sight—or out of sight, either.'

Oh, that grin. She remembered that grin. It did things to her.

Or not. Past history, she told herself fiercely. That grin could not be allowed to influence her in any way at all.

'How are you?' he asked, and it was as if he was holding himself back. He was still standing by the door. Unsure.

Maybe he wanted to hug her, too, she thought, and then she decided of course he did. Josh did comfort in a big way.

'We're both excellent,' she told him, cradling Lea close. Lea was still fussing a little, not hungry, just wide-eyed and not inclined to sleep. 'Me and Lea both.'

'What did Keanu say? Is he worried about infection? You tore a little. Has he put you on antibiotics? And how is Lea? I couldn't clean that cord stump properly. And has he checked both your lungs?'

'You know, if you're going to play doctor you need to find a white coat,' she told him. 'Boxers just don't cut it.'

'Maddie, I'm serious.'

'And so am I. Keanu's my doctor.'

'He's not an obstetrician.'

'Neither are you, though you did do a neat job of filling in,' she conceded. 'I wasn't too fussed about lack of white coats underground.' She smiled, forcing herself to stay light. 'But we're aboveground again now. Normal standards apply. We're both patients for the duration. Keanu's demanding I stay here for a week. I was due to fly back to Cairns today, but with Cairns airport closed I'm stuck. Caroline's been very kind.'

'It's her house?'

'It's her father's house, though it's been used by her uncle Ian. But until she came back a couple of months ago it's been empty. It seems Ian's done a runner. Apparently he's been ripping off money from everywhere. That's why the islanders were down the mine—they haven't been paid for months and they decided to do a bit of gold-mining for themselves.' She shrugged. 'But that's the island's problem, not yours.'

'But you care.'

'About the islanders? Of course I do.' She bit her lip. 'Kalifa died. He had no business…' And to her annoyance she felt tears welling behind her eyes. 'Damn, I'm as weak as a kitten.'

And Josh was over to her bed before she could begin to swipe the stupid, weak tears away, tugging her into his arms and holding. Lea was in there, too. He was cradling them both. His…family?

And it felt right. It felt like home. She could just sink into his shoulder and have her cry out, and let him comfort her as he'd comforted her so often in the past.

'Maddie, we could build again.' What was this? He shouldn't be speaking, she thought. She didn't want him to speak. This was Josh in his let's-make-things-better mode. Let's distract Maddie from what's hurting. She didn't want it but he ploughed on inexorably. 'We could make things right. Neither of us is happy apart. What you've done is extraordinary. You've rebuilt your life and I'm in awe. But, Maddie, I should never have walked away. I should have tried harder. I love you so much, and I love Lea already. We could buy a house with a view of the sea near the air rescue base. It's close to your mum. I can afford a housekeeper. It's near the base hospital, too, if you want to continue medicine. We could share parenting. We could start again.'

He was still holding her. She was still crumpled against his chest. She couldn't move.

She took time to let his words sink in. She needed to take time. The last few days had left her hurt and shocked, and now... Josh's words felt like a battering ram, threating to crumble what was left of her foundations.

To calmly leave here... To go and live in Josh's beautiful house—she had no doubt he'd buy her something special... To have a housekeeper on call...

Share parenting, though... Was that a joke? That'd be where the housekeeper fitted in, she thought. Josh would be flitting in and out in between rescues, playing husband, playing father.

'You don't get it, do you?' she whispered, still against his chest because it was just too hard to pull away. 'You still want me to need you. You want us to need you.'

'What's wrong with that?'

And she did pull away then, anger coming to her aid. How could he be so stupid? How could he be so blind?

'Because love doesn't work one way,' she whispered, and then suddenly she was no longer whispering. She'd had five years to think this through, five years to know she was right. 'Love's all about giving. Giving and giving and giving. And how can I love you if all I can do is take?'

'I don't know what you mean.'

'Of course you do. It's why you walked away. Josh, after Mikey died, you tried to do it your way. You did all the right things. You said all the right things. You supported me every inch of the way. You stood by my

side while we buried our son and your whole body was
rigid with trying. You had to be everything to me. You
couldn't crack yourself because I needed you. You
couldn't show one hint of emotion, and you know why
not? Because there's a vast dam of emotion inside you,
and if you let one tiny crack appear then the whole lot
will flood out, and you're terrified.'

'Maddie—'

'Don't "Maddie" me,' she bit out. 'You walked away
from me. Sure, you stuck around after Mikey died. You
held yourself together, you hugged me and I let myself
be hugged because, yes, I needed you, but it hurt even
more that you didn't cry with me. You still hurt from
losing Mikey. I saw it on your face when Lea was born
but you won't admit it. You'll hardly admit it to yourself. And then Holly died and it was worse. You were
wooden, as if admitting even a little bit of grief would
make you implode. I was so sad for you, but when I tried
to get close, when I needed to share, you walked away.'

Hell. He went to dig his hands into his pockets but
boxers have a dearth of pockets. He felt exposed. He was
exposed. Boxers and T-shirt and bruises and...emotion.

'It was five years ago,' he managed. 'It's history.'

'You mean you have your armour back in place so
we'll start again? That'll be fine as long the need all
stays one way.'

'Maddie, you care for your mother. You'll care for
Lea. You don't need—'

'Another person who needs me? That's what I mean.
You still don't get it. Not letting me close hurts, Josh.
After five years I should have built my own armour
but I don't want to build armour. I love it that my mum
needs me. I love it that Lea needs me and I love it that

I have a working life where this community needs me, too. But you know what? I need them, too. I sit and read to Mum and it warms my heart that she can still smile and hold my hand. I cradle Lea and I'm warm all over. The islanders bring me their problems but they also include me in their lives. They share, and when I'm off the island I miss them. Kalifa died when the mine collapsed and I'll go to his funeral and I'll weep. I loved him. I needed him as I need so many.'

'You can't—'

'Don't tell me what I can and can't do, Josh Campbell. You don't have the right.'

And suddenly she was almost shouting and Caroline was gliding into the room and putting herself firmly between Josh and Maddie and giving him a glare that might have turned lesser mortals into stone.

'What do you think you're playing at?' she demanded. 'I told you—you upset Maddie, you upset the whole island. Maddie, you want me to call in a few good men to cast this guy to the fish?'

'I… No.' Maddie choked on an angry sob and fell back on her pillows. Lea whimpered and Josh felt sick.

'What's he been saying?' Caroline demanded. 'Tell Aunty Caroline.'

'He wants to marry me—again.'

There was a moment's stunned silence. Then Caro's lips twitched. It was a tiny twitch. She had herself under control in an instant but he saw it.

'So he proposes in Keanu's boxers and T-shirt,' she managed. 'I can see why that would upset a girl. And where's the diamond?'

'I don't want a diamond.'

But Caroline had moved back into professional mode.

'What you want,' she said, lightly now but still just as firm, 'is a sleep. I'm going to take your obs and then close this room off to everyone. Whatever Dr Campbell has been saying, forget it. What's most important, for you and for baby, is sleep.' And then she lifted Lea from Maddie's arms and turned and handed the tiny girl to Josh.

'Here,' she said, and Caroline might be young but right now she was every inch a Lockhart of Wildfire, with a lineage obviously stretching back to the dinosaurs. No old-fashioned hospital matron had ever sounded more bossy. 'Lea looks like she needs time to settle,' she decreed. 'I need to care for Maddie and if you're proposing marriage then maybe you could take this small dose of domesticity and try it out for size. Keanu wants you to walk, just a little, slowly but getting the circulation moving in those legs. We don't want clots, do we? Can you hold her without hurting your arm? Excellent. I want you to take Lea for a wee walk around the veranda, then settle down outside until I come and get her. You're banned from here, Dr Campbell. Now, Maddie, do you need some pain relief? Yes? Let's get you sorted.'

And she turned her back on Josh, blocking his view of Maddie.

He was left with an armful of baby.

He was left with no choice but to leave.

CHAPTER ELEVEN

HE STOOD IN the hall, holding Maddie's daughter, and he thought...

Nothing.

Maddie's words were still echoing in his head. He should try and make sense of them, but he couldn't sort them out.

In his arms Lea wuffled and opened her mouth to wail.

And at that, the professional side of him kicked in. Caroline had given him Lea for a reason. She knew he was more than capable of caring for a baby. She also knew that Maddie was distressed and needed to sleep, and the one thing that'd stop her doing that was to hear her baby crying. That was the reason she'd handed her over to him. Professional concern.

So be professional. How to stop a baby crying?

He hadn't actually read that in any of his textbooks.

Still, it was a professional challenge and he was a professional. How hard could it be?

'Hush,' he told Lea, and he lifted her onto his shoulder and let her nuzzle into the softness of his T-shirt while he made his way outside.

He walked for a little, as ordered, until the threat

of wails was past, until he heard only gentle wuffling. Then he headed for a mammoth rocker on the side veranda. He settled—cautiously—into the softness of its faded cushions, and rocked.

It was a good place to sit. There were herons wading at the edge of the lagoon, seeking tiny fish in the shallows. The veranda was shaded, cool and lovely. In the distance the sea was a sheet of shimmery, turquoise glass.

There was a cyclone threating Cairns, but here there was nothing but calm.

'There's no threat here,' he murmured to the baby in his arms, but she seemed singularly unimpressed.

She whimpered some more. He lifted her from his shoulder and cradled her in his hands. Why did newborns feel so fragile? He knew from training that babies were born tough but she didn't feel tough.

She felt precious.

He laid her on his knee. He expected to hurt a bit as her weight settled on his bruised thigh, but she nestled as if this was a cradle made for her. Her eyes were drifting with newborn lack of focus but she seemed to be taking in this strange new world.

She looked like Maddie.

Who was the father? he wondered. Who was the unknown sperm donor?

He wished it could have been him.

No. He didn't wish that. Fatherhood… He remembered clearly the agony of loss.

His son and then his sister.

How could he hold himself and not crack? That's why he'd had to walk away. He couldn't help Maddie when he was hurting so much himself. He was no use to anyone.

'If you were mine I'd be useless,' he whispered. 'If you hurt… Or if your mother hurt…'

So why had he offered marriage again? What had changed?

Hope that this time it could be different? Hope that there wouldn't be a time when he was needy?

'Excuse me?'

He turned to see a woman maybe in her late sixties standing at the foot of the veranda. She was short, slightly overweight, breathless. Her soft, white hair was tugged into a wispy bun and her eyes looked swollen, like she'd been crying.

'Excuse me,' the woman said again. 'I knocked on the front door but no one answered.'

'I'm Dr Campbell,' he told her. 'Can I help?'

She'd been climbing the side steps, but as soon as Josh spoke she stopped short, looking at him in shock.

'You're a doctor?'

'I don't look like one, but yes.'

'So… Keanu said…you were helping when my husband died.'

It was a simple statement, said with dignity and peace, like a jigsaw puzzle was coming together in a way she could understand.

'You're Kalifa's wife,' he ventured, remembering the big man, the desperate fight to save him, the hopelessness he always felt when he lost a patient. He'd been gutted, and then the trauma with Maddie had stopped him following up. Normally when a patient died in his presence he'd seek out the relatives and talk them through it.

Too much had happened.

'Kalifa Lui was my husband,' the woman agreed, looking to the baby, to him, then back to Lea. 'My name is Nani Lui. The nurses told me that you and Keanu tried very hard to save him. I thank you.'

'I wish we could have done more.'

'It would seem that you've done more than you could be expected to do,' she said, and the echo of a smile washed across her tired face. 'Did they teach you mine rescue in medical school?'

But then she was interrupted. 'Nani?' It was Maddie, calling through the open window. 'Nani, is that you?'

Uh-oh. 'You're supposed to be asleep,' Josh called back. 'We'll move farther along. Caroline will have us hauled before the courts for disturbing you.'

There was a sleepy chuckle. 'Caroline's gone across to the hospital to get more diapers and, oh, I need to see Nani. Quick, Josh, bring her in.'

'Nani, if you go through that door…'

'No,' Maddie called out, suddenly imperious. 'Come in with her, Josh. I want Nani to meet both you and my daughter.'

He was wearing boxers! 'I'm hardly dressed—'

'Nani won't care. She's practically family and I guess…after all we've been through, so are you.'

So he ushered the elderly woman into Maddie's bedroom—keeping a wary eye on the door. Caroline seemed a woman it was better not to cross. But Maddie's distress seemed to have evaporated. She hugged Nani to her as Josh had seen her hug her mother and he thought…maybe it was true. Maybe Nani was family.

He stood silent, feeling superfluous, until the hugging finished, until Nani stepped back, tears streaming down her face, and turned back to see Lea in Josh's arms.

'And this is your little one,' she whispered. 'They tell me you've named her Lea. For my daughter?' She forced her gaze from the baby to Josh. 'Lea was my daughter,' she whispered. 'She did the cooking at the hospital. She was so full of love and laughter. Then she got the encephalitis. It was so bad, so fast. Maddie worked desperately to try and save her but she died before she could be evacuated. And now... To call your little one for her... My Kalifa would be so proud.'

And Josh looked down at Maddie and saw her eyes fill with tears. It was true, then. She'd named her baby for a patient she'd lost.

Part of her extended family? Surely not. He hadn't asked, though...

He hadn't had the right to ask why she'd decided to call her baby anything.

It hurt that he didn't have that right. It hurt a lot.

'She's beautiful,' Nani whispered. 'A new life from this tragedy. This is joy. And you called her Lea.'

'I wanted to share.' Maddie's voice was weak but determined. 'I know all of you will love her. She'll need you all.'

'And we'll need her,' Nani breathed. 'Oh, Maddie, I'm so happy for you.' She glanced up at Josh. 'Maddie's wanted this little one for so long.'

'I know.'

And Nani's gaze sharpened. She looked from him to Maddie and back again. 'It's true then,' she said forcefully. 'They're saying you two were married.'

'I... Yes.'

'And you walked away.' Her tone was accusing.

'I couldn't help her,' Josh said helplessly.

'Maddie said she couldn't help you.'

'Maddie talked to you about us?' He turned to Maddie, incredulous.

'I'm a grandmother,' Nani said simply. 'Everyone talks to me.' And then she paused, the present crashing home. 'But not my Kalifa. No more. People tell me things and I weep for them, but then my Kalifa holds me…'

'We'll hold you, Nani,' Maddie said. 'You know we will. Whenever you need us. Just as you've always held us.'

And Nani's face crumpled. She stooped and hugged Maddie and she sobbed, just once. And then she sniffed and braced herself and rose and faced Josh again.

'She will, too,' she said. 'Maddie is part of my strength, part of this island's strength. I knew Maddie would be sad about Kalifa's death. She told him to stop smoking. She told him to lose weight. He didn't listen but she tried, and she was there for him when he needed her. As she always is.'

She stopped and stared down at the tiny child and her face softened. 'Life goes on,' she whispered. 'With no blame. With love. This little one…she's our faith in the future. She gives me strength, and, heaven knows, we all need to take strength where we can find it.'

'You find it in yourself,' Josh said, and Nani stepped back and looked at him as if he'd said something that didn't make sense.

'Is that what you think? That you're born with strength enough to hold you up for your whole life?' She groped backwards and sat and held Maddie's hand. 'Is that what drove you apart?'

'Maybe,' Maddie said, and Josh heard exhaustion in her voice.

'We shouldn't be here,' he told Nani. 'Caroline will be after us with a shotgun if she finds us in here. Maddie, go to sleep, love.'

'I'm not your love,' Maddie whispered, and Josh flinched.

But what she said was true. He might love Maddie. She might love him but the chasm between them was still miles deep.

He ushered Nani out. Nani looked as if she was bursting to say more but she held her tongue. Out on the veranda she touched Lea's face again and then gave Josh a searching look.

'There's time,' she said enigmatically. 'You can't be the only one to take care of you.'

She left. Josh looked down at the baby, now sleeping soundly in his arms. He thought of the web of love and dependence and need that held this island together.

He thought he'd head back to his rocker.

Babysitting was easier than thinking, he decided. It was just a shame he could do both at the same time.

She wasn't asleep. She was tired and drowsy, her body was as comfortable as Caro could make it and there was no reason she shouldn't sleep, but she lay in her beautiful bed and looked out at the distant sea and thought about Josh.

He was on the veranda. He'd be rocking back and forth, looking out over the lagoon.

Holding her baby.

He'd called her 'love'. He still wanted her. He even wanted marriage.

The idea was preposterous, crazy, even heartbreaking, so why was there an insidious voice hammering away in her consciousness?

Go on. You know you want to.

And part of her did want to. Despite what Nani had said, this island wasn't her all.

There was still a part of her that ached for Josh.

Down the mine he'd massaged her head and shoulders, and, despite the shock, the danger, the physical battering her body had just been through, his touch had swept back all the memories of the fire between them. He just had to look at her and her knees turned to jelly.

Lovemaking with Josh.

There was a memory she had to suppress. It was still there, though. The perfection.

Five years. Surely she should have moved on by now?

The problem was that she'd made vows.

With my body I thee worship.

Had she made that vow? For the life of her she couldn't remember. Her wedding day had passed in a blur of happiness, and the words she'd spoken, with love and with honour, had blurred, as well.

With my body I thee worship.

If she hadn't said it out loud, she'd said it in her head.

It wasn't enough. It had never been enough. Not when the caring was only permitted one way.

If Josh loved, he protected, and protection for Josh meant never letting her close enough to see his hurt.

'It's impossible,' she whispered into the stillness. 'The island has to be enough. I can't love a man who won't let me love back.'

The only problem was that she did.

* * *

'Josh?'

He'd been dozing a little, the rocking chair stilling as he and Lea drifted towards sleep. His legs made a secure cradle. His hands still cupped her. Lea was peaceful and seemingly content, and for this moment so was Josh.

He had to be. Listening to Nani had left him…discombobulated. He'd tried to figure it out but the effort had left him too tired to sort the tangle that was in his head. For now all he could do was soak in the sun, the peace, the feel of this little girl sleeping between his hands.

Everyone should have a Wildfire Island, he thought sleepily. And a baby called Lea.

'Josh!' It was Caroline again—of course. She was standing in front of him, smiling her approval. 'What a great job,' she told him. 'We'll give you a job in the children's ward any day.'

'Do you have many ill children?'

Why did he ask that? Because he wanted to shift the focus onto medicine? Okay, maybe he did. Ever since he'd arrived on this island, things had been personal and it was time to back away.

'We have too many ill children,' Caroline told him, obviously ready to follow his lead. 'As well as normal kids' stuff we have a vicious ulcer caused by the local mosquitoes. It starts out as a mosquito bite and grows. If left untreated it needs to be cut out and requires skin grafts. What's worse, we also have encephalitis caused by the same mosquito. There's a local remedy—a plant that seems to give immunity—but sometimes parents forget how important it is to use it. We aim to send the encephalitis patients to the mainland but that's not always possible. In the meantime, we need to do the front-line treatment here and the cases are increasing. The island's desperate for more medical staff but there's no money. The government funding's limited and we're running out. And now the encephalitis cases are increasing.'

'Why?'

'Because the money's run out, for education and also for mosquito eradication,' she said bitterly. 'My uncle seems to have been embezzling funds for years. Heaven knows how we can attract any more staff. We're just blessed that Maddie's decided to stay.'

And he'd asked her to leave.

But for her to stay here… With Lea…

Ulcers. Encephalitis…

'You needn't worry. We take very good care of our staff,' she said, seeing him glance at the sleeping baby and guessing his concern. 'And our staff's children. This baby will be cared for by the whole island. But that's not what I came to talk to you about. Keanu's just had a call from Cairns Air Sea Rescue. From Beth. She says to tell you the cyclone's tracking north and the airport's open from dawn tomorrow. So, unless you don't want it, they're flying out to collect you. She wanted to know if Maddie wants evacuation, too, but Maddie's adamant that she stays. Keanu doesn't see any reason why she shouldn't. Oh, and the plane's bringing our permanent doctor back, Sam Taylor, so we'll have a full medical contingent again, or as full as we can afford. Can you be ready to leave at ten tomorrow? Keanu's trying to find you some decent clothes to wear on the way home.'

Unless you don't want it.

In all that she'd said, those were the words that stood out.

Ten tomorrow morning, unless he didn't want it.

His boss would insist he take a break, he thought, at least until the cut on his arm healed. He could…

What? Stay here?

What was the point? He'd only upset Maddie.

'Of course,' he said, and the matter was decided.

She left, taking Lea with her. He stayed sitting on the rocker, staring sightlessly out over the island.

What was the point?

He'd rescued Maddie. He'd played emergency doctor because that was what he did. That was who he was. There was no use pretending he could be anything more.

It was time to move on.

At nine the next morning, Maddie had just finished feeding when there was a knock on the door.

'Come in,' she called, and it was Josh. Of course it was. Caroline had told her he was leaving. She'd warned her he'd want to say goodbye.

He was wearing clean jeans and a crisp, short-sleeved white shirt. He was washed and brushed and almost impossibly handsome. He looked like Josh again. If it hadn't been for the dressing on his arm she'd say he was back to being her invincible Josh. No, not *her* Josh. *The* Josh. The Josh who was in control.

'Caroline says if I promise not to upset you I can have ten minutes,' he said, and part of her wanted to say he could have the rest of her life. But she was sensible and there was no way a sensible woman could say such a thing. Even if he looked like Josh.

'I won't get upset,' she managed. 'You'll be glad to get back to work.' Of course he would. An idle Josh was like a bear with a sore head. Or a sore arm? 'Will they let you work with that arm?'

'Office duties.'

'You won't take a holiday?'

'No.'

'You need to rest.'

'Says you. Are you sure you don't want us to take you to Cairns?'

'I'll go in a week or two, when I'm recovered,' she told him. 'I need to see Mum, but I can't for a little while yet.'

He understood. She couldn't push a wheelchair. She couldn't spend a whole day with her mum.

'I'll go and see her if you like. I'll send word back.'

'That'd be...kind. She'll remember you. She l—'

But then she bit back the word. *Loved.* It was too big to say, and Josh was moving on.

'Going back and forth to Cairns will be hard with a baby.'

'It won't be.' Her chin tilted, a gesture he knew and loved. His brave Maddie. 'It'll be the same as before, only this time I'll have Lea, too. I'm thinking Mum will love her.' And she did say the L word then.

'Maddie, how can you manage?'

'How I can is none of your business,' she said, gently but firmly. 'I'm not asking you to care. In fact, I'm asking you not to care. You've cared before and it almost broke you. You walked away from our marriage because of it and nothing's changed. Lea and I have nothing to do with you, Josh.'

'Yet…'

'There are lots of yets,' she murmured. 'But none of them work.'

'I love you.'

'Not enough.'

'Maddie…'

'When Lea cries, I'll comfort her,' she said, trying to make sense of what didn't make sense at all. But it did—in a stupid, muddly way. 'And you know what? She'll comfort me back. Oh, she won't—she can't—care for me. Even in old age I hope she won't need to care for me, but she'll hug me and she'll be there and just knowing I'm her mum, knowing I'm loved, that's enough. I won't ask for more. But to be there for her when she hurts? What a privilege to be permitted to be so close to someone. And when I hurt and she hugs me…that's a gift, too. A gift you could never accept.'

'You know I can't.'

'I know you can't,' she said, sadly now, and she hugged Lea tightly. 'All I can do is hope that one day you'll meet a woman strong enough to crack that armour.'

'Maddie—'

'It's time to go, Josh,' she said, and her bottom lip wobbled a bit. 'It's over.'

Only it wasn't. He stooped as if compelled. He put his hands on her shoulders and he bent so his eyes met hers.

And, as if she was compelled in turn, her face tilted to meet his. Her eyes were wide, her lips parted, just slightly, in just the way he remembered.

And he kissed her. Properly this time, not like the kiss they'd shared in the darkness and the stress of the mine.

Some things were the same.

Some things were mind-blowing.

He remembered the first time he'd kissed her, the sweetness, the taste, the rush of heat. He remembered the way his body had responded—like here was the other half of his whole.

He remembered thinking it must be something in the water—or what they'd eaten. It had been their first date. They'd bought hamburgers and eaten them on the beach at sunset.

They'd kissed and when they'd finally drawn apart he'd felt like his life had just changed.

He remembered thinking it was ridiculous. She was a colleague. She was just someone…nice.

Nice hadn't come into that kiss.

Nice didn't come into this kiss.

The heat was still there, and the power.

Two bodies, fusing.

They might just as well be naked between the sheets. This kiss said they knew each other as they'd know no other.

Two becom one? They'd made their wedding vows but vows didn't come into this. It was the way he felt.

It was the way she made him melt.

Her lips were parted and the kiss she gave him was all Maddie. Generous. Holding nothing back.

She was soft and strong, warm and wanting.

She gave everything.

He remembered that about her. Her love for her mother. Her generosity to her friends.

The way she gave her body to his.

He'd thought he could lie with this woman forever. He thought he'd found his home, and somehow it was still here, this sweet, perfect centre. This aching, loving perfection.

Her kiss said it all. Her hands were in his hair, tugging him to her, kissing him back with a passion that made his heart twist. That made him want to gather her into his arms and carry her.

To where?

To where he could protect her forever?

She must have felt the discordant note, for suddenly the fierce hold eased and she was pushing him back. When their lips parted he felt as if their bodies were being wrenched apart, but she was smiling.

Sort of. He knew this woman. He could see the glimmer of tears behind the smile. But he could also see the strength—and the decision.

'Time to go, Josh. If I ever need rescuing again you'll be the first person I call on, I swear.'

'I'll come.'

'And if you need rescuing?'

Silence. Her smile stayed, but there was infinite sadness behind it.

'If ever you change your mind…' she whispered. 'If ever you want to hop off your white charger and let me have a turn…' But then she bit her lip. 'No. I won't make a promise like that. I've tried to move on, and I'll keep trying. You go back to your life, Josh Campbell, and I'll stay here with mine.'

'Maddie…'

'No more words,' she whispered, and put a finger to his lips, a feather touch, almost a blessing. 'Just go.'

He was gone.

She lay in her too-big bed and hugged her baby. Her body ached.

Her heart ached.

She'd made the right call—she knew she had—but, oh, it hurt. And it was hurting Josh, too.

'Impossible,' she murmured to herself, but then Lea wriggled and opened her eyes and screwed up her nose and told her mother in no uncertain terms that all was not right with her world.

She was a mother and she was needed.

'But not by Josh,' she told herself. 'I'm on my own.'

Only she wasn't. She had her baby. She had her mother, her friends, the islanders.

It was only Josh who was alone, she thought bleakly.

He had no choice. With the demons he was carrying he'd stay alone forever.

CHAPTER TWELVE

'I'M NOT LYING on any stretcher.'

'Honey, we came to pick you up on the grounds that you're a medical evacuation,' Beth told him. 'If we told the powers that be you're fine, apart from a gashed arm, you'd be told to have a nice holiday on Wildfire and come back with the supply boat next week. But you've a gashed arm, a haematoma and shock. Post-traumatic stress disorder is yet to be ruled out. Lie down, like a good boy, and let me give you an aspirin.'

'I'm not lying down,' he said, revolted, and she raised her brows.

'Um…I have backup. The medical opinion on your bruised leg is that sitting upright for the flight is asking for clots and you're not growing clots on my watch. You lie down or we land again and I'll have Sam and Keanu come in here and sit on you. Straitjacket if necessary.'

'You wouldn't dare.'

'Try me,' she said, and grinned and crossed her arms and kept her brows raised. 'Down!'

He had no choice. He lay on the stretcher. She smiled and strapped him in.

'Mind, we could have left you there,' she said serenely. 'We gave you that option.'

'There's no point.'

'Maddie's moved on?'

'I… Yes.'

'Funny things, marriages,' she said. 'Unless they end really bitterly, you always leave a bit of your heart behind.'

'I haven't.'

'No?'

'No,' he said, and then decided if he was to be treated as a patient he could act like a patient. He lay back and closed his eyes as the plane raced down the runway and took to the skies.

He'd have kind of liked to sit up and look down at the disappearing islands behind him.

Saying goodbye hadn't been enough.

It had to be enough. They'd go back to Christmas and birthday cards and that'd be it.

You always leave a bit of your heart behind.

Philosophy of Beth, he thought dryly. After two marriages and four sons, she had an opinion on everything.

She was wrong this time. It wasn't a bit of his heart. It was a lot.

No. It was the whole box and dice. He lay back with his eyes closed, and it felt like he was leaving a part of himself down there. It wasn't just Maddie, either, he thought. He'd delivered Lea. He'd cradled her in his big hands and he'd felt…he'd felt…

Like she was his?

She wasn't, though, and neither was Maddie.

They could have been his wife and his daughter.

He'd walked away.

And all of a sudden it was just as well he was lying

down, as the sweep of emotion flooding through him might have sent him reeling.

He wanted them with a fierceness he'd never experienced before. He wanted to be part of their lives.

He wanted his marriage back.

Marriage... In sickness and in health. Why did that line suddenly slam into his head?

Because he remembered Maddie saying it. To love and to honour, in sickness and in health.

He'd said the words as well, and he'd meant them.

But he hadn't let Maddie mean them.

He'd met Maddie just as her mother had suffered her stroke; when Maddie had been in distress. He'd been able to help. He'd been strong, capable, ready to move heaven and earth if it could make Maddie smile again.

He'd loved helping her and he'd fallen in love.

Because she'd needed him?

Why should he have these insights now, after all these years? It was impossible to understand, and suddenly his thoughts were everywhere.

He remembered the night Mikey had died, trying desperately to hold on to his rigid control. 'It's okay to cry,' Maddie had said, more than once, but he hadn't. He'd held her while she'd broken her heart, and then he'd walked off his pain and his anger where she hadn't had to see.

His job was to protect.

And then, five months later, the policemen at the door. *Your sister, sir...*

He remembered Maddie moving instinctively to hold him, to take him into her arms, and yet he'd backed away.

He'd failed even more. He couldn't protect his sister.
He couldn't protect his wife.

They'd been in the air for over half an hour now.
Back on Wildfire a funeral would be starting.

Kalifa Lui. Nani's husband.

His thoughts were flying every which way but suddenly they were centred on Nani. Mourning her husband but finding the strength to visit Maddie.

Nani, touching Lea's face, taking strength from a
baby.

Maddie, taking strength from Nani.

Loving was all about giving? That had been his mantra, but in Maddie's world loving worked two ways.
Giving love and receiving love. Giving comfort and
receiving comfort.

Just loving, no strings attached.

Maddie would be at the funeral now, he thought.
No matter how sore, no matter how much she'd prefer to be in her magnificent bed with her sea view and
her beautiful baby, she'd be at the funeral and no one
would send her away.

There'd be no objection from Nani. He knew it. Nani
knew that accepting love was the same as giving it.

To accept love wasn't a weakness?

To accept love might even be a strength.

How had it taken so long for him to see it? Was he
stupid?

Could he admit he'd been stupid? More, could he
act on it?

His thoughts washed on. He lay so silent that finally
Beth moved from her seat to check on him.

'Don't you dare die on my watch,' she told him.
'We're only an hour from Cairns.'

'No, we're not.'

'Not?'

'No.' He was trying to unclip the straps holding him in place. 'Give me the radio.'

'What? Why?'

'This is a medical emergency,' he told her. 'I believe Maddie is attending a funeral without proper medical attention. She needs an emergency physician.'

'You're kidding.'

'I would never kid about anything so serious,' he told her. 'But this isn't your decision.'

'Josh…'

And then he softened. Start now, he told himself. Share.

'Beth, I'm in love,' he told her. 'I've been stupid and blind and any number of adjectives you want to call me, but I'm over it. I need your help.'

'You?' she said in disbelief. 'You need my help?'

'I need your help,' he said humbly. 'Dear Beth, please help me unfasten these straps and hand me the radio. And then let's get this plane back to Wildfire.'

The day thou gavest, Lord, has ended, the darkness falls at thy behest…

If there was one thing the islanders of M'Langi prided themselves on it was singing, and the combined voices of what seemed at least half the population was enough to bring tears to Maddie's eyes.

Actually, there were a few things bringing tears to Maddie's eyes right now.

First and foremost was that Kalifa had been a friend and he'd died too soon. If he'd been sensible, stopped smoking, lost weight—if he hadn't decided to embark on a harebrained scheme to make money out of a patently unsafe gold mine—she wouldn't be standing here.

Then there was the sight of Nani, surrounded by her children and her grandchildren. It'd be desperately hard for Nani now, she thought. The elderly woman lived out on Atangi, the biggest of the island group, but her children mostly lived on Wildfire.

She had no money. Kalifa had given it all to his son after he'd lost his fishing boat. He'd mortgaged their house and Nani would have no hope of redeeming it.

She'd lost her husband and her home, yet her shoulders were straight, she sang with fierce determination, and Maddie looked at that sad, proud woman and felt tears well again.

And then there was Josh. Gone.

He'd left five years ago, she told herself. One visit and here you go, falling in love again.

Or still loving?

It's just hormones, she told herself fiercely. She'd given birth only three days ago. Caroline was on one side of her and Hettie was on the other. They both thought she shouldn't have come.

And I shouldn't if I'm going to sob, she told herself. I will not cry.

The hymn came to an end. Kalifa's sons and brothers took up the coffin and carried it out of the chapel into the morning sun. From here it'd be taken to Atangi to be buried in the place of his ancestors.

Maddie wouldn't follow. Burial was the islanders' business. There'd be a wake later on but she wasn't up to a wake yet.

She turned away drearily, immeasurably sad for her friend. But life went on, she told herself. She needed to return to her daughter. She needed to get on with living. She turned towards the hospital—and Josh was right in front her.

Just…there.

'Hi,' he said, and she couldn't think of a single thing to say.

She was facing her husband. No. He was her ex-husband. He wasn't even the father of her child, she told herself desperately. He was someone who had nothing to do with her.

But that was a lie. He was someone who held her heart in his hands.

'I thought you were gone,' she said at last. It was a dumb thing to say but it was all she could think of. But she'd watched his plane take off. He should be in Cairns.

'I had a couple of things I forgot to say,' he said, and then he fell silent.

The hearse drove away, towards the harbour where a boat would carry Kalifa, in all honour, out to Atangi. The islanders followed.

The rest of the mourners drifted off. Maddie stood at the foot of the steps of the little island chapel and felt empty.

'Hey!' It was Caroline, flanked by Keanu and Hettie and Sam. Her people. 'Maddie needs to be back in bed,' Caroline said sternly. 'Thirty minutes tops, Dr Campbell, or we'll set Bugsy onto you.'

'See me terrified,' Josh called back, and Caroline chuckled and linked her arm in Keanu's and said something that made them all laugh—and then they were gone.

Her people.

Her husband?

'What...what did you need to say?' Maddie asked at last, because the silence was getting to her and, in truth, her legs ached and she wouldn't mind sitting down. And as if he guessed, Josh took her arm and led her to a wooden seat that looked out over the headland to the sea beyond.

It really was the most beautiful island. They were facing west, where the sun set. The island's sunsets were where the island got its name, for Wildfire was what they resembled.

Had Josh ever seen a Wildfire sunset?

She was babbling internally. She let herself be propelled to the seat and she tried to empty her mind.

Josh was still holding her arm. How could she empty her mind when all she could do was...feel?

'Two things,' he said into the stillness, and her heart seemed to stop.

'Two?'

'The first is that I'm sorry.' He wasn't looking at her. He was staring out at the distant sea, reflective, sad, almost as if looking back at those five past years. 'I'm sorry I left you. I'm sorry I was so weak.'

'You weren't weak.' She paused and stared down at her feet, thinking of all the times she'd tried to comfort him, all the times he'd held himself back. The bracing of his shoulders as she'd reached for him. The rigidity of his body, the sheer effort of holding emotion within. 'You were so strong I couldn't get near you.'

'But I wasn't strong enough. That was what I didn't see. That admitting weakness, admitting need, takes its own form of strength. That sharing is two-way. And that's the second thing I want to say to you, my Maddie. It's that I need you.'

I need you.

The words hung in the warm morning air.

Need.

He'd never said such a thing. Their relationship had been based on their love and her need. It hadn't been enough.

'How can you need me?' she whispered, hardly daring to breathe, and still he stared out to sea. His hands were clenched, as if things were breaking inside him, as if he was deliberately taking apart something he'd built over a lifetime.

'Because I'll shatter if you don't take me back,' he said, and then he shook his head. 'No. That's blackmail and there's no place for that here. I'll keep on going. I'll stay doing what I'm doing. But, Maddie, something inside me has changed. It's melted. When we were down the mine, when we'd delivered your daughter, when I thought we might die together, Maddie, I wanted to be held. I wanted to admit to you how scared I was. I was terrified for all of us. I was terrified of losing you, yet I couldn't admit it. And then...'

'Then?' How hard was it to whisper?

'Then we were safe and things were as they'd been before. I knew life could go on. I knew you didn't need me. But then I saw Nani come to visit you. She was bereft but she still came, to say to you that she knew you'd done your best, that there was no blame. And I thought, how strong was that? It's the kind of thing I might try—I have tried. When I'm hurt I try to make those around me feel better. It's what's been instilled in me since birth and I don't know any other way.'

'So what's different now?'

'I watched you,' he said simply. 'I watched you admit

that you needed her. That you needed this island. Giving and taking. And all you've said to me… Everything over the years… It was like that moment coalesced it all. Maybe if I could have gone straight back to work, straight back into needed mode, I wouldn't have had time to sort it out, but Beth made me lie on the stretcher in the plane and I stared up at nothing and that moment kept coming back. And I thought…how selfish was I? To not let you care.'

'Josh…'

'I do need you, Maddie,' he told her, simply now and humbly. 'I've always needed you. I just didn't know how. Mikey's death shattered me and all I knew was to try and comfort you. I didn't see that sharing the hurt could have helped heal us both. And then, when Holly died so soon after, I was a mess and I kept thinking I couldn't lay that hurt on you. So stupidly, selfishly I stepped away. I told myself it was protecting you, but all the time it was about protecting my armour. I thought I'd shatter if I admitted need. But, Maddie, I do need. If anything happened to you now, I'd fall apart. If anything happened to Lea…'

And his voice broke.

Enough. She took him into her arms and pulled him to her. And he came. After all these years she felt him melt into her, merge, warmth against warmth. She felt him hold, not in passion but in need.

To take comfort.

To love.

How long they sat there she couldn't say. Up at the house Caroline would be caring for Lea, but she'd fed her just before the funeral. For now time didn't matter. It couldn't be allowed to matter.

All that mattered was that she was holding the man she loved.

'I wouldn't mind a kiss.'

She wasn't sure when she said it, or even why she said it, but suddenly it was needful. Comfort was all very well, she thought, but if she was getting her Josh back... Well, she wanted her Josh back. Bravado and all. Hero, except in the most dire of circumstances. Her knight in shining armour—but with the ability to take off his armour and leave it in the hall cupboard.

But then she was no longer thinking. There was no room for thinking because she was being soundly, ruthlessly kissed. She was in Josh's arms and there was nowhere else in the world she would have rather been.

She was with her Josh. He needed her.

She had her baby. She had her Josh.

She had her family.

Afterwards, when there was room for words again, when the world had somehow righted itself on this new and wonderful axis, she did check the hall cupboard. It took some doing but Josh had been gone for five long years and she wasn't about to let him back into her world on a promise. The sensible side of her—the part that had learned to distrust and could never completely be ignored—wanted to know just what terms that armour would be let out.

'So...' she managed, breathlessly because that kiss had taken energy and she didn't have much energy spare at the moment. 'So how could we work this? Because... Josh, you know that I love you but...'

'But my proposition about a house close to my work didn't make you happy?'

'You make me happy,' she said simply. 'But, Josh…'

'You love this island,' he said, cupping her face and kissing her again, lightly this time, tenderly, as if he had all the time in the world, and kissing her was almost as natural as breathing. 'I can see that. And you love this community and this community needs you. And you love your mum. Your mum needs you and you need your mum. And of course there's Lea, who we both love…'

'You don't…you don't mind that I used a sperm donor?'

'If I ever meet him I'll give him half my kingdom,' Josh said simply. 'He's given me a daughter—if you'll let me share.'

'Oh, Josh.' She could feel the tears. It was weakness, she thought desperately. She hated tears, but Josh smiled and kissed them away and she thought maybe she didn't hate them so much.

'Proposition,' he said simply. 'I've been talking to Keanu.'

'When?'

'Yesterday. When you were faffing about, learning how to feed your daughter. When he was faffing about, worrying about clots on my leg. He talked to me about these islands. He talked about how desperate the islanders are for a full medical service. Apparently the Lockhart money has run dry for the mine, but there's still Australian government funding for doctors—if you can get doctors to come here. They work on a doctors-per-head-of-population ratio, which means the islands are short by at least two, possibly three doctors. So I thought, if it's okay with you, I could come here. This is really tentative—I need to talk to Keanu and Sam— but it seems to me that a couple of doctors settled out on Atangi could work well. I could be part of the emergency on-call roster from there. It's only three minutes by chopper to pick me up. We could run a permanent clinic. We could build ourselves a great house overlooking the sea—'

'Josh…'

'We could be happy there,' he said, urgently now. 'I know we could. Sure, we'd be two doctors dependent on each other for backup, but…' He shrugged his shoulders and gave a rueful smile. 'I guess that's what you already know and I'm finding out. We could depend on each other. I'd need you, my Maddie, and you'd need me.'

'Josh.' Dammit, her eyes were brimming again. It sounded wonderful—it sounded brilliant—but there were still things…complications…

Love.

'Josh, I need to stay flying in and flying out.' It nearly killed her to say it but she had to. 'Or…or leave the islands and live in Cairns. It might need to be in your house near your work. Because Mum…'

'Your mum needs you.'

'I need my mum.' She said it simply. It was two-way, this loving business, and he had to see it. 'I can't walk away.'

'I would never ask you to.' Once more he kissed her. 'It's a whole, complex web. I need you, you need your mum, I need you to be happy and you can't be happy without your mum. But there are needs and needs. There's another thought, as well. Your friend, Nani, loves Atangi and wants to live there, only of course she and Kalifa mortgaged their house to try and get her son out of debt. She loves you. This is early days, there's so much to sort out, but I thought, if we build big with a

housekeeper's apartment, maybe we could bring your
mother here. And Nani could be our housekeeper-carer.
It'd mean your mother would be near Lea as she grows
up. You'd have company if I'm called away. Maybe…
maybe we could all be happy?'

And that pretty much took her breath away. She sat,
astounded, as what he was proposing sank in.

A house on Atangi. No, a home. Her daughter, her
mother, Bugsy, Nani…

Her husband.

Maybe even…

'Two or three?' Josh said, and grinned because he
knew what she was thinking—he'd always known what
she was thinking. 'We wouldn't want to be lonely. And
maybe another pup to keep Bugsy company. After all,
he saved your life—he deserves his own happy ending.'

'You'd do all that for me?' she whispered, and he
cupped her face in his hands and his gaze met hers. He
was loving her with his eyes.

'No,' he said softly. 'I'd do all that for me. I'd do it
because I need it. I need you. I need family. Yes, I need
to be needed, but I can be, and it will be two-way. I
promise you, Maddie, love. If you'll marry me again I
swear that I'll need you for as long as we both shall live.'

And what was a woman to say to that? There was
only one answer and it was a soundless one.

She drew him to her and she kissed him, tenderly this
time, lovingly, an affirmation of everything in her heart.

The armour was melting, she thought. Wherever he'd
stowed it, she could feel it disappearing.

He had no need of armour.

Her heart was beating in sync with his. She loved
and she loved and she loved.

Soon her daughter would need feeding. *Their* daughter.

They'd walk back to the house together, and they'd walk slowly because both of them hurt.

They'd hold each other up, she thought as he helped her to her feet.

They needed each other, and together it didn't hurt at all.

* * * * *

A SHEIKH TO
CAPTURE HER HEART

BY
MEREDITH WEBBER

Published in Great Britain 2016
By Mills & Boon, an imprint of HarperCollins*Publishers*
1 London Bridge Street, London, SE1 9GF

© 2016 Meredith Webber

ISBN: 978-0-263-25435-8

Printed and bound in Spain
by CPI, Barcelona

Dear Reader,

The very best thing about writing this book was that I shared the experience with two very good friends. Together we set up Wildfire Island, and over a couple of years we got together to refine the stories and make them work together.

Recently Marion Lennox, from Victoria, Alison Roberts, from New Zealand, and I were on the Gold Coast in Queensland, where I live. They'd rented a lovely apartment high on a hill above the beach, from where they could look out at the whales passing south after the annual pilgrimage to our shores. Together we sat watching the stunning views and talked about our characters, who were very real people to us by then, and we sorted out the very last chapter of the last book so all our readers would know what had happened to everyone a year or so later.

Such fun! We hadn't done a series together since Crocodile Creek, and it was a great challenge to have.

All the best,

Meredith Webber

To all my writing friends,
but in particular Marion and Alison.

Meredith Webber lives on the sunny Gold Coast in
Queensland, Australia, but takes regular trips west into
the Outback, fossicking for gold or opal. These breaks
in the beautiful and sometimes cruel red earth country
provide an escape from the writing desk and a chance
for the mind to roam free—not to mention getting
some much needed exercise. They also supply the
kernels of so many stories she finds it's hard for her
to stop writing!

Books by Meredith Webber

Mills & Boon Medical Romance

Visit the Author Profile page
at millsandboon.co.uk for more titles.

CHAPTER ONE

RAHMAN AL-TARAQ WAS BROODING. At least, that was what he assumed he was doing, but, never having been what he'd consider a moody man, it had taken a while to reach that conclusion.

If asked, he'd have described himself as a—well, *driven* was probably the only word—man. Driven to succeed, to prove himself, to be the best he could and garner admiration for his achievements rather than for having, purely by chance, been born into royalty.

Wealthy royalty!

It wasn't that the servants at the palace where he'd grown up had bowed and scraped, but very early on he'd realised that every whim would be granted and treats of all kinds supplied, not because he'd done something to deserve them but because of who he was.

What other six-year-old boy would be given an elephant for his birthday, simply because he'd happened to mention in passing that the elephant he'd seen in a travelling show shouldn't have to live with a chain around its foot?

That thought made him smile!

Imagine bringing Rajah here, to this tropical paradise in the South Pacific! He'd love the rainforest, but would decimate the villagers' gardens in a week.

Maybe less.

Besides which he was getting too old to travel.

He sighed, a sure sign he was brooding, and as brooding was a totally pointless occupation and achieved precisely nothing, a man who was into achievement—or had been—should do something about it.

He stood up and paced the bure he'd had built for himself as part of his exclusive resort on Wildfire Island, his eyes barely registering the beauty of the natural stone, the polished, ecologically sourced timber, the intricately woven local mats. From outside it might look like a typical island home, but inside…

In truth, he might be driven to achieve recognition for his work, but he didn't mind a few trappings of luxury.

Work!

There was that word again.

No matter how hard he tried to convince himself the work he was doing now was important and worthwhile, which it was, there was always a but.

His drive to be himself apart from his background had begun as a child sent to England at ten to a top boarding school. On arrival he'd introduced himself as Harry so his more exotic name didn't mark him out.

And as Harry, he'd been driven to succeed, to be the best, and his rise through school and university had been marked with success. But he'd found his true passion to be for surgery—general at first then specialising in paediatric surgery, helping save the lives of the most vulnerable small humans.

But one could hardly operate on a newborn with a

right hand that trembled, legacy of a touch-and-go brush with encephalitis. His initial reaction to the loss of the work he loved had been fury—fury with the weakness of his body in doing this to him.

Eventually he'd realised the pointlessness of his anger, so he'd sought and found a new focus—to provide facilities for scientists working on a variety of vaccines for the disease, as well as developing mosquito eradication programmes in the worst affected areas.

It was worthwhile work, and it had him roaming the world almost continually, checking up on the services he'd set up. Which left him tired. But it didn't become the passion his surgical work had been, and he felt a lesser man because of it.

He sighed and went back to brooding, but on the woman this time—better, surely, than brooding on the past and the loss of the work he'd loved.

What was done was done!

The woman!

Sarah Watson…

He *had* met her before, he was certain of that.

But having come close to death from the encephalitis virus had obviously killed some brain cells and though his memory of her was vivid in his mind, he couldn't place it in context anywhere.

He'd asked her at the cocktail party, caught up with her in the crush at the opening of the refurbished research station and resort, reminded her they'd met.

And she'd denied it—brushed away from him—telltale colour in her cheeks suggesting it was a lie.

But why?

And why in damnation did he care?

Worse, care enough to have returned to the island

in order to see her again when he could have been in Africa, or, if he really needed a woman, in New York, where there were beautiful, fun, sophisticated women who wanted nothing more than a brief sexual relationship with no strings attached?

It was her hair!

How many women had hair the colour of rich, polished mahogany?

And the scent of it—tangy—like vinegar mixed with the rose perfume his mother always wore, and the rose-scented water that splashed in the fountains at home.

But vinegar?

Could he really have picked up vinegar in the scent—*and* been drawn to it?

Who was drawn to vinegar?

Whatever!

The fact remained he *had* to have brushed against her some time in the past, for the scent to have been so evocative as they'd passed in the crush of people at the cocktail party! He'd asked his friend Luke about the woman and had learnt nothing more than that she was the general surgeon who flew into the island for a week every six weeks, and that she was English.

Big help!

Although her being English *did* make it possible he'd met her before, as he'd been based in London all his working life.

It was now six weeks since the cocktail party to celebrate the opening of the luxury resort and the reopening of the research station funded by him in the same small piece of paradise.

Six weeks, and here he was back on Wildfire when he should be at another research facility he'd set up in

West Africa, or in Malaysia, organising the mosquito eradication programme. Should have been anywhere but here.

Brooding!

Enough!

He picked up his phone and got through to the island's small hospital.

'Is Dr Watson there?' he asked the woman who answered.

'Finished for the day, probably down on Sunset Beach,' was the succinct reply.

Sunset Beach—just around the corner, a short walk to the rock fall that separated his resort beach from the next small curve of sand. Walk around that and there was Sunset Beach.

He'd meet her there, as if by accident, and work out where they'd met—ask her again if necessary.

Action was better than brooding.

He dropped the phone and left the bure, not giving himself time to consider what he was doing in case he decided it wasn't a good idea.

He'd see her, ask her again where they'd met, perhaps smell her hair…

Was he mad?

Wasn't he in enough trouble with women at the moment, with his mother, three sisters, seven aunts, and Yasmina, the woman he was supposed to be marrying —for the good of the country, of course—insisting he come home and prepare to take over his role as ruler when his aging father died?

They all knew, as did his father, that his younger brother would be a far better ruler than he, and the very thought of returning home to the fussing of his horde of relatives made him feel distinctly claustrophobic.

While marriage to a stranger… That was something else.

He's spent too long in the West but deep in his bones knew that some of the old ways were best.

Some!

He was at the rock fall now.

Stupid! He should have stopped to put something on his feet as the rocks were sharp in places. But the tide was going out, the water at the base not very deep.

He'd wade…

Sarah came out of the cool, translucent water, towelled dry, then slipped her arms into the long white shirt she wore as covering over her swimsuit. Even at sunset the tropical sun had enough heat in it to burn her fair skin.

Fair skin and red hair—a great combination given she was slowly finding peace and contentment on this tropical island. Slowly putting herself back together again; finding a way forward in a life that had been shattered four years ago, sending her to what seemed like the end of the earth—Australia—and then finding a job where she could move around—a week here, a week there—not settling long enough for anyone to dig into her past, bring back the memories…

A loud roar of what had to be pain startled her out of her reverie and she looked towards the rock fall at the other end of the beach where a man—the roarer, apparently—was hopping up and down in thigh-deep water.

Some kind of local ritual?

No, it was definitely pain she'd heard—and could still hear.

Pushing her feet into her sandals, she ran across the white coral sand to where the man was struggling to get out of the water, clutching one foot now, slowly becoming the man she'd seen briefly at the cocktail party—the man they'd all called Harry.

Sheikh Rahman al-Taraq, in fact, a man she'd once admired enormously for the expertise and innovations he'd brought to paediatric surgery. Admired enough to be flattered when he'd asked her to have a coffee with him afterwards, babbling on to him about her desire to specialise in the same surgery. So she had been late for David, who'd said he'd wait at work and drive her home rather than letting her take the tube—half an hour late—half an hour, which could have changed everything.

She closed her eyes against the memories—the crash, the fear, the blood…

It hadn't been Harry's fault, of course, but how could she remember that meeting without all the horror of it coming back—not when she was healing, not on the island that had brought peace to her soul.

But right now that man was in pain.

She reached him and slipped to the side of what was his obviously injured foot, taking his arm and hauling it around her shoulders to steady him.

'What happened?' she asked, once they were stabilised in the now knee-deep water.

'Trod on something—agonising pain.'

The man's face was a pale, grimacing mask.

'Let's get you back to civilisation where we can phone the hospital,' she said, hoping she sounded more practical than she felt because the warmth of the man's body was disturbing her.

In fact, the man was disturbing her, and, if truth be told, the memory of her chance meeting with him at the cocktail party had been niggling inside her for the past six weeks. Reminding her of things she didn't want to remember…

But reminding her of other things, as well.

Not that he'd know that.

'I'm Sarah. We met at the cocktail party.'

'Harry!'

The name came out through gritted teeth but they were out of the water now and heading slowly, step hop, step hop, for the first of the bures in the resort.

'Did you see what it was?' Sarah asked, thinking of the many venomous inhabitants that lurked around coral reefs.

'Trod on it!'

They'd reached the door.

'That probably means a stonefish. They burrow down into the sand or camouflage themselves in rock pools so they're undetectable from their surroundings. You should be wearing shoes. Is your hot-water system good? Water hot?'

The man she was helping—Harry—seemed to swell with the rage that echoed in his voice.

'Need a shower, do you?'

Sarah decided that a man in pain was entitled to be a little tetchy so she ignored him, helping him to a chair and kneeling in front of him to examine his foot.

'You've got two puncture wounds and they're already swelling. I'll get some hot water and then phone the hospital. Hot water, as hot as you can stand, should ease the pain.'

Sarah looked directly at him, probably for the first

time since she'd arrived at the bottom of the rock fall. Even with gritted teeth and a fierce expression of pain on his face, he was good looking. Tall, dark, and handsome, like a prince in story books. The words formed in her head as she hurried to the small kitchen area of the bure in search of a bowl and hot water.

No bowls, but a large beaten copper vase. The stings were in the upper part of his foot—he could get that much of his foot into it.

Back at the chair, she knelt again, setting down the vase of hot water but keeping hold of the jug of cold water she'd brought with her.

'Try that with the toe of your good foot,' she said. 'If it's too hot I'll add cold water but you need it as hot as you can manage.'

He dipped a toe in and withdrew it quickly, tried again after Sarah had added water, and actually sighed with relief as he submerged the wounds in the container and the pain eased off.

Looking up at her, he shook his head.

'How did you know that?'

But she was on the phone to the hospital and someone had answered, so she could only shrug in reply to his question.

Quickly she explained the situation, turning back to Harry to ask, 'Is the pain travelling up your leg?'

He nodded.

'Like pins and needles that turn into cramp, although it's easier now.'

Sarah relayed the description to Sam, who was on the hospital end of the phone.

'We'll pick up a few things and be right down,' Sam said. 'Put his foot in hot water.'

Sarah smiled to herself as she hung up, glad some tiny crevice of her brain had come up with the same information, although it had been at least ten years since she'd practised general medicine and, having been in England, had never encountered a stonefish sting before.

Grabbing the jug, she returned to the kitchen for more hot water, knowing that as the water cooled, the pain would return.

'I *did* know you before the cocktail party,' her patient said as she returned, his dark eyes on her face, unsettling her with the intensity of his focus. 'I remember now. You were at the talk I gave at GOSH on the use of transoesophageal echocardiography for infants. We had a coffee together afterwards.'

His voice challenged her to deny it a second time!

Great Ormond Street Hospital—GOSH—of course she'd been there. How could she ever forget? She'd been so excited to be invited because back then she'd been considering paediatric surgery, and listening to the mesmeric speaker—this man—had crystallised her ambition.

But further memories of that fateful day brought such anguish she couldn't stop herself hitting out at the man who'd provoked them.

'The man *I* had coffee with was one of the foremost paediatric surgeons in the world, an innovator and inventor, always finding new ways to help the most vulnerable but important people in our society—children. I know you've been sick, but still there's so much you could offer.'

She shouldn't have let fly like that, and knew it, so guilt now mixed with the anguish churning inside her.

The recipient of the tirade just sat there, eyes hooded and spots of colour on his cheeks as warning signs of anger.

'The cart from the hospital is here, I'll go,' she said, her voice still taut—angry—hurt...

Ashamed?

Yes, very, but—

She thought she might have got away, but as she stalked out the door, jug of hot water still clenched in her hand, the man spoke.

'Well, the woman *I* met was ambitious to do the same work!'

Sarah closed her eyes, feeling stupid, useless tears sliding down her cheeks, almost blinding her as she made her way back to the beach to collect her things.

She'd deserved that comment, lashing out at him the way she had, but his insistence she remember that day had brought back far too many memories—just when she was beginning to think she'd healed.

How could he have said that?

Something so personal, and obviously very hurtful.

Because her words had struck a nerve?

More like a knife in his chest, directly into the similar doubts he had about himself.

Doubts he refused to face...

Which was no excuse for him to hit back at her!

What was happening to him that he could say such a thing?

'Done something stupid, have you?'

Sam Taylor, senior doctor at the hospital, charged into the bure.

It was impossible to brood with Sam around! He was a cheerful, capable man, who deftly delivered an analgesic to the wounded foot before suggesting Harry move to the hospital so the wound could be cleaned, while the antivenin and any further pain relief could be given intravenously.

He helped Harry out to the small electric cart that was the common transport on the island, and drove them up the hill from the resort to the neat little hospital.

Out of the hot water, the analgesic yet to work, the cramping, burning pain returned to both Harry's foot and his lower leg. But his mind had other things to handle.

Despair that he'd flung those words at Sarah Watson returned. Ultra childish, that's all it had been. *Her* words had stung, probably because there was an element of truth in them. In fact, they'd gone so deep he'd hit back automatically, and from the way her face had grown even paler, he'd hurt her badly.

She hadn't deserved that, for all she'd earlier denied knowing him. She certainly hadn't deserved it after getting him back to the bure and providing pain-relieving first aid. With agonising pain shooting up his leg, he'd not have made it alone.

'You brooding over something or is it just the pain?' Sam asked, as they pulled up at the small hospital.

'I *don't* brood!' Harry snapped, then regretted it.

More to brood over!

'I didn't think so,' Sam said cheerfully. 'Come on, we'll get you inside.'

Keanu Russell, the second permanent doctor at the hospital, had appeared and with Sam helped Harry through the small emergency room and into a well-equipped treatment alcove.

Harry checked out the paraphernalia by the bed.

'All this for a sting? Or are the spines lodged in my foot? Is it one of the deadly marine creatures that seem to flourish in these parts?'

Sam smiled and shook his head.

'You're here because we have good monitoring equipment in here. We can hook you up to oxygen, use a pulse oximeter, and a self-inflating blood-pressure cuff. And with a few wires on your chest, the screen will tell us all we need to know. And no, it's not deadly. Just painful.'

'Tell me about it!' Harry grumbled. 'I see myself as a tough guy but it was all I could do to not whimper while Sarah was helping me to my bure.'

'Going to keep him in?' Keanu asked Sam, as the two men efficiently attached him to the monitoring equipment.

'Nah, he's strong, and he just told us he's tough, so he'll survive. We'll drip the antivenin in, let him rest for a while, check everything's working as it should be, then send him home. He might only be a surgeon but I reckon he knows enough general medicine to yell for us if he has any further problems.'

Harry had to smile at the laid-back, teasing attitude of these men who worked on the island. They did enormous good, providing medical assistance and support to the whole M'Langi group of islands. It was a complicated programme of clinic visits, preventative medicine, rescue work and emergency callouts, yet they made everything seem easy.

Maybe if he stayed here long enough, he might pick up some of the relaxed island vibe.

Impossible right now, though. The woman he'd just hurt was walking into the room, still in the long white shirt she wore over a black bathing suit, a black and white striped beach towel slung over her shoulder, and an obviously anxious expression on her face.

Anxious about his well-being?

Well, she *was* a doctor!

'Is he okay?' she asked Sam.

'Ask him yourself,' Sam retorted, and the sea-green eyes set in that pale creamy skin turned towards him, narrowing slightly.

'Are you?' she demanded.

'Hey, be nice. He's a patient,' Sam reminded her.

'Yours, not mine. I just happened to be there when he strolled through reef waters without anything on his feet.'

She didn't actually add *the idiot*, but the words hung in a bubble in the air between them.

But even with her contempt there for all to see, she was beautiful. He knew it was probably her colouring that he found so fascinating: the vibrant hair, the pale skin, the flashing green eyes. Things he'd noticed way back when they'd first met.

But now he sensed something deeper in her that drew him inexorably to her.

Hidden pain?

He knew all about *that*.

Didn't it stab him every day when he felt the tremor in his hand as he shaved?

So grow a beard, a mocking voice within suggested, and Harry closed his eyes, against the voice and the woman.

'I just popped in to make sure he'd made it safely up here,' the woman said. 'So, see you two tomorrow.'

Sam stopped her retreat with a touch on her arm.

Harry suppressed a growl that rose in his throat. It had hardly been a lover's touch and, anyway, what business of his was it who touched her?

'Actually, Sarah,' Sam was saying, 'if you could spare a few minutes, I'd like you to stay around until the drip's finished. We were actually at a staff meeting up at the house and your phone call switched through to there. Mina's here for the other patients, but I think Harry should be watched.'

I have to *watch* him?

Sarah nodded in reply to Sam's request, telling herself it didn't mean *watch* watch, just to check on him now and then.

But watching him—he'd opened his eyes briefly as Sam spoke but they were closed again—actually *looking* at him might be a good idea. She could start by confirming her impressions of his physical appearance and maybe that would help sort out why the man made her so uneasy.

Why he stirred responses deep inside her that she hadn't felt for four years...

For sure he was good looking. Olive-skinned, dark-haired, strong face, with a straight nose and solid chin. The lips softened it just a little, beautifully shaped—sensual—

Get with it, Sarah!

Stop this nonsense!

'Are you looking at me?'

Surprisingly pale eyes—grey—opened, and black eyebrows rose.

'Not looking, just watching—that's what I was asked to do, remember.'

'Not much difference, I'd have thought,' the wretch said, with the merest hint of a smile sliding across those sens—

His lips!

She turned her attention to the monitor. The blood-pressure cuff was just inflating, so at least she had something to watch.

A little high, but the pain would only just be subsiding, so that was to be expected.

'Tell me if you feel any reaction to the antivenin,' she told him. 'Nausea, faintness…'

He opened one eye and raised the eyebrow above it as if to say, is that all you've got?

She almost smiled then realised smiling at this man might be downright dangerous, so she walked out into the main room and found a magazine that was only four years old, grabbed a chair, and returned with it to the emergency cubicle to sit as far as possible from the man as she could get in the curtained alcove and still see the monitor.

He appeared to be asleep, and she tried hard to give her full attention to an article about the various cosmetic procedures currently in vogue in the US.

And failed.

The stonefish wound was in his right foot, so it had been his right arm she'd had around her shoulder as she'd taken some of his weight to get him back to the bure.

Had she felt a tremor in it?

Looking at him now, the arm in question was lying still on the bed. Or was it gripping the bed?

Parkinson's patients she'd encountered in the past found tremors in their arms and hands worsened when

they relaxed but lessened when they held something.
Would that hold true for tremors induced by encephalitis or was a different part of the brain affected?

And just why was she interested?

She sighed and tried to tell herself it was because the
surgery world had been shocked to learn the results of
his brush with encephalitis. Shocked that such a talented
and skilful man had been lost to surgery.

But she wasn't here to wonder about his tremor. That
was his business.

She was here to watch him, not worry about his past
or the problems he faced now.

She turned her attention from the monitor to the man.

His eyes were open, studying her in turn, and although she'd have liked to turn away, she knew doing
so would be an admission that he disturbed her.

'I'm sorry,' he said, those strange pale eyes holding
hers. 'I had no right to throw such a petty, personal,
ridiculous remark at you. All my friends tell me I'm
over-sensitive about the results of my illness, but that's
no excuse.'

Now she did look instead of watching, looked and
saw the apology mirrored in his eyes.

She almost weakened because the man had been
through hell.

And to a certain extent hadn't she opted out as well,
heading away from home as fast as she could, taking
a job that meant she didn't have to settle in one place,
make friends, get hurt by loss again?

But she hadn't been a genius at what she did and this
man had. The world needed him and people like him.

Straightening her shoulders, she met his eyes and
said, 'Well, if you're expecting an apology from me,

forget it. I meant every word I said. You must have any number of minions who could run around checking on the facilities and programmes you've sent up. By doing it yourself, you're wasting such skill and talent it's almost criminal.'

And on that note she would have departed, except she was stuck there—watching him.

Watching him raise that mobile eyebrow once again.

'Minions?'

The humour lurking in the word raised her anger.

'You know exactly what I mean,' she snapped, and he nodded.

Thinking she'd got the last word, she prepared to depart, or at least back as far away as possible from him.

'But we *had* met before—you'll admit that now!' he said.

So much for having the last word! He'd not only sneaked that one in but he'd brought back the memories—of that wonderful day at GOSH *and* the horror of its aftermath.

Her heart was beating so fast it was a wonder the patient couldn't hear it, and a sob of anguish wasn't far away. The curtain sliding back saved her from total humiliation as she burst into tears in front of this man.

Caroline Lockhart, one of the permanent nurses at the hospital, appeared, flashing such a happy smile that Sarah couldn't not smile back at her.

'I'm to take over,' Caroline said quietly. 'Sam says thanks for the hand. We were discussing how best to spend a rather large donation we've just received—working out what's needed most. Since you overwhelmed us with the equipment needed for endoscopies and keyhole surgery, the theatre's pretty well sorted. But if you have any other ideas, let someone know.'

Sarah nodded and stood up, wanting to get as far away as possible. Caroline's words had added a further layer to her pain. Getting compensation for the accident that had taken her husband and unborn child four years after the event had been traumatic to say the least—how could money possibly replace a husband and son?—so her immediate reaction had been to get rid of it as quickly as possible.

And because it was the leisurely pace and overwhelming beauty of this magic island where she'd finally begun to put the broken pieces of herself back together again, wasn't it right she give something back?

She made her way out of the rear of the hospital, down to the little villa where she stayed when she was here, and tapped on the door of the villa next door to remind her anaesthetist they had an early start in the morning.

Ben was clad in board shorts, his hair ruffled and a vague expression on his face.

'Did I catch you at a bad moment?' she asked.

'Halfway through dismembering a body,' he replied, and Sarah grinned.

Ben was an excellent anaesthetist and didn't mind the travel, but apparently he was an even better writer, his sixth murder mystery hitting top-seller lists. It was only a matter of time before he was making enough money from his writing to support himself and she'd have to find a new anaesthetist willing to travel to isolated places in outback Queensland, and to Wildfire in the M'Langi group of islands.

'We're doing that thyroidectomy tomorrow. You all set?' she asked.

He raised his hand in a mocking salute.

'Ready as ever, ma'am,' he said, the words telling her he was still lost in his book—one of his characters talking.

But lost though he was at the moment, she knew he'd be fully focussed in the morning.

'Our patient came in this afternoon, if you want to pop over the hospital tonight to talk to her. I'd say the op will take three to four hours, depending on any complications, and she's had some complications with her heart so we'll have to watch her.

Ben nodded.

'Don't worry, we'll be right. I've already read up on her and checked with my old boss back in Sydney about the level of drug use. We'll be fine.'

Ben was about to back away, obviously anxious to get back to what he considered his real work, when he paused, then reached out and touched her cheek.

'Have you been crying?' There was suspicion and a touch of anger in his voice, and in his eyes. 'Did someone upset you?'

Sarah forced a smile onto her lips and fixed it there. She was only too aware of how protective Ben was of her, once taking on the boss of an outback hospital when he'd wanted her to work beyond regulation safe hours.

'I'm fine,' she told him, taking his hand from her cheek and giving his fingers a 'thank you' squeeze.

'Well, I hope you are,' he said, before disappearing back into his villa, from which Sarah could almost hear his computer calling to him.

But the little white lie had made her feel better, so

instead of hiding away in her island home, she walked to the top of the cliffs above Sunset Beach to catch the last fiery blast of the sunset.

Except she'd missed it. The soft pinks and mauves and violets, however, were still stunningly beautiful and like a soothing balm to her aching heart.

CHAPTER TWO

KEANU DROVE HARRY back to his bure, offering to stay for a while, though Harry could see he was itching to get into the newly refurbished laboratories. As well as Harry's team working towards clinical trials of an encephalitis vaccine, other scientists were welcome to use the facilities, and Keanu's passion at the moment—apart from his fiancée, Caroline, and saving the island's gold mine—was examining the properties of M'Langi tea, a project started by his father many years ago.

'Are you getting anywhere?' Harry asked the young doctor.

Keanu shook his head.

'We know we have fewer encephalitis cases than other South Sea islands and the only difference as far as diet is concerned is this tea we drink.'

Harry nodded.

Keanu's work fitted with what his team was doing, but the two strands needed to be studied separately.

Keanu pulled up outside the bure and came around to help Harry inside.

But he sat for a moment, wondering if he might not be better off going up to the lab, making himself useful.

Or would he be a nuisance to his 'minions', as Sarah Watson had described them?

Of course he would, limping and still in some pain as he was. Besides, meticulous research work was not his thing—he was far too impatient.

Though not in surgery...

'Thanks, Keanu, I can hop from here,' he said, waving away the man's assistance, his traitorous mind thinking of the last person who'd helped him inside the building.

Maybe it was lemons, not vinegar—or something a little tarter...

Limes?

Hobbling up the two steps, his foot still in pain, he shook his head at his stupidity. Sarah had made her feelings clear when she'd let fly about his behaviour, neither could he have failed to feel the contempt in her words.

Deserved contempt?

Probably!

Forget the woman!

Easier said than done.

Women usually lingered pleasantly in his head, small, special moments of past relationships stored neatly away like boxes in a storeroom in his brain.

But this woman...

No way she'd stay in a box!

Perhaps because they *hadn't* had a relationship.

They'd been nothing more than ships that had passed in the night!

She'd been pregnant. She obviously had a family—husband and child—or at least the child.

So why the job of flying surgeon?

She'd be home, what, one week in four or five? Hardly a good arrangement for family life.

And none of his business…

Sarah loved operating in the small but brilliant theatre at Wildfire. Double-glazed windows let in natural light while allowing the room to be airconditioned, and through them she could see the tangle of treetops and vines in the rainforest that ran up the hill behind the hospital.

Added to which Sam was an excellent assistant, competent in his own right to perform routine operations but unable to take time out of his busy schedule to do regular surgical work. Hettie, the head nurse, and Caroline both enjoyed theatre nursing so, with Ben, she had a great team.

The patient was sedated, breathing through an endotracheal tube, and Sarah was about to begin when she sensed, rather than saw, another person enter the room.

Sensed who it was, too.

'Glad you felt well enough to come up,' Sam said cheerfully to the newcomer, who was still somewhere behind Sarah as she lifted a scalpel off the tray, ready to begin. 'It's not often we can show off our theatre to someone who's seen the best.'

'Thank you for inviting me.'

The deep voice reverberated down Sarah's spine, and she had to focus on the lines she'd drawn on the patient's neck and breathe deeply for a moment to steady her nerves.

Sam glanced at her, the retractors in his hand, ready to begin, while Hettie shifted a little impatiently, ready to cauterise tiny blood vessels.

Sarah began, although a tiny portion of her mind was protesting that it was *her* theatre right now and she could ask him to leave.

When the hospital boss had invited him?

She focussed fully on the patient, cutting into the throat in a crease in the woman's neck so the scar would be next to invisible. The parathyroid glands lay directly behind the thyroid, so at the forefront of her mind her brain was locating and isolating them so they wouldn't be damaged.

The area was also filled with important nerves and blood vessels, not to mention the larynx, just above the gland, so it was easy to lose herself in the meticulous work, excluding all outside factors.

Three hours later the glands had been removed and Sarah was checking they'd cauterised all the blood vessels in the incision.

'I'll close for you if you like,' Sam offered, and, knowing how much he enjoyed being part of the surgery, Sarah stepped back, only too happy to let him finish the job.

'Do you want a drain in place?" he asked, and she checked the open wound again.

'No, it's clean,' she said. 'Good job, team.'

She crossed the theatre towards the washrooms, stripping off her gloves and gown and dumping them in a bin by the door. Still clad in the highly unflattering green hospital scrubs, she turned to push her way through the door, finally catching sight of the unexpected onlooker.

He'd obviously been masked as he'd stood outside the sterile area of the theatre. Now the white strip of paper hung around his neck, resting on the collar of a dark blue polo shirt that clung to a chest any athlete would be proud to display.

And just why had she been looking at his chest?

To avoid looking at his face?

Probably!

But what was it about the man that drew her eyes?

More than her eyes… Her senses.

Forget him!

She felt strongly about his opting out of the world of paediatric surgery. From all she'd seen and read, he'd been truly gifted.

And he'd made her cry!

Twice!

So why was she even thinking about him?

She stripped off her clothes, showered, and pulled on a pair of white slacks and a black and white striped tee that was old and faded but very soft and comforting. Pushing her feet into sandals, she went out the back door of the changing room and along the corridor to the rear of the hospital, heading for her villa.

Ben was in charge of their patient now, and would keep an eye on her in the recovery room. Sarah would see her in the morning.

The first thing she saw as she walked into the villa was the jug from Harry's bure—the jug she'd carried away with her as she'd fled the man's taunt.

Well, he was up at the hospital with Sam right now, so she'd duck down to the resort and leave it outside his door. She grabbed her hat, a large droopy-brimmed black creation, off the hook by the door.

The ducking down to his island home would have worked if he hadn't overtaken her as she strolled down the track, admiring the beautiful, lush gardens and isolated bures.

Finding he'd lost interest in the hospital once Sarah had departed, Harry made his way across the airstrip and onto the track that led through the resort.

The figure striding ahead of him was instantly recognisable despite the floppy black hat covering her glorious hair.

Glorious hair?

He really was losing it with this woman…

This woman he'd hurt when he'd hit out at her.

Unforgiveable, really.

'Going my way?'

She started at his voice, but perhaps because it was
such a corny thing to say she also smiled and held up
the jug.

'Returning your property, but now you're here I can
give it to you.'

She turned towards him, pushing the jug into his
hands, their fingers touching, time suspended.

'Have lunch with me?'

The invitation coming out like it had startled *him*,
and apparently was so unexpected Sarah could only
peer up at him from under the hat.

What did she see?

His regret?

Or had she heard a hint of desperation in his voice?
She thought for a moment then said yes.

She seemed as startled as he'd been by the acceptance, but he couldn't hide his pleasure, smiling as he
took her elbow to walk her down the track.

His foot still pained him but he tried to hide it, then
wondered if was kindness because he *was* limping that
had made her say yes and hadn't shaken off his hand.

Probably!

Harry's light touch on her elbow was causing Sarah's
body all the same manifestations of attraction she'd

first felt as she'd helped him out of the water the previous day.

The same manifestations that had *so* confused her she'd ranted at the man about his life choice!

He didn't speak until they'd reached his island home. He walked her through the room where she'd given him first aid and out to a trellis-covered deck.

He waved his hand towards a cushioned cane chair, then sat down opposite her, looking at her, studying her as she pulled off the hat and shook out her hair— studying her as if to really look at her was the sole reason he'd brought her there.

The strange part was she didn't mind, not when it gave her time to study him—to try to work out just what was at play here.

A subliminal link from the past—back when *both* their lives had been so different?

Or something more basic, even earthy… Simple attraction?

Was attraction ever simple?

And not having experienced it for so long, how could she be sure that's what it was?

'Cold drink? Juice?' he finally asked, and Sarah wondered if she'd imagined that brief moment of mutual interest.

'Cold water would be great,' she said, then sank thankfully back into the chair as he disappeared inside.

Relief washed through her but it didn't entirely release the inner tension she was feeling—or the strange, almost magnetic force this man exerted over her.

Saying yes to lunch—sitting staring at him—this wasn't her. Sarah Watson was practical, organised, totally self-contained, and content with the new life she'd made for herself.

He reappeared carrying a large tray, the jug she'd just returned set in the middle of it, surrounded by platters of sliced tropical fruit, curls of finely cut meat, chunks of cheese and a cane basket filled with soft rolls and bruschetta.

'One moment,' he said, disappearing inside again, then reappearing with plates, glasses, cutlery, napkins and a smaller tray containing little dishes of butter and relishes.

'Wow? You did all this in a matter of minutes?' Sarah said, looking up at him as he checked they had everything they needed.

'Minions,' he said briefly, placing a plate and glass in front of her. 'The resort staff bring me a lunch this size every day, although I keep telling them there's only one of me and I can't possibly eat it all.'

'So you asked me to lunch to help you out?' Sarah teased, looking up at him.

He held her gaze for an instant then shook his head.

'Heaven only knows why I asked you to lunch,' he growled, a puzzled frown drawing his dark eyebrows together. 'It just seemed to come out of me, but as both Sam and Caroline have ripped strips off me for upsetting you, maybe my conscience made the call.'

So Sam *had* seen her crying as she'd left the bure, and Caroline had definitely seen she'd been upset in the ER yesterday...

But tearing strips off him?

She concentrated on the lunch, forking some sliced fruit onto her plate, taking a piece of bruschetta, some cheese—

'You obviously know my recent history, but what happened to you?' he asked, his voice gentler now, his eyes on hers, not on the plate already filled with meat and cheese that he was holding in his hand.

She frowned at the intrusive question, selected a piece of melon, didn't answer.

'You don't have to answer, of course, but I've obviously upset you, and I wouldn't knowingly do that. Not for the world.'

She *had* to look at him now, and she saw not only concern but empathy in his eyes.

It would be so easy to tell him, to excuse her rudeness to him by revealing why remembering the night they'd first met had caused her so much pain.

Yet still she hesitated, until he moved his chair closer, lifted the plate from her hands and set it on the table, then took one of her hands in both of his and looked deep into her eyes.

'What happened to your ambition to practise paediatric surgery, to the child you carried? What was so terrible it sent you halfway across the world to take on the itinerant work you do?'

His words were almost hesitant, so much so she knew it wasn't curiosity but some deeper need to know.

The same need to know that she felt about him—a need to know more of this man.

Although she left her hand where it was, she couldn't look at him, chewing at the melon when it had already dissolved to mush in her mouth.

'I watched you today,' he continued, genuine interest in his voice. 'You're a natural surgeon, the instruments are like extensions of your fingers, and your hands move almost without messages from your brain. You were so enthusiastic about paediatric surgery—'

'So were you!' She shot the reminder at him. 'Stuff happens, as well you know.'

He didn't reply, studying her again, then gave a rough shake of his head.

'I'm sorry, I really hadn't meant to bring all this up, to pry into your private life. It's none of my business what you do or why you do it and if I hurt you yesterday I'm truly sorry.'

Sarah met his eyes, and saw the apology there as well, but behind it the questions lingered, questions she didn't want to answer—probably couldn't.

Not right now, anyway…

Harry moved his chair away—fractionally—then picked up the plate he'd removed from Sarah's hands and gave it back to her.

Was he out of his mind? Here he had the company of this attractive woman and he'd ruined the lunch by demanding to know why her life had changed.

He'd already upset her twice, obviously by the things he'd said about the past, so why was he pushing for answers she equally obviously didn't want to give?

And why should she?

What business was it of his what she did or why she did it?

He was attracted to her—he'd got that far in sorting things out—but he'd rarely, or possibly never, pried into the pasts of other women to whom he'd been attracted.

He had accepted them as they were, enjoying a relationship that brought pleasure to both of them, always with the understanding that that was all it would ever be.

He knew some of the reasons it was all the women concerned wanted—their careers came first, or they'd been hurt before and just wanted the fun and companionship, and, yes, sex.

While ever conscious that for all he'd built his own life away from his family and the place of his birth, he still had obligations there—and a woman his family had pledged him to marry.

So relationships had been, well, fun, and many of the women remained his friend.

But this woman?

He pushed his plate away, his appetite gone, and looked at her.

'For all we seem to have done nothing but fling accusations at each other and probably hurt each other more than we should, there's something between us,' he said, hoping that bringing things out into the open might help.

She smiled, which didn't help.

'You mean a cup of coffee nearly five years ago and a stonefish sting?'

'No!'

He hadn't meant to snap, but even in his own ears it sounded snappy.

'A link, an attraction—a strong attraction that I think you can feel, too.'

She looked up from her plate then looked down again, very deliberately choosing a slice of pineapple and lifting it to luscious pink lips.

Every sinew in his body tightened—attraction? Or nerves about what, if anything, she might reply?

'And?' she said finally, when she'd chewed the pineapple far more than was necessary and swallowed it, the white skin on her throat moving up and down, the tip of her tongue sliding out to wipe the juice from her lips.

The tightening this time definitely wasn't nerves.

'And what?' The words scratched out from a throat thickened by emotion.

She almost smiled, her lips widening just slightly, indenting the faintest of dimples into her cheeks.

'And what would we do about it if, as you say, there's something there?'

'I don't know!'

He threw up his arms in exasperation. This wasn't how his courtships usually worked. He met a woman, they liked each other, went out for dinner then usually ended up in bed.

No, he shouldn't have thought about the bed part, especially as his bed was so close and he could already picture a naked Sarah Watson spread out on it, while he licked the cream of her skin from her toes to her forehead.

Possibly pausing on the way, here and there...

He blanked the image and forced his mind to shut down the thoughts accompanying it.

'It's a long time since I've been in a relationship,' she said quietly, setting down her plate and leaning back in the chair, the faded T-shirt she was wearing pulling tight against her full breasts.

'Because?'

He *had* to ask but all she did was shake her head and look so lost he wanted to scoop her into his arms and hold her tight against his chest until the sadness left her lovely eyes.

'But I probably wouldn't mind one.'

Had he heard her right?

'With me?' he managed to get out, any semblance of the suave man of the world he thought himself completely gone.

This time she smiled properly.

'Well, you're here, and I think you're right, there *is* something between us, isn't there? We're both old enough to recognise attraction, and should be able to admit to it, for all it's weird when neither of us seem to *like* each other particularly, and I don't really believe in instant…'

'Lust?' he suggested when she faltered in her almost clinical dissection of what lay between them.

'I suppose that's as good a word for what we're experiencing as any,' she admitted, 'and given I'm only here for a week—well, five days now—it wouldn't have time to get complicated. It'd be like a holiday romance only without the holiday part—a fling.'

He nodded, partly because he couldn't find the words but also, in part, because he had no idea where to go from there.

Taking her into the bedroom and peeling off all her clothes was one option, but it seemed a little abrupt—even more clinical than her words had been.

Damn it all, how did he usually get a woman into bed? He must have some technique—some idea of how to get from a shared lunch to the bedroom!

She was smiling, probably at the confusion that must be evident on his face.

Had she *really* just suggested they have an affair—well, hardly an affair, surely they took longer…?

I wouldn't mind one. She'd definitely said that.

Put the words right out there in the open, in a cartoon bubble above her head!

Well, the man *was* the most handsome, sexy member of the species she'd ever met, and if you counted tingling nerves, and a racing pulse, and shallow breathing, then he was right about there being something between them.

But an affair?

Well, hardly that, a fling.

A very short fling…

What the hell!

She looked into those slumberous grey eyes, studied the moulded lips, and, as panic yelled at her to go, to run for her life, she heard herself saying, 'Well, what happens next?'

He looked so stunned, she helped him out.

'Either I kiss you or you kiss me, I guess. Do you have a preference?'

He made a growling kind of noise and drew her close, studying her face, running his fingers through her hair, eyes wide now with a kind of wonder.

'You're serious?'

'Well, I think I am, but the more you mess about the more worried I'm getting. Perhaps we should sleep on it, decide tomorrow.'

This time the growly noise was more like a purr.

'And miss tonight? No way.'

Now, finally, he *did* kiss her.

Well, she guessed it was just a kiss, although it was unlike anything she'd ever experienced, sending her brain cells into a muzzy cloud and her body into a frenzy of desire.

Lust?

What the hell? Did it really matter?

She concentrated on the kiss, on kissing him with as much heat as he was kissing her.

Kissing *him*...

He felt her momentary hesitation, remembered her tears, and lifted his head, cupping her face in his hands, and looked into her eyes.

'You're sure about this?'

Well, nearly sure...

She didn't say the words but he read it in her eyes. Nearly sure wasn't good enough—not this time, for some reason, not with this woman.

Though at other times would he have hesitated?

Hell, what did *he* know?

Except he wanted her to be sure, so he kissed her lightly on the lips and tried a smile, although he knew it probably looked as false as it felt.

'Think about it,' he said quietly.

She eased her body away from his and nodded.

'I think I need to,' she responded.

And with that, she stood up, thanked him politely for the lunch, and walked away.

Out of his bure, but not out of his life?

He had no idea...

CHAPTER THREE

SARAH HEADED STRAIGHT for the rock fall. Sunset Beach was her sanctuary on this island and the sooner she got there the sooner she might be able to work out why she'd suddenly taken leave of her senses.

Calmly telling that man she wouldn't mind an affair!

That *was* what she'd said, wasn't it?

And from what part of her obviously impaired brain had those words sprung?

Although, remembering the heat of that one long kiss, she doubted her brain had had anything to do with it.

Even so…

She was clambering over the rocks now as the tide was in, but her mind raced to find an explanation for her behaviour.

Once on the beach she sat in the shade of the rocks—it was really far too early for her to be out here—and let the beauty of that special place calm her racing heart.

In the beginning, all she'd had room for in her heart and mind had been her grief, the grieving process isolating her from others, so she'd barely noticed that the sensual part of her nature had died along with David and her unborn child.

But seeing Rahman al-Taraq—Harry—again at the cocktail party had not only brought back memories of that dreadful day but, contrarily, had reawoken her senses. She'd been so startled by the unmistakable surge of attraction she'd felt towards him that she'd denied ever having met him and fled the party.

Yet, once reawoken and stirred, those parts of her that had lain dormant would no longer be denied, and over the following weeks she'd dreamt, at times, not particularly of Harry but of the pleasant, teasing sex she'd shared with David, although sometimes in the dreams he wasn't David, and sometimes in the dreams she'd wanted more…

She shook her head, sighed, and stared out at the translucent water that ran over the reef through the lagoon and splashed on the beach near her feet.

Was it because she'd finally got her life back in order—had put herself together again, albeit like a jigsaw with more than a few pieces missing—that her libido had returned?

Whatever!

It wasn't the whys and wherefores of her returning hormonal rush that she had to consider but what she was going to do about it.

Have a brief affair?

A fling?

Get it out of her system?

But could that happen?

Might she not want more?

She sighed again then reminded herself that if she did there were other men out there—for companionship, a bit of fun and pleasant, perhaps even exciting, sex.

She glanced up at the sky, hoping that wherever David's spirit was he wasn't privy to her thoughts.

Then she smiled!

It was David who'd taught her it was okay to enjoy sex—more than okay. David who'd taught her it could be fun as well as unbelievably intense.

David…

Harry felt as if he'd been pacing his room for hours. The woman—Sarah—had calmly told him she wouldn't mind having an affair then, equally calmly, had walked away.

Well, probably not as calmly—that kiss had been *hot*!

What made it worse was that she hadn't actually said it was him she wouldn't mind having an affair with!

No, she'd just wandered off as if the whole almost clinical discussion had never happened.

He had to find out.

Would she be at the beach?

He'd been told she went there at sunset every day when she was on the island, but today?

His body was so taut with wanting her he felt the slightest bump might shatter it. He'd been okay until she'd more or less said yes.

He tried to analyse his feelings.

Attracted, yes.

Desire spiralling within him, definitely.

But strung tight like this?

This was new and he was unsure what it meant.

Best not to think about it. Go around to the beach—with something on his feet—and see if she was there.

He saw her as he reached the rock fall, long white

arms stroking rhythmically through the water, little splashes as her feet kicked, her wet hair appearing almost black against her pale skin.

He crossed the small sandy area to where her clothes were piled under a pandanus palm and picked up her towel, carrying it down to the water's edge and waiting for her to come out.

She rose like Venus from her shell, shaking her head to clear the water from her hair, the paleness of her skin seeming lighter against the black swimsuit that moulded a perfect body with full breasts, a narrow waist drawing the eye to her hips and from there to her long, long legs…

She looked up, saw him—and smiled.

The tightness in his body zeroed downwards, and his hands trembled as he draped the towel around her shoulders, holding it closed beneath her chin.

'You're shaking,' she murmured, looking up into his face, perhaps reading the naked need he was feeling.

'You've bewitched me,' he muttered, his reaction to this woman so strong he wondered if maybe the encephalitis had returned and he was delirious.

He breathed deeply, calming himself, then wrapped the towel completely around her, leaving his hands at the back of her waist, easing her body closer.

Kissing was close, but for now it was enough to hold her, more than enough that she didn't push away…

Sea-green eyes looked up into his and her pink lips widened into a shy smile.

'This is weird.'

The words were little more than a breath of air, but her face told him so much more. She was uncertain, vulnerable…

And he wanted to hold her forever.

'You wanted something?'

She'd shifted slightly and her lost look had been replaced by a mischievous grin.

'You!' he muttered gruffly, although he knew he was rushing things.

This woman wasn't one of the career-focussed businesswomen with whom he usually dallied, and he, for certain, wasn't, right now, the attentive, caring, casual lover *he* usually was.

That man had romance and seduction down pat, while the man on the beach right now, the man in his skin, was so damned uncertain he was *shaking*.

She'd eased away from him, dried herself—hell, he should have done that, not stood there holding her. *He* should have been running that towel down her legs, over her curves, drying the pale skin between her shoulder blades.

For the first time in his life he understood the phrase 'pull yourself together'. It had always seemed asinine to him, but right now it was what he needed to do.

As she dropped the towel on the beach he recovered sufficiently to reach down for the shirt he knew she wore over her swimsuit, then hold it for her, watching her slide long, slim arms into the sleeves, turning her gently so he could button the shirt, right there above the swell of her breasts.

He could barely breathe as his fingers brushed against her skin, and felt her tension as she stood, statue-still beneath his touch.

'Have dinner with me.'

He'd meant it to be a request but it had come out as a demand.

Expecting her to be offended, he was surprised when she relaxed and moved just a little away from him, smiling as she said, 'Minions do dinner, too?'

He hoped the wild swoop of pleasure he felt wasn't making him look like an idiot as he smiled in turn.

'It's that kind of resort. I can order anything. What do you fancy? The crayfish is particularly good at the moment.'

'I'll try it,' she said, then she bent down to spread the towel on the sand, slapped the huge hat she wore onto her head, and straightened to look at him again.

'What time?'

There was a challenge in the words and he guessed it was aimed more at herself than at him. It had been a while, she'd said, and now she was obviously nervous.

But game!

He liked that, liked it a lot.

But then, there were so many things he was beginning to like about this woman...

'Will you stay and watch the sunset with me?'

As soon as Sarah had said the words she regretted them. As an invitation they weren't in the same league as 'Have dinner with me', but on top of that, didn't she usually enjoy the splendour of the sunset on her own?

Wasn't it *her* special moment of the day?

'I'd like that.'

Her gut twisted. Things were really getting out of hand when she was having physical reactions to three simple words.

And now she'd asked him, would she have to share the towel?

He solved that problem by dropping to the ground

beside her towel and picking up a handful of the coarse coral sand.

'So white,' he murmured, as she settled beside him. 'Not as fine as the sand back home, but beautiful in its own way.'

He'd turned to look at her as he'd said the last phrase but she refused to take the words personally.

'For real beauty we have to wait,' she said, nodding to where the sun seemed to be almost diving towards the horizon, the sky around it a brilliant red and gold. 'As it drops lower the colours in the sky reflect not only on the water but on crystals in the sand, as well. I've seen it pink and red and even purple at times. A painted world!'

He nodded, and she wondered about his country, about his apparent exile from it, and whether the sunset painted the desert sand with colour...

And for the first time since the accident she felt curious about a place—felt an urge to travel, see a desert at sunset, maybe other wonders the world had to offer.

'Oh, yes,' he murmured, and she set her wayward thoughts aside.

Thin bands of cloud made the explosion of colour even more dramatic, the western sky alive with fire.

He took her hand and somehow that was okay.

Comfortable even, for they were sharing something special.

The colours faded to beautiful, hazy pinks and mauves, and Sarah stood reluctantly.

'Night falls swiftly,' she reminded him. 'I need to go so I can navigate the path safely.'

For some reason she was still holding his hand.

He had taken it to help her to her feet, so had her hand just decided to stay there in his—warm and comfortable?

Seeking a distraction, she looked towards the now dark shadow of the rock fall.

'You shouldn't go back that way,' she told him. 'Come up the path and walk back down to the resort.'

He didn't answer, but walked with her to the foot of the path.

'I'd have walked you up anyway,' he said. 'I do have *some* manners.'

She paused on the first step on the path and looked down at him.

'You realise the jungle drums will be beating before long?'

He laughed, a rich, unexpectedly joyful sound that made her smile.

'So let them beat.' He came abreast of her and turned towards her, his voice softer as he added, 'Is that all right with you? Or will it make you uncomfortable?'

She smiled at his concern.

'I think I've been uncomfortable for years,' she told him, and took a deep breath to steel herself before continuing. 'They died, my husband and unborn son, in an accident, that same night I met you at GOSH. We were on our way home. Seeing you again—at the cocktail party—it brought it all back.'

'Oh, Sarah, what can I say?' He stepped up onto the narrow step, and put his arms around her. 'Nothing that would help, I do know that. I cannot even imagine such a loss, or the pain it must have caused you.'

She allowed herself to be held, perhaps even snuggled closer, the physical contact, the security of being held healing another bit of her that had been lost.

He kissed the top of her head, then asked gruffly, 'And since then?'

'People tiptoed around me, thought carefully about what they'd say, or didn't say much at all, which suited me just fine because I had no time for anything but grief.'

She eased away and climbed again, but this time with him in the lead and her hand still in his.

It had been too dark to see his face as she'd blurted out the past, but his voice had been so deep and understanding she caught up with him and stopped beside him.

Looked at him as she tried to find the words she needed.

'I've been busy putting myself back together—like a jigsaw, or a broken vase. Coming to Australia—as far as I could get from where my life had been—gave me the base, then slowly, bit by bit, I've got it just about done.'

'But pieces are still missing?' he asked, resting his hand on her cheek, his thumb wiping at a tear she hadn't realised was there.

'Oh, yes, pieces are missing.'

She smiled although she knew it was probably a weak effort, so she, in turn, laid her palm on *his* cheek.

'Even if nothing happens between us, you have given me another piece—the bit of me that can be stirred by a man—the bit that feels desire and lust. And it being a fling, well, that's right, too...'

She hesitated, unsure how to go on, surprised when he finished the words for her.

'Because losing love was too hurtful? Because you don't want to be hurt like that again?'

She pressed against him, silently acknowledging that

truth, feeling his arms around her, holding her safe from hurt for what seemed like a long time.

He kissed her then, just gently on the lips, demanding nothing but somehow making a promise of the kiss.

They turned and walked again.

'We're there now,' she said, and hoped he didn't hear the hoarseness of desire in her voice.

The man seemed to have unleashed a monster...

'My villa's second from the bottom. What time tonight?'

She was talking too fast, rattling out the words because she'd suddenly realised she had no idea how she *would* react to those jungle drums. Her private life had been private for so long, and now, inevitably, there would be talk.

Could she handle it?

'Eight o'clock?' she suggested, when he didn't answer. That would give her time to be alone, to think things through.

So many things...

'No, no, come earlier. We'll have a drink, talk. Come as soon as you're ready.'

He spoke quickly and Sarah realised he was as uncertain as she was about whatever it was that was happening between them, and somehow that made her like him more.

Not that she knew him, or anything much about him, apart from his illness and opting out of surgery.

'I'll just shower and change and walk down.'

He opened his mouth and she knew he was going to offer to come for her, to drive her down, but she put her finger to his lips and said, 'I'll walk. Jungle drums, remember?'

'And you think no one will notice you walking down to the resort?'

'They will, but I walk a lot, all over the place. "There goes Sarah again" is all they're likely to say.'

'And dinner? They won't miss you at dinner?'

Was he holding her here with fairly meaningless conversation because he didn't want them to part?

'I usually eat in my villa—I like simple meals and I'm in the habit of preparing them myself. Anything I can eat with a fork and keep reading whatever I happen to be reading while I eat.'

She knew it was time to turn away again, get inside to think, but she was enjoying standing there, looking at him, taking in the little details of this man she didn't know.

A faint white scar, like a crescent moon, on his cheek by his right ear, the little lines that played around the corners of his mouth as he smiled, the dark lashes that could hood his eyes in a split second, hiding any hint of emotion.

'Come soon,' he said quietly, and every nerve in her body ran with fire.

Harry wasn't sure how he felt as he headed back down past the laboratories and kitchens to go through the resort to his bure.

Hearing the bare bones of Sarah's story had probably cut into him more than if he'd had the details.

Not that he needed more information when he'd heard the pain still echoing in her words as she'd laid them matter-of-factly before him.

It made him want her more, yet warned him to be careful—to take this pursuit more slowly than he usually did, for, like a skittish horse, Sarah could, at any time, back away from him.

Which only made him want, even more, to hold her in his arms.

Hold her in his arms?

When had he ever wanted to do that with a woman?

Apart from during foreplay or sex…

So he had to pull back, cool off, treat this as just another attraction, a fling for their mutual enjoyment.

Not get too involved…

He *never* got too involved, mainly because he knew he couldn't offer more than an affair. Eventually he'd have to give up his nomadic lifestyle—was he a modern-day throwback to his ancestors who'd roamed the desert on camels?—and return home, to duties and to a woman his family had chosen for him to marry…

'You and Sarah made up your differences?'

Sam had emerged from the shadows of the gardens around the laboratories, and Harry could only shake his head that the message of the jungle drums had spread so quickly.

Not that he intended to respond to Sam. Whatever it was that lay between himself and any woman was private. With Sarah, it felt even more intensely private.

'How's the research going?' he asked Sam instead, and his friend laughed.

'Well fielded,' he said, patting Harry's shoulder. 'But since you asked, like any research—slowly!'

'Yet you keep at it?' Harry persisted, thinking now of Sarah's accusation that he had simply given up on the career he'd lived for.

'I love it,' Sam said simply, and Harry felt his gut tense.

He, too, had loved his job.

Could Sarah possibly be right?

Could he continue to work in the field, even if he couldn't operate?

The realisation that the encephalitis had left him with a tremor had been shattering, especially, he realised now, because it had also left him so weak.

So he'd backed away as quickly as he could—found new challenges...

Sam was saying something about the hospital, how they intended to use his donation, but he was no longer listening, his mind too busy denying that he *could* have stayed on in his field of work.

Making excuses?

They parted on the path, but the joy he usually felt walking through the beautiful resort he'd created—an oasis of peace for people harried by the busy world— was missing.

Better to think about Sarah, about courtship—well, sex if truth be told.

And *that* thought brought a degree of discomfort somewhere inside him. She was obviously vulnerable. Nothing like the strong, focussed women he usually dallied with.

So could she handle a short affair?

Well, that was all she wanted and he could understand that now. Understand her shying away from emotional involvement, understand her fear of loss...

For her this would be a kind of trial run before moving on with life.

Which, for some unfathomable reason, made him feel even more uncomfortable.

He ignored it.

They'd keep it simple, nothing too intense—keep

it light and fun, so it would be nothing more than the holiday romance, as Sarah had suggested…

Sarah sat in front of the meagre assortment of clothes in the villa wardrobe and sighed.

After the accident, she'd insisted her mother give all her clothes to charity, unable to bear the thought of wearing things that David had touched.

'So what *shall* I get you to wear?' her practical mother had asked.

Sarah hadn't been able to answer, burrowed down under the duvet, where she'd been since her release from hospital.

'I'll sort something,' her mother had said, and she had.

'I just got black and white,' she'd announced, re-turning to Sarah's flat loaded down with bags. 'Black, or white, or black and white. That way everything will go with everything else and you won't have to make choices.'

After a week of asking what Sarah might fancy for breakfast, her mother had realised her daughter couldn't make even the simplest of decisions so she'd just pro-vided a variety of meals, most of which had remained, at best, half-eaten.

Hence the poor selection of clothes Sarah still owned—black, white or black and white!

For the first time since the accident she longed for colour—for a bright emerald scarf or a red shirt…

'Nonsense,' she muttered to herself. 'You're going down there for—well, for sex, to put it bluntly. The hol-iday romance thing was just a way of making it sound better. As if it matters what you wear!'

She pulled a black shirt out of the cupboard—soft and silky, it felt wonderful against her skin, and even without an emerald scarf it *did* suit her colouring.

Loose white linen trousers came out next. They looked good with the shirt—they'd do.

She waved a mascara brush at her eyelashes, a touch of blusher on her cheeks, and added lipstick—bright red.

That was something she hadn't given up, defiantly sticking to the same brand and colour because someone had once told her redheads shouldn't wear red lipstick.

David had laughed and dared her to wear it always— so she did.

Oh, David, is this okay?

Stupid question! He'd be jealous as hell, but beyond that he'd probably understand that it was the next part of moving on and he'd pat her shoulder and tell her to go for it.

Pushing David very firmly to the back of her mind, she picked up her beach bag, threw a hairbrush, the lipstick and her phone into it, took a final look at herself in the mirror and headed out, her heart thudding so hard it was a wonder it wasn't bursting out of her chest.

She slipped down across the airstrip and into the shadows at the gate to the resort. During the rebuilding, the gate had been guarded but the area was now open to hospital staff either using the laboratories or deciding to get a meal in the small restaurant near the kitchens.

Sarah smiled to herself.

Restaurant meals prepared by Harry's 'minions'!

As she walked down towards his bure she felt a sense of peace—serenity—wrap around her, and could understand why people in stressful jobs or those in the public eye would enjoy the resort.

Here they could be totally private, each bure carefully concealed in a bountiful display of tropical plants.

And right at the end, Harry's bure. He had apparently sensed her approach for he was out his door and walking towards her, taking her hands in his, looking her up and down, nodding.

'Very stylish!' he said, then, as if they'd been lifelong friends, he kissed her on the cheek.

'Come in.'

Come into my parlour, said the spider to the fly! For the first time since she'd agreed to dinner, Sarah felt a shiver of apprehension.

Or was it doubt?

Was she ready for this?

She shook it off. Of course she was, and, anyway, it wasn't as if he was going to rip her clothes off right then and there, and she could leave at any time.

He had lights burning on the deck outside, some kind of scented oil throwing flames towards the sky and casting shadows on the greenery around them.

Inside the lights had been dimmed and soft music played, music that she didn't recognise but that was soothing to her suddenly tightened nerves.

A platter of fruit, cheese and biscuits had been set on a low table in front of a divan—*the* jug, water beading on its sides, stood beside the platter.

'I do have wine,' he said, 'but try this juice first. It is a mix of pomegranate and rosewater, my mother's special recipe.'

'No wine, thanks,' Sarah said. 'I don't drink much

and never when I'm on the island. Who knows when I'll get a call to the hospital?'

'Do you get many night calls?' Harry asked as he waited for her to be seated, then poured a long glass of the brightly coloured juice, adding ice blocks from a matching bucket beside the jug.

'Very rarely, but I'd hate to get one and find I couldn't operate.'

The words were no sooner out than she regretted them. Harry couldn't operate and she could only imagine the loss that must've been to him.

But he said nothing, pouring himself a juice, settling beside her on the divan, and raising his glass.

'To no callouts tonight,' he said, the words and the slight huskiness of his voice causing a shiver to run down Sarah's spine.

She clicked glasses with him and for the first time actually noticed the slight tremor in his hand.

She wanted to touch it, to set down their glasses and hold it in both of her hands, not exactly regulation behaviour for someone embarking on an uncomplicated holiday romance.

Except she'd told him about David and the baby, so couldn't she...?

She did put down her drink, and took his hand in both of hers.

'I imagine your loss was probably as bad as mine. I lost beloved people, but you lost your life's work.'

She looked into his eyes, leaning forward to kiss him lightly on the lips.

'I *do* apologise for what I said! Was it only yesterday?'

'Yesterday or a lifetime ago,' he said quietly, retrieving his hand and using it to touch her cheek. 'But tonight is about new beginnings, not the past, so raise your drink in a toast.'

He waited until she'd lifted her glass.

'To us and our fling. May the memories we make here on Wildfire help draw a curtain across the past.'

Sarah raised her glass to touch his, and as he clinked he added, 'We're big on curtains in my country, I think because we were nomadic people originally and lived in tents, divided, to a certain extent, by curtains. And gauzy curtains soften even the harshest of landscapes.'

The curtain idea was lovely, Sarah decided as she sipped her drink, but it was forgotten as she was tantalised by the tastes she could and couldn't identify. Yes, rosewater was there—just—and the pomegranate of course, but there were hints of spices less easy to discern.

'It's beautiful,' she said, giving up on her analysis. 'A truly exquisite, refreshing drink.'

'For a truly exquisite woman.'

He raised his glass again, toasting her, and Sarah felt the blush start somewhere in her toes and race through her body to heat her throat and cheeks.

'Hardly exquisite,' she managed to mutter, then she took too big a sip of drink and promptly choked, coughing into a hastily grabbed handkerchief.

Much to her embarrassment, he slid closer, patting her gently on the back, his thigh against hers, his heat generating even more confusion in her body.

The hand that had been patting her back somehow seemed to settle around her shoulders, and although she told herself she was turning her head to thank him for the help, deep down she knew she was waiting for a kiss.

Inviting one?

Not quite, but close!

So his mouth settling on hers wasn't altogether surprising, but the effect of it galvanised nerves in parts of her body she had forgotten existed.

The kiss was gentle, explorative, persuasive rather than demanding, yet her heart rate accelerated, her breathing became unsteady, and she clung to his shoulders to anchor herself to some kind of reality.

But even that was lost when his tongue slipped inside her mouth. She gave in to desire, or need, or whatever it was that had her pulse racing and her body burning with a heat she hadn't felt for what seemed like far too long.

They were lying on the couch now, lips still joined, although his hands were inside her shirt, her fingers in his hair, holding his head, his lips, to hers with a desperation she had never felt before.

A discreet cough broke them apart.

'Minion?' she whispered, as she dragged her lips away from his, and checked the buttons on her shirt before sitting up.

'Minion!' Harry muttered back at her, hastily adjusting his own clothing.

'You stay here,' he said, as he stood up and strode to the kitchen area, where a local worker was standing with a trolley laden with silver-covered dishes, rising steam suggesting the trolley was well heated.

Harry spoke quietly to the man, who disappeared

through a rear door, while the man she'd been so busy kissing on the couch pushed the trolley towards her.

She studied him, this man she'd just been kissing, trying to work out how and why she'd felt such a strong attraction to him.

Yes, he was good-looking—strongly moulded features, clear olive skin, dark eyebrows arched above his surprising grey eyes. But there was something else that drew her to him.

Then his wry shrug, and his muttered 'Jungle drums beating wildly now' gave her at least part of the answer. As well as being possibly the sexiest man alive, he was thoughtful and considerate, worried how gossip might affect her.

'Not to worry,' she assured him. 'It's time the islands had something new to talk about. Your friend Luke's romance with Anahera had them buzzing for a while, but it's old news now.'

He pushed the trolley over to a table already set for two, before turning around to face her, the mobile eyebrow raised.

'Does it really not bother you?' he asked.

'Not at all,' she said, then she smiled as she realised just how true the words were.

Whether it was the appeal of this man, or that the healing process was nearly complete, she didn't know, but something, probably a combination of both, had released her spirit and reawakened not only a need to live but an almost urgent desire to live life to the full.

A brief affair was just what she needed, the first step in the discovery of the new Sarah Watson.

She stood up from the couch and crossed to the table,

pausing to lift the lids off some of the dishes, sniffing the delicious aromas with renewed appreciation of good food.

'Thank you,' she said to Harry as she took her seat.

The bemused look on his face made her want to explain.

'For bringing me back to life,' she said. 'For reminding me of simple pleasures like a great meal or a really, really good kiss.'

The candlelit gloom made it difficult to be sure, but she was almost sure he blushed...

She was glowing, and more beautiful than any woman he had ever seen.

Surely one hot kiss couldn't have caused the transformation but, whatever it was, he hoped it stayed. Sitting there at the table, in her prim black blouse with the top button undone—had he done that?—revealing just a hint of shadowy cleavage, she was so enticing he doubted he'd be able to eat.

But he was the host so he lifted the first covered dish from the trolley and placed it on the table in front of them.

'The chef seems to have provided for all tastes. Do you like oysters? He's done Kilpatrick and Mornay and, on a special dish of ice, just natural ones. *Do* you like oysters?'

She smiled and his heart jolted in his chest.

'I could force some down,' she responded, 'although only for the zinc, of course.'

The teasing suggestion of the supposed aphrodisiac properties of the shellfish hung in the air between them.

Using the tongs provided, she selected half a dozen differently prepared shellfish for her plate.

'For the zinc, of course,' he agreed, but although he loved oysters he was far too mesmerised by the crispy, pancetta-topped Kilpatrick disappearing between her pale lips to serve some for himself.

'Here,' she said kindly. 'Try a Mornay.'

She held the fork towards him and he leaned forward to let her slide it into his mouth.

He was bewitched!

Incapable of doing anything more than sit in dumb silence, watching as she ate another one then offered the next to him.

He had to get real here, to take control. He was the host!

'More?' Sarah asked softly, and he ignored the innuendo in her words and placed the platter of oysters on the table between them.

And to show he was in control, he lifted one on his fork and offered it to her, his senses on overdrive as she opened her slightly kiss-roughened lips and sucked it from the fork.

So dinner became a prelude—a long, teasing period of foreplay—as they ate the oysters, crayfish and salad, then fed each other some kind of coconut mousse, as delightful as any dessert he'd ever tasted.

Or was it the company that made it so special?

She was leaning back in her chair, this red-headed woman he'd kind of pursued across the world, looking rosily replete and so damned beddable he had to keep reminding himself not to rush things.

'So?' she said finally, and although she managed

a very small smile he could almost feel her tension across the table.

He rose and took her hand, leading her back to the divan.

'We could just chat for a while then say goodnight, and I'd drive you up to your villa...'

'Or?'

Her smile was a little stronger this time, and her green eyes glittered in the candlelit room.

'Or I could kiss you like this,' he responded, sitting down beside her and demonstrating gently.

'Or like this!'

The kiss deepened, and now she was kissing him back, inviting him into her coconut-sweet mouth, her tongue teasing at his, her hands sliding underneath the back of his shirt, touching his skin so lightly he was almost sure he moaned.

Or someone had.

His body was so aroused it was only a matter of time before their movement on the narrow divan made her fully aware of it.

'Bed?' he whispered into her mouth.

'Bed!' she responded, firmly enough to excite him even further.

He quelled a mad urge to lift her into his arms and make a dash for the bedroom.

Except he'd probably drop her! He might think he was fighting fit, but, as Luke had warned, it could take years before he fully regained the strength and mobility he'd lost in the fight for his life.

He drew her close again, and somehow, still kissing, they made a less dramatic move into the bedroom.

Where she stiffened in his arms and he realised just

how big a step this was for her. He'd lost a bit of strength and the ability to do the one job he'd excelled at, the job he'd loved, while she'd lost the man she loved and a child she'd have been expecting to welcome into their family.

He eased away and took her face between the palms of his hands, looking into her eyes, at her reddened, swollen lips, remembering the taste. No, this was about her.

'We can stop right here if you like,' he told her.

And for a moment she hesitated. Then the glowing smile returned.

'And miss a night of our very short fling?' The smile widened, and he found himself wanting to watch that smile forever.

As if!

Sarah pressed her body against his, feeling his reaction to her teasing, hearing his growl as he plundered her mouth once again, backing her towards the bed while his hands roved at will over her body.

And her body responded to every move he made, so by the time he'd manoeuvred her onto the bed and was slowly undoing the buttons on her shirt she was trembling and helpless, her fingers touching his face, his hair, his chest, almost begging him to take her but lacking the words after so long a time.

And probably because he wasn't David?

A new love, even for a brief affair, needed new words, new language—language she hadn't yet learned.

Then, suddenly, words were not required. Instinct and need and want and desire all took over and although the first time was too frantic, too mind-blowing in its intensity, the second time, when their bodies had lain close and probably spoken a secret language to each other, was slow, and languorous, and so intensely fulfilling she clung to Harry, like a limpet to a rock, remembering the pleasure of maleness—the strength and sinewy toughness that differentiated men from women.

'Tomorrow?' he murmured in her ear, as they lay, spent and sweaty, once again. 'If you like, we could take the resort boat out and snorkel along the edge of the reef. It's another world of beauty out there.'

'Tomorrow,' she whispered back, 'I have a day of extremely unromantic and unbeautiful endoscopies to do, and the day after that, if I remember rightly, a double hernia op and a breast lumpectomy.'

'Ouch!'

He shuddered as she nipped her fingers on his nipple, although earlier it had excited him.

'It's a holiday romance without the *holiday* part, remember?' she said, easing away from the enticing maleness in the bed, knowing she had to get back up to the villa for the little that remained of the night. 'But I'm here to work, so daytime canoodling is out.'

'Canoodling—what a great word. Is that what we've been doing?'

'It is indeed,' she said quietly, standing up now, searching around for clothes.

It had been David's word and although she felt no guilt, the memory somehow brought him closer.

'Do you have to go?'

He was sitting on the bed, this Sheikh Rahman al-Taraq, his lower body covered by a rumpled sheet, his chest bare and smooth, slightly muscled beneath the

skin, the smile that had accompanied his question so
beguiling she almost slid back in beside him.

Almost!

'And wander back home at dawn with the eyes of
the entire island on me?' she asked. 'I don't think so.'

'Then I'll drive you back.'

He was out of bed in one lithe movement and she almost gasped at her body's reaction to this naked male—
this magnificent naked male.

'You d-don't have to drive me.' She stuttered out
the words, aware that one touch or, worse, a goodnight kiss would have her back in bed with him in
less time than it took for a single drumbeat, let alone
a chorus of them.

He had things to do!

He'd told himself, when he'd made this mad dash
across the world to a very small Pacific island to see
again the woman with the red hair, that with the marvels
of the internet he could work from anywhere.

But that had been before just one night with that
same woman had blown his mind.

Now every time he closed his eyes he saw an image
of her milk-white skin, the teasing smile, and long, slim
arms and legs, and full breasts, and—

Open your eyes and do some work!

But although the voice he used with himself was
stern, himself wasn't obeying, seeing Sarah now even
when his eyes were open.

He'd go for a walk, clear his head, or go up to the research station to see what was happening there.

Or he could take the resort helicopter over to one of

the uninhabited islands and gather some of the bark and leaves Sam needed for his research into M'Langi tea.

Or just take a long, cold, shower…

Sarah worked slowly and carefully, aware that any deviation in her concentration could have, well, not fatal but nasty results.

And there were so many new tracks to follow in her head that a deviation would be easy.

So she concentrated even more than usual, calling out results to Caroline, who was note-taking, although the new machine she'd bought for Wildfire computed the results.

Somehow, seeing them on paper made diagnosis easier for Sarah, and her assurances to patients that all was clear were far more heartfelt and meaningful.

Another patient was wheeled out to the top ward, today being used as a recovery room. Hettie held sway in there, keeping an eye on all the patients as they woke from their mild anaesthesia, helping them dress, then offering juice or cups of tea. Vailea, the hospital housekeeper, made sure there was a steady supply of both, and plenty of sandwiches for people who'd been nil by mouth for at least twelve hours.

The day wore on, finally finishing, and Sarah stripped off in the washroom and turned the shower to very hot. That way, if Hettie or Caroline happened to come in while she was dressing, they might think the red marks left on her body by the adventures of the previous night were from the water, nothing else.

Not that either of them came in, so Sarah dressed in the clothes she'd hastily pulled on that morning—for some reason all black—and headed to the small office to write up her notes.

The sun was almost setting, and she wasn't on the beach. They'd made no arrangements, she and Harry, but would he look for her there?

Think she was avoiding him?

She shook her head and sighed.

Fancy complicating her life like this, even if it was only a holiday romance.

But would she not have done it to avoid complication?

No way!

Her body tingled in secret places even as she sat in Sam's chair and pulled up the information she needed from the computer.

Tingled even more when she heard his voice.

His voice!

'Anyone need a hand, someone to stand in while someone takes a break?' he was saying.

A gust of laughter from Keanu confirmed what they both already knew—jungle drums!

'You don't need an excuse to see our Sarah,' Keanu said. 'She's in the boss's office, writing up her notes. But before you interrupt her, will you take a look at an X-ray we've just done? For some reason the pictures aren't coming through from the machine as clearly as we'd like—we've an expert coming out next week to fix it. It's a little boy with an injured arm, and Sam and I both think greenstick fracture, but another pair of eyes on it would be good.'

Aware in every nerve in her body that they'd have to walk past Sam's office to get to X-Ray, Sarah held her breath, though obviously the X-ray had been taken to Harry, wherever he was out the front—maybe outside—as the murmur of their voices had grown softer.

A brief affair, she reminded herself, but her ears strained to hear his voice again, and her body continued to misbehave.

Much as he'd have loved to spend more time with her, Harry realised that a woman as dedicated as Sarah wasn't going allow herself to be distracted from her work. So he'd learned to live with her absence during the day.

He would drift up to the hospital most days, hoping to catch a glimpse of her, hear her voice, accepting the inevitable on the majority of days when it was nothing more than exercise and a time to chat with the other staff.

But late afternoons and evenings were theirs. They'd meet on the beach at sunset, swim together in the placid waters of the lagoon, then, now that the tides were kinder in the late afternoons, walk around the rock fall to his bure.

There, they'd shower, where the simple action of soaping her back had become an erotic pleasure that invariably led further. Then they'd dress and sip their juice on the deck outside until the stars were out and their dinner had been delivered.

The second night, they hadn't eaten until midnight, when hunger had forced them out of bed.

But today was the last day—the final evening of their time together lay ahead.

The thought of never seeing her again, except perhaps occasionally if their visits to Wildfire coincided, made his gut ache, but he was a man with his life in tatters; a man with family responsibilities tugging at him; a man who could see no fixed future even for himself, let alone for anyone else.

And Sarah deserved someone better. She would never be over the losses in her life, but now that she was moving on, she deserved the best.

'Are you all right? When you didn't arrive on the beach, I—'

But he could see what she'd thought. She was breathless, her skin sheened with perspiration. She'd run from the beach to the bure thinking what? That he'd collapsed? That the encephalitis that had done so much damage to him had returned?

Not that it did, but he did suffer periodic weakness and he remembered confessing that to her.

He held out his arms and she came into them.

'I hadn't realised it was so late,' he said. 'I was thinking how much I didn't want to say goodbye.'

She pulled him closer and held him tightly.

'A fling,' she reminded him. 'It's been fun and so very good for me I cannot thank you enough, but we've still got tonight.'

'We've still got tonight,' he echoed, but as he began to unbutton her shirt he heard the helicopter take off, and a sense of foreboding made his fingers shake more than normal...

They were out on the deck, swinging lazily in a double hammock, bodies tangled together, and suddenly she wanted to know more about him and about the land where even the fountains were rose-scented.

'Tell me about your home.'

Had the fact that it was their last night together prompted the question?

Who knew? But now he was talking, his voice deep with the love he obviously felt for his homeland.

'At night in the desert the stars seem so close you could reach out and pluck a handful of them from the sky to keep in your pocket for a dark night, or to lay at the feet of a woman as homage to her beauty.'

Would you gather stars for me? Sarah wanted to ask, then reminded herself it was a holiday romance and the holiday ended tonight.

'And the sand stretches as far as the eyes can see, right up to the red and gold mountains, waving dunes of it, tempting the unwary to cross just one more hill. It is a barren beauty but I can imagine nothing more beautiful.'

Sarah moved closer, snuggling up to him.

'More,' she demanded. 'The sand, tell me about the sand.'

She felt his smile against her cheek.

'It is soft and fine, and runs through the fingers like the most expensive silk. Warm to the touch—well, too hot to touch at times, but in the shadows it will warm you, provide a bed for you, and weave itself into your life.'

And she would never see this beauty, feel the fineness of this sand—what lay between them would be memories, and on her part gratitude for his help in moving on in her life.

But was that enough?

Was that all it could be?

Of course it was, it had to be. A fling with Harry was one thing, but Sheikh Rahman al-Taraq had responsibilities to his family, to a tradition that stretched, she'd realised from snippets of conversation, back almost to the beginning of time itself.

And he also had, she remembered, a woman pledged to marry him—a woman chosen, he'd said one night, by his family—his mother. It was the way things were always done.

He was easing away from her, as if aware of her thoughts, but apparently it was hunger driving him.

'Food has yet again miraculously appeared,' he told her, holding the hammock steady as he climbed off it. 'My traditional food tonight, but little bits and pieces of it, like Spanish tapas. Do you want to sit at the table out here to eat it?'

Sarah swallowed the lump of melancholy that had formed in her throat and agreed that sitting at a table to eat was probably more sensible than handling food of any kind in a hammock.

He helped her out, held her to steady her—or perhaps just to hold her—then took her hand and led her to the small table where a platter of delicacies had miraculously appeared.

A round silver tray held myriad little dishes while a second platter had a variety of flatbreads, some thick and crusty, some wafer thin.

'Sit and taste!' Harry told her. 'The smaller, inner dishes are sauces of various kinds. You can try them by dipping bread in them, or perhaps pick up a *kibbeh*…' he lifted a small, round ball in his fingers '…and dip it in here like this.'

And he held it to her lips, his fingers trembling slightly—but, then, so were her lips and all of the rest of her body.

Whatever it was, it was delicious, a crusty outside protecting something soft and delicious—

'Eggplant?'

Harry nodded, then chose a piece of flatbread, dipping it into a steaming dish of…who knew?

'This is one of my favourites. It is *mujadara* with meat and pine nuts.'

He offered her a bite and a host of flavours she could only guess at hit her tastebuds.

'Wow!'

Harry smiled.

'Now you know how to eat our food, you must help yourself. Fingers and bread are our cutlery.'

How could the sound of a man's voice speaking about cutlery make her bones melt?

To distract herself, Sarah leaned forward and selected a small red pepper stuffed with who knew what.

'Shrimp!' she said, as once again an explosion of taste filled her mouth.

It was a culinary exploration, and with Harry's thigh tight against hers as she tried the different delights, braving all the sauces eventually, it became again a kind of foreplay.

'There are sweets,' he said, when she finally sank back, replete, against the back of the divan.

Sarah shook her head.

'If I eat again this week I'll be a pig,' she complained.

'So, we walk it off? A walk on my beach instead of yours? A *short* walk!'

He was prolonging this, their last night together, and Sarah understood, even agreed.

So they walked together past the long infinity pool at the edge of the resort gardens and onto the private beach.

'Your stars can't be much brighter than these,' Sarah told him, waving her arms towards a heaven alight with brightness.

'Don't you believe it,' he said, turning to walk back along the beach to the bure.

Sarah opened her mouth to say she'd have to see it to believe it, then closed it again.

Theirs was a brief affair, a fling—it began and ended right here on Wildfire.

Harry held Sarah tightly against his body, his mouth opening to say, *You must come and see them*, then closing again. Remembering their decision that it would be a fling, and also the complications of his life back home.

He knew of the young woman his parents had arranged for him to marry. Had even mentioned her existence to Sarah. The chosen one was everything a man could want in a wife—beautiful, well educated, a far-removed cousin in the strange marital dance of alliances the royal family had practised for centuries.

The perfect match for a ruler!

Except he didn't wanted to rule.

His brother would be better, fairer, more involved with the people.

But the woman had been chosen. She would be expecting to marry him. To let her and both their families down would be unthinkable.

So this romance would end with this last night…

CHAPTER FOUR

'SARAH, ARE YOU down here somewhere?'

Sarah broke away from him and hurried towards Caroline.

'We tried to get you on your phone, then at Harry's. I'm so sorry, Sarah, but we've brought in a baby from one of the outer islands. Will you look at him?'

Sarah turned back towards him.

'I'm sorry,' she said. 'I have to go.'

And she hurried with Caroline along by the pool, through the quiet gardens of the resort and, presumably, up to the hospital.

Although he'd wanted to go with them, Harry knew it wasn't his place. Besides, hadn't he set aside his medical career, refusing to consider practising general medicine, which would have been more or less possible with the tremor in his hand?

So that was it!

The end of an idyll!

Maybe not!

The recent collapse of the mine having damaged the extensions to the airstrip so his jet couldn't land here, it meant they'd both be on the same plane back to Cairns in the morning…

Then he laughed at the thought!

As if anything could happen on the local, gossipy plane that was more like a holiday coach jaunt than an international flight.

No, the flight would just be something to be endured, torture, really, if that was the last he'd see of Sarah.

He wandered back to his bure, kicking at the rough coral sand, remembering other sand, his sand.

Maybe it was time he went home…

His phone was ringing as he entered the bure and for a moment he was tempted to ignore it. But something about the insistent tone made him pick up.

'Harry, I'm at the hospital. I need you!'

The urgency in Sarah's voice rang in his ears as he drove the little cart as fast as it would go up towards the hospital. Thankfully no one was around, although the privacy he'd built into the place meant you rarely met with other guests and all the staff should be home in their beds by now.

Lights were dim in the ward side but burning brightly in the small ER room and farther on in Theatre.

Sarah was waiting for him, her usual black and white replaced by theatre scrubs.

'There's a baby boy, born thirteen days ago on one of the outer islands. His mother has reported no bowel movements since birth and although he appeared to be feeding normally, he's had a lot of projectile vomiting.'

'Pyloric stenosis?' Harry asked.

Sarah nodded, her green eyes meeting his.

Pleading?

'Harry, he's badly dehydrated and Sam's working on his electrolyte balance and correcting his fluid balance, but it's there, the little olive you can feel on palpation.

They called me in—they often do if I'm here and it's a child, because I do have a fair bit of paediatric experience—but he needs an op. Now! Not after the eight hours that it would take for someone to fly over, pick him up and fly him back to Cairns.'

She paused and he wondered if she could possibly be going to ask him to operate.

On a newborn when his hand trembled?

Impossible!

'I've never operated on a child so young,' she said, hurrying on as he thought, here goes, 'so I wondered if you'd guide me through it? Stand beside me and be my brain telling my hands what to do?'

'Be your brain telling your hands what to do?'

She couldn't be serious.

'Yes, it will work, I know it will. You must have done the operation a hundred times—well, a dozen at least—so what difference will it be if it is your brain telling *my* hands what to do instead of your hands, if you know what I mean?'

The words had come out in a rush, out of the lips he'd kissed only hours earlier, but the idea was ridiculous.

Impossible!

'Please, Harry!'

Lips and green eyes pleading now.

'Just take a look at him, see how urgently he needs this op.'

Harry closed his eyes and wondered if prayer would help.

He'd left this all behind, put it away from him, lived from day to day for a long time, with the loss of something he'd set his heart and soul on doing.

Forever!

But now he was healing, getting over that loss. Wouldn't this drag him back into that time?

He looked at the woman in front of him, the woman he'd held in his arms, had kissed, had made passionate love to, and—

'We can't guarantee it would work,' he said, and knew it for a pitiful excuse.

Sarah must have known it, too, for she just waited.

'He'll need a nasogastric tube for continuous gastric lavage,' he said, and the woman in front of him positively glowed.

'Oh, Harry,' she murmured, then she became the total professional he had already seen she was. 'Come on, let's get you gowned then see our patient. Ben's okay with the anaesthetic—he did a big stint in paediatric surgery before he decided to become a writer and needed something less full time.'

Ben was a writer?

Harry shook his head. That was *so* insignificant, yet it had caught his attention in the maelstrom of emotions he was feeling as he followed Sarah down the corridor.

She could do this! Sarah told herself as she led Harry to the theatre.

With one of the world's best paediatric surgeons there to guide her, she could do this.

It would be like her first surgery experience again, only this time the guiding voice would be Harry's, not some older unknown surgeon, and her hands would be steady on the instruments.

No way could she let Harry or the baby down by being hesitant or unsure.

She turned around at the door into the changing room

and smiled at the man she'd probably pressured into helping her.

Rahman al-Taraq, his name at the top of innumerable papers on paediatric surgery, considered among the top ten in the world.

Until…

She left him to change and returned to the theatre, stopping at the door to tuck her hair into a cap, pull on a sterile apron, new booties, then went to the wash basin, scrubbing carefully—newborns were so fragile—gloving up and moving to the middle of the room, where Sam and Ben stood beside the tiny baby boy, Hettie standing behind Sam, Caroline near Ben.

Waiting…

'Will he do it?' Sam asked.

Sarah nodded.

'He's changing now.'

She didn't add *I hope it works* because these people, these friends who'd helped put her life back together, were already worried enough, without her dumping any doubts on them.

Harry came in and her heart skipped a beat.

It shouldn't be doing that when it was just a passing fling.

Neither could she have it misbehaving during the operation. Little Teo was far too important for that.

Harry moved towards the operating table, his focus on the patient lying there, his eyes taped shut, wires and tubes already attached to him, overwhelming the little body.

A trolley beside the operating table held everything Sarah had felt they would need, but Harry checked it anyway.

Already gloved, he touched the child with gentle fingers, palpating his stomach, feeling the little lump that was proof that his stomach was blocked where it should empty into the intestines, and the operation was a necessity.

'So!'

He looked around at the assembled crew.

'Not my usual team but I couldn't ask for better,' he said, waving Sarah towards him.

He looked at Ben.

'You ready?'

Ben nodded and injected the anaesthetic into a tube already in place.

'You happy with the nasogastric tube, Sam?'

'It's secure and we've a gentle suction attached to it.'

'So, let's go!'

He smiled at Sarah as he said it, and for all his voice fired every nerve in her body, she set everything else aside and focussed on the little boy they needed to save.

Praying this would work, Harry began.

'Three-centimetre incision just below the right rib cage, careful of the liver, see…'

Sam was cauterising the small blood vessels, and as Harry talked he could watch Sarah's steady gloved hands following his instructions. The teacher in him kept coming out as he explained things to the others— how gentle traction with a damp sponge just here— Hettie followed that order—could bring a curve to the stomach to allow best access to the pylorus.

Each step seemed to take forever, but with such a tiny baby there were so many things that could go wrong.

Cutting too deep could be as disastrous as not cutting deeply enough.

Sarah followed his instructions with neat, sure movements, finding the side of the pylorus that lacked blood supply, placing the longitudinal cut along the wall of the tiny bead, cutting into the outer skin but not going deep enough to do any damage to the inner walls.

'Now, gently spread the lips of the cut apart until the mucosa puffs up—there, you've got it. Excellent. Now, who has the slow absorbable sutures? I use a running stitch but you can use interrupted ones.'

He watched as, with more confidence now, Sarah sewed up the layers of tissue and muscle through which she'd cut, finally asking Sam to add butterfly closures across the wound to ensure its closure.

Harry was uncertain what he felt as he left the theatre, Sarah staying on as if unwilling to leave their fragile patient.

Satisfaction, certainly, but…

Was Sarah right?

Did he have something to offer to paediatric surgery, even if he couldn't operate?

Probably, but surely it would never be enough.

No, what he was feeling must be nostalgia. He had new interests, more than enough to keep him busy, and maybe, just maybe, he could fall in line with his family's wishes and go home to learn at least something of his country's politics.

Yet the words Sarah had thrown at him that night still rankled.

And the fact that their last night together—the one

night he'd known she'd stay with him—had been cut so short rankled, as well.

How selfish was that!

Of course Sarah would want to stay with the baby.

Hadn't he needed to watch over babies he'd operated on?

They'd always seemed too fragile for the indignities he'd made them suffer, too small for him to be invading their bodies.

The dull ache of all he'd lost returned, and he realised it was the first time since he and Sarah had made love that he'd felt what had been an ever-present pain before.

Because he'd known their time together would be so short?

Surely not!

Sarah wasn't sure why she'd stayed. There were plenty of more than competent people watching over little Teo, yet somehow she couldn't leave the quiet room where machines still helped him breathe, and wires taped to his chest showed all his vital signs on the monitor above his bed.

Yet still she had to stay, as if in apology to the little one whose body she'd invaded.

She thought of Harry, wondered if he'd be expecting her, yet somehow knew he'd understand her needing to be here.

So, tomorrow on the flight back to Cairns would be their last time together. She had a few days off then a flight to Emerald in Central Queensland, a week of surgery there, patients brought in from hundreds of miles around the large country town.

While Harry, well, she'd seen the blue-and-gold-painted executive jet on the tarmac at Cairns airport from time to time. It matched the colours of the little helicopter that sat on the tarmac here at Wildfire, always ready to take visitors on a trip to one of the outer islands, or simply a flight over the marvels of the reef that surrounded M'Langi.

Harry would be whisked away in his pretty plane to places she could only imagine. Not back to the desert with its silken sands but probably to Africa to check up on his projects there, or to South-East Asia to see for himself how his mosquito eradication programme was progressing.

Harry!

Weird how they'd started out hurting each other, then—

Well, all holiday romances must come to an end.

'How's our patient?' Harry asked when Sarah appeared at the airstrip while the place was still being unloaded.

She flashed a radiant smile that hit him in the gut.

'Brilliant!' she said. 'The staff know how to treat him, and they're the best, so he'll be fine.'

Now beneath the happiness he saw her exhaustion.

'You haven't slept,' he said, and heard an edge of what couldn't possibly be anger in his voice. As if her sleep—or lack of it—was any of his business.

'I usually sleep on the plane,' she said. 'And I've a few days off to catch up anyway.'

It shouldn't be like this. Harry's mind, or maybe some other part of him, was protesting. This shouldn't be how it ended, polite nothings on an airstrip.

But what else was there?

The two of them in a bubble of—what, emotion?—

amongst the bustle of people coming and going. All words said, their time together was already becoming nothing more than a memory.

'Hi!'

The bubble burst as Ben arrived, a wodge of papers stuck untidily under one arm, a duffle bag in the other.

'Maybe I won't be sleeping on the plane,' Sarah said, smiling at the new arrival and taking the papers from under his arm.

'Did you finish this last night?' she asked Ben, who nodded happily, although he looked even more tired than Sarah.

'I'm his first reader,' Sarah explained, turning back to Harry, explaining politely, as if this was all perfectly normal.

Wasn't her body shouting that it hadn't had enough?

Weren't her fingers longing to touch his shoulder, his cheek, perhaps run a thumb across his lips?

How could she just stand there chatting about Ben's latest book, which she apparently was going to read on the plane? Now even sitting next to her was probably out of the question.

He had obviously been mad to start something he couldn't finish properly. To begin an affair that couldn't possibly come to its natural conclusion.

Holiday romance, indeed!

Yet Sarah seemed unfazed. Tired, yes, but remarkably at ease, as if their few nights together were already forgotten. As if the passion with which she'd kissed him could be turned off so easily.

Like flicking a switch!

Whereas he just wanted to rip off all her clothes—

or maybe undress her slowly—and finish what they'd started in a way more suited to a holiday romance...

Sarah hugged the mess of papers that was Ben's latest masterpiece to her chest, thankful it would excuse her from sitting next to Harry on the flight back. Ben would claim the seat next to her—previous experience told her that. He'd want to know, every ten minutes, what she thought of it so far...

But sitting next to Harry would have been agony. Already she was having trouble controlling fingers that wanted to stroke his cheek, hands that wanted to rest lightly on the back of his waist, or on his neck, or head, or, really, anywhere at all on Harry.

She wanted the licence her fingers and hands had had to roam his body, learning him by touch, while other senses devoured him, inhaling the scent of him, thrilling to the roughness in his deep voice when he made love, seeing the light in his grey eyes when she made him laugh.

Oh, Harry...

She looked his way, caught his eyes on her, and knew he, too, felt the urge to touch.

It was because their last night together had been cut short that their little romance felt unfinished. It had to be that, for her body to be wanting him so badly.

Thank heaven for Ben.

Sitting next to Harry for four hours and *not* ripping off his clothes would have been unbearable.

'Okay, folks, remember we go through customs when we land, so leave anything illegal here on the island.'

The pilot and co-pilot were ones Sarah had flown with before, and the co-pilot, in charge of loading, always began the flight the same way. At the top of the steps leading into the plane one of the two cabin staff waited, a list in his hand.

Sarah smiled to herself. The flight crew would all know who was going to be on the plane and also which of the various islanders could cause problems, often trying to smuggle a live chicken or even a piglet on board, to be part of a celebration feast with their family in Australia.

Sarah lifted her bag then felt the weight go from her hand, fingers brushing hers, sending a shock along her nerves.

Hadn't she just put all thoughts of touching Harry from her mind? Cooled down her over-active imagination and her body?

And told herself to think ahead, not backwards? It was finished, done, nothing more than they'd intended it to be—a holiday romance…

'I can carry it!' she snapped, disturbed by that shock wave when everything between them was over.

'Fight me for it?' he suggested, in the husky voice he used in bed, the same husky voice that fired her entire body with waves of heat and desire.

She shrugged but kept her fingers on the handle.

How weak are you, Sarah Watson, to be pretend holding hands when the holiday is over?

The seemingly never-ending flight finally ended, the plane touching lightly down in Cairns, releasing Sarah from the agony of knowing Harry was directly behind her, his body bombarding hers with subliminal messages as she battled to read Ben's book.

Harry stood up to lift her bag from the overhead

compartment, then quelled her protest with a look as he carried both her bag and his from the plane. So they stood together in the queue for Customs, the messages no longer subliminal as their bodies touched when the new arrivals pressed forward.

Memories of other body-touching made her knees go weak, and it was only with the utmost resolution that she shut down the memories.

She was saying goodbye to this man, and had to be cool, calm and clinical about it.

Deep breath!

'I don't know what to say, other than goodbye,' Sarah murmured to him, knowing her voice would be lost in the hubbub and only Harry would hear it. 'And to say thank you. It was really, really special to me and I'll always remember our time together.'

'Wow, that seemed to come right from the heart!' Harry muttered angrily at her. 'Did you really feel it necessary to offer polite nothings?'

'Well, what have you to say?' Sarah demanded, wondering just why this particular man could fire her temper so easily.

He didn't answer and, looking into his face, she realised he didn't know—any more than she had when she'd struggled to find words.

The tightness in her chest eased, and she touched him on the arm.

'There are no words,' she said softly, 'other than goodbye.'

'Or I might need to be in Wildfire in six weeks,' he suggested.

Sarah shook her head.

'I'm taking time off after this next trip—six weeks—

time enough to go back to England and spend some decent time with the family, rather than a rushed three-day Christmas visit.'

Although the prospect of going home no longer had the appeal and excitement that had been there when she'd booked the trip.

Damn the man, he really *had* got under her skin!

Flurried, she repeated her goodbye but more firmly this time...

Goodbye?

Harry's brain struggled to grasp the concept.

This was goodbye?

Of course it was. What had he expected her to say?

And as she'd said, what did he have to say that would be better?

He was still struggling with these thoughts when she stepped up to the arrivals desk, had her passport stamped, then lifted her bag from the floor near his feet, opened it ready for a cursory inspection, and moved through the barrier.

Getting farther and farther away from him, especially when the man stamping passports wanted to talk about his country.

Ambelia!

The word stuck in his head and a sudden rush of homesickness all but overwhelmed him.

He wouldn't go to Africa. His pilot would have to change their flight plan.

He'd go home.

And perhaps there he'd forget the woman with the vibrant red hair and slim white body who had just disappeared through a door and out of his life...

CHAPTER FIVE

IT WASN'T EXACTLY BORING, Sarah's trip west. In fact, there were some interesting patients and she liked Emerald as a town.

But something was missing and, loath as she was to admit it, she knew it was Harry's presence—Harry's lovemaking, and just Harry himself.

Stupid, really, because now that she'd rediscovered her sexual self, she could enjoy a relationship with anyone she fancied.

Providing, of course, they fancied her back.

Not that she'd be slipping straight into bed with them as she had with Harry. No, she could take her time, get to know someone, let a relationship build.

Perhaps that was why she was missing Harry—because the time they'd spent together could hardly be called a relationship. They'd done it all backwards.

Maybe, given time, she'd have got over the need to brush her fingers across his skin, or trace the tiny scar beside his ear, or stroke her hand down his firm thigh.

Got over the need to touch him at all.

'You want to come into town for a bite to eat? There's that great Indian restaurant just off the main drag.'

Ben had knocked on the door of her motel room and poked his head through the gap.

He'll want to talk about his book, Sarah thought, and shook her head, then regretted it when she saw the disappointment on his face.

But tonight she just wanted to brood.

To try to work out why a certain Rahman al-Taraq had stirred the embers of her dead emotions back to smouldering life.

In five days?

Well, less, in the end.

The attraction had begun, on her side anyway, from the moment she'd helped him from the water with the stonefish sting.

And the discomfort—the shock, really—of that slow burn through her body had made her hit out at him.

But he *was* wasted, doing what he did.

Thankfully, her mobile belted out a jaunty tune at that stage of her brooding over Harry, and a desperate search for it distracted her completely.

So when she finally found it and answered, and a deep, sultry, masculine voice said, 'Sarah, I need you,' she almost fainted on the spot.

Had she conjured him up out of her thoughts?

And was need the same as want?

But he was still talking, and she had to listen. Apparently, Harry had touched down in Ambelia to complete chaos. His youngest sister had just given birth to her first baby, and he suffered from exactly the same problem as the baby boy on Wildfire Island: pyloric stenosis.

'She wants me to do the op, Sarah, and you know I can't. But we've done it together once before and could do it again. Will you help me?'

'Oh, Harry, how can I? We're at opposite ends of the world.'

'My plane is on the way to Cairns as we speak. Will you come?'

She *had* to go!

She'd needed him and he'd come.

'Can your pilot fly into Brisbane? It's easier for me to get quickly from here to there than from here to Cairns. I've one small op in the morning, then I'll get an afternoon flight to Brisbane. Should get in around five in the afternoon.'

'He'll be waiting at the airport for you,' Harry promised.

Sarah didn't know what to say—even how to say goodbye. Not without sounding over formal, which would come across as cold.

Harry broke the silence.

'Thank you, Sarah.'

Then he was gone.

Had that really happened? Or had she imagined it?

But, no, she was still holding her mobile in her hand so she'd been talking to *someone*.

And now excitement began to build. Changing her flight was easy on the internet and she messaged Harry to let him know her flight details.

Then she sat down, ran her hands through her hair, and considered what she'd agreed to do.

Which was when the enormity of it all hit her.

She'd see Harry again, see the desert and feel the sands run through her fingers like silk. Of course, she'd have to check she could fly from there to London, and if it was summer here would it be cold in...

She dug through memories of her time with Harry but nowhere could she find the name of his country.

Back on the net, she ran a search on Rahman al-Taraq and discovered the country was Ambelia and that Harry was heir to the throne.

A sudden sadness filled her when she saw Harry still listed as a gifted and world-renowned paediatric surgeon.

She shied away from that, looking up Ambelia instead, reading that the discovery of copper as well as the ever-present oil had made the country very wealthy.

'The wealth is spread amongst the people,' the article continued, 'although many Ambelians live in traditional ways, with nomads following ancient trade routes in the desert, and fishermen using the traditional dhows to ply their trade.'

Excitement stirred, the thrill of the unknown mixing with the physical sensations she was experiencing at the thought of seeing Harry again.

It was only when he'd ended the call, heart hammering in his chest at the prospect of seeing Sarah again, that Harry realised it had a downside.

He had his own suite of rooms and his own staff in a section of the palace, but his mother would insist that Sarah stay in one of the guest suites.

On the far side of the rambling building!

And while jungle drums might be quick to pick up gossip, they were as nothing compared to the speed of palace gossip.

It came of having too many staff with too little to do, but most of them were fourth- or even fifth-generation retainers to the royal family, which made sacking any of them inconceivable.

So Sarah would be here, but not here for him—not close enough to touch, to slowly undress, to lie in his bed and make those little breathy moans when he pleasured her.

His body tightened.

There had to be a way.

But even reserving a suite for her in one of the six-star hotels was out of the question.

Hotels, too, had staff, and though he'd spent little time at home in the last years—in fact, since he'd been ten and had gone to boarding school—he was still easily recognisable...

He sighed, cursing himself for not thinking this thing through. To have her here, so close, but untouchable—

Hell and damnation, he couldn't touch her anyway. His engagement was due to be announced, already postponed because of Miryam's baby...

He had to see speak to his mother, ask her to speak to Yasmina—to explain.

Explain just what, exactly?

That a woman with whom he'd had a brief holiday romance was coming to the country and he'd like to continue their relationship?

Great thing to dump on any woman, but to someone who was related, whose family had already agreed to the marriage...

Impossible!

But it was equally impossible to marry Yasmina when he had feelings for Sarah. The exact nature of the feelings were a little confused, but they did exist...

Didn't they?

He sighed.

Even with the little he knew of Sarah, he knew she'd laugh at the situation—the two of them close but not close enough…

He gritted his teeth and messaged her the name of the acting consul in Brisbane who would meet her plane and take her to the private section of the international airport. Youssef would see her onto the Ambelia-bound jet.

Damn!

He could have flown out with the plane, met her in Australia, then at least he'd have had the ten hours' flight time to…

Make love to her?

Because that *was* all he wanted, wasn't it?

Now uncertainty raised its head, but he decided to ignore it. He had enough to do organising someone to meet Sarah at the airport, visiting Miryam at the hospital, arranging staff to be on standby for the op on his little nephew.

More than enough to do, so why was his mind stuck on seeing Sarah again?

Perhaps because she might not be quite as excited about seeing him?

A brief affair, a fling, she'd said.

Finished when their time on the island ended.

But we didn't have that final night, a pathetic voice cried in his head, and he quelled it firmly, called someone to take a message to the stables for his horse to be saddled.

He'd forget about Sarah, go for a ride and watch the sunset from his own beach—hundreds and hundreds of miles of it.

* * *

Sarah sat back in the plush leather chair in the luxury jet, playing with the buttons that made the chair lie flat or worked the small TV in front of her.

She'd been offered champagne, juice or water before the plane had even taken off, but had stuck with water, aware she could become dehydrated on the flight and wanting to arrive as alert as possible. The operation had already been delayed just getting her to Ambelia.

Ambelia—Harry's home…

Once in the air, she was fed, the spices in the food, the little dishes of sauce reminding her of her last night on the island.

That last night they were supposed to have been together.

Reminding her of their mutual desire to drain as much pleasure as possible out of it.

But that had been then and this was now, and as it had been nothing more than a brief fling, it was best to tuck it away in her memory and think of the future.

Her future!

The four years in Australia had helped her heal, but maybe it was time to think of returning home permanently. Her parents weren't getting any younger, and Australia was a long way off if she was needed urgently.

And operating on the baby had reminded her of her ambition…

She sighed and settled back into her seat, letting it recline so she could put her feet up and doze.

As if that was going to be possible, when Harry was at the end of this journey and memories of their short time together played like movies on the inside of her eyelids.

* * *

The ride had been a good idea—racing his stallion across the dunes behind the palace had been invigorating. The problem was, he shouldn't have dismounted, shouldn't have picked up a handful of sand and let it run through his fingers.

Was this to be his fate in life, that even the simplest of pleasures would remind him of Sarah?

He rode home less swiftly, and went to visit Rajah in his palatial enclosure. The big animal trumpeted softly in greeting, and not for the first time Harry wondered just how old his friend might be. He'd been born in the circus and the man who had owned him had been sure he was at least twenty when Harry's father had bought him.

Too old, the man had said, to be retrained to live in the wild. But that was thirty-five years ago.

Could elephants live into their fifties and sixties?

Rajah's trunk explored Harry's pockets, seeking a treat that he'd usually find.

'Nothing today, old boy,' Harry told him, scratching at the more tender skin behind the animal's ear. 'I'm too out of whack to have thought of it,' he continued. 'There's this woman, you see…'

And he poured out the story of Sarah, and attraction, and the frustration that lay ahead for him—perhaps for both of them—while she was a guest at the palace.

Rajah nodded wisely, but Harry knew he probably needed more than an elephant's wise nod to sort out his mind and body.

The sun was rising over a distant horizon as they came in to land at Ambelia, and Sarah stared with wonder at the world she was about to enter. There were the dunes Harry had told her of, stretching to red and golden mountains, and there was the sea, dotted with fishing boats so small they looked like toys.

The tall towers of a modern city glinted in the early morning sunlight, but it was the large walled estate beyond the city that drew her eyes. Minarets reached towards the sky, round domed buildings stood among rectangular ones, courtyards seemed to be scattered like embroidered handkerchiefs between the buildings and the whole complex within the walls was ringed with more greenery and formally laid-out gardens.

Then it was gone, the city and the old walled complex, and they were coming in smoothly to land.

Now there were no distractions.

Very soon she would be seeing Harry again.

Or maybe he'd be at the hospital with his sister and her child, and she would have to put up with the flock of butterflies dancing in her stomach for even longer.

The crew unlocked doors and a stairway slid into place, then Harry was there, right in front of her, his face tense and pale as if he, too, was feeling uncertain about this meeting.

Only it wasn't Harry, it was Rahman al-Taraq, a gold-braided circlet holding his snowy white checked head-cloth in place, more gold dribbling down the front of his immaculate white gown, tiny embroidery stitches outlining an opening in the front.

And she stared—probably open-mouthed—at the man she knew yet didn't know, then his eyes looked deep into hers and her lungs seized up.

A slight smile twitched on his lips.

'Sorry about the regalia. There was stuff I had to do on the way to the airport.'

Still trying to regain control of her lungs, and other rioting body parts, all Sarah could manage was a vague nod.

Had he read just how paralysed she was? He bent over, reaching out to undo her seatbelt, his voice shaking slightly as he said, 'Thank you for coming, Sarah,' in that deep, husky voice that played havoc in her dreams.

She had to get with it—she was here, this was Harry, they would operate on the baby and then she'd be gone.

His being dressed in his traditional garb reminded her of just how big a gulf lay between them culturally, and also reminded her he had a wife-to-be waiting somewhere in the shadows—possibly in one of the white buildings she'd seen from the plane, the ones in the walled complex.

So forget the husky voice and dreams and show some strength.

All she could muster was the smallest of smiles.

'My pleasure,' she said, as his hand took hers to help her to her feet. 'I was coming in this direction anyway,' she added, because if she didn't talk she'd forget about strength and do something stupid like throw herself into his arms. 'It's on the way home to England, more or less, so it's no trouble...'

Her voice trailed away as Harry pulled her towards him and held her in a gentle hug, then kissed her on both cheeks. She could feel his heart hammering against his ribs, probably in tune with hers, but the cabin crew was waiting for them to leave the plane, so there'd be no proper kiss.

Not in Ambelia! Not now she'd met Rahman al-Taraq and realised just how impossible this situation was.

Would there ever be a proper kiss again?

Hardly!

It had been a brief affair—they'd both understood that.

So why was her body betraying her with its heat? And, come to that, the tight grip on her hand felt like Harry's rather than Rahman's.

But this *wasn't* Harry from the resort. Here he was the ruler-in-waiting, and here he had a woman pledged to marry him and subjects who'd take a great interest in every move he made.

The robes made those facts perfectly clear.

Sarah sighed.

Unless there were very roomy linen cupboards at the hospital they might have to forget the attraction side of their relationship—put it behind them.

For the duration of her visit?

She sighed again, but softly.

In truth, it was probably forever, given his position, and the wife in waiting, and the fact that it had only ever been a holiday romance.

Warmth hit her as she exited the plane, but it was pleasant, soft and dry as it enfolded her body. She was following Harry down the steps, and he stopped at the bottom and turned to take her hand, presumably to help her make the last step safely.

His fingers gripped hers hard, and she squeezed his in return.

'This is possibly the most ridiculous mistake I've made in my entire life!' he muttered angrily. 'I must know at least twenty excellent paediatric surgeons in

London that I could have flown in, but no, I had to complicate my life—and probably yours—by demanding you.'

And Sarah smiled.

At least they were both suffering.

No matter who he was—Harry, heir, husband-to-be—it was obvious their affair felt unfinished to him, too.

Not that that was much consolation so she forgot about the man who was now striding ahead to a waiting limousine, and forced her mind to think about what lay ahead—to think about a tiny baby who needed the expertise of both of them.

'Did you sleep on the flight?' he asked abruptly, opening a rear door of the car for her.

'Most of the way,' she replied. 'I spend a lot of my time in planes far less comfortable than yours, and have learned to sleep on all of them.'

She looked directly at him, refusing to be distracted by the robes and headdress, and looking instead at his pale, hypnotic eyes and the grim set of his lips. At the tiny scar she'd traced with her fingers, and which she knew grew paler when he was stressed.

Very pale. The way it was now.

His tension was evident, but she was here to do a job, not to dally with this man, no matter how appealing more dallying might be. So right now she had to make it plain that the visit was for work.

She took a deep breath and, well, prattled…

'I think we learn to sleep at any time in any place during our training, don't you? It's probably nearly as important as learning anatomy, given the lives we lead, especially during our early days in hospitals.'

Now it wasn't just his lips that looked grim. He was positively glowering at her.

But she wasn't to be put off by a glower.

She waited until he'd stalked around the car and got in the other side behind a silent driver, then, determined to keep things as casual as possible between them, she asked, 'How's the baby? Is the op urgent? I'm confident I could go straight into Theatre, although a shower and a cup of tea would be a nice way to relax first.'

'A shower and a cup of tea?' he repeated, the disbelief in his voice so strong it was like a physical force. 'Is that all you can say?'

She turned towards him and, hoping the driver who was now concentrating on getting the vehicle through the airport traffic wouldn't see the motion, she took his nearest hand and held it in both of hers.

'What else is there to say, Harry?' she said softly. 'Or should I call you Rahman here?'

She squeezed his fingers.

'What we had was wonderful, but I know, and you know, that we can't take it further—not now you're home and definitely not here, where word of any relationship between us would get back to the woman you are going to marry and so, I'm sure, shame your family as well as hurting her.'

He bent his head, his hand still in hers, although now his fingers gripped hers as if he thought she might let his go.

'The baby,' she repeated quietly. 'Tell me about the baby. Let's concentrate on that and think about the rest later.'

He raised his head but didn't look at her.

'He's doing well. He arrived fourteen days early,

which was hardly a problem, but the stenosis wasn't picked up until the projectile vomiting started three days ago. I think the pylorus wasn't totally blocked at first. Since the diagnosis, he's been having limited amounts of parenteral nutrition, and the doctors are keeping a constant check on his electrolyte balance and hydration.'

'And his mother, your sister?'

Now he turned to look at her, and she saw the ravages that concern for his sibling and her child had left on his face.

'Miryam's been wonderful. She stays by his bedside night and day, her gloved hand through the window in the sterile crib, touching him, talking to him. Her husband is there as well, most of the time, but I've learned women are far better than men at handling things like this.'

His face lightened and he almost smiled.

'You'd have thought I'd have worked that out long ago, but until it becomes personal there are things you don't see. Miryam's husband has to leave the room to go into a corner somewhere and cry from time to time. It's the only way he can keep going for his wife and child.'

Harry squeezed her fingers, adding, 'I've felt for him—felt his tears—teared up myself. Pathetic, really.'

'Nonsense,' Sarah said, removing her hand before he broke the fingers she'd need for the operation. 'This is your family, people you love, in pain and trouble. You're entitled to get emotional about it because you're human. Miryam probably cries sometimes as well, and her husband holds her and gives her strength to continue. But, being a man, he won't let her see *his* tears in case she loses faith in his strength.'

Grey eyes studied her face for a moment, then the slightest of smiles touched his lips.

'Maybe I *was* right to call you…'

Was that a compliment? Sarah wondered, then told herself to stick to the plan—be practical, do the job, go home to England…

'We're nearly at the hospital. If you're sure you're happy to go ahead—after your shower and cup of tea—I'll let them know.'

He lifted a cell phone out his pocket and spoke words Sarah didn't understand. Soft, strange words that touched her heart, while her eyes were on the man himself, on the hand that held the phone and the fingers that had brought her body such pleasure, on the lips she'd kissed, the neck—

'They'll be ready. I didn't know what tea so they'll make a selection and you can choose.'

CHAPTER SIX

THE HOSPITAL WAS UNBELIEVABLE, reasonably new and laid out in spacious, beautifully maintained gardens. The buildings were white, two and three stories high.

'Each unit is complete,' Harry told her, as the limo pulled up at a portico entrance, 'ER, Outpatients, Radiography, Theatre and wards. There's a central pathology lab that does all the blood and culture work. This is the children's block. You can see it's built around a central courtyard. Even after generations of urbanisation, we still like to be close to the outdoors. Many family members of hospitalised children will sleep in the portico outside their relative's room.'

'So the hospital was built to accommodate families?' Sarah asked, looking around in wonder at the beautiful interior—the entrance was like that of a five-star hotel.

'Family is important to us,' Harry said, although she realised it was Rahman talking, and Harry only when he touched her lightly on the arm and added, 'I am sorry. Talk of family must be painful.'

She turned towards him, wanting to look at him, to make sure it *was* Harry under the unfamiliar clothing.

'I only lost part of my family. The rest of them helped me through, kept me going, until I ran away from their kindness because I knew I *had* to do it myself—to put myself back together again, possibly in a way that was different from their expectations. Do you understand that?"

She need not have asked, because the understanding was there in his eyes and in the little extra pressure of the hand that rested on her arm.

He had to stop touching her, had to take his hand off her arm, yet how could he? A friendly touch like this was all the contact he would be able to make with her, surrounded as he was by the ever-present interest of the people of his country.

He'd been away so long he attracted extra interest wherever he went and he knew the gossip would be rife.

Was he here to stay this time?

Would he take over from his father, as had been ordained by his lineage?

Had he come home to be married?

It was time he produced an heir...

He guided Sarah towards the theatre area of the building and handed her over to a young woman who was hovering near the tea room.

'Would you show Dr Watson the bathrooms when she finishes her tea?' he said, then weakened. 'No, don't worry, I'll have tea with her. We can talk about the operation, then I'll show her the way to the showers.'

'How weak am I?' he said gruffly, aware his annoyance was with himself. 'Wanting just a few more minutes alone with you, but not in the way I'd like to be alone.'

Sarah turned her green eyes on him, her pain clear to see.

'Harry, we *have* to put what happened between us in the past. You have duties to your family here, a woman expecting to marry you. We'll do the op then I'll be gone. Why torture ourselves needlessly when we know this can't go anywhere?'

The shock was like a knife going into his chest.

'But you have to see the sand—my sand—and meet Rajah. I have so much to show you—'

She lifted her hand in front of her, an obvious stop signal, and shook her head to emphasise the point.

'No, Harry,' she said softly. 'I cannot do anything with you. With a guide, perhaps, but not with you. You know as well as I do the attraction is still there and being alone together would be stupid. You have—'

Now *he* stopped *her*.

'A duty. I'm sorry, that was stupid, but…'

She poured a cup of tea, and sipped at it.

'There are too many buts, Harry. Too many ifs and buts and whys and maybes. We had fun together, shared passion for a while, but now it's back to real life for both of us.'

He felt anger flare, and wanted to rage at her, or more probably at himself. She was just too calm, talking about passion without a hint of it in her face or voice.

And hadn't it been more than that?

She finished her tea and stood up, collecting the small bag he'd carried off the plane and set beside their chairs.

'Bathroom?' she asked, and now she smiled and he was back on Wildfire, soaping her long, white back, counting down the vertebrae with his fingertips, inciting them both to—

Passion!

'This way.'

He spoke abruptly and led her out of the room, pushing open the door to the women's dressing room, calling to someone inside to show Dr Watson where everything was kept.

'See you in Theatre?' Sarah asked, and he heard anxiety in her voice.

Instead of calmly and quietly discussing what lay ahead of them, he'd been fuming over her withdrawal from him—a withdrawal he deserved. After all, *he* was the one with commitments.

He nodded a reply then calmed himself down before seeking out Miryam, wanting to speak to her, reassure her, before he had to change for Theatre.

His youngest sister was in the theatre waiting room, together with his mother, two other sisters and a horde of aunts and cousins crammed into what he'd always thought a reasonably sized room.

His mother seized him first.

And right at the back of the crowded room, his father, sitting in an armchair, two grandchildren on his knee, quietly watching over his family.

'She's here, the doctor?' his mother demanded, and Harry assured not only her but all the clamouring relations that Dr Watson had indeed arrived and would be in Theatre within minutes.

He took Miryam's hands in his.

'I know it's hard to think so young a baby, your baby, has to have an operation, but it is simple and Dr Watson is an excellent surgeon. I will stand behind her and tell her what to do. She will be my hands, so your baby's life will be in my hands, as you wished.'

He kissed her cheek then held her close for a moment, though inwardly aware that it was his sister's insistence he operate that had brought him and Sarah together again.

Having done the same operation with Sarah once, he had known this was the safest way to proceed. Other paediatric surgeons would have their own ways of working and would not want him hovering over them. But while having Sarah close again when he'd been trying to convince himself it was all over was bad enough, having her close and untouchable was even worse.

He had to stop thinking about their relationship—or lack of it—and direct all his thoughts to what lay ahead.

Focus on his sister's baby—his nephew. This was family.

All his attention must be focussed on the baby.

He could do this, he reminded himself as he introduced Sarah to the team already in place, then stood beside her but a little behind her, to keep out of the way of people operating instruments.

He *could* do this, although as he spoke and her hands moved, he felt as if they were not two people but two parts of a whole, working in tandem, the feel of her body close to his so familiar it was like part of him, her fingers on the scalpel his as well as hers.

It was a slow and careful process. So tiny an infant had a lot of very necessary paraphernalia tucked into his little body, all of which must be kept intact.

But Sarah never lagged, never slumped or hesitated, her hands sure and steady as he told them what to do.

And when the job was done, the baby taken to Recovery, he touched Sarah on the shoulder. Her hair was hidden by the theatre cap, her face pale from the strain of the work she'd done, but to him she was as beautiful as he had ever seen her.

He couldn't let it end.

Not the way it had, and not now, with hard words between them.

Yes, it had been a fling, but there'd been something deeper between them, something he was sure Sarah felt as keenly as he did. It was up to him to give them more time together—time to look past the passion that they'd shared and maybe just a little way into the future.

Time…

'I have a few things to do,' he said, 'the family to see. Will you wait for me in the tea room?'

She looked at him as if trying to assess his reasoning, but in the end smiled and nodded.

'I could be a while,' he added.

She simply said, 'I'll wait.'

Right! Family first—reassurances for Miryam, then a quiet word with his mother. She would know the best way to go about things, and, though undoubtedly she'd be disappointed in his decision, she'd understand it was the right thing to do.

Probably!

Sarah waited in the tea room, nibbling at the delicate pastries that were brought to her, chatting to other staff who'd been in Theatre with her as they stopped for tea or coffee before heading back to whatever jobs they had to do.

They came and went through an inner door, so when the outer door opened she turned, expecting it to be Harry, feeling disappointment when she saw the tra-ditionally dressed woman, a long black cloak covering whatever she was wearing underneath, a headscarf wrapped in some mysterious fashion around her hair.

Miryam, the baby's mother!

She moved on soundless feet across the room, sinking down beside Sarah, taking her hand.

'I must thank you for what you did today, for saving my baby. I know Rahman feels the loss of his profession very keenly, and he must have great trust in you to ask you to do it.'

Sarah, embarrassed by the praise, tried to brush it away.

'It was nothing—anyone would have done it—'

'No, not anyone. Only someone who has lost a child would understand my terror. Rahman told me of your accident. It makes your action today even braver.'

Tears were sliding down Miryam's face, and Sarah put her arm around the woman, blinking away her own tears.

'There, he'll be all right now and I would think he'll be out of Recovery very soon. You'll want to be with him, I know.'

Miryam nodded, then found a tiny scrap of lace handkerchief somewhere in her voluminous robe and wiped her eyes.

'I'll go but you will be in my heart, forever in my gratitude for what you did.'

She rose gracefully, touched Sarah on the shoulder then glided away—soundlessly again.

Sarah mopped her own eyes. The young woman's gracious words had touched her heart, and once again she wondered about her future.

Was it too late to go back—to join a paediatric surgical team and start again at the bottom to achieve that old dream?

She heard the door but no footsteps—not Harry, then—and turning saw another figure robed in black.

The grey eyes told her all she needed to know even before the woman introduced herself as Hera, Rahman's mother.

Uh-oh!

Sarah put aside the discomfort she felt at this gracious woman's presence.

'Hera is a pretty name—wasn't she a goddess in ancient times?'

Hera smiled.

'The goddess of women and marriage. Our families go back a long, long way,' she said, and although she possibly didn't mean as far back as Greek gods and goddesses, she was making a point.

A 'keep away from my son' point?

An 'I'm in charge of his marriage' point?

Sarah didn't have a clue, although she didn't feel any animosity as the woman settled on the couch beside her.

'I wish to thank you for coming to help our family and invite you to stay with us for as long as you like. Your luggage has already been taken to the palace, and my son will bring you there when he finishes his business.'

Oh, dear—what now?

'That's very kind but I don't know that I can stay,' Sarah began, while her mind searched wildly for an excuse. She was too superstitious to say one of her family was ill in case it came true and she brought illness on someone she loved, but—

'Rahman, or Harry, as I suppose you call him, would

be disappointed if you didn't stay,' Hera told her. 'He is looking forward to showing you his country and introducing you to his family—and Rajah, of course.'

Not wanting to argue that her hanging around was probably the last thing Harry wanted, Sarah seized on Rajah.

And smiled!

'Yes, I'd like to meet Rajah. Harry talked so much about him, but—'

'But there is something between you and my son that would make things awkward?'

Sarah could only stare at the woman by her side. How could she know if Harry hadn't told her?

The she felt the softness of the woman's hand on hers.

'Harry is seeing to things now. We women—and women all over the world—make plans for our children, but the children don't always follow those plans. We know this even as we make our plans, and know not to be disappointed when they don't work out, because all we want is for our children to be happy.'

'But the plans you had—they're important for both family and political reasons, aren't they? Harry loves his country, I can hear it in his voice whenever he speaks of it. He's not a man to walk away from his responsibilities!'

Now Hera smiled, her grey eyes twinkling.

'We knew he was going to be different from the beginning. It wasn't only his passion for an elephant but his insistence on choosing "Harry" for his school name, and his determination to make it to the top of his chosen profession. After the encephalitis, he came back to us a broken man, but now he's back, and whatever path he's chosen will probably be tough because he's not a man who does things the easy way.'

She paused but Sarah knew there was more coming.

'But whatever he does his family will always be behind him. Always!'

She repeated the last word very firmly, although Sarah was still trying to fathom the entire conversation, not just the final declaration.

Uncertain how it had happened, Sarah found herself accompanying the gentle Hera back to the palace in another long, dark limousine. Hera pointed out the city sights, but the city fell behind them as they drove out along a wide, flat road that ran along the shoreline, sunlight dancing off the slightly ruffled blue water.

'I will leave it to Harry to show you around,' Hera said. 'But for now you must rest. The flight, the operation… We have been taking advantage of your good nature. And if you need to contact your family to let them know you will be a little late, there is a private phone in your room.'

If she was dazed by being practically kidnapped by this woman, Sarah was even more dazed—or perhaps dazzled was a better word—by the sight that met her eyes as she entered the palace.

The floor of white marble, veined with fine threads of gold and stretching, it seemed, forever, was littered with bright rugs. Having left her shoes with others outside the door, Sarah found the rugs so soft beneath her feet it felt like walking on a cloud.

An arched opening on the left led into a room even more spacious than the entrance hall. Within, a crowd of women in dazzling dresses ceased their chatter when they saw Hera, rushing towards her like a flock of bright budgerigars.

'The baby is all right?'

'The doctor came?'

'Rahman saved the child?'

The questions flew through the air and, understanding them, and the accents, Sarah realised that all the women must have been educated in England or America.

Although maybe they spoke French and Spanish and even Russian with equal ease.

This was a country that would be full of surprises, and now she wanted so much to stay, to talk to the women, listen to the things they talked about, learn just a little about their culture and customs and how they lived in a world that was being fast-tracked into the twenty-first century.

But staying would mean seeing more of Harry, staying would mean seeing Harry knowing what they'd had was over—unable to touch him, to lean into him, to share his bed...

Unless?

What had Hera meant when she'd said that Harry was seeing to things?

And would Hera have asked her to stay—insist she stay—and that Harry show her around if her presence would be an offence to a bride-to-be?

But being here, being with Harry and not able to touch him, kiss him, sleep with him would be torture.

These frantic thoughts were tumbling through Sarah's head as Hera was hushing the women, telling them she would speak with them soon, and summoning a slight young woman to show Sarah to her room.

'You must rest,' Hera said to Sarah. 'Your luggage is

already in the room, and there is a bell to ring for anything you want. Anything at all!'

And Sarah believed her, for hadn't a six-year-old been given an elephant?

Not that she wanted any exotic creature—only Harry.

Although here, wasn't *he* an exotic creature—so far out of her realm she'd barely known him?

Although her body had.

'This way,' a soft voice said, and Sarah sensed she'd said it earlier, while thoughts of elephants and Harry had swirled in her head.

She followed the woman along the length of the great entrance hall, passing rooms off to both sides, done in different colours, but all with the bright carpets on the marble floors and silky-looking curtains swathing all the windows.

At the end of the hall they turned down a passage to the right.

'This is for visitors,' the woman said. 'Madam Hera says you are to go in Yellow—because of your hair she said, although your hair is red, is it not?'

Sarah agreed her hair was indeed red, and as some of the women who had surged around Hera on their arrival had touched her hair and murmured to each other about it, Sarah had realised it made her different.

'Maybe she thought the red hair would clash in another colour of room,' she said, and the woman smiled.

'And maybe, too, it is because Yellow opens to its own courtyard and you can be private.'

Private alone, or private with Harry?

Surely his mother wasn't giving tacit consent to their continuing affair?

Well, hardly affair. And there was no way they could

be having sex in a courtyard at the palace no matter how private it might be.

Could they?

No and no and no. It had been a fling and it was over. Harry had duties here, and his position demanded respect, so he could hardly be seen dallying, or even thought to be dallying, with a guest—especially when he was due to marry someone else.

Sarah looked around a room that could have been lifted out of a very posh decorating magazine, and sighed.

It was beautiful, no doubting that. Not *yellow* yellow but more lemon, with some hints of lime thrown in. Pale lemon silk curtains hung across the wide doors that opened onto a covered area outside, with steps leading down to an oasis of green in the small, enclosed garden beyond.

An embroidered silk spread in the same colour as the curtains covered the bed, where pale lime cushions were piled at the end. The lime colour was repeated in the ornate bedside cabinets and the carved-legged writing desk over by the windows that held the phone and heavy writing paper.

Through an arch opposite the windows was what must be a dressing room, walls of cupboards with the same lemon silk on the doors, padded and indented by lime-green buttons.

And through that door a bathroom, the floor and walls the same white marble that provided flooring throughout the palace, with stacks of pale lemon towels on an antique cabinet, a shelf above it containing a range of toiletries to shame most department stores.

'You will be comfortable? I will bring tea and you can rest, Madam Hera says.'

So what Madam Hera says is law, Sarah thought as the woman left the room. Well, she'd take the tea but she doubted she would rest. There were too many thoughts and impressions swirling in her head. Rahman al-Taraq was there—a little too often—but other things, like right and wrong, and Harry and fiancées, and family, and traditions, swirled in the mix until her brain gave up in sheer exhaustion and she pulled back the coverlet on the bed, flung the cushions to one side, and slept.

So much for not resting. That was Sarah's first thought when she woke two hours later. A tea tray sat on the little writing desk and to her delight the teapot was insulated and the tea still piping hot.

Either that or the almost silent servant had come and gone at intervals to replace the pot.

However, it had happened, the tea was wonderful, and the little pastries, hidden beneath a snowy-white napkin, delicious. So, with something in her stomach, Sarah debated. Did she want to explore the little courtyard, or shower before she went exploring?

Shower, she decided, but first she had to find her clothes.

Not difficult when she opened the first cupboard door and saw her things hanging there, her underwear neatly stacked in a drawer beside them.

But the clothes brought a sigh. She'd packed for an English winter and because she'd been in air-conditioned vehicles or the hospital or this coolly luxurious palace, she hadn't felt hot, but she was relatively certain it would be hot outside.

The thought had barely left her when the silent woman returned.

'Madame Hera said there are other clothes you might

wish to wear, both European and traditional. You will find them here, and here.'

The woman walked to the other side of the dressing room and threw open more cupboard doors.

It was like walking into an upmarket boutique, as the clothes came in all colours, shapes and sizes and all still held store tags dangling from them—though no sign of price!

Feeling she'd look foolish in a local outfit no matter how the colours called to her after four years of black and white, she chose instead from the first section, sticking to loose linen trousers—black—and a silk shirt.

She'd reached for the white shirt but something seemed to nudge her hand and she lifted out a similar one in emerald green—the colour of the scarf she'd wished for on the island.

'Thank you,' she said, smiling at the woman before collecting her own underwear and heading for the bathroom.

In there, she took a deep breath. She wouldn't take advantage of these people, kind as they were, but would wear the black slacks and some simple shirts while she was here.

And she'd use her own toiletries and cosmetics, no matter how enticing some of the expensive body lotions and face creams might look.

But she did wonder just what happened with this kind of generosity. She had no idea how many guest rooms the place might hold, but if all rooms were supplied with brand-new toiletries for every guest, there must be awful wastage.

That or the servants must all have perfect skin!

CHAPTER SEVEN

HERA HERSELF CAME to collect Sarah to take her to dinner.

Sarah had just returned from a short sortie into the courtyard and realised that whatever she wore during the day it would have to cover all her skin, as, at dusk, the air was still hot, so by day the sun must be fierce.

Although maybe she'd be gone tomorrow.

Maybe Harry would realise the impossibility of their being here together, and what?

Ask his mother to rescind the invitation?

Hardly.

So he'd avoid her. That would be the best. Hera would ask someone else to show Sarah Ambelia...

'Please don't think we are offering gifts with the clothes we have for visitors to wear,' Hera said, after checking out Sarah's outfit. 'We have the clothes available for those who don't intend a visit here and would have nothing suitable to wear. I think it would be best for you to choose some of our traditional tunics and trousers for daytime, to protect your beautiful skin.'

'But—' Sarah protested, before a small hand on her arm stopped her objection.

'You must not think that anything is wasted. If visitors do not wish to take with them the clothes, or, for that matter, the toiletry items they have used, we pass them on to several houses we have for women from less fortunate circumstances, women who are escaping abusive husbands or families, or who have nowhere else to go.'

Sarah nodded. She knew such organisations existed back at home, and in Australia, even some that took half-used bottles of shampoo and other toiletries.

But here?

Hera must have read her thoughts, for she smiled a little sadly and said, 'Unfortunately it happens everywhere, my dear. People are people all over the world. But, come, we have only a few of the family in to dinner tonight, but they will be anxious to meet you.'

Because of the baby? Or to check out suspicions of a connection between her and Harry—Rahman?

Sarah followed Hera back towards the front of the building, turning off through another arch about halfway down the hall. Although the room was large, it was so full of people she had to wonder just how big the al-Taraq family was if this was just a few of them.

Then Harry was there—Rahman, for he was in his robes—but the hand that touched hers and fired her skin was definitely Harry's.

This was bad, worse than bad—horrendous. How could she be close to him and not look at him, touch him, remember what they'd shared?

'I will not introduce you to all of them at once,' he said, and she realised she should have added listen to him to the list. 'But my other sisters and my brother-in-law and a favourite aunt or two—that will do for tonight. Are you up to it?'

He sounded as if he was flirting.

But they'd never really flirted.

Maybe because she'd forgotten how and their attraction had been strong enough to skip that bit.

But looking up at him, seeing the smile in his eyes, yes, he was definitely flirting.

'And just how many more relations are there that that will do for tonight?'

'Countless,' he said, with a chuckle that stirred every nerve in her body.

Heaven forbid, she was here in a palace, with the man she…loved?

'I don't think I should be meeting any of them,' she muttered at him as the possibility that her feelings might run that deep shocked her into anger.

'It is all right, Sarah,' he assured her. 'Everything will be fine. Just relax and enjoy yourself.'

Relax and enjoy herself in a room full of exotic strangers?

'Just for me?' he murmured, and her bones melted at the smile accompanying the words.

'Why not?' she responded, deciding he was right. Whatever happened in the future, there was no reason not to enjoy the present—and what a stupendous and astounding present it was.

So she allowed herself to indulge in the pleasure of Harry's hand on her elbow, in the warmth of his body close to hers.

He guided her through the crowd and she nodded and smiled and turned away thanks and praise for her coming to help the family, all the time wondering how many of the women were seeing through their 'professional colleagues' act and wondering just how well they knew each other.

Probably all of them because in between introductions Harry was whispering in her ear, teasing her with memories of other whispers.

And she was responding, with quick retorts and, well, almost flirting.

'Time for dinner,' Harry said, giving her elbow a secret little squeeze.

He ushered her towards the back of the room, and Sarah realised it was nothing more than a very large ante-chamber, opening out through more arched doors to a splendid spacious area, a huge mat already loaded with platters of food dominating the middle of it.

'We do have rooms with dining tables and chairs,' Harry said quietly in her ear, 'but tonight with all the women's gossip antennae twitching in the air, the sheer numbers meant we needed to eat in here.'

He led Sarah to one of the long sides of the mat where Hera already sat, her legs tucked neatly to one side. Several other women were sitting now, so Sarah followed their lead, tucking her legs to the side, the cushion beneath her making the position quite comfortable.

She looked around, noticing for the first time that there were children present—a lot of children. They must have been lost in the crowd of adults or maybe had been playing outside.

'The men, like men everywhere, I believe, will gather at the far end,' Hera said, nodding her head to where Harry was striding along the side of the room.

'That way,' Hera added with a sly smile, 'they can pretend to be above the gossip, although they will insist on hearing every word of it from their wives when they get home.'

'You are comfortable to sit like this?' a voice on Sarah's other side asked.

Sarah turned to look at the woman. She was one of Ha—Rahman's sisters, she was sure.

'When I came home from school and university, it would to take me ages to get used to it again, and even now we sit on chairs at a table at home, so my legs aren't as supple as they used to be.'

The woman was beautiful, a red tunic giving her classic features, smooth olive skin and deep brown eyes a radiance that Sarah could only envy.

'What did you study at university?'

Sarah wished she remembered the woman's name but most of her mind had been on not revealing just how much pleasure a simple touch on her elbow could bring.

'I got a First in psychology,' the woman said. 'I thought it might help me fathom just how this family works.'

She smiled and gave a little shrug.

'It hasn't helped,' she added, 'but I'm useful around the hospital both with patients and staff.'

She studied Sarah for a moment before speaking again.

'I suppose you're sick of people thanking you for what you did for Miryam's baby, but we do all appreciate it. You're probably wondering why Rahman didn't ask one of his old colleagues from London, but—'

'But apart from having to see and talk to them, which would have hurt him immeasurably, he wouldn't have wanted to insult them by standing in on the operation, which was obviously what your sister wanted.'

'And *I* did psychology!' Neela—she was Neela,

Sarah remembered—said, smiling again and patting Sarah's hand.

'You must love him very much to have seen all of that,' Neela said, and Sarah was so flummoxed she dropped the piece of bread she was eating and stared at the other woman—probably with her mouth agape.

'Me?' she finally managed. 'Harry? Love? No, no, you have it wrong—we're colleagues, maybe friends, although we've not known each other long, that's all.'

The words must have come out in such a mangled mess that Neela patted Sarah's hand again, while Hera, on the other side, nodded as if with satisfaction.

The meal was superb, platter after platter of delicious food, some with tastes Sarah recognised, others new and different.

'You have seen the resort Rahman has built?' Hera asked.

'Yes. It's very beautiful and the research he's funding at the laboratories there is very important.'

'Ah, but is it enough?' Neela asked, and without thinking Sarah shook her head.

She turned her attention to a small ball of nuts and seeds that Hera had put on her plate, but Neela was persistent.

'And?' she asked.

Sarah shrugged, still hoping to avoid the discussion.

'I know him well,' Neela said, 'and love him so I—all of us—only want the best for him.'

Sarah turned to look at the woman who was still probing—a psychologist's probing or a sister's?

'When we first met,' she admitted to Neela, 'I accused him of opting out of the paediatric surgery he was so good at—of walking away when he still had so much to offer current and future surgeons, even if he couldn't operate.'

She paused but something in Neela's eyes forced her to continue.

'I think I hurt him quite badly,' she admitted.

'Did he hit back at you?'

Sarah stared at the other woman in disbelief.

'It's not witchcraft or even psychology, but I know my brother well. He only hits back when he's cornered and refuses to admit to something he's accused of.'

Sarah just shook her head.

How they'd got onto the topic of her and Harry's meeting at Wildfire—memories of which still had the power to hurt her—she didn't know, but the way Neela spoke of her brother only made Sarah feel more deeply for him and his pain from the loss of the work he'd loved.

'So what are you going to do about getting him off this wild circling of the world, checking this, checking that, and back into the work he loves?'

'Me?'

Sarah was so astonished by the question the word came out as a squeak.

'Yes, you! You're a colleague.'

Something gleamed in Neela's dark eyes. Was it suspicion they might be more than that, or was she simply attempting to sort out her brother's life?

'Yes, but in a minor way. Not in the same league as your brother—not anywhere near where he was, and even could be.'

'Yet you've had him back in Theatre, a place he'd sworn he'd never see again, not once but twice.'

Sarah breathed deeply. She was drowning here, drowning in Neela's persistence.

Yet still she had to protect the man she...

Loved?

Surely not—not in four or five days. Love didn't happen that way.

'Well?'

Had her face changed? Had Neela read something in it as the shock of the random thought hit her?

She could handle this!

'They were both emergencies,' Sarah said firmly. 'Now, tell me, I don't think Harry ever said where he was kept, but is Rajah here at the palace?'

'Nice change of topic,' Neela told her, but she was smiling as she spoke so Sarah guessed she wasn't offended.

'You haven't met Rajah yet?'

It was Sarah's turn to smile.

'I arrived, went to the hospital, played Harry's hands for the operation, then came here, slept, showered and here I am.'

'I suppose it has been a big day for you, but I'll tell Rahman you were asking. He'll probably introduce you to Rajah tonight. It's not far to walk.'

Neela was smiling again but although Sarah couldn't read guile in the lovely eyes, she guessed it was there.

But why?

She had to have missed something somewhere. Harry—Rahman—was supposed to be marrying some woman chosen by his family, so why was his sister suggesting the pair of them have a walk after dinner, probably in moonlight?

Please, let there not be moonlight...

Sarah looked along the rows of people seated comfortably at the sides of the mat, and in spite of his traditional clothes picked out Harry easily.

Because he was looking at her?

You *will* not blush, she told herself, although she could already feel the heat crawling up her neck.

She coughed to cover her confusion then remembered Harry moving close to her, patting her back, turning it into something else—a first embrace.

She glanced his way again but he was speaking to a man in a business suit by his side.

'That's my husband he's talking to,' the super observant Neela told her. 'Most of the menfolk aren't here tonight. My father and Miryam's husband will be at the hospital until they are sure the baby is out of danger, while my other brother is overseas at present—America, I think, maybe at the United Nations—and the husbands of the other women avoid what they call "gossip gatherings".'

Neela paused then added, 'But that doesn't stop them giving their wives the third degree when they get home. I think men are probably worse gossips than women, although they'd never admit it. Do you agree?'

'I've not really thought about it,' Sarah answered honestly, not having had many men close to her in recent years to judge such a thing.

Although…

'My husband hated gossip,' she said. 'Working in a hospital, which are always hotbeds of it, he used to talk about how even the smallest of stories doing the rounds could grow into something large enough to break up a marriage, or hurt someone badly in some other way.'

'Your husband?'

Of course Neela had seized on that!

'He died,' Sarah said, and turned her attention to Hera before Neela could probe further.

'This pastry is delicious,' she said to the older woman. 'Is it a traditional recipe?'

Hera smiled at her.

'Neela wearing you down, is she? I'd like to say it's because of her job, but she's always been the most inquisitive of all my children and definitely closest to Rahman.'

'She's been very kind,' Sarah said weakly, suddenly aware that Hera would have heard most, if not all, of the conversation.

But Hera must have understood because she talked about the pastry, soaked with lemon and honey, and other traditional dishes; about the bread that was made fresh every day, and how oil and dates had been stored in the nomadic days of the family.

Sarah listened, mesmerised by the stories of the past that Hera told, Neela joining in from time to time, prompting her mother's memory or offering her own favourite stories.

'I'm glad to have a settled life,' Neela said, 'but the desert stays in the soul of our people. All of us have to get out beyond the palace walls to listen to the silence or the wind shushing the sand against the dunes, to feel the sun warm us through to our very souls. I think maybe Rahman forgot that in his frenetic journeys around the world.'

Hera nodded then smiled as she added, 'But he is home now, and for that we must be thankful.'

'That and other things, I suspect,' Neela said, but

Hera ignored her, instead directing Sarah's attention to a new platter of desserts that had arrived in front of them.

She tasted coconut in the dessert and again looked along the mat...

He couldn't help but glance her way, checking her as she sat demurely there beside his mother.

It was an unbelievable sight in some ways, but there she was—visible as well as present in the air around him, for he could feel her presence, too.

Sarah...

Neela's husband was telling him about some great business deal he'd pulled off, but Rahman—he *was* Rahman here, although to Sarah he was Harry—well, whoever he was, wasn't quite as fascinated in the story as his companion thought him.

He was too caught up in wanting Sarah—Sarah, who'd entered the ante-chamber with his mother, a vivid green shirt framing her pale face and flaming hair.

Having only seen her in black and white, the sight of her had somehow filled his heart with gladness that she was here, in his home, except...

He wanted her, wanted her more badly than he'd ever wanted anything, even the continuation of his career, but of course he couldn't have her, not physically, not here in Ambelia, where jungle drums were as nothing compared to the whispers of the sands.

So the want ached inside him as he nodded to keep his brother-in-law convinced he was rapt in the story, and ate, and tried not to look along to where Sarah sat.

Neela was beside her—that was dangerous. Neela could draw out secrets from a stone.

Beautiful, that's how she looked—Sarah, not Neela.

'Are you actually interested in what I'm telling you?' his brother-in-law demanded, and Harry smiled and shook his head.

'Not really. I must be tired—the flight home, the baby...'

Stupid excuses really when all of the family were almost as at home in their jets as they were on the ground, and the baby's situation had never been drastic.

'Worried about the changes to your future? Neela tells me the woman's changed her mind.'

Harry shook his head at the speed with which news travelled in this country. He and his mother had only spoken to Yasmina's mother that afternoon.

Now, *that* had been fun!

He'd felt such a worm, but even if nothing eventuated between himself and Sarah, he'd known he couldn't, in all fairness, marry another woman.

Meeting Sarah again, maybe even loving her—could it be love? He had no idea—but even if it wasn't love—

'I cannot believe this!' he muttered to himself.

'That the woman broke it off? You didn't even know her. It shouldn't bother you,' his brother-in-law protested.

Harry—he was Harry when he was thinking of Sarah—shut his lips tightly so the growl that had threatened to escape was captured unspoken.

But not unfelt—

Was this what frustration felt like?

He'd been shocked and angry when he'd learned he couldn't operate again, but he'd slapped away the useless emotions and plunged into other work.

Probably so he didn't keep thinking of the loss.

But he hadn't been frustrated.

Only too aware the word was more used in a sexual context than a general life kind of frustration, he was now feeling both.

Frustrated that he couldn't touch the woman he— well, wanted to touch, and frustrated that his life no longer provided a clear path in front of him.

When he'd taken up the search for an encephalitis vaccine he'd been drawn into other activities that had kept him constantly busy, but now?

Was it because the vaccine, for some forms of the disease, was about to go to clinical trials that he was no longer satisfied, or had Sarah's dig about minions being able to do what he did, dug deeper than he'd realised?

Then, being back in Theatre again, not once but twice…

This time the growl did escape but fortunately his brother-in-law was telling his neighbour on the other side about his latest business coup so it probably went unnoticed.

He glanced towards Sarah again and saw his mother rising from her place, Sarah and Neela with her. As the senior male present, it was his *duty* to escort his mother from the room, wasn't it?

He rose lithely to his feet and moved quickly towards them, taking his mother's arm to lead her to one of the sitting rooms where coffee would be served.

Behind him, people were standing, jostling each other, talking in louder voices now the feast was over, but he only had eyes for Sarah, and ears for the mur- mur of her voice as she asked Neela what happened next.

'Next I think Rahman takes you to meet Rajah,' his

irrepressible sister said, throwing him a wink over their mother's head.

'What a good idea,' his mother said, and Harry frowned.

It would be just like his sister to have sussed out that there was something between them, but for his mother to be pushing them together?

'Go with Rahman,' his mother said, detaching her arm from his hand and easing Sarah towards him. 'I will explain to the family that you are tired but need some fresh air before you retire.'

After which, for his benefit, he knew, his mother repeated, 'Fresh air.'

Neela grinned at him, but Sarah was looking so lost he took her elbow and drew her away from the head of what had become a procession towards the room where coffee would be served.

'You look beautiful,' he told the woman beside him, as he led her down the long hall towards the rear of the main palace building.

'Well, I'm not sure about that, but I can tell you I've never been so nervous in my life. I had no idea what was going on in there.'

'Neela pressuring you for answers?'

Sarah looked at him now, and smiled.

'Just a bit!' she admitted. 'But I doubt she got much she didn't know. She's aware you're unhappy away from the job you love. I think your mother knows that, too.'

Harry shook his head.

'Perceptive women in my family,' he muttered. 'Did they, perhaps, come up with answers to my plight? They know full well I can't operate any more.'

'But you could still be involved,' Sarah insisted, stopping to look directly at him as she spoke.

He shrugged his shoulders, and nodded to the man who was opening the wide back door for the pair of them, and producing, to Sarah's obvious surprise, the shoes she had kicked off at the front door what seemed like another life ago.

'I think that's where we came in,' he said. She heard what could only be a rueful note in his voice.

'That was only my opinion,' Sarah protested, 'and you'd awoken bad memories, so I struck out at you, but that doesn't mean what I said was wrong.'

'Heaven save me from opinionated women,' Harry grumbled, but the woman by his side didn't respond. Instead she stood and gazed around her, apparently taking in the beauty of this, the kitchen garden, with its neat rows of citrus and stone fruit trees, a fountain playing in the centre of the path that lay between the rows.

'It's an orchard but you've made it beautiful with symmetry and patterns like the carpets inside,' she murmured.

It was Rahman who appreciated the compliment but Harry who took pride in the woman who had seen the design for what it was.

'We try to echo the patterns of carpets in all our gardens,' he said, taking her hand and bringing it to his lips to kiss it lightly on the back.

He felt her shiver of response, and his own acceleration of the need he'd felt since she'd first arrived in Ambelia.

And cursed…

It was a dream.

Being here with Harry, in this fantasy palace with

smooth marble floors and carpet gardens beyond the doors, and on her way to meet an elephant.

She was asleep—it had to be a dream—but the surge of feeling through her body when Harry's lips brushed her hand suggested that she must have been awake.

Awake, and oh, so aware of the man beside her...

But he was who he was—Rahman here, not Harry—so a furtive kiss beneath a sculpted apricot tree was not going to be an option.

She could smell the faint hint of roses in the water in the fountain—more fantasy, a land where fountains sprayed rosewater—and walked towards it by the side of the man she couldn't kiss.

And she knew with terrible certainty that she shouldn't have come—shouldn't have answered his plea for help, for all he'd answered hers.

For seeing him again, having him beside her like this, she couldn't help but realise the holiday wasn't over—if what they'd had had really been a holiday romance.

Not for her, anyway.

'He's down this way,' Harry said, breaking into her musings and guiding her down a side path where raised beds, set out in precise geometric patterns, held garden vegetables.

Sarah told herself to lighten up, to relax and enjoy the wonder of this new experience—to set aside all other thoughts and feelings and live for the moment.

Easier thought than done when Harry's light touch on her arm joined them, providing a conduit for messages to hum between their bodies.

Although that would probably be happening without the touch, she admitted to herself, then realised they'd left the garden through an arch in a tall earthen wall and were entering what appeared to be a jungle.

'A jungle in the desert?'

Harry laughed.

'With water we can grow anything, even jungles, and while the sea along one of our borders provides us with water for desalination, we will never be without it.'

Another gate, again through high earth walls, this one carefully locked with a key code for entry.

Harry called and to Sarah's delight an animal—probably an elephant—answered. Then, rumbling towards them from the shadowed trees appeared the huge bulk of the animal he called Rajah.

'But he's beautiful,' Sarah whispered, awed by the huge beast who stood so quietly in front of them.

She reached out and touched the rough hide on his trunk as Harry made formal introductions.

'Sarah, Rajah. Rajah, Sarah.'

The big beast seemed to nod, and Sarah stepped back a little, needing to take him in more fully.

'I've never been this close to one before—never realised just how big they are.'

'He's a beauty,' Harry said, so much pride in his voice Sarah had to laugh.

Harry looked at her for a moment, then he, too, laughed.

'Some first date for a woman—being introduced to an elephant.'

Sarah studied his still-smiling face.

'Is it a first date, Harry?' she asked.

'I think so,' he said. 'I know we skipped that bit on the island but, given the circumstances, I thought I could make up for it here. Take you places, show you things, while we get to know each other better.'

'But are you free to do that? Your mother said something about you seeing to things, but are you free?'

He frowned and she wondered, if he'd broken the arrangement, just how hard it must have been for him.

'I could never have married another woman while feeling the way I do about you. I'm not even sure how that is, which is why we need to go back to the beginning, leaving out the lust part and just get to know each other.'

'And why would we want to do that?' Sarah asked, as too many emotions jostled in her head.

He grinned at her.

'Well, for a start the lust part is impossible here, where every move we make will be watched and broadcast far and wide. I do have *some* responsibility to my family. I hadn't thought it through—I needed you for the op, but I also needed to see you, not even considering that *seeing* each other would be all we'd be able to do.'

'And fully clothed at that,' Sarah teased, as she realised just how he must have felt. 'But why the courtship?

The smile disappeared, and he frowned slightly.

'Because it's the right thing to do,' he said firmly.

Whatever, she decided. If it meant spending a little more time with him, even time made agony because they couldn't touch and kiss, she'd take it.

'Okay,' she said, then to her surprise he took her carefully in his arms and kissed her. Not a heated kiss of passion, like ones they'd shared before, more a first-date kiss, a goodnight kiss...

Or was *goodbye* lingering behind it?

CHAPTER EIGHT

SARAH DIDN'T ASK, simply satisfied to be with Harry as they talked beside the elephant then wandered back through the beautiful orchard, hands linked and bodies touching, and back into the palace.

'I think I'll show you the souks—the markets—tomorrow,' Harry announced as he handed her over to another young woman. 'Lea will take you back to your room and bring breakfast in the morning. Is eight too early for you? I would like to get out before it gets too hot.'

It was beyond weird, Sarah decided, listening as Harry spoke to Lea, apparently giving her orders for the morning.

'I have told her to make sure you have something suitable to wear—well covered so the sun doesn't damage your skin.'

Such ordinary words, but his eyes were saying other things.

Saying that he cared about her?

Loved her?

She frowned and he reached out and smoothed the frown away.

'Don't worry, everything is arranged,' he told her. 'And tomorrow I will show you the souks.'

His fingers slid down to rest lightly on her cheek.

'Goodnight, Sarah,' he said, then turned and walked away.

'This way,' Lea said, her English clear, unaccented.

So why had Harry spoken to her in their native tongue? Had he said more than telling her to make sure Sarah covered up?

'He told me to make sure I take special care of you,' Lea said, apparently reading Sarah's mind. 'It is unusual for him to speak our language in front of a guest so you must be very important to him.'

Was she?

He'd said not to worry—everything was sorted—but was he speaking of the marriage arrangement? Was it because it had been sorted—his betrothal broken?—that he could take her out on dates? He'd said he could never marry another woman while he felt the way he did about her, but what way did he feel exactly? And if that feeling ceased, what then?

Sarah shook her head, suddenly exhausted. She sank down on the bed in the beautiful room and shook her head when Lea offered help.

'I'll be fine, thank you. I'll see you in the morning.'

The girl disappeared on silent feet.

Too tired to do anything more than brush her teeth and wash her face, Sarah stripped off her clothes and climbed into bed. She had pyjamas somewhere in her luggage, but again they were for winter in London.

London. She must phone her parents, let them know when she'd be home.

But when *would* she be home?

And what time would it be there now?

Her brain refused to think about it, so she turned over and went to sleep on a mattress that seemed more like a cloud than something solid, and with a faint rose scent lingering in the pillows beneath her head.

Roses and Harry and an elephant called Rajah— they'd be entwined in her mind forever.

That was her first thought on awakening to a bright, sunny day—perhaps all days were bright and sunny here—and Lea bringing in a tea tray, asking what she'd like for breakfast, offering to fix a platter of the things they usually ate.

'That sounds lovely,' Sarah told her, sitting up with the bedclothes wrapped around her.

As soon as Lea left, she leapt from the bed, had a quick shower, and pulled on a clean towelling dressing gown that was folded on a shelf in the bathroom.

Decent now, she poured some tea and took it across to the window so she could look out at the small court-yard garden while she drank it. There was something magical about it because, just looking at the patterns of the hedges and paths and the different greens in the garden, she felt at peace with the world.

Yes, she had a 'date' with Harry, and had no idea what would happen next, so she'd just take life as it came, enjoying the company of the man she was pretty sure she loved, for all the impossibility of it.

For now, just being with him would have to be enough.

Harry had an early breakfast with his mother, enjoying the traditional tastes of the yoghurt with honey, thick date bread and milky coffee.

'Are you happy, my son?' his mother asked, and he could only stare at her, for she rarely asked personal questions. But when she did, she would expect an honest answer.

'Not entirely,' he admitted, 'although having Sarah here, being able to show her a little of our country, that makes me happy.'

'You are from very different worlds,' Hera said, watching him over the rim of the wide cup while she sipped her coffee.

'I know that, little mother,' Harry said. 'Just as I know, and I think you know, that my little brother would be a better ruler.'

'So you could move to her world?'

Harry shook his head. He had no idea where Sarah's world would be. She'd escaped to Australia to get over a tragedy but she was rebuilt now. Would she want to continue to live there? Might not her parents want her nearer as they aged?

London! Could he live in London again without regretting every minute of every day that he had lost?

'I don't think the question of either of our worlds will arise, little mother. I think now Sarah has found herself again, she will realise how much the future has to offer her. I may not be part of it.'

His mother was silent. Which was just as well, because when he said those words, he suddenly realised that since breaking the arrangement with the family of the woman he was supposed to marry, he had not considered whether marriage lay ahead for him and Sarah.

He'd just known he couldn't continue to see her— even for a date—while he was promised to someone else.

But in saying the words—the 'not being part of her life' bit—he'd felt pain, deep within his body, and he knew he wanted her, perhaps needed her, beside him forever.

Somewhere...

'When you look at all the sandals and shoes outside the different doors, I have to wonder how my shoes always end up outside the door I'm going out of,' Sarah said, turning to Harry with a puzzled frown as she slipped on her shoes.

'There's no mystery,' Harry told her, 'as those of us who live here probably have sandals at every door, so the servants know the strange shoes in the line.'

'And know what door the strange-shoe wearer will be using next?' Sarah teased, and Harry smiled.

His mind might be in turmoil over what lay ahead, but his body was so happy to be with Sarah, even if it was only for one more day, that he probably wouldn't stop smiling.

How asinine!

But she did look beautiful. She was wearing traditional flowing trousers in a pale orange colour and a long-sleeved tunic over them, with embroidery around the hem and cuffs of the sleeves in a darker colour, almost the red of her hair.

On top of it all, she'd slapped on a wide-brimmed orange hat.

'Your mother found this for me,' she said, pointing to the hat. 'She's worried I might get burnt but I've used plenty of sunscreen, and you said we'd be back home before the day got too hot.'

Home?

Could Sarah ever think of Ambelia as home?

It was important because he'd realised on this visit that no matter where he lived, Ambelia would always be home.

Just happy to be with Harry again, on their own, out on a date, Sarah sat in the big four-wheel drive vehicle and looked out at the country they were driving through as they left the palace.

It wasn't desert, but rocky, red-gold country, and red cliffs scoured by the wind.

'They're like the cliffs at Sunset Beach, aren't they?'

Harry smiled.

'I thought you'd like them.'

Like I like you, Sarah thought, as her eyes remained focussed on the countryside while her mind mused over 'like' and 'love'—two small words, but very important in the whole scheme of things.

Because they led to bonds, and, no matter how much people thought they could manage on their own, most needed friends and family, people they liked and loved.

And 'hated', probably, but that was a far uglier four-letter word—

'This road ahead is my father's pride and joy.'

Harry's voice brought her out of the internal debate she was having, and she looked ahead to see a wide motorway, lined by palm trees and with a median strip planted with smaller, squatter trees that still looked like palms.

'Dwarf date palms,' Harry said, pointing to the smaller trees. 'My father likes to play around with plants and helped develop those. He says they make it easier for children to eat dates straight from the tree, and every child should have such pleasure.'

The pride in Harry's voice told her how close his family were, something she'd suspected when she'd met so many of them the previous evening.

'That's a lovely idea, but how many of them are skittled by the cars roaring down this motorway?'

'Not one,' Harry replied, pointing an overhead walkway, looking more like an exotic sculpture, with steps twisting down to the median strip.

'Those walkways are scattered along the road—about every two hundred metres—and are built to resemble climbing frames in playgrounds so the kids can have an adventure on their way to grab some dates.'

Sarah was about to ask if they were used when she heard the excited shouts of children racing each other down the twisting stairway.

Children!

There'd been children at the dinner, so obviously they were important to the families.

Don't think about it, just enjoy them.

'Where do they come from?' she asked, seeing the little forms darting among the small trees.

'Beyond the noise barriers are quite large housing developments. A lot of the overseas workers live out this way. Many come from very poor and crowded cities and having space is paradise to them. As the city has grown we have needed them for the skills they bring, from architects and doctors down to people who can drive a back hoe.'

Looking beyond the taller palms, Sarah could now see the noise barriers, painted with various scenes of both desert and the sea.

'And here's the city,' Harry announced, and there it was, tall towers rising from the barren ground into the bluest of blue skies. 'We skirt around it to the old town. There are shopping malls and other stores in the city, but for a taste of Ambelia as it was, we keep the old city mostly undeveloped.'

Ahead, earthen walls like she'd seen at the palace came into view. Harry pulled into the shade by a wide arched gate.

'You can take vehicles inside, but do so at your own risk. The roads are jammed with old cars, bikes, donkeys and camels, but, come, you'll see for yourself.'

They walked through the gate into a world of noise and colour.

'Here on the right are the camel markets. Once a week, breeders bring their camels here to sell or trade. Many people still live in the old way and use camels for transport, but today they are mainly bred for tourism and for racing, and as tourists like pretty camels, there's great competition to breed the prettiest.'

Sarah smiled.

'A camel beauty contest,' she said, looking around the covered stalls where a few of the animals rested.

Harry took her hand and squeezed her fingers—first-date style—and although she tried to tell herself it didn't mean anything, her heart leapt at the touch.

'Now we're into the markets proper,' he said. 'This area is for fabrics and clothes.'

'Yes, well, I could have guessed that one! But how could anyone choose?'

Sarah looked around in disbelief as traditional outfits danced on hangers on both sides of the narrow alley. Bolts of brightly coloured cloth stood amongst

the outfits, and trimmings dangled temptingly from
rods across each stall.

'No prize for guessing this one,' Harry said, when
suddenly they were surrounded by metalware. Large
jugs and huge pots, silver, bronze and brass, gleamed
in the sunlight, the intricate patterns incised into them
flashing out 'buy me' lures.

'The shapes are so beautiful,' Sarah murmured, lifting up a tall, graceful jug, running her fingers down its
exquisite lines, thinking of the jug in Harry's bure that
had brought them both together.

'They are traditional shapes, going back thousands
of years,' Harry told her, as she thought of her luggage
and reluctantly put the jug down. 'All such household
items, even plates and platters, were made in metal so
they could be easily transported without fear of them
being broken.'

Sarah moved behind him through the crowds, as
aware of him, in this crowded alleyway, as if they'd
been alone together. Wanting to touch him, brush lightly
at his shoulder, his hand...

'Now the gold. Prepare to be dazzled.'

Harry led her to the right, and she *was* dazzled.
Jewellery of every type hung from hooks and rods
and stands like trees, right out in front of their eyes
in places, so to get down the alley at times they had to
walk sideways.

Delicate filigree earrings hung beside chunky gold
chains, trailing gold necklaces, up to eight strands in
each one, competed with gold bangles and bracelets.

'Who buys it all?' Sarah asked, stunned by such an
array of wealth.

'Families,' Harry explained. 'Or lovers, I suppose.'

He grinned at her, then explained.

'It is mainly families. If their daughter takes gold into a marriage, it is hers forever, so if the marriage breaks down, or her husband dies, she will still have money to live on. These days it is not so important because a husband has to support his wife even if they part, and his family would support his widow. But going back, when people lived in tribes, to avoid too much intermarriage a woman would often be married to a man from far away. The gold meant she would always be able to make her way back home if the marriage didn't work out.'

'I think that's lovely in theory,' Sarah told him, hefting a heavy chain in one hand. 'But would her husband let her go?'

'Usually, yes,' Harry replied, 'although there have been, and always will be, bad husbands and probably bad wives.'

Sarah nodded. It was only too true and confirmed what Hera had said about the necessity for women's shelters.

'So, may I buy you something?'

The question startled her and she looked at the man she was with—then shook her head.

'Not on a first date—or even a second date if we count meeting Rajah as the first.'

Harry smiled at her, and her insides melted.

This was *not* a good idea.

She should have left, flown home that morning. Her and Harry's lives were already complicated enough, and being here, especially in the souk, was a reminder of just how different their worlds were.

But the tour continued, through fresh fruit and vegetable markets, then the smell of fresh baked bread drew them down another alleyway.

'We will stop for coffee and a cake here, if you would like,' Harry suggested, leading the way into the dim interior of one of many small shops and cafés.

The man at the door bowed his head briefly in Harry's direction, and Sarah realised it had been going on throughout their ramble along the alleyways, people nodding deferentially to the man she was with.

She'd taken the first nods as those of passing acquaintances, but unless he knew everyone in Ambelia the nods must be acknowledgement of his royal position.

Had he nodded back?

Sarah couldn't remember, but thinking of it now as the nodding café owner showed them to a table, she realised just how different this world was.

Not only the wealth displayed at the palace, the wardrobes full of clothes for guests who might never wear them, but the acceptance of and acknowledgement by the people that this man was someone special.

And there she'd been, wandering along behind him, because to her he was just Harry.

Well, not *just* Harry!

'If you've fallen asleep on your feet it's definitely time for coffee, but, I warn you, our coffee is thick and dark and sweet and comes in tiny cups with water to drink with it.'

He took her elbow and guided her to a seat.

Sarah watched him as he sat down opposite her and spoke quietly to the man who was serving them.

But all her attention was on Harry, although in his robes he had to be Rahman, and Rahman *was* a prince.

Not only that but he was, for all his dislike of the idea, heir to the throne.

Expected to produce more heirs, to keep the family dynasty going…

The tiny coffee cups arrived with a platter of small buns and cakes and a jug in the shape of the one Sarah had admired in the market, condensation from the cold water inside beading on the intricately engraved design.

She traced the line again with her fingers, picking up a little moisture, thinking about Harry and Rahman and families and history and tradition…

And although she hadn't given it much thought, the robes definitely defined him as regal, as did his bearing and the sense of authority that hung like the robes around him.

He was slipping away from her—from being Harry—or maybe distancing himself from her, hence the platonic 'dates' they were enjoying.

And she *was* enjoying this exploration of a country so different from her own, so she decided the only sensible thing was to keep enjoying it and work out the rest later.

After the coffee and cakes, they went back to the palace, Harry having promised his mother not to keep Sarah out in the midday heat. He touched her cheek as he left her at the door to her room.

'I have some things to discuss with my father, but you have a rest, and at four I will collect you to take you to see *my* sunset!'

His fingers lingered on her skin, caressing it gently, and she longed to put her hand on his, to hold it where it was.

Because right then he was definitely Harry, although

the man she'd known was already slipping away from her, leaving Rahman in his place.

'Later' came much sooner than Sarah had expected. She *had* slept, her body clock adjusting itself, no doubt, and was woken by Lea bringing tea and offering delicacies in case Sarah was hungry.

But sleep had left her head muzzy, too muzzy to think about anything that might lie ahead—too muzzy to think, really.

She showered and allowed Lea to choose her outfit—blue loose trousers with a gauzy blue and green top, embroidered around the neck with green thread and sequins.

'Surely that's too fancy for a drive to the desert?' Sarah protested, but Lea insisted it was perfect.

When Sarah was dressed, Lea handed her a scarf, draping it around Sarah's face.

'I don't think so,' Sarah said. 'I don't want to pretend to be someone I'm not. The tunics and trousers are common sense, but unless it is a special day and I need to keep my hair completely covered, I think I'll take the hat.'

'But it's orange,' Lea protested. 'And the scarf is big enough to wrap around your shoulders if it becomes cool.'

Sarah took both, but the hat, when she put it on, did look terrible with the outfit, so she slathered on extra sunscreen and hoped the setting sun would be gentle on her skin.

Harry was waiting by the door in the big entry hall, and he was Harry again, dressed in pale cream chinos and a dark grey shirt. Her heart did that silly flip it insisted on doing when she first caught sight of him, and she realised that, instead of sleeping, she should have been doing some serious thinking.

Too late now, her body told her, reacting with delight to his touch on her elbow.

She was ravishing, Harry decided, as Sarah, escorted by Lea, seemed to glide towards him.

From her long, slim feet to the tip of her vibrant red hair, she was just gorgeous! The colour of the tunic brought out the green of her eyes, and made her skin seem even paler in contrast.

He wanted to touch her, to hold her, to whisper some of what was in his heart, but good manners and protocol dictated he simply take her hand and raise it to his lips.

Colour crept into her face, and a flash of something lit her eyes. Excitement? Happiness?

'You look beautiful,' he said, and she smiled.

'Thank Lea for it—she tells me what to wear.'

She turned to Lea, but the girl had already disappeared on soundless feet.

'It is not the clothes that make you beautiful but the woman inside them,' he said, hoping he was making sense because for some reason he felt like a schoolboy—a youngster on his real first date. 'Come,' he said, steadying her while she put on her shoes. 'Today you're going to see my sand.'

That was better. He was back in control.

'And feel it run like silk through my fingers?' she asked, and he smiled, remembering the conversation on the beach.

His body tightened as he remembered the aftermath of that conversation and the aftermath of most conversations on the beach. He wanted her so badly, but having spoken to his father about his brother succeeding to the throne instead of him, and receiving his father's blessings for a marriage to this woman, he now had to be extra-careful how he was with her, for he didn't want the faintest hint of gossip to sully her name.

Bearing in mind, of course, that she might not want him.

That thought disturbed him so much he shut the door of the car more forcibly than he should have, winning raised eyebrows from the beautiful woman who was causing him so much gut-wrenching stress.

He reached out and touched her thigh, his hand low where no prying eyes would see the gesture.

'I want you so badly it's driving me insane,' he muttered, then he removed his hand, placed it on the steering wheel and drove sedately out of the palace grounds, raising his hand in salute to the gatemen who stood as the vehicle approached.

'Are they guards?' Sarah asked, and, glad to have his mind diverted, he explained.

'We do have some security but it's largely electronic today. Specialists sit in a room surrounded by monitors to keep an eye on things, but the gatemen have been here always, the jobs passing down through generations. I think originally they acted as watchmen in the nomad camps. They are family, too, you know, and these days their sons and daughters go to university, yet there always seem to be some gatemen around.'

'And do they live here?'

Was she asking out of interest, or to keep the conversation going?

To take *her* mind off things she might like to do to him?

He doubted it, although the more time he spent with

Sarah the less he felt he knew her, yet a certainty that she was his remained.

He was explaining that all the servants had apartments within the walls when he realised he'd lost her attention.

'Ahh!'

The long, soft sigh came as he turned off the motorway and almost immediately the land on either side of the road gave way from palm trees to red desert sand.

'It *is* beautiful,' she whispered, gazing around at distant dunes and the smaller baby dunes shifting towards the road.

'Do they shift all the time?' she asked.

'All the time,' he agreed, 'but unlike the sea the tide of sand is always coming in. Those little dunes will blow across the road unless they're blown back by machines. We don't like to interfere with nature if we don't have to, but in time the sand would cover every road if left to its own devices.'

He turned into the desert now, along a track that was barely there, driving through a dry wadi then up along the wall of a tall dune. From the top, he knew, they'd have a perfect view of the sunset, and to watch the sunset there with Sarah had suddenly become extremely important.

CHAPTER NINE

THE RED-GOLD DUNES rose and fell as far as Sarah could see, although on the western horizon there were mountains, purple in the distance.

Harry stopped the big four-wheel drive at the top of one of the tallest dunes, and sighed with what sounded like total satisfaction that he was back in his land of sand.

'Sit there for a moment,' he said, turning to her and touching her lightly on the hand.

And while Sarah battled her reactions to a simple hand touch, Harry got out of the vehicle and opened the rear, obviously unloading things.

Whatever he was doing was around his side of the car, but as a flock of birds flew towards the sunset, leaving black shadows on the sand, she looked around more carefully, because this seemingly empty place obviously had life within it.

Here and there little tufts of what looked like the salt-bush that grew in outback Queensland could be seen, some so nearly covered with sand that only a few leaves showed.

And leading away from those leaves, the footprints of a small animal.

Harry blocked her view. He was at the door, opening it, putting out his hand to steady her as she climbed out.

And he kept her hand in his as he led her to where he'd unrolled a carpet and thrown large cushions down on it. A small fire had been lit just off the edge, while on it sat a silver tray with two matching glasses and two tall jugs. Little dishes of nuts and dates surrounded the jugs and a single red rose lay beside them.

Sarah's heart flipped at the rose then she reminded herself that in this country red roses probably didn't mean *I love you*. In fact, they probably had no significance at all…

'You've made us a picnic,' she said, delighted by the scene, whatever the red rose meant.

He led her to the carpet, and she sank down on it, tucking her legs sideways, as she'd learned to do.

He sat between her and the tray, shifting it so they could both reach the offerings.

'I've water or my mother's special juice,' he said. 'Or there's coffee in the car if you'd prefer that.'

'Definitely the juice,' Sarah told him, watching hands that had fondled her body lift the jug and pour juice for her.

'Cheers,' she said, lifting her glass to his, mainly to break the tension that, for some reason, was coiling inside her.

You're here to see the sunset, she reminded herself. Nothing more.

She sipped her drink, Harry lounging now beside her, the sun dropping swiftly and the colours of the sand reflecting back the sky of brilliant orange, red, and yellow.

'It's beautiful,' she murmured, as the full extent of this special sight struck her. 'So beautiful!'

'But wait,' Harry said, touching her lightly on her thigh and starting all the physical reactions again. 'Wait until it sinks and the softer colours come.'

And come they did, the pinks and mauves, and blues and purples, making the desert seem more like the sea than a vast stretch of sand.

'It's like the colours of the water over the reef.'

Harry smiled.

'That's exactly what I thought the first time I flew into Wildfire, only the other way around, of course. That the colours of the water over the reef was like my desert sands at sunset.'

He eased himself to a sitting position and took her hand.

'Do you like my sunset, Sarah?'

He sounded so serious, as if this was very important to him, that Sarah could only nod.

He moved closer, put his arm around her shoulders.

'I know it's a strange question for a third date,' he said, his voice so deep and husky it reverberated in her bones. 'But will you marry me?'

The shock struck Sarah like a lightning bolt, solidifying all her body as if she'd turned to stone beside him.

She stared towards the fire, now more visible in the gathering dusk.

Harry had asked her to marry him.

Marry Harry?

As her body began to return to flesh and blood and nerves and even tingling excitement, she knew she had to tread very carefully.

To think before she spoke…

But who could think through such a startling question?

So don't answer—well, not right away.

'Did you bring me out here to ask me this?'

She'd shifted slightly away from him and turned to look at him, catching a small, wry smile playing around his lips—lips she'd kissed with such passion that simply seeing them made her feel hot all over.

'I brought you out here to see the sunset,' he said, and she believed him, although his hands were shaking as he lifted the jug to pour more juice. 'The question just seemed to come out, as if it was the natural thing to do.'

Sarah took a deep breath. Somewhere inside her a voice was prompting a 'yes' reply, but she'd had enough trouble working out who she was—and making a new life for herself after the accident—without marrying a man who was as torn and broken, although in a different way, as she had been.

She took his hand and traced the back of it, the veins and bones and tendons, with her fingers, before lifting her head to look directly at him.

'I don't think I can, Harry,' she said quietly. 'It's not that I don't love you—I've been fairly certain about that for some time, but our worlds would clash, we wouldn't fit. Your life, when you're not off doing the encephalitis stuff, should be here, with your family, keeping the traditions going, caring for your people, while me, I have to finish out my contract in Australia, then I think I'll return to England.'

She couldn't tell him why—afraid it would be too painful for him, hurt the man she loved too much.

'To try to get back into paediatric surgery,' he said quietly, a statement, not a question, as if he could read her dreams.

He put his free hand over hers, trapping it between his, and to Sarah it felt like goodbye.

'Yes, I've dithered long enough,' she said. 'The two operations… They recharged that desire that your talk at GOSH first aroused in me. I want to put the past behind me and move on.' She paused, but knew she had to continue. 'And I need to get home—now. I've loved every minute of being in this amazing country, but I need to get home and see my family, talk to people, and then get back to Oz to finish that job before I can start again. I can't say I'm all that confident, but at least I'll know I gave it a go.'

She was prattling but the tension between herself and Harry was so tight she felt it could explode at any moment, with a force that would hurt them both.

'Can you ask someone to arrange a flight?'

Harry sat on a carpet on his favourite sand dune, watching the final flickers of colour from the dying sun, and felt his world collapse around him.

Not that he'd been expecting Sarah to say yes… Well, how could he have been when he hadn't realised he'd intended to ask her?

It had been a daft idea. Their worlds *were* far too far apart, and although he'd told his father earlier that he didn't want the throne, his life was still a mad rush around the world, checking up on things that were happening in both the scientific and the practical measures he'd set up.

He'd be back on Wildfire before long, to check on the progress of the clinical trials, and in Bangladesh soon after that.

What woman would want a husband who was never there?

And when he was at home, wherever that might be, how could he live with someone who was doing the job that had been taken from him?

The job that had been his passion?

He squeezed the fingers on the hand he held in his, and much as he wanted to argue and protest, he knew that she was right to turn him down.

'I love you,' he said quietly, and knew he should have said it sooner.

Not, he suspected, that it would have made much difference...

The hand in his moved to tighten its grip.

'I love you, too,' she said, her voice so full of sorrow he longed to take her in his arms and hold her close.

Forever?

She'd made it clear that couldn't happen, so he lifted a handful of sand and placed it in her hand, where she let it slip between her fingers.

'Sand like silk,' she said, remembering his description of it, 'but it's like life as well, isn't it? If we're not careful it slips away because we're too afraid to grab it and cling to it and wring whatever satisfaction and joy and pleasure that we can out of it.'

He kissed her then, restraining the passion burning within him for this was a goodbye kiss...

So much for booking a flight for her, Sarah thought as the limo carrying her turned into the private part of the airfield where she'd arrived.

It pulled up at the foot of stairs leading into the same, or a similar, jet to the one in which she'd arrived.

'Welcome, Dr Watson,' one of the cabin crew greeted her as her chauffeur held open the door. 'If you would give me your passport, I'll see to the formalities while you get comfortable inside.'

Another member of the crew beckoned her up the stairs.

But halfway there she turned and looked back, disappointed that all she could see was the airport and the city beyond it.

'You'll see the desert when we take off,' the crew member told her.

But Sarah knew that had been only part of her disappointment.

Not that she'd expected him to be here.

They'd both agreed last night that their goodbyes would be said in private. Not in the desert but, after dinner with the family, when she'd gone to say goodbye to Rajah.

And remembering Rajah she had to blink back tears, telling herself it was certainly the goodbye and not the kiss that had followed it that she would miss.

But she'd miss more than a kiss from Harry. She'd miss his closeness, miss sharing little moments of the day with him, miss his touch, and the feel of his skin beneath her fingers.

She'd miss him with an ache deep inside her but in time she'd find a smile as well—a smile for the happy memories.

Settled in her seat, seatbelt on, the engines whining as the pilot revved them, she reminded herself that pain lessened with time, and the memories became good friends instead of hurting.

She waited until the plane had crossed the desert,

giving her one last glimpse of the red-gold sand, then closed her eyes and slept, waking only for a snack as they approached Farnborough, where, according to one of the crew, they were due to land.

He'd also told her that a car would meet her to take her to her family home in Roehampton, only a twenty-minute drive, she imagined, although she'd never been to Farnborough before, even for an air show.

Harry threw himself back into work, travelling first to Africa where his scientists were struggling to balance mosquito eradication with the preservation of the natural ecosystem.

Spraying worked for a season, but the swamps were still there, and the swamps and waterholes were an integral part of the local landscape and home or source of food to the inhabitants of each area.

The vaccine was the answer, and although clinical trials of the Wildfire vaccine were under way, there was doubt it would work here. The disease mutated according to the area, and sometimes success seemed a long way off.

But he persisted, needing work and the frantic dashing around the world to keep his mind off Sarah.

He could tell himself it had been nothing more than a short affair—a holiday romance, as she'd kept insisting—but images of her played in his head and a word here or a sight there reminded him so strongly of her he'd often have to stop what he was doing and breathe deeply for a moment.

The invitation came as a surprise.

It was waiting for him when he returned home for a brief visit before heading to Asia.

Real mail—a letter—white and thick, like an invitation...

But there was always mail waiting for him, and always invitations to speak at this or that convention.

He threw it in the bin, part of his past, then contrarily pulled it out and shoved it in his travel bag.

He might read it on the plane.

Or not!

But although that part of his life was over, it might be interesting to see who the speakers were going to be and whether any of them might have something new to offer.

He thought no more about it as one of the engineers he'd employed to look at draining a flooded rubbish dump in Bangladesh, with a view to reclaiming the land, was on the flight so it was back to business.

He avoided Wildfire for as long as he could, knowing he had competent people there who could carry on the work.

But even thinking about Sarah brought a clear image of her into his head, right in the middle of some theory about reclaimed land—a smiling, teasing image.

Sarah spent the first week home with her parents doing family things like visiting aged aunts and walking through Richmond Park with the dogs, remembering Bugsy on Wildfire who'd loved a walk...

The second week she began tentative enquiries about the possibility of getting an opening on a paediatric surgery team. She was only too aware that most of the people who could offer such training would be friends of Harry's and one word from him might have made her job easier, but she couldn't hurt him more by asking this of him.

He was with her day and night—well, more at night—because it was easier to escape her thoughts during the day.

But at night she dreamed of the time they had shared, of the passionate and gentle lovemaking between them, of their conversations, and shared laughter, and sitting together on Sunset Beach.

She didn't think about the desert sunset, although its magical beauty was burned into her brain.

That memory was too painful…

He phoned one evening. She was just back from a walk and the smell of the roast beef her mother was cooking for dinner hung around the house.

She answered the phone, thinking it would be an old friend calling back, a doctor with whom she'd trained and who was now a GP.

They were making arrangements to get together for a meal, so there was no premonition of it being anything other than an ordinary call.

'Sarah, I need you.'

Harry's voice…

Harry's voice almost pleading…

Her heart was bouncing around in her chest, her lungs had seized, and her stomach cramped painfully.

'A baby?' she managed to croak.

To her surprise she heard a smile—well, half a smile, a little bit of a smile—in his voice as he answered.

'No, more a pillar—that's what I need.'

'A pillar?'

She took the phone from her ear and checked to see she wasn't dreaming.

'One of those things that support other things,' he

continued, although she might have missed a bit. 'I need you to support me, be my pillar.'

Long pause.

Was he gone?

No-o-o-o!

The wail came from her heart and then he was back again, his voice in her ear.

'To prop me up.'

She heard a deep intake of breath then his words came out in a rush.

'I've been asked to speak at a symposium in London, at GOSH, and at first I threw the note away, then I picked it out of the bin and tucked it into my luggage, and when I had to go back to Wildfire I looked at it and saw what it was and I heard you in my head telling me it's what I should be doing—working in the field I loved and was good at. So I phoned someone and said yes and now I'm getting nervous. It's next Tuesday and they've booked me into a hotel, the Russell, quite close to GOSH and the British Museum, if my talk gets boring for you, and it's at the opening of the three-day talk-fest and I wondered if you'd come.'

'Yes!' Sarah said, and wondered if he could hear her smile, which was so wide he could probably see it reflected on the moon if he was looking.

'That's it?' he asked—or maybe demanded.

'Yes,' she said again, because that really *was* all there was. The rightness of it all, and seeing him again, and maybe, just maybe, talking him into returning to the work he'd loved and lost.

'I'm coming in on Sunday. I'll phone you with the time. Someone will collect you to meet me at the plane.

We'll have a couple of nights together before the show begins. Time to talk…'

Pause…

'Is that all right?'

'More than all right,' Sarah said. 'I'll pack a bag.'

CHAPTER TEN

'THERE'S A VERY large car outside,' Sarah's mother said on Sunday morning, sounding a little put out by the ostentatiousness of a very large car.

'It's how they get around, Mum,' she said. 'But the people are ordinary, friendly, hospitable—just like you and me.'

'Except they live in a palace,' her mother countered, and Sarah realised that although she'd listened to Sarah's tales about Ambelia with interest, she was obviously concerned about Sarah's possible future amidst such wealth.

'Wait till you meet him,' Sarah said, hugging her mother, although the car was waiting. 'He gives his talk on Tuesday evening and we'll come out here on Wednesday, take you and Dad to The Crabtree for lunch and we can sit by the river if it's fine.'

Sarah could see her mother still had doubts, but those, Sarah guessed, were about meeting Rahman al-Taraq, and would be banished when she met Harry.

She said a quick goodbye and went out to the waiting car.

'First to Farnborough to meet the plane,' the driver told her, and this time Sarah actually noticed what Farnborough airfield looked like.

It was, she realised, like some great futuristic city, only too small to be a city—a village maybe.

It had developed from a small, wartime landing strip to an airfield that catered to the wealthy and privileged, flying in on their private jets for business, a shopping trip, or simply pleasure.

The high-arched dome was more intimidating than welcoming, but Sarah guessed it looked better from the other side.

She waited, moving from one foot to the other in an effort to keep her excitement in check, then, finally, he was there, walking out through sliding doors and just appearing in front of her.

He dropped the small bag he was carrying and drew her into his arms, holding her so close and for so long she wondered if he'd ever let her go.

Not that she wanted to be let go!

Eventually they made their way to the car, joined at shoulder and hip, his arm around her waist.

With the miracle of organisation she was beginning to accept as part of Harry's world, his luggage was already being loaded into the boot, and the driver had the rear door open for them.

Harry spoke quietly to him, then slid in beside her, reclaiming her hand and drawing her close to kiss her again.

'I have never before understood the concept of missing someone,' he said, when he finally raised his head from hers, and brushed his fingers against her cheek. 'But every moment of every day since you left, I have missed you. In my head, and in my heart, and in other parts of my body that we'll leave nameless, you've been a gap and an ache and a sorrow all run together.'

Sarah nodded, her heart too full of happiness for words to form.

'You, too?' he asked, and she smiled and nodded, then kissed the lips that had haunted her dreams for so long.

They spent a very enjoyable hour or so in the car, until the driver announced 'Hotel Russell, sir' and Harry and Sarah broke apart like naughty schoolchildren caught kissing behind the gymnasium.

The driver opened the door on Sarah's side, while uniformed hotel staff appeared from all directions, whisking away Harry's large suitcase and Sarah's much smaller bag on a trolley that would have held five times as much luggage.

Harry took her hand to lead her into the hotel, but Sarah paused, wanting to take it all in. The big old red and cream brick building had large inset windows, and the quiet dignity of a dowager of older times. Inside, it was breathtaking, with marble floors and pillars and a huge chandelier over the central foyer.

'It's not six stars but it's very comfortable,' Harry was saying, 'and close enough to walk to GOSH.'

'I love it already,' Sarah said, although she knew she'd also have loved some cheap flea-pit hotel with Harry for company.

Once registered, they were shown to their suite of rooms, with views out over Russell Square. But views were soon forgotten, because Harry was behind her, holding her close, his desire for her making itself felt.

She turned in his arms, and held him close as she kissed him, remembering how well they fitted together, remembering touches that brought him pleasure, and revelling in the fingers that roamed her body.

'We will *not* hurry this,' he said very firmly. 'I've been waiting so long I refuse to be rushed.'

But somehow that didn't work because, once naked on the bed together, not rushing wasn't an option, the fire between them driving their bodies to take and be taken, to give and be given, to touch, and kiss, and tease, and come together until they both lay exhausted on the bed.

'Maybe next time we'll take it slowly,' Sarah teased, propping herself on pillows so she could look down at Harry's beloved face.

She traced her fingers down his profile, around his lips, and her heart filled with love for this man she'd met by chance, and who had given her back her love of life itself.

She'd slowly put herself back together again, but to find love as deep as this a second time—that was special.

'Thank you,' she said, dropping a kiss on his lips. His eyebrows rose. 'For loving me, for letting me love you.'

For now, that was enough, Sarah decided. The future could take care of itself...

Tuesday dawned bright and sunny, and because Harry had people to see at GOSH, Sarah walked with him to the hospital, a little bit of new excitement fizzing inside her as she'd been accepted on a paediatric surgical team, not here but at Arcadia London Children's Hospital, due to begin in six weeks.

She'd be going back in time to the long and irregular hours of hospital work, with study on top of that, but it was something she definitely wanted to do.

And something that would occupy all her attention

if this little visit with Harry proved to be just that—a small piece of heaven stolen from time.

'Well, are you coming in?' Harry asked as they stood by the statue of Peter Pan and Tinkerbell outside the front door.

'Not until tonight,' she said, then wondered at the look of concern on his face.

'You'll be all right?' he asked anxiously. 'Not too many bad memories?'

She had to smile.

'My memories of that life are all good ones now, Harry. Yes, I wonder about the baby, but all the rest are safely stored away. I've made new memories now and am happy with them, and happy to make more.'

She didn't say 'with you' because beyond tonight she had no idea where Harry's future might lie. She hoped it would be here, but knew it would be a huge step for him to take, to get back into paediatric surgery without being able to operate.

'I should be done by lunch but just in case, let's meet back at the hotel at three—I'll stand you high tea!'

Sarah laughed. Harry was standing her everything on this little holiday and she felt pampered and thoroughly spoiled by his attention.

She kissed his cheek—lip kisses were too hard to break and they were in public—and left, wanting to wander through the museum again, to look at artefacts from the past and think about her future.

It would be with Harry, wherever he was, she'd decided. She could travel with him, learn about his projects, forget the idea of further study...

Couldn't she?

As thinking only confused her, she headed for the

Egyptian rooms and peered at mummies preserved for thousands of years, wondering if love had been as hard for people then as it was for her now.

She had lunch in the café beneath the vast, high steel and glass roof, built to provide more space and facilities for the museum, then walked back to the hotel to shower and change before meeting Harry again.

He was late, coming in at four, telling her he'd booked a table for high tea, urging her off the bed, where she'd been reading and dozing, and insisting they go now.

He was fizzing with excitement, and as they stood together in the elevator she could feel it buzzing in his body.

'So tell me what this is all about,' she said, but he smiled and shook his head.

'Soon,' he promised, and because the elevator was empty but for them, he dropped a quick kiss on her lips.

They sat in style at the back of the big open foyer in high-backed armchairs, a table with a snowy white cloth over it in front of their knees.

Sandwiches came first, tiny delicate sandwiches made from different coloured breads with fillings so delicious Sarah ate the lot.

'Now tell,' she said when the waiter brought scones and jam and cream, the scones covered by a pristine white napkin to keep them warm.

He looked at her, grey eyes dancing with excitement, although she thought she could read doubt on his face.

'There's a job,' he said, 'teaching and research. It would give me time to keep an eye on my managers who'll take over the overseas programmes but get me back into what I love.'

He paused, took a scone, and carefully broke it open and buttered it.

'It's the research that interests me most as it involves development of new techniques for operating on babies still in the womb, correcting a lot of congenital problems before the infant is born.'

Sarah's heart lurched, and she reached out and covered his hand with hers.

'It's perfect, something new,' she said, 'something to excite you, and the teaching... That's a bonus for your students because you're the best.'

'Was the best,' he said quietly, and she understood the doubt she thought she'd seen.

'That was then, and this is now,' she said, refusing to let him dampen her excitement. 'And the first breakthrough you make in your research will have you back on the top of the tree again, if that is what you want.'

He didn't answer, studying her instead, thinking...

And now his smile was free of doubt.

'It's not what I want,' he said, confusing her for a moment. 'To be top of the tree again,' he explained.

He reached out and took both her hands in his slightly buttery fingers.

'You're what I want. To live with you, be with you, have children with you if you want them. I want you for my wife, by my side, whatever lies ahead. I learned that when you left, but couldn't see a way forward until now, when we're together again. I know you have your own ambition and I'll be with you all the way, but being offered this position means we can be together, here in

London, and it's the being with you that's the most important thing.'

'But Ambelia? Your home? The throne?'

He smiled so gently she thought her heart might break.

'That's all been decided. My brother will make a far better ruler than me, and, deep down, I think my father knows it. Well, the rest of the family does anyway.'

The smile was better this time, but still Sarah held her breath.

'So now I'm yours, if you'll have me? I have my parents' blessing—they both love you already because they have seen how happy you make me. So, my Sarah…'

I will not cry, Sarah told herself, but felt the tears sliding down her cheeks anyway.

The waiter brought little plates of cakes and pastries but she was beyond eating.

'I'll pack them in a box and send them to your room,' he said, when Sarah waved him away. 'Nice for a midnight snack.'

She smiled weakly, then realised they probably would be good at midnight—a midnight feast with the man she loved.

Harry stood on the dais, a lectern before him, dressed as she'd never seen him, in a dark suit, grey shirt and darker grey tie.

He was beautiful, she decided, then wriggled in her seat, for he'd told her the same thing—that she was beautiful—before they'd left the hotel.

They'd returned to their room after the abbreviated high tea, where she'd found an exquisite outfit waiting for her.

'I told the woman in the boutique all about you and she chose it all,' Harry had said proudly, and 'all' it was, right down to filmy underwear and sheer stockings and black high-heeled shoes.

The suit itself was grey, the colour of his shirt, with an emerald-green silk blouse to go beneath it and a small black handbag to finish the outfit.

'Oh, Harry,' she whispered, shaking her head. 'It's lovely, so stylish. I did't have much reason to wear suits in Cairns.'

He smiled and pulled her close so it was a little while before they both dressed in their finery and made their way to the hospital.

This would be a test for her, Harry thought, holding tightly to Sarah's hand as they made their way through the building to where conferences and symposiums were held.

He was pretty sure it was the first time she'd have been here since the day the accident had taken her husband and child, and it must be taking tremendous courage on her part to be returning.

And she was doing it for him—to be there when he spoke, for the first time in nearly five years, about the work that had been his passion.

'New starts,' she whispered to him as they entered the main lecture theatre, and her fingers returned the squeeze he'd given hers.

'Are you all right?' he asked, and found her smile as reassuring as her words.

'With you beside me, how could I not be?'

He wanted to kiss her, but it was too public a place,

and too many old friends and acquaintances were hailing him.

'It may be a crush later,' he said, realising he'd have to speak to these people. 'Do you want to join me?'

'And meet a couple dozen strangers all at once?' Sarah teased. 'No, if you lose me I'll be waiting by Peter and Tinkerbell.'

Expecting nerves, Harry was surprised to find himself at home behind the lectern, talking easily about the history of paediatric surgery, the first operations that now seemed clumsy, even inept compared with work done today.

'But we must move on,' he said, 'to a future where many congenital defects can be repaired in the womb, and investigate ways for problems that can't be handled that way to be done with minimally invasive surgery. Keyhole surgery is commonplace in most theatres now, but less is known about the procedures where that technique can be used on small children, even neonates.'

He paused and felt the attention of every person present in the room, although his eyes found Sarah first.

'For that is the way ahead. That is our holy grail, and here at GOSH, through the generosity of some of our supporters, it will be happening before long.'

He surprised himself as he mentioned a few possibilities, surprised by the fact that part of his brain must have been working on these matters for some time.

Sarah sat and watched him, barely listening to his words. She'd been happy just to be with him, even if only for a few days, but now she could be happy in the present and look forward to even more happiness in the future.

The crowd rose as one, and she realised she'd drifted

away from the words he was saying, content just to listen to his voice.

She stood up, clapping with them, clapping because the man she loved had returned to the world he loved.

Sure, there were things they both had to do, but before long they could be together forever.

Forever?

Was she jumping the gun?

No, he'd said forever and she knew he'd meant it. It was just that marriage hadn't been part of the conversation—not since she'd turned him down in Ambelia.

She looked around for him, but he was being mobbed by admirers and well-wishers and she didn't want to deny him that, so she eased out of the room and walked back through the hospital to the little garden where Tinkerbell perched lightly on one of Peter Pan's fingers. Tinkerbell had been added later, she remembered, but the delicacy of the bronze casts always amazed her.

To her, tonight, they were symbols of David and her unborn child, the bronze statues as strong as the memories tucked away inside her head. They would never be forgotten, but it was time to move on, and to move on with joy and anticipation into the life that lay ahead.

That's if Harry did ask her to marry him…

He appeared, as if by magic, and took her hand.

'Will you marry me?' he said.

And this time she said, 'Yes.'

They wandered back to the hotel together, content to be alone.

CHAPTER ELEVEN

GETTING MARRIED, THEY REALISED, was harder than it seemed.

'Dratted people,' Harry muttered, as he shut off his cell phone for the third time that morning.

'Leave it, for the moment,' Sarah told him. 'You're nervous about meeting Mum and Dad, and phoning government offices isn't helping. Besides, Dad will know what to do. He worked in the local council for years, and loves knowing everything that goes on.'

Dad did, and over lunch in the open garden of The Crabtree pub, looking out over the Thames at its most beautiful as it twinkled in rare sunlight, he explained the procedures at the register office.

'You can print the forms off the internet. The first, your request to get married, has to go in twenty-eight days before the date, and another, which lists all the information about yourself, you have to take with you when you deliver the notice.'

He turned his attention to Harry.

'You lived and worked here—do you have residency?'

Harry smiled.

'Scottish grandmother, hence the grey eyes, so I have

dual citizenship, and not only do I have a British passport, I also have a flat in Fulham. It will need a bit of refurbishing as I haven't lived there for a while, although some of the family have used it from time to time.'

'Well, that's the next consideration—proof of residence—a tax notice of some kind.'

The conversation continued, Harry certain he'd be able to provide all the evidence required, but Sarah's evidence would be harder. She knew she had David's death certificate tucked away somewhere but had always refused to look at it.

She felt Harry's hand find hers beneath the table and knew he understood what she was feeling, as did her mother, no doubt, who got on to practicalities.

'With twenty-eight days' notice you might just be able to squeeze it in before you have to go back to Australia and Harry's due in Asia,' she said.

So they discussed dates.

Harry was leaving for Africa the following day but could be back whenever he was needed.

'And if I have a date I can get my parents over,' he said, and Sarah nodded. They'd already decided that the only people they wanted at the wedding were both sets of parents, although Harry had warned her there would be big celebrations to be endured—or enjoyed—when they next returned to Ambelia.

So it was sorted, the wedding date set, Harry seen off to Africa, and Sarah left to wonder just how this had all happened in what seemed like a millisecond of time.

'No time for dreaming,' her mother chided her. 'You might not be doing the full bride thing, but I want you looking beautiful for that man—he deserves it.'

* * *

She was beautiful!

So much so she took his breath away.

Dressed in a deep cream-coloured suit, very simple with a calf-length skirt and fitted jacket, and very pale green shirt underneath it, her red hair swinging free, he just stood and looked, until his mother prodded him and he managed to step forward and take her hand.

They'd had dinner the previous evening, all six of them, so the two sets of parents could meet and talk.

And talk they did, embarrassing both him and Sarah with their reminiscing.

Now they were waiting, waiting to witness the marriage of their children, and he was waiting, too, waiting for a future with this woman he loved beyond all words.

Tomorrow they'd be parting, the jet dropping Sarah at Cairns airport before taking him on to Wildfire. They both had jobs to complete before beginning their London life.

But today and tonight she was his, his to love and be loved by.

'I love you!'

She mouthed the words at him as they went into the very functional room at the register office used for weddings.

He squeezed her hand in response.

A short ceremony, lunch at the five star hotel where his parents were staying, then home to his flat, already refurbished, the renovations overseen by Sarah while he'd made his final mad dash around the world, minions trailing after him to learn the way of things.

* * *

Sarah managed to get through the ceremony without crying, enjoyed lunch with their parents at the posh hotel, but as it drew to a close her nervousness increased.

Soon, too soon really, they'd be back at the flat, and she was worried what Harry—or maybe Rahman—would think of it.

The flat, when she'd first seen it, though spacious, had been student style with a bit of minimalist thrown in. Fortunately for her, Hera had come over, and with her mother the three of them had shopped.

Now it was a home, with polished wood floors, soft leather armchairs, a settee with a bright angora throw to wrap around the two of them, and small but functional tables scattered around.

And on the wall and floor were carpets, small and large, colourful, intricately woven pieces Hera had brought over with her.

The dining room was more formal, the glass and chrome table, which Harry had bought at some time, softened by the large silk on silk Persian carpet underneath it, while a long cabinet against one wall held a collection of the beautiful jugs, goblets and platters Sarah had so admired in Ambelia.

And in here the only ornamentation on the walls was a large picture of Wildfire, the cliff ablaze with the colour of the setting sun.

Harry wandered through the rooms, his hand holding tightly to Sarah's, a catch in his breathing the only comment when he saw the living room. But in the dining room, in front of the picture, he took her in his arms and kissed her.

'Beautiful!' he said. 'Both you and my new flat.'

But if he'd liked the beginning of the tour, the bedrooms knocked him off his feet. Three bedrooms, the smallest of which Sarah had refrained from changing much, hoping in the near future it might need balloons and flowers and small animals involved in its decoration. The spare bedroom had the colours of the island, the translucent blue-green waters on the spread, chair and cushions covered with bright reef colours.

'And you're saving the best for last?' Harry asked, as she led him to the main bedroom.

Which she was—well, she hoped it was the best.

She'd used the colours of the desert here, the red-gold of the sand, the paler silk curtains and embroidered quilt, and a soft cream carpet so the colours came alive.

He loved it and apparently he loved her, for the delicate silk quilt was soon thrown aside, and they collapsed together on the bed, holding each other and laughing at the sheer joy of being together—together for now and together always.

They undressed each other slowly—teasingly slow—but Sarah was determined not to crush her wedding finery. This suit would always be special to her, and this time when they returned to the bed it was to make love slowly but passionately, their actions better than words to explain their feelings at that time.

Talk came later, little memories they'd shared, talk of Wildfire and their meeting, of the work that lay ahead—their hopes, their dreams, their futures.

When Harry slid from the bed, Sarah felt his absence but he was back within a minute, kneeling by the bed, opening a box and drawing out the most beautiful necklace she had ever seen.

'This has been given by my family's eldest son to his wife on their wedding day for as long as my people can remember. My mother gave it to me last night.'

He leaned forward and clasped it around her neck, Sarah still wide-eyed in wonder, her fingers going up to touch the brilliant emeralds and small diamonds that glittered between them. The gems were cold against her skin, yet her body burned when Harry added, 'And I doubt they've ever looked more beautiful than they do on you.'

She understood now why he'd insisted on an emerald for her engagement ring, a ring that was now protecting that more precious ring, her wedding band.

She drew him to her, back onto the bed, and they pledged to each other without words but with the jewels between them shining as a bright token of their love.

* * * * *

Don't miss the next story in the fabulous
WILDFIRE ISLAND DOCS *miniseries:*
THE FLING THAT CHANGED EVERYTHING
by Alison Roberts.
Available next month

MILLS & BOON®

Helen Bianchin v Regency Collection!

16_MB520

MILLS & BOON®

Let us take you back in time with our Medieval Brides...

The Novice Bride – Carol Townend

The Dumont Bride – Terri Brisbin

The Lord's Forced Bride – Anne Herries

The Warrior's Princess Bride – Meriel Fuller

The Overlord's Bride – Margaret Moore

Templar Knight, Forbidden Bride – Lynna Banning

Order yours at
www.millsandboon.co.uk/medievalbrides

MILLS & BOON®

Why not subscribe?
Never miss a title and save money too!

Here's what's available to you if you join the exclusive **Mills & Boon® Book Club** today:

- ✦ *Titles up to a month ahead of the shops*
- ✦ *Amazing discounts*
- ✦ *Free P&P*
- ✦ *Earn Bonus Book points that can be redeemed against other titles and gifts*
- ✦ *Choose from monthly or pre-paid plans*

Still want more?
Well, if you join today, we'll even give you
50% OFF your first parcel!

So visit **www.millsandboon.co.uk/subs**
to be a part of this exclusive Book Club!

MILLS & BOON®

Why shop at millsandboon.co.uk?

Each year, thousands of romance readers find their perfect read at millsandboon.co.uk. That's because we're passionate about bringing you the very best romantic fiction. Here are some of the advantages of shopping at www.millsandboon.co.uk:

* **Get new books first**—you'll be able to buy your favourite books one month before they hit the shops

* **Get exclusive discounts**—you'll also be able to buy our specially created monthly collections, with up to 50% off the RRP

* **Find your favourite authors**—latest news, interviews and new releases for all your favourite authors and series on our website, plus ideas for what to try next

* **Join in**—once you've bought your favourite books, don't forget to register with us to rate, review and join in the discussions

Visit **www.millsandboon.co.uk**
for all this and more today!